MY ANTI-HERO

SPECIAL EDITION PAPERBACK

TIJAN

Edited by: Jessica Royer Ocken
Proofread and beta-read by: Kara Hildebrand,
Paige Smith,
Kimberley Holm, Amy English, and Crystal Solis

TW: Mentions of domestic abuse, mentions of murder, attempted abduction.

For all those who've been waiting for Brett to have his book.
For those who didn't know they were waiting,
but now know they were.
For those who enjoy serial killer documentaries.
For those who are obsessed with chickens, or goats, or alpacas, or
basically any animal.

———

A note:
Billie is a brand new character.
Brett was first introduced in the Fallen Crest series,
in book 2 & 3.
(Fallen Crest Family & Fallen Crest Public.)
This book is intended to be read as a standalone so it is not necessary
to read those books before reading My Anti-Hero.

1

BILLIE

This was the most moronic, stupid-endous, idiotic move of all moves I'd made in the last ten years. And I'd done some seriously stupid shit. But agreeing to be interviewed on a local news channel when I lived mostly as a hermit was, yeah, just plain dumb.

My armpits looked like they'd been dipped in buckets of water, and there were red splotches all over my arms.

I'd already been in the hair and makeup chair, so not only was I screwed, the news people were screwed. No touchup was going to fix the mess my nerves were making of my body.

"Willow, are you ready...?" One of the show's staff came in, saw me, and promptly trailed off as horror flashed over his face. He clutched his clipboard to his thin frame and reached for his radio. A forced smile plastered over his face. "If you'll excuse me? One moment."

He was in the hallway in a flash, and I could hear his slightly panicked voice. "We need a fixer in guest room two ASAP." *Click.* "Also, we'll need to switch segments. Alert the prompter." He continued speaking, but his voice grew quieter, so he must've been walking away.

This was my fault. All my fault.

I worked alone, dealing with clients over the internet. Graphic design. Any contact was through email or private messages. Or sometimes a phone call, which was fine.

It's not like I was some social recluse. I could be around people. I was around people growing up from the time I went into foster care at age twelve until I got lucky on my tenth home. The couple took a liking to me, and though they'd never adopted me legally, they'd raised me in every other way. I lived with them until I turned eighteen, then took over their guesthouse, and I'd been there ever since. They charged me almost nothing, just enough to cover their gas and electric, and I'd been able to finish high school, put myself through community college, and take a few extra classes in Photoshop. That had gotten me to where I was now. Well, not exactly here. Only my dumbass self was to blame for my current predicament.

"Oh dear." Frantic energy brought my attention to the doorway, where the makeup guy now stood. He shook his head, talking into his radio. "We'll need wardrobe. A new shirt for sure." He spoke to me. "Honey, you'll need my chair again. Come on. You can tell me what's going on too. You got nerves? Is that it?"

I followed him through the back of the studio.

"I guess with what you went through, you wouldn't want to talk about it? I wouldn't either. If I were you—" He prattled on, but I mostly tuned him out. It was all things I'd heard before.

Still, I was able to respond when he said something that required a response—a nod when needed and a grunt or *yeah* of agreement when it was appropriate. I'd learned to do that a lot over the years, mentally checking out. Usually, if and when people recognized me or heard my story, they wanted to talk because everyone knew about my story.

It used to be overwhelming.

Because I was more focused on studying the wall as we

walked along the hallway, I wasn't expecting what happened next that happened next. We passed a doorway—and *it* hit me.

It wasn't love at first sight, but it was most definitely lust at first sight.

It hit me hard, right in the sternum, and I stopped in my tracks. Actually and literally stopped. My mouth wasn't on the floor, because I was too reserved for that, but it was definitely open. Some drool action might've happened.

Coming out of another room was a giant. Or he looked like a giant.

He was massive. There was no softness about him. He was all muscle, and holy gods, I was reeling.

Tan skin.

Rich black hair.

A *yummy* looking beard that made me want to rub myself all over it.

A thick neck.

Square jaw.

Massive shoulders.

Massive pectorals.

Holy—his entire chest was large and in charge but ended in a tapered waist.

The guy, whoever he was, had me seeing stars. And I wasn't like this. Ever.

My last relationship had been with a guy in community college. I'd had a brief relationship with a girl before then, but that was it. I didn't do casual sex, and I'd learned it was easier just staying away from most people in general, for everything. But this guy made me ache for things I'd never experienced in my life.

I wasn't sure how to handle it.

I was usually locked down, or actually, I didn't even need to lock down. I'd just learned not to expect a whole lot of good from people. So I was completely unprepared for the whiplash of need and want and yearning that now raged inside me.

The guy looked me over, and when he caught my eyes, his narrowed. A different look came over his face. A wall came down, but his eyes held a gentle concern. He'd been talking to another man, both in some serious business suits. Each of them filled out those suits to where I was realizing how the right suit could be a weapon. Funny how I hadn't known before.

The first guy stepped toward me. He ran his hand over his face, flicking through his dark beard, and he angled his head down.

Jesus. He was probably a foot taller than me.

I was five foot six, average height. Average weight, though I dropped to a size four during stressful times. And there wasn't anything remarkable about me, a fact I'd loved growing up. I could always blend in. Pale skin. Shoulder-length strawberry blond hair and dark eyes.

My face was normal, and a few people had said I was attractive growing up.

I hadn't cared. I'd never been a makeup girl, and Vicky, my foster mom, had once told me I had natural beauty so I could get away with it. I could do lipstick, but mostly kept to lip gloss. I did indulge in pedicures. Keeping my toes painted light pink with sparkles made me happy. Sometimes I did a manicure too, but working on a computer every day chipped my nails, and since I never saw anyone outside of my foster family, what was the point?

Yet somehow, as this massive giant studied me, I wished I'd done my face up.

Then I remembered, I had. *The show.* But wait, I was a mess. I was on my way back to the makeup chair because I was such a mess.

"Are you okay?" The giant spoke, a deep baritone rumbling out of his chest. Smooth.

The sound of it washed over me, calming me. I closed my eyes, savoring the feeling. His voice settled me, cementing something inside me, just as it had woken at the sight of him.

What is going on with me?

"Miss Harm?" The makeup guy was back. "We need to fix you up. Can you follow me?"

I needed to go. I needed to fix my face.

The giant was still staring at me. The guy with him was now also staring at me.

Man, oh man. Those business suits...

Oh God.

Now the makeup guy was staring.

My face and neck got hot, probably breeding more of those red splotches. I ducked my head. "Yes. Sorry."

There was another beat of silence. "Follow me, please."

We continued down the hallway. I kept my head down, becoming mute—another habit I'd learned growing up. It helped with the attention. When you didn't respond, people just talked about you instead of to you. Eventually they forgot you were in the room.

I got back into the chair, and he started fussing.

A new shirt was brought in.

All the while, I sat there, my eyes anywhere except making eye contact, and I waited for the usual numbness to settle over me. It was like a blanket. My system would return to being empty but peaceful.

I liked the emptiness. I could function if I felt empty.

It wasn't happening.

Whoever that guy was, he'd stirred something in me that wasn't settling.

Slight panic laced through me. *What do I do with this?*

"You met our newest Kings football player," the makeup guy said. "Defensive end, I believe. He's delicious, ain't he?"

My mouth went dry. "He plays football?"

"Mmm-hmmm." He kept working on my face. Another person was smoothing my hair because I had messed that up as well. "He's one of those big, burly guys who tackle the quarterback."

The hair guy laughed. "You think every football player tackles the quarterback."

"They don't?"

Both laughed.

"Or maybe that's just what I would like to do," Makeup Guy clarified. "Colby Doubard. Hmmmm mmmm mmmm. Either way, this one is the newest sports celebrity in town. Brett Broudou is here to promote a charity."

Brett Broudou.

I couldn't believe I hadn't recognized him.

I started to nod with them, dazed.

He made a disapproving sound. "Don't move, sweetie. They switched your segment so the football hottie is going on first, in your place, but we don't have a lot of extra time."

"Right. Sorry." I was horrified, but still... Football. It's one of the few things I knew. I enjoyed watching all the trades, seeing how the teams worked together with new players on the roster. The trash talking. The egos. The politics. The continuously evolving door of all the coaches going from one team to the other. The personal relationships too.

And the Kings had won the Super Bowl last year.

I'd been on a high for two weeks after the game. I'd even indulged by ordering pizza and Chinese food the next day because I was still celebrating. I almost immediately regretted it, but it'd been worth it. It'd been my own little personal party that lasted two days, or more if the diarrhea counted.

I was kicking myself because I should've recognized him when he spoke.

I was glad I hadn't in the moment. My reaction would've been worse. I'd already made a fool of myself. He thought there was something wrong with me. The first guy in ten years who'd made me feel something thought... I didn't know what he thought. Nothing good, I'm sure.

"Okay, sweetiekins." The makeup guy stepped back to admire his work. "You are back to being gorgeous! And you're just in time for your segment."

"What?" But we were moving, a staff person drawing me along—off the chair, down a hallway. I heard the audience applauding, and I saw him again.

Brett Broudou.

A shiver went through me.

He was delicious.

He stood to the side, off-camera, talking with a bunch of the show people. That made sense now. That had probably been his agent or manager next to him, the other guy in a business suit.

The staffer brought us to a stop.

I felt Brett's eyes coming my way.

I felt the punch of them landing on me, and oh boy, my body heated all over again.

This wasn't good. Just a look and I was hot and bothered?

"Okay!" The staff person touched the small of my back and pushed. "You're on, Willow."

I started but looked back. "My name isn't—" I didn't go by that name. I went by Billie. It was the nickname my little brother gave me. He could tell the host through their earpieces, and I wouldn't have to endure being called Willow during the whole interview. Only when I tried to tell him that, my feet weren't paying attention.

One kept going.

The other started to turn back.

They twisted and *slam!* Down I went.

Or I would've gone down.

The audience gasped.

A few cursed.

I felt myself melting into a puddle of shame. All the work they did to make me look good and this? I was a disaster.

A pair of hands caught me.

It was happening in slow motion and my heart literally did a backwards flip in my chest.

I was held before being lifted up against a strong and massive chest.

My throat was up in my mouth.

I didn't know what to do because part of me didn't want to pull away because I knew who had caught me and I didn't want to pull away from him. Who would? And the other part was already thinking about what happened, where it happened, and oh no.

I hoped that hadn't been caught by the camera, but then I was being lifted back to my feet and released from the chest behind me.

It was like magic.

I knew, but I hadn't known. Though, I *knew.*

Brett Broudou was standing in front of me.

The defensive end out of Cal U who never played football in high school but got recruited because he'd been scrimmaging with the right guys at the right place, right time, and a scout saw him. Saw his size. Saw his speed. Saw his reflexes, and he was asked to try out. He got a full scholarship and then went on to college stardom. Cal U won the National Championship, and Brett went in the first round of the draft to Kansas City. He was given a five-year contract, and they kept renewing until he'd come to the Texas Kings last year. He'd been a perfect combination with Stone Reeves, Jake Bilson, and Colby Doubard. The Kings were going to be unstoppable.

And he was still touching me. On television.

"I—" I couldn't talk. My face felt so hot. I was going to break out in splotches all over again.

He gave me the kindest smile, which almost broke my heart because I knew it must've been filled with pity. "They're waiting for you."

Right.

Interview.

I jerked around, smoothed a hand over my hair, and strode out.

The host had stood from her table, starting to come toward me. I waved her back. "I'm good. I'm so sorry about that."

She laughed, and the audience joined in. Everything was getting back to normal. *Though, God, how humiliating.*

She extended a hand for me to take a seat, and as I did, I smiled, hoping to hide my mortification. "I can be clumsy sometimes. I'm sorry again."

"No, no. As long as you're okay?" Her eyes held mine.

I managed a nod. I'd blanked on her name.

The back of my neck was so hot.

She turned to the audience and started our interview. "Ladies and gentlemen, Willow Harm is the only person to have come face-to-face with the infamous serial killer known as the Midwest Butcher. She is the *survivor* who helped bring him down. Welcome to the show, Willow."

2

BILLIE

Lo: How'd the interview go??? I recorded it so I can watch it when I get home.

I'd escaped the stage in one piece, my interview complete. Now I was back in the green room, trying to remember how to breathe normally and staring at my phone.

Lo: Mom said the chickens are upset. They've not been producing the normal amount of eggs. She's worried about you, so I'm going to stop out at the place and bring some from the store. They'll be organic and free range, don't worry. Or I can grab some from my neighbor's place. They love their chickens. They built a whole playground for them. She messaged they had extra. I'll try her first, and if she doesn't have any left, I'll go to the store. Anywho, let me know how the interview went!! I'm sure it went great. You always think you do worse than you do. Love you lots. Want to have some wine tonight? I know Mom has some on hand, but I can grab some extra too. BYE!

Elowin was like a sister. That's what I called her in my head —like a sister. But Elowin, or Lo, would call herself my actual sister. It was easier for her, easier for them, her parents, Vicky and Harold Mitchell. They were a bit more reserved than Lo, but I knew the sentiment was there. They considered me their daughter, their second girl. But for me, on the outside, it was safer to remind myself I wasn't blood.

I wasn't really family.

I did love them. All of them. I'd never be able to express how grateful I was to have met them at fifteen. It was an awkward age, so bless their hearts for that as well. Lo was three years older than me. I was a freshman, and she was about to graduate, so we got one year in the same school together. After that, she went to Texas A&M, and I spent time with her during her school breaks.

Me: The interview was okay, but I tripped on the way out and I think the camera got it. I was mortified.

Lo: Heyyyy!! Don't worry about that. Even when you trip, you look like a little swan. Graceful and elegant and all class. Plus, with your story, no one will laugh.

Me: Hopefully. Wine sounds good tonight.

Lo: REALLY??? Yay!! I'm excited. Want me to come alone or should I bring Roger and the kids?

Me: Bring Roger and the kids. You know your mom and dad will dote on them.

Lo: I'm asking because *you know* Roger is going to want to have wine with us, and if he wasn't as head over heels for me as he is, I'd be worried! He adores you. But you're warned. He's going to be on cloud nine since you finally agreed to be interviewed.

I sighed. Roger had this delusion that if I put myself out there more for publicity, my story would make me money. A few writers had reached out, asking to interview me, but I'd turned them down. Roger wanted a movie, and he thought a bestselling book would be the ticket to that. I'd had a few inquiries, but Roger didn't understand that I flat out wanted nothing to do with any publicity—no books, no newspaper articles, no blogs, no television shows, and most certainly no movies.

They didn't entirely need my permission, but I'd kept details quiet, so without me, all they had were theories and rumors. Only I—and certain people in law enforcement—knew what had happened that morning when I came across the Midwest Butcher.

I blamed the wine Lo had supplied me and my own soft heart for agreeing when the local news channel had contacted me. They were doing a segment on domestic abuse and violence and said they thought my story would draw even more viewers. I'd agreed only for that reason.

Me: Roger is hilarious. Bring on Wine Roger!

Lo: I'm going to remind you of this when he's badgering you tonight about why you're not dating.

She was right, but I had a soft spot for Wine Roger. He would be considered a golden boy, or now a golden husband—one of those guys who grew up popular, good-looking, and nice, yet it never changed him. He was nice in school, nice in college, and still nice. He could've had a huge ego with his perfect tan, sharp jawline, smoldering blue eyes, and broad shoulders. Roger could've been famous himself if he'd wanted. He played baseball in college but chose to marry Lo and start a family instead of going pro. Lo always got choked up when she talked about it, because they'd made a conscious decision to have her pursue law and her career. Roger got a job at his father's golf course and took care of the kids while Lo went to law school.

Man. Thinking about them again, thinking about all of them, I realized just how lucky I was.

None of them should've loved me. None of them should've accepted me. With my past, my very heavy baggage, all my therapy, all my issues? Yet still they let me live with them.

I didn't deserve them.

I gathered my things, exchanged the borrowed shirt for my sweaty one, and headed for the elevator.

"You did great, Miss Harm," said one of the staff as he walked past me.

I should've lifted my head and squared my shoulders with confidence. But that wasn't me. Instead, I ducked my head and mumbled, "Thank you." Learning to be invisible had saved my life, literally, but Lo's text was on my mind. She was right. Roger was always asking to set me up. He had two friends he said would love to go out with me.

Roger and Lo didn't get it.

Sometimes the way to get through life was to be as small as possible.

There were reasons I didn't date.

"My agent says your trip is already trending." That same deep baritone from earlier, smooth like whisky, sounded from behind me in the elevator.

Gah! I'd been looking at the floor as I got on. I'd not even noticed him. Brett Broudou was there, staring at me. This guy wasn't small. At all. How had I *not* noticed him?

Where are my survival instincts now?

His words penetrated. My gaze jerked to his. "What'd you say?"

Those eyes, man. So dark and deep and looking inside me.

I squirmed until his lips twitched and I got distracted by how good *that* looked on him.

"I believe the term is that you've *gone viral*," he said. "It's a good thing."

My face was probably all red, but horror pushed aside my normal shyness. "Viral?"

This was my worst nightmare. I didn't want attention, and why had I done the show today? I shouldn't have agreed. I should've kept to my usual policy of no publicity at all.

This was horrible.

"You look good in it," the giant—Brett—assured me. "You don't need to worry about any negativity. Trust me, and anyway, the assholes are assholes. Fuck 'em."

I was now in a daze. He meant that. I could tell. I blinked. "Huh?"

The side of his mouth lifted. He was almost smiling, and I swear, I was pretty sure he leaned toward me. The top half of his body shifted forward. Just a little.

That meant something. Right?

"I said, fuck 'em. That's always been my motto."

I was vaguely aware of the elevator moving, aware that the doors opened. He started forward, then paused.

I moved ahead of him, and he walked beside me off the elevator.

"That's always been your motto?" I asked.

He kept watching me, not looking where we were going. Something about me amused him. "Yes," he said seriously. "Only people's opinions that should mean anything to you are the people you love."

I started to say I didn't have anyone like that, but I stopped because it wasn't true. Vicky, Howard, Lo, Roger, and their three girls loved me. Vicky's chickens loved me. Miss Sylvia Rivera really loved me.

"Miss Sylvia Rivera?"

My face flooded with heat. "I said that out loud?"

He nodded, no longer smiling. "Who's Miss Sylvia Rivera?"

"My—where I live, this woman has a bunch of chickens. Miss Sylvia Rivera is my favorite hen. I named her after the real Sylvia Rivera. She was at the Stonewall riots. She also cofounded a homeless shelter for LGBTQ+ youth. And—" I stopped myself. My love was true and genuine. I could've talked for hours about all the great things the real Sylvia Rivera did. "She's just someone I really respect."

"I'm getting that." His tone was kind again.

Why was it kind?

"Broudou! Hey, my man," a voice said. "Could I get a selfie with you?"

"Oh man! It's Brett Broudou. You kicked ass in the Super Bowl last year. The Orcas didn't know what hit them."

His buddy laughed. "Literally, man. I could tell Doubard was happy you're on his team. Hey! Is it true you and Mason Kade are archrivals from high school?"

"Was it about his woman?" the first guy piped up, handing over a pen and paper. "Aren't you, like, screwing a supermodel?"

I'd gone tense at the first question, not paying attention to where we were going, and boom, here we were, out on the street. What was I doing on the street? My car was in the parking lot.

I was tense and confused about our location.

Brett said, his voice went low. "You want a selfie with me, and you expect me to sign your shit while you speak disrespectfully about people I know? You serious right now?"

Whoa.

Brett's jaw was clenched, and he hadn't moved a muscle to do anything for these guys. Pose. Sign. Nothing. He scowled at them to the point that it seemed he was keeping himself from putting his hands on them.

I'd known this about him earlier. It was a sixth sense I had, knowing when someone was capable of violence. There was a difference I could feel between people—those who had never needed to use violence but were capable, people who weren't capable of it, and those who had needed to be violent and would and could be violent again if a situation occurred.

Brett was in that last category.

Brett?

I was on a first-name basis with him?

I suppose anyone who knew about Miss Sylvia Rivera should be on a first-name basis with me. I didn't talk about her with just anyone. I held her in such high regard, like the real Sylvia.

But also *whoa*, because I knew Mason Kade. He'd gone over to join the San Diego Orcas, a brand-new team, and they'd shocked everyone by almost winning the Lombardi. Brett knew him in real life? From childhood? I was trying to remember who Mason Kade's woman was, but I couldn't. My football knowledge centered mostly on the players themselves, their college playing history, and the general game gossip about them. I didn't pay attention to the blogs that wrote about their personal lives, unless they'd been arrested for some reason and that interfered with their career. I'd never heard about that with Mason Kade. Most newscasters just talked about his athleticism and whether he was going to stay with the Pats, his old team, which he hadn't.

"Whooooaaaa! The Brood Machine is activated."

That guy's voice was annoying. It was high and shrill. There was a wide smile on his face, like he was watching a show play out in front of him. The other guy looked more chastised. His head was down, and he looked back at the group of guys waiting for them. There was a girl with them, and she eyed Brett like he was covered in whipped cream.

She probably needed a hamburger.

The guy shoved his paper and pen out again. "Just sign, man. We didn't mean anything." He moved closer, lowering his voice. "My girlfriend is two seconds away from coming over here and pressing her breasts against your chest. I love her, but she's a fame whore." He looked to me now. "No disrespect, ma'am."

"Ma'am?" I barked, all my usual hesitancies forgotten. Who was this? I didn't recognize myself. "I'm thirty-two. Not old enough to be your mama."

He flushed. "I call every woman older than me ma'am. It's just a thing."

The other guy hooted. "He just insulted Broody's woman. This is classic. Hey, wait a minute." His laugh died. His head straightened, and his eyes got big. "You're the chick who tripped this morning. On CBX. It was a clip from their show. HOLY SHIT! You guys." He stepped to the side, pointing at me. "This is the hot chick that took a nosedive." He looked between Brett and me. "That like *just* happened, didn't it? It was loaded an hour ago, and ESPN already added it to their Sunday highlights. It's all a joke, that Broody's magic is so powerful, even a girl who survived a serial killer is affected. And shit, girl. I'm real sorry about what you went through." A keen look flashed in his eyes. He tilted his skinny head to the side. "Can I have your autograph?"

"Fuck's sake." Brett's hand wrapped around my shoulder, tucking me against his side.

Tingles shot through me. Humiliation raged inside me, but it warred with the fact that he was touching me again. *Oh no. Yay. No. Yay! Shit, no. But also, yay!*

He smelled good. Like fresh laundry. That was the best smell.

And his chest was so tight. There was no softness to him at all—not that a little softness was bad. I liked a little cushion. Dad bods. Brett Broudou *definitely* did not have a dad bod. All muscles. And strength. And hardness.

I needed to stop thinking.

"I mean this with the utmost respect," Brett clipped out. The guys quieted. I waited. "But fuck off." He moved us back and returned to the lobby.

An hour ago?

I'd stayed after to talk with one of the producers because she knew Vicky, and then to calm down, but it'd been over an hour?

I'd lost track of time.

"Mr. Broudou?" One of the front lobby guards approached, likely concerned about how livid Brett seemed. It was radiating off him.

Yet somehow I felt protected and safe. None of the violent tendencies emanating from him affected me, which was shocking, because with my past, with anyone else, I wouldn't be anywhere near him.

I would've sensed them on the elevator immediately. And I would have gotten the hell out of there.

"Yeah. Stupid dipshits outside," Brett explained. "Can you have my car brought to the parking ramp? Is there a connecting door to it from this building?"

The guard nodded. "Do you want the police called?" He had a walkie out and was walking quickly beside us, an arm stretched ahead, showing the way.

"No. They're just young shits. We were all young shits at some point."

"Of course, Mr. Broudou. And yes, we got ahold of your driver. He needs to go around the block in order to pull into the ramp. It'll be a short wait, if you'd like me to stay with you?"

"No. I'll be fine. Thank you. It's not a big deal." There was a slight pause, and the guard's gaze moved my way. Understanding dawned.

He nodded. "Yes, of course. Miss Harm, would you like me to arrange for a ride home?"

I felt Brett tense again as we arrived at the skyway connecting the ramp with the building. I stepped away, feeling the loss of his body heat. I shook my head. "I parked in here. It's just over there. I'll be fine."

"Ah. Yes." He looked Brett's way one last time before inclining his head. "I hope you both have a good day." He left quickly after that.

The door swooshed closed.

"I want to see you," Brett stated.

"What?" My stomach fell out of my body.

In a good way. *I think...*

A set of headlights swept up over the lane as a car came inside.

Brett sighed, tightly. "Of all days for me to get a ride from my agent and Jason has to leave early." His eyes found mine, ignoring the SUV now waiting. "I drive myself. I always drive myself. Why the fuck did I start not driving myself today?" He grinned.

God. Even that was smoldering.

I had a problem.

I was horny.

I never had this problem. Or rarely. I'd been horny, of course. That was normal, but not to the point where a smile could fry my brain.

I was horny for Brett Broudou.

I'd have to stop watching the Kings. That would suck. I really liked watching the Kings.

He took a step toward me, his gaze holding me in place. "Why do I feel like you're going to rabbit if I let you out of my sight?"

My mouth opened, and I said it before I knew I was going to say it. "Because I will."

His eyes flashed before darkening. "Why?"

"Because you scare me."

This was why I didn't like hormones. They complicated, well, everything.

He froze.

"I mean, not in a bad way," I rushed out, holding up a hand. "In a good way."

His hand took mine and he tugged, gently. With purpose. "Leave your car. Come have coffee with me." He entwined our fingers. "Right now."

Flames zipped through my body. My hand was on fire. I kept staring at his big fingers next to mine, how his hand almost swallowed mine. "Right now?"

He tugged again, until I was almost touching the front of his body. "I want to learn more about Sylvia Rivera."

"You do?" I breathed. "She did so many things. I've had her Wikipedia page memorized since it was created—"

"I meant the chicken."

My chest deflated but then inflated. I also loved talking about my favorite hen. "Oh, Miss Sylvia Rivera. She has no nickname. It's the full name. You either commit to it or you just call her Hen One. It's the rule around the flock." I could've said more, but noticed his lip twitching again, so I bit the inside of my cheek to shut up. "You don't really want to know about Miss Sylvia Rivera."

"You're wrong. I want to know about anything you like. You shut down, but when you talk about Sylvia Rivera, your eyes light up. Your face gets this glow. I want to know what else makes you glow."

He watched my every move, studying my face as if he needed to memorize it.

I confessed, softly, "This doesn't happen to me."

"What doesn't?" A slight pressure from his hand, and I was pressed against him.

Ooh. That felt nice.

He moved his thumb along the inside of my palm, and more sensations raced through me. He held me in place, not pushing any closer, just keeping me there, with his front touching my front.

My horny needs exploded in me, reminding me it'd been years since I was touched like this. Did that make me pathetic?

"I've only dated two people in my life," I said, faintly.

His smile was quick, and it was stunning, flooding my body

with warm feelings. Warm aches. "I was thinking we could start with coffee first. Then see what happens."

"I could do coffee."

His smile flared again, and yep, my knees actually knocked together. "Perfect."

He must've given a signal, because suddenly there was a man behind us, opening the rear door of the SUV. "Mr. Broudou."

Brett guided me inside.

The man gave me a nod. "Ms. Harm."

"Miss." I said it without thinking as I moved to the far side.

"Miss Harm."

Brett got in next to me, but he didn't crowd me. He stayed on his side, his body seeming relaxed. "Do you have a favorite coffee place?"

I shook my head. "I usually just make it at home. I have the best almond creamer. Can't get that quality anywhere else. Except the grocery store, where I bought it."

He was smiling again and leaned up to ask the driver, "Where do you get coffee?"

"Miss Walters' is local and has the best coffee there is." The SUV started forward. "Also got a nice back area for privacy."

"I think that'd be perfect," Brett said.

"I know the owner. I'll give them a call ahead."

"Thank you."

The divider went up after that, and it was just Brett Broudou and me in the backseat.

And my horniness.

"I KNOW WHO YOU ARE, you know."

We were still in the back of the SUV. Brett had been looking out the window, letting me sit with silence, which I was grateful for. That's the kind of person I am, and it was like he could sense that and give me what I needed.

Major points there, on top of everything else about him.

I swallowed over a nervous knot and picked at my seatbelt with my fingers. "The football you. Your career. I know all your stats. I know who scouted you for Cal U, that you never played in high school. I know all of that. I just felt like you should know since you've made your interest known. You know, your interest in maybe seeing me naked." I rushed on, ignoring how he'd gone still after that last statement. "I'm a football person. It's something I like to watch."

He remained quiet, an eyebrow raised.

I frowned. "I don't know what that look is for. I'm putting my cards on the table."

"I don't think it's fair."

I frowned again. "What?"

"You know all about my career, and I know almost nothing about you." He grinned. "Except that you love chickens and also Sylvia Rivera, who I will learn everything about now that you've gotten me intrigued."

I perked up. "I can tell you all about her."

He leaned toward me, across the seat. "I'd like to know about you."

I slumped down. "Well, that's the problem."

"What do you mean?"

I shook my head, my tongue feeling heavy. What was there to say about me? Trust issues galore? Baggage to the excess? "The chickens are kinda my selling point," I admitted.

His head leaned back, and he laughed.

I never would've expected that response, and I was fascinated by the sound of it, wanting to hear it more, hear it often, and let it settle over me like a warm blanket—on a cold night, not a warm night. That's an important difference.

"Do it again," I breathed.

He stopped. "What?"

"Laugh. It sounds amazing. Do it again."

He didn't, but he did give me a rueful grin. "I'm not a laugh-on-command type of guy."

"You should be. You could make millions on Cameo."

His next laugh was abrupt, as if it was out before he knew it, surprising himself.

I grinned. "I'm telling you, millions. Not that you need more millions. You're one of the best defensive ends in the business. You and Chase Hart, but you have longevity. He won't be where you are at your age."

"Thanks."

"Not that you're old. You're not, but for football and for your position, you've lasted a long time. The average is a little over three years. For linemen, it's just slightly longer. Unless you're a first-round pick, which you were. Then the average is nine years, so you've exceeded that by three years and counting." I noticed a peculiar look on his face and stopped. "What?"

His voice was soft, just as the vehicle came to a stop. "You love female icons. You love chickens. You just rattled off stats that a normal person would not know without looking them up, and you sit here and say 'what' like you have no idea how you're wrapping this entire package up for me." His eyes went hard. Cold.

Shivers went down my spine.

His tone was deep, a warning. "The tripping? It was a nice meet-cute. The fanboys? I can't decide if they were a plant or not. They seemed real, but all of this? You stepped too far over the line. Here's something you missed in your research. I grew up with criminals, but I must be losing my touch. It took this long for me to spot the con."

The door opened, and Brett got out.

I was too stunned to move.

He turned to the driver. "I'll find my own way home. Please take Miss Harm back to her vehicle."

What?

It felt like he'd calmly walked up to me, stone-faced, lifted his leg, and kicked me deftly in the sternum.

Again. *What?*

3

BILLIE

"Pssst, Billie!" Lo fake whispered, laughing as she climbed into my bed with me. The whole thing rocked from side to side and she landed against my hip, still laughing. "You're famous! And not because of your past, but because you're gorgeous and who knew the hotness Brett Broudou had hiding under those pads and helmet. Wowza, the second clip is giving me steam factor."

I rolled over. "What second clip?"

The first one, where I tripped, was still trending. I was pretending it hadn't happened, which was easy because none of my clients knew my real name and I barely went out. My plan was to hide at my place, continue working, and take care of the chickens. In a week or two, the clip would blow over. No one would remember me until the next anniversary of when the Midwest Butcher was apprehended. I'd go into hiding again.

Lo cued up her phone and handed it to me. This clip showed the fanboys on the street. I was in the background. Brett was shielding me. I hadn't remembered him doing that in the moment, and snapping at one of the guys. It showed Brett's statement to the guy, not what the guy had said to him.

"He's protecting you," Lo said. "That's mega sweet."

"No, they didn't include the beginning part. The guy asked if Broudou was rivals with Mason Kade because of Mason Kade's woman. Broudou knows both of them."

"What?" Lo hiccupped, which made her start laughing all over again. "You mean that second clip has nothing to do with you?"

I had to grin a little. I'd been in a dark hole, stinging more from Brett's utter and complete rejection than anything else. I'd almost forgotten about the trending clip, now clips. "This one is really trending?"

She shrugged. "Not as much, but it got some juice yesterday. Assholes, though. They're capitalizing on your shitty situation."

When I'd gotten home after the disastrous interview, I'd made my excuses to skip Wine Roger night, wanting to do just this: hide out in my dark room. But Lo being Lo, she hadn't gone for that. She'd dragged me back to the patio table and gotten the story out of me. She kept up to date on anything viral and trending. She would've found out about the clip no matter what. Roger had actually been the one who found it first, nearly spitting out his second glass of wine as he jerked forward in his chair. He'd been leaning it back so the front two legs were in the air, which Lo and I and his mother-in-law always told him not to do, but after the first glass of wine, he always forgot.

"Why were you guys on the street together? Were you walking to your cars or something?"

Lo knew me, knew I wouldn't have been walking with him for any other reason, because let's face it. Brett Broudou was Brett Broudou. Super famous. Super hot.

And super out of my league.

Except he said he was interested, a tiny voice whispered in my head.

I'd not told them about the coffee date that almost happened.

Pain sliced through me.

Gah. The way he'd looked at me at the end, as if he hated me.

There was no con. I couldn't believe that's what he thought. That made me ache for him. What had happened to make him think like that? Though, he *was* a celebrity professional athlete. I'm sure all sorts of people tried to target him for money, attention, or whatever other reasons people target people.

It was laughable how far I was on the *opposite end* of being a person like that.

I ran away from attention. In my life, attention never brought anything good.

I shrugged. "Just wrong place, wrong time kind of thing. I was trying to get to the food truck."

Lo snorted. "Are you serious? That's even more hilarious. Also, I looked up this Mason Kade guy. Holy effin hotness, man. He looks like a way rougher Superman Henry Cavill kind of guy. I've been sleeping on football. You watch the sport. Who are the other supreme hotties?" She poked my shoulder before settling beside me, lying on her back. "Man, and those uniforms. They knew what they were doing, accentuating their shoulders. Then how tight it gets on the bottom? Those asses." She sighed. "Next Halloween, Roger's going as an NFL player. We'll have some good sex that night."

A corner of my lip curved up.

"I prefer a guy with a beard." Such as Brett Broudou.

Lo shared a smile with me. "Roger's been hinting that he wants to grow a beard. He's been trying with his mustache, but it just makes him look like a super villain in some cartoon movie."

I barked out a laugh. "Not a cartoon movie."

"I mean, he can't even look like a villain from a cool movie. He's got cartoon vibes."

"Tell him about the football costume tonight when you tell him he can't grow a beard."

She smiled. "He'll go out and buy it tomorrow. And he'll wear it around the house. God. He'll so totally do that. He'll pose, asking how he looks in this position or that. He might even carry a football around the house with him, trying to make it look all casual, as if he's just getting home from practice."

We were laughing all over again.

Then we fell into a comfortable pocket of silence.

"All jokes aside, you got the dark-room effect going here," Lo noted. "Should Vicky start making a meal plan for you? Scheduling who brings you your tray for breakfast, lunch, afternoon snack, and dinner?"

"Afternoon snack?"

"Everyone needs an afternoon snack. No shame in that."

Her concern was disguised as a joke, but she was gauging how upset I was about the trending videos. Any attention tended to bring more fanatics out to find me—reporters, bloggers, writers convinced their book about the Midwest Butcher would land them a deal.

Hiding in a dark space kept me alive, so it was my go-to when I needed to feel safe. Vicky and Howard had found me many times in a dark room, but they'd always coaxed me out.

My current dark-room situation wasn't about the videos going viral, but I couldn't bring myself to tell Lo. The rejection stung, more than it should've. That made it sting even more.

What was my issue? So what? He asked me for coffee.

So what if I'd wanted to go?

I could go to coffee with another guy.

That was the thing. I didn't want to go with someone else.

I'd not been interested in anyone for so long. It felt nice, just to have that feeling, and he crushed it so quickly. So cutthroat too. That side of him was evident in football. He was one of the best defensive linemen for a reason, and I'd always been intrigued by him. I was elated when he came to the Kings. He hated doing press, except for the times he'd promote a charity. He was kind in those moments, no matter what. But there was a deeper, darker, rough side to him—an asshole side. The fans called it the Brood Machine, a play on his last name, when he was on the field. Most quarterbacks feared him. Colby Doubard, the Kings' quarterback, had said many times that he was glad Broudou played with him and not against him.

Maybe I wanted to have coffee with him because something was healing inside me? Maybe it wasn't even about him, but about the coffee, about going and having coffee with another person in a date-like setting?

I opened my mouth.

Don't do this. You know it ain't about the coffee. That tiny voice was back in my head, this time reprimanding me.

I spoke anyway. "Maybe Roger should set me up with one of his friends."

Lo went rigid in the bed, then jerked upright with a gasp. "WHAT?!" Her eyes were huge, a wide smile stretching her face. "Okay. No. Don't answer me. I'm not even going to try to connect the dots for whatever thought train you used to get to that suggestion, but yes! Yes! Travis. It should be Travis. I would never let him set you up with Doug. Nothing against Doug, but as your sister, you need to go with the guy even I would date if I wasn't already madly in love with Roger. Travis is the guy."

Girl, what did you do?

I ignored my inner voice. "Okay. Travis it is."

"Oh! Do you want to double date? OH! Yes. I know you. You're probably already freaking out inside at the idea of a date.

Let's do a hangout. Group hangout. I'll invite some of our other
friends so it's not so obvious it's a setup for you and Travis—"

"No." I was determined now. This was not about Brett
himself. It was about the coffee. "A date. If he's a friend of
Roger's, I know he's a good guy. I can meet a good guy for a
meal." *Thought it was about the coffee?* "Or for coffee."

"Coffee?" Lo wasn't privy to my inner voice. Lucky her.

"Either. I don't care."

See? This was not about Brett Broudou.

"We can turn the light on now," I announced.

4

BRETT

We'd had a game yesterday, so I was coming in this morning later than usual. The elevators opened at the stadium, and I stepped off, heading for the reception area in our publicity offices.

The woman behind the desk smiled as she lifted the phone to her ear. "You can have a quick seat, Brett. I'm just letting Kim know you're here."

I gave her a nod and helped myself to some water from the little fridge. By the time I turned, Kim was coming out of her office and bustling my way, her suit jacket flapping to the side. Dressed in her normal business top, usually silk, and a business skirt on the bottom with pointed flats on her feet. She was fierce like a bull. Caucasian. Maybe five feet and an inch. Red hair that was cut at her jawline, and a bunch of her strands lifted in the air from how fast she was walking. A pretty face, except for the perpetual scowl she always seemed to have when dealing with me or any of the players. Kim was a no-bullshitter, and seeing the sharp look in her eye, I wasn't sure what to expect from this meeting. I didn't often get called to the office. At my old team, they'd learned I wasn't the one to handle the usual press questions, but if they wanted a player to promote a nonprofit, I was all about that.

"Brett." Kim signaled for me to follow as she ducked through another door. "Come on in here. My office is overrun by interns right now, trying to find something to dig us out of a Colby-sized hole. By the way, I know you've not been here long, but thank you for never making a Brett-sized hole. At least so far." She sat with a frantic air around her.

"You want the door closed?"

"What?" She looked up. "Oh, yes. Please. Thank you." She typed on her phone. Once the door was closed and I sat at the far end of the table, she stopped. "Okay. Tell me about CBX news. They said you did well last week."

She paused, but I just waited. I knew a bait when I heard one. She wanted something from me.

She kept eyeing me. "The clip is still trending."

I grunted. *Fuck that clip.* I was still pissed a week later, but I couldn't figure out her hook—not Kim's, Willow Harm's. I'd been interested the moment I saw her walk past my room, and I'd stayed by the stage on purpose because I wanted to see her walk past for her segment on the show.

Then she'd tripped.

And after I'd watched her do her segment, and holy shit. She'd gone to a friend's house for a playdate when the Midwest Butcher showed up. He'd killed everyone except her. She'd been hiding, and the speculation was that he hadn't been looking for another child in the house. I was jaded from knowing the worst of the worst, and nothing much shocked me.

Her story shocked me. It made me feel cold to the bone that she'd gone through that.

She'd gone into foster care after that, which made me wonder what had happened to her real family. Had something already happened, and that's why that friend's family was watching her? That made sense. Foster care was hard. It pushed my buttons. Anyone who fucking decided to foster children, not for the children but for the money, deserved to be destroyed. Which I'd done. And I enjoyed it, especially when it was my fucking sister, who'd tried four times to foster a kid. I'd never let her do that, not when she barely raised her own.

If my sister had a heart of gold and was doing it for the right reasons, I'd be a big supporter. She didn't. She was a parasite on society.

Shit. Was my sister after the con? It *was* something Shannon would do. Find someone she knew I'd like. Prep her with the right things to say. Willow Harm likes football. She likes odd shit, like chickens. She even named a fucking chicken after an activist. I liked all of that, a lot. It'd been too good.

I didn't know how she'd done it, but it all made sense now. My fucking sister. She could do the long con, do her research, find out when I'd be doing another promotion on CBX. *Shit.* It was within her abilities to make friends with someone on staff and get her "friend" booked because somehow surviving a serial killer was related to highlighting domestic abuse?

This was the month for it, for fuck's sake.

And having the girl trip? That was also classic Shannon. Make me feel like a stud, like I needed to save the damsel. Though if Shannon had been the one who'd tripped and been rescued, she would've already had a hand snaked around my back, lifting the wallet out of my pocket.

Willow Harm's face flashed in my mind—her big, doe-eyed, deer-in-the-headlights look. She was a knockout.

She also had no fucking clue she was a knockout.

I'd fallen for it. All of it.

Now what? This was take two?

I waited to hear Kim say they wanted me to do an event with Willow Harm.

Or hell, maybe I needed to step back and stop thinking like

a fucking calculating asshole like my sister. Maybe none of it
was a con and I'd misjudged everything?

Jesus fucking shit. I wasn't sure what to do right now.

"You have nothing to say?"

Kim was hella smart. She had eyes like a hawk, missing
nothing.

I didn't respond.

She tapped on her phone. "Okay. Not that you're a big talker
anyway, but what's this?" She turned her phone around and
slid it my way.

Street noises came first, loud and invasive, and my voice
came second. *"...I mean this with the utmost respect. But fuck off."*

Kim took the phone back. She left it on the table in front of
her, sat back in her chair, and folded her arms over her chest.
"The rest of the video shows you manhandling Willow Harm
back into the station."

I cursed again. "That's not what happened."

She raised an eyebrow. "Care to fill me in? This is the third
video that's been released since that show. I'm sure they're
doctored for a negative slant, but this month is domestic abuse
awareness. Not to mention, Miss Harm isn't just some survivor.
She survived a monster who killed sixty-two people up and
down the entire middle section of this nation. She's the only
one who survived, and his story is *still* selling headlines. People
love sports, but they also love the shit out of serial killers.
Willow Harm is this shiny toy everyone wants to talk to, love,
protect, shield—and by the way, she's notorious for wanting
nothing to do with any press. Nada. Zilch. No one even knows
where she lives. People used to try to follow her. After a while
she caught on and drove to a farm outside of town. The guy, no
joke, met their cars with a rifle. After that it was widely known
that if you wanted to find out where Willow Harm lived, you
needed two extra tires because that rifle wasn't a toy. He shot
out the tires."

I'm sure. This fit the script as if Shannon had written it herself... But fuck. It wasn't like that. This woman, all her life? "She's never done press?"

"Hardly ever," Kim clipped out. "You were the cherry on top for the show last week, but the real headline was her. She only came out because of the cause. Obviously, violence in any form hits close to home for her." She leaned forward, her sharp eyes never leaving my face, and she tapped again on her phone screen. "This is a problem for the team. This is a problem for you."

That opinion might've explained why I had two missed calls from my agent and three from my manager. "It really wasn't the way it seems."

She nodded. "I talked to someone at the station. They said you seemed friendly with Willow Harm."

I narrowed my eyes. "You knew the video was bullshit and you dragged me in anyway?"

"Fuck yeah, I did. You've got a reputation in the NFL world. You will support any and all charities. You do your job, almost like you hate quarterbacks and it's your mission to rid the world of them. Though thank you for always doing clean hits when you take them down. And the other reputation you have? Don't push you on anything that's not explicitly in the contract. I'm telling you as a woman, you're hot, you're quiet, and you're dangerous."

I frowned. "Speaking professionally here?"

"Yes." She leaned forward in her seat, her arms crossed over her chest. "My opinion as a woman matters. I got a call from the higher-ups, and they want this shit squashed immediately. I have no clue how to get in touch with Willow Harm. I've been told there was an email address the show used to contact her. That was it. No phone. Nothing else, and that email is gone."

"Gone?"

"Like it never existed." Her eyes were hard. "So riddle me

this, Brett Broudou. You were friendly with her when you went back into the station after running into those dipshits. What happened between then and now? I need to stress this for you. Very little is known about Willow Harm—how she was found, how she helped the police apprehend the Midwest Butcher. It's like that by her design, and I'm guessing with the help of some people who sit seriously high up in the FBI. Again, she is *protected*, and not just by the American people, who *love* her. They watched videos of her being carried out of that house, covered in blood. She looked half starved. Why she was there for a playdate, who the fuck knows? Details weren't released because she was a child."

She was still looking at me as if I'd manhandled Willow Harm. "Fuck. I didn't grab her. I'm *not* like that."

"I know, but I need to know if anything happened between you two." At my pause, she added, "The station said Miss Harm had a vehicle in their parking ramp but chose to get into the car with you. Did you fuck her?"

This bitch. My fury was building, but I clamped it down. "Because she's like that?" I said through gritted teeth. "That's what you're saying?"

She relented, a little. "Again, you're hot, you're quiet, and you're dangerous. You're also a goddamn professional athlete, and you're rich. Yes. Even girls like Willow Harm might, on occasion, decide to throw caution to the wind and hike up their skirt for a guy like you."

"Shit, Kim. I'm blushing." I was boiling under the surface, and she knew it.

Her smile turned cold. "Did you fuck her? In this world we live in, it's a very reasonable question to ask."

"No. I asked her for coffee and changed my mind on the drive."

She went quiet, scrutinizing me. "Why? What'd you do?"

"I did nothing."

"I highly doubt Willow Harm suddenly turned stark raving crazy on a car ride. What happened?"

"I'm not giving you shit for details. You just need to know what I said. I asked her to coffee. We were going for coffee. She was talking, nothing stark raving crazy, though she has a thing for chickens, and I changed my mind."

Kim's head lowered. "Chickens?"

"She's got a thing for Sylvia Rivera."

"The drag queen?"

I frowned. "A female activist."

Kim flicked her eyes up. "Yes, I know who Sylvia Rivera is. Willow Harm is a fan?"

"She named her favorite chicken after her."

"*...Miss Sylvia Rivera. She has no nickname. It's the full name. You either commit to it or you just call her Hen One. It's the rule around the flock.*"

She'd been protective of the name, of the chicken, of the activist. She cared.

Shit.

Shiiiiiit.

Shit!

It hadn't been an act. None of it.

No con.

She was probably someone people tried to con.

My fucking sister—no. I couldn't blame Shannon for this. This was on me. My fuckup. My serious and very real fuckup. I really did need to step back and get my sister's scheming out of my head. It wasn't right to live this way.

"What's going on now?" Kim indicated my face with her finger circling in the air. "Something just happened in that head of yours. Clue me in."

"No." I grunted. They didn't get my personal life. I'd made that a boundary early on. They'd found out about my brother. Knew about my sister. It was Shannon herself who'd reached out for interviews. She'd liked getting paid, until I started suing the tabloids and websites because they were printing lies. It took a while, but eventually the media learned not to take my sister's calls. They also learned that I was relentless. I had to be, because my sister was a shark, always looking for someone's blood.

"Do you have suggestions on how to fix this clusterfuck?" Kim asked.

The video was only a hot item now because of the other two clips. Backtrack two weeks, and a video like that wouldn't even get an email in acknowledgement, much less a phone call, a call to the office, and a whole sit down. Kim was right. This was because of Willow Harm's effect, not mine.

I was *seriously* a dick.

"Look, I don't have anything for you," I told her. "I have no clue how to get ahold of Miss Harm. We didn't exchange numbers. Or anything else," I added at her look.

"They're asking for a statement on this video," she informed me. "We're going to put something out."

The team's stance on drama was that none existed. For them to want to respond said a lot.

"Is that necessary?" I asked.

"It'll help stop the video from getting any more attention. In this situation, we need to say something. Of course we'll deny the insinuations. But Brett, you need to tell me if anything else will come from this. It's apparent you pissed these guys off, and they're claiming their fifteen minutes of fame."

I swore, because hell, there could be.

"What?" she asked immediately.

I told her about the guys' initial question, about Kade and his woman.

"Samantha Kade? Or Strattan? She was an Olympic runner, wasn't she?"

I nodded. "She competed three times."

"What's the answer to their question?"

"No. There's no rivalry where she is concerned. Mason and Sam were together in high school. I stepped in on a situation to help Sam once, but that was it. She was wifed up already with Kade, even back then."

Kim mulled over what I'd said, her mouth twisted in a snarl. "I don't like it, *but*—" Her finger came up as if I was going to interrupt her. I wasn't. "—Kade is almost as bad as you are about putting out statements. He'll handle press if he has to, but the only thing I can think of is that they might go to him, put a twist on what was said, and see if they can get a rise out of him." She thought another moment. "There's no bad blood there? I watched their documentary. Your towns were rivals."

"We had dinner after the Super Bowl."

"No shit?"

"No shit."

She grunted. "Okay. We'll consider this whole fuckup no longer a fuckup, as long as it dies down. And these little assholes will receive a threatening letter to cease and desist their games or be slapped with a lawsuit." Her grin was wolfish. "What I'd do to see their faces when they read it. The room will smell of their piss, and I'll love knowing I was the driving force behind it." She nodded and finally seemed more relaxed. "Off you go. You have tapes to watch."

5

BILLIE

Turned out Travis was a cop. A detective.
And he was hot.

Light brown skin, kind dark eyes, and a *very* nice square jaw. He was lean, and I figured he knew how to handle himself. Plus, he was smart. He asked about the chickens. I told him all their names, and he never blinked once. He listened attentively through the entire dinner. He was engaging. He asked questions.

He told me about himself, about his two golden retrievers. About his father who was Hispanic. About how his mom and grandma, both Caucasian, would get together every Saturday for coffee, then brunch, then shopping, and they ended the day with an early dinner, which consisted mostly of appetizers and martinis.

They had nicknames for each other. His grandma was Bunny I and his mom was Bunny II. They greeted each other by wiggling their noses like bunnies, which started off every Saturday on just the right note.

He had three sisters, all older, and they picked on him. He very much respected women—he'd learned he had to in order to survive their household. He'd been joking when he said that, or so I hoped. His sisters had liked to practice putting makeup on him, and he knew the difference between leave-in conditioner and detangler. He knew the protocol for women and getting ready, and his own personal protocol was steering clear of the bathroom for two hours before going anywhere.

He got an odd look on his face when he said that and laughed to himself. But then he put his beer down and refocused on me. "Sorry. Just went down memory lane."

He'd said he'd been married. He wasn't now.

I hadn't asked Lo about the story. "Was your divorce recent?" I asked.

"God, no." He laughed awkwardly. "I mean, she cheated on me with my best friend. It was five years ago. I've learned to pick better friends since then, and I promised myself I'd only date again if she knocked my socks off." His eyes found mine, an unspoken message there. "Roger is *very* protective of you, which told me right away that you're someone worth waiting for. I'm glad you agreed to go out with me."

"It was between you and Doug, but Lo said she'd only set me up with someone she would date." *Oh, God.* I'd said way too much with that statement. I felt my face getting warm. "Uh..."

He grinned. "Lo would date me, huh?" He laughed, sitting back and picking up his drink. "I'm going to love rubbing that in Roger's face. I'll wait for the perfect time, when I need to distract him during a game of darts." He raised the glass to me. "Thank you, Billie."

I laughed, and I didn't know why, but I relaxed.

He grew somber, taking another sip. "You know, I'm a cop."

I knew where this was going. "I do."

Sadness flared briefly in his eyes. "I'm a homicide detective, so I see shit. A lot of it. All of it bad, but you're one of the reasons why I do my job. You walk into a crime scene, see all that death, and your low opinion of humanity just gets lower.

But then you hear a noise. Someone's alive. Someone survived, and everything comes back into focus. You're going to do your job anyway—for the mere fact that you just hate motherfuckers who hurt others—but if there's a survivor... You have no idea what that does to us. All the bullshit, all the politics, all the corruption, all of it goes away because someone lived, and you've got someone to avenge, and you can see them still walking around, breathing, hurting, but *alive*. And actually getting the fucker? Knowing that survivor will never be physically hurt by them again? Knowing they can feel safe now. Well—" His voice grew hoarse. "—it gives you life, and you think you can keep doing your job for another few years. So I have to say it, because I'm a cop. Thank you. Just, thank you for being one of the ones found alive." He looked away, clearing his throat. "I should—bathroom. I'll be back."

He shoved out of his chair.

My chest felt like a black hole had appeared in it as he spoke.

"...thank you for being one of the ones found alive."

Tears swam in my eyes. I needed a minute. Just one...

I headed for the back door of the bar and stepped out, bypassing a staff person entering for her shift.

"...and actually getting the fucker."

"...knowing they can feel safe."

"...then you hear a noise."

"Someone survived."

I held my hands over my face and bent over, needing to get it to the back of my mind, needing to forget so I could function again.

"...thank you for being one of the ones found alive."

This was a date. Laughter. Joy. That's what we were supposed to be doing.

Drinking. Flirting.

Drinking so I could flirt because I was horrible at sober flirting.

Who was I kidding? I was horrible at flirting in any capacity.

"Willow?"

Goddammit!

I gritted my teeth, recognition not clicking until my hands fell away and I turned to whoever this was, because for once, I was going to have my say and someone would respect it.

"I hate that nam—" I stopped, my eyes widening. "Holy shit." It was Brett Broudou with another guy, who was big, Black, and bald—holy shit! "You're Olvander Barrio. You sacked Hawk Maldonado three times in a game, and that was just the first half. Of course, you were the only reason the Kings were still in it, but you held that record until—" My gaze swung to Brett, and I remembered how I felt about him. I scowled. "You're a dick."

"Damn!" Olvander barked out.

"You're so off the mark with me," I continued. "A part of me felt bad for you, because for you to think I was some sort of con set for you? That's horrible. What must've happened in your life for you to think that way? And then I remembered you thought that about me. *Me!* I was going to have coffee with you. I've not gone on a date for seven years. *Seven.* I don't do casual sex, so think on that."

Brett glanced to the door, which was being held open by a staff person trying to pretend they couldn't hear us. Brett nodded to his friend. "Ole, can I meet you inside?"

Olvander choked back laughter, his giant shoulders shaking. "Sure. Yeah, buddy. Have fun groveling. If she dusts you, I won't bring a broom. I'll show up with a whole vacuum cleaner, because you done *blew* it with this one."

He went inside, and the door closed.

Brett swung his head back my way, and *whoa*. He'd been

holding back with his buddy here. Now he was all intense, and the air felt sweltering around us. He moved toward me, slowly, and I only had two steps until I was against the wall.

He was in my space, leaning down.

I gulped.

"First off, what name do you prefer? I don't want to keep messing up with you."

He...what? I blinked. "You don't?"

He growled, moving in another step, "What name?"

"Billie." Oh, boy. He was super close. Like, I could feel his body heat kind of close. "My little brother called me Billie. Most everyone in my life knows not to use that other name."

"You have a little brother?" His voice was still intense, but softer.

What is going on here? I nodded, faintly. "Had. He's dead. He and my mom got in a car accident."

"I'm sorry about that."

I started to shrug, an old habit to deflect because I never liked talking about him, but then I was. "His name was Ben. He kept calling me Willy, and that got changed to Billy because he decided one Christmas that we should both have B names. I spell it with the '-ie' because I felt it was more girly. I used to like being a girl back then."

His eyebrows lowered. "You don't now?" And he took one more step, the last step. His hand moved to the wall beside me. The other went to my stomach, touching me slightly.

His touch seared me.

It was overwhelming, welcomed, and alien all at the same time. It'd been so long since I felt anything remotely close to this, but even when I had, it didn't compare to...whatever this was between us.

"I thought you hated me?" I asked.

His eyes were grave as he shook his head. "This is not an excuse, because I fucked up royally, but my football stats aside,

I don't know if you're aware of my personal history. I didn't grow up good. I have a twin brother—"

"You do?"

"—who's in prison."

"He is?"

"He went in for attempted rape, and never left because of all the bad shit he's done in there."

"Oh." I frowned.

"That's not all."

"It's not?" I whispered, feeling his hand sliding around to my back, aligning his front against my front.

"My dad's been a drunk all my life, so I have nothing to do with him. My mom never left the trailer park. We had a house at one point, but for the most part, we were in the trailer park. We can get into that later, but there are good trailer parks and some that aren't. She came from the stereotyped kind. If that doesn't make sense to you, that's a good thing, but if you meet her one day, you'll understand. I gave up on her a while ago."

"Oh." I reached up to comfort him, but when my hand found his arm, a different zing went through me. *"Oh."*

"I got two more siblings. One is the reason I thought you were trying to con me. The only contact I have with her is when I block her from hurting more people. She's not good news, and I'm trying to turn over a new leaf, keeping communication with her to the bare minimum and as nice as I possibly can, while not letting her fuck with the way I view people. I almost missed out on you, because darling—"

Darling?

I liked that. No. I *loved* that.

His head inclined toward me. "You know how you sometimes have milestones that change your life?"

I nodded.

"If I'd missed out on a chance with you, that would've been a milestone in regret."

Oh, whoa. A milestone in *regret*?

"I got a half-brother who grew up in the next town over with his mom, which probably saved him, and I've got no intention of fucking that up in some way, so I steer clear." He stopped, holding my gaze for a beat. "So now you know something about me. I don't talk about my family. Football saved me, plain and simple. Also, you were crying before. Why were you crying?"

I frowned, remembering that too. "Where did you come from?"

"We like eating here. We get escorted in from the back and slip into a booth. Most people have no clue we're here. Olvander needed to talk about his woman, and honestly, I could use some drinks trying to figure out what to do about you."

"About me?" Also, holy crap. He needed to be escorted in the back? He was that kind of athlete. Which I knew, but seeing it firsthand? Wow.

"Because I messed up. Bad. I'm sorry."

His hand slid from my back to my front, and he toyed with the bottom of my shirt. His knuckle grazed against my skin, teasing me. Little wisps of lust grew, dancing inside me.

"That's okay." I wanted his whole hand against my skin. Under my shirt. "We all mess up now and then."

He chuckled. The sound washed over me.

I loved the sound of that.

"I can more easily count the times I've *not* screwed up. That's also the kind of guy I am, so you know."

"Why are you telling me all of this?" I was also touching him. My hand smoothed down his arm to his wrist.

"Because I don't want to fuck up with you. I just dumped out most of my skeletons, and now that you know all that, you can decide."

"Decide what?" I tilted my head up and was caught again by his eyes.

They were so close.

His whole face was so close.

His lips... If I stood on my tiptoes, mine would brush against his.

It'd be so easy.

"I want to know you. Do you want to know me?"

"Want you?" My mind was all muddied. Desire blanketed me, making everything fuzzy at the corners. Except his mouth.

What would it feel like to touch those lips? Press against them?

Taste them?

Taste him?

How would he feel?

He groaned. "Billie."

"What?" I breathed.

"I gotta ask. Do you—"

"What *the fuck* is going on out here?" An angry voice sounded, intruding.

Brett lifted his head, and I felt cold seep in, but he kept his hand pressed against my stomach, under my shirt. He hadn't altogether pulled away.

Thank God.

"Give us some fucking privacy." He wasn't asking.

"I would, except that's my date you got backed against the wall."

What? Date?

Brett went tense.

I was disoriented.

"You're here on a date?" he asked.

Am I? My brain was having a hard time catching up. It kept wanting to pull Brett back toward me, to feel all those wonderful feelings I'd never felt before, not the way he was making me feel them.

Then, *shit*. I blinked again.

Reality set in.

Travis had come looking for me, and both men were *not happy*.

I bit on my lip. "Uh..." *Wait a minute. Wait a goddarn minute.* I jerked from the wall and had a finger up. I stepped toward Brett. "This is *your* fault. And you." I swung to Travis. "You said some seriously heavy stuff in there. Really heavy. It's a first date, Travis." I went back to Brett. "And I'm only here because of you."

"Me?"

"Yes, you. You met me. You made me feel things. You made me *feel*, and that was just in the back of an SUV. Then you turned asshole. So yeah, I'm here on a date because I thought maybe, just maybe, it wasn't you. Maybe it was me. Maybe I actually did want to date someone again. Maybe I do want to let someone in, though after round two, I'm realizing no one could make me feel what you do. But I needed to find that out. So excuse me, both of you, because I've not done anything wrong here. And both of you, stop—" I wavered on Travis, who looked admonished, but also like something else I couldn't place. "— dropping emotional bombs on me and being all up in my face." The next was for Brett. "And making me forget who I even am in the process. I'm going inside, and *I'll* have a drink with Olvander because now I need one."

I huffed, stalked inside, and slammed the door behind me.

6

BRETT

Billie left the dude and me staring at each other.

"I'm a cop, so you know. Homicide."

"You brought her on a date?"

He grunted, shaking his head. "Lo, who's like her sister, set us up. Said Willow gave the go-ahead."

"She prefers Billie. How long have you been waiting for a date?"

He laughed abruptly. "Clocked her two years ago, but I was in a relationship. Once it ended, I made it known six months ago that I was interested. She's a ball buster, and she doesn't even know it."

I nodded. "Got no clue."

"She told me tonight she hadn't even asked for me. It was between me and another guy. Lo picked me."

I had to laugh. "This was just my second time meeting her, but that sounds right."

"Jesus. Your second time?"

I eyed him. "Yeah."

He raked a hand over his head. "Shit, man. I should back

out. I can see your connection, but a woman like that? All that
she *just* did? That sealed it for me. I'm in."

Well, fuck. "Are you serious?"

He gave me a glimmer of a grin. "I know who you are, you
know."

I slanted him a dark look. "I know who you are too."

His chin lifted.

"You're the dickhead who took my girl on a date."

He burst out laughing. "You messed up, and I got a chance,
so thank you. Now if you'll excuse me, I'm here on a date."

I bit off a growl as he strode back inside. I went right after
him, having never imagined myself in this position or that this
was how the night would go. He went to a table, and I cut
through to the area where Olvander and I always sat. He and
Billie were in the back booth, her head barely visible as she was
scrunched all the way against the wall. When I got there,
Olvander was laughing his ass off—bent over, his beer spilling
because his body was shaking, and he pounded the table with
his hand. "I can't even! My man. My boy. And you—I should've
stayed." He let out a long laugh, resting his hand on his chest.
"I'm going to regret that for so long." He saw me, and his head
tipped back in another round of laughter, loud and not caring
about the attention he was attracting.

I ignored him. "I'd like to give you a ride home," I told Billie.

She had stopped laughing, her eyes getting big, just like all
the other times I'd been forward with her. She was so unlike
the other women I came in contact with. So many of them were
the aggressors. I hardly had to say anything. But here Billie was,
always having a different reaction to me. I never knew what I
was going to get.

I caught movement behind me, and saw the date coming in.

"Billie, I'd like to give you a ride home," he said.

"I..." Her eyes trailed behind me as he rounded my side and
stood next to me.

He stopped short at the sight of Olvander. "Whoa. Hi." He smirked, motioning between Ole and me. "Do all footballers hang out like this? I heard some do and some don't."

I growled. "So glad you found us. Now you can go. I'll give Billie a ride home."

"I—" Billie started.

"I brought her. She's my date," the guy countered. "I'll make sure she gets home safely."

I faced him. "She will, because I'll take her."

"I don't think so. Lo entrusted her to me. Lo has no idea who you are."

"She will when I introduce myself, when I get her home."

"She doesn't live with Lo."

"We'll make a stop on the way."

"Then you'd be interrupting either bath time, teeth-brushing time, or if the kids went to bed early, something else." His grin was tight. "I don't think that'd be a great first impression."

I narrowed my eyes. "You have an answer for everything?"

"Pretty much, yeah." His grin became more relaxed, and he settled back on his feet. His shoulders loosened. "Look. Get her number. Let me take her home. I brought her here. It goes against the man I am to not make sure she gets home safe."

"And for you to take your shot."

He shrugged. "You've had two shots."

"You've had six months where you could've gotten that done."

"A woman like that you'd wait years for, and you know it."

He had me there, and seeing that, he scanned the rest of the table. His head whipped around. "Wai—where'd she go?"

"Oh yeah." Olvander lounged, one of his arms along the back of the booth. "She called an Uber thirty seconds ago, but keep going. I am thoroughly enjoying this. I don't need to talk about my wife anymore. I got that hashed out with her before you two even joined us. Also, Kayla will love meeting her."

Travis cursed, reaching for his wallet as he took off.

I wasn't going to race him out of the place. Billie'd be gone by now. I was starting to know her, and I knew that much. I slid into her vacated seat. "You called Fred?" Fred was Olvander's cousin, and on the nights when Ole wanted to drink, Fred was his driver.

Ole beamed. "I called Fred. He'll get her home."

I knew he would. I'd witnessed Fred's ability to handle himself. He had skills, and I never wanted to ask where he'd gotten them.

I'd not gotten her phone number. I'd not asked where she lived. I didn't know that Travis guy's last name, or what Lo's full name was.

Fred wouldn't tell me if she didn't want me to know. The only thing better now than an hour ago was that I'd gotten to her.

I'd gotten under her skin. That meant something.

"I was going to draw this out. I was going to enjoy watching you wallow in your misery, but I can't handle the fucking crestfallen look on your face." Ole pulled out a slip of paper he'd hidden under his napkin and slid it over to me. "She left her digits for you."

I snatched it up. "I got her number?"

"You got her number." He studied me thoughtfully. "First time I've seen you like this."

I didn't respond to that, but it was the first time for myself as well. I wasn't sure I liked it, but I was sure I liked her.

I got her number.

7

BILLIE

My phone buzzed as I crawled into bed.

Unknown: This is Brett. Thank you for leaving your phone number.

My tummy fluttered, and my heart lifted.

I smiled as I rolled to my back and texted a response.

Me: I'm glad we ran into each other tonight.

Brett: Me too. You got home safely?

Me: Yes. Just going to bed now.

Brett: Can I see you tomorrow?

The flutters tripled.

Me: Yes.

Brett: Great. I'll call you tomorrow.

Me: Night.

Brett: Night. *(smile emoji)*

I stared at that smile emoji for five full minutes before I put my phone away.

I went to sleep smiling.

8

BILLIE

I *need to be smaller.*
  I need to be quiet.
Thump.
My heart is so loud.
Thump.
Mom, where are you?
Ben?
I want to cry, but Mom would tell me not to cry.
I can't cry.
If I do, I'll die.
Another bloodcurdling scream rose from the living room.
I can't make a sound. Not a sound.

I jerked awake, a scream already building in my throat.

I wasn't there, hiding at my friend's house. I was in my own place, at Vicky and Howard's farm. I closed my eyes, counting things I knew to be true in the now.

I was in a bed. Not Jojo's hiding space.

I was thirty-two. Not twelve.

I reached for my phone. I had a cell phone. I hadn't had a phone then.

I was in my house, in my own bed. I rarely had a bed then.

Chickens.

I could hear the chickens. *Cluck, cluck, cluuuuck.* That would be Marsha P. Johnson.

I was here. In Texas. I wasn't there anymore.

I'd not been there for so long.

He can't get to me.

He couldn't get to me.

He couldn't get to me.

I kept repeating that as my heart slowed, and slowly, I came back. I was okay.

I pushed the fear away. There'd always be residue. There'd be residue as long as I lived, but I was functioning.

I could manage this.

It'd been a long time since I'd had a nightmare. I was tempted to use the bathroom, then curl back in bed with the lights off. I doubted another one could happen so soon after this one, so I would probably be fine. I could sleep normally. Though, who I was kidding? There was no normal sleeping for me. If I got four hours a night, I was happy. Medications had me sleeping fourteen hours and barely functional during the day, so I'd stopped using them. Four hours got me through, usually.

I got up, washed, and made coffee. Vicky came out to check on the chickens, and I dressed for my day. I had a job where I could work anywhere, and I was my own boss, so sweats and a tank were just fine.

Vicky wouldn't be in the coop long, not if she let them out. I filled two cups with coffee and headed over to the patio table. I was just sitting down when clucking filled the air.

Miss Sylvia Rivera was running around, her chestnut head bobbing. She kept circling, which wasn't normal. Usually she'd do a run, then settle and go back to doing whatever she and the other hens felt like doing for the free-range part of their day. I figured they had their own schedule.

She kept circling and clucking, until I frowned and stood up. "Miss Sylvia Rivera, hey."

Her head turned. I was never sure how much they could see, but whether she heard me, smelled me, or saw me, she took off running right toward me. She'd never done this. I sat back down and once she got to the patio, she jumped up and flapped her wings, landing in my lap.

Her clucks quieted as she settled into my arms.

"Well, I never." Vicky stood just beyond the patio, her eyes wide. She was a tiny woman, around five foot three inches, with meat on her bones, but nothing in excess. She liked working in the garden and around the farm, and it showed, but she had pale skin so she often wore a giant hat to protect against the sun. And she was strong, which her size didn't show. Her red hair used to be amber, but it'd faded to pale strawberry, with silver highlights mixed in. Today it was pulled back in a loose ponytail at the base of her neck, her sun hat pulled low to cover her eyes. She wore working gloves, hands at her hips. "Has she ever done that before?"

I shook my head.

"Never seen that in my life." She chuckled, stepping up and taking a seat, her eyes still on the hen. "She must've missed you, I guess?"

"I guess I'm sitting tight."

"Absolutely." She picked up the coffee I'd brought for her. "It's considered sacrosanct. If a chicken flies into your arms, you have to hold her until she decides to move. If you move first, the wish you've wished for is considered broken."

"You just made that up."

She laughed, sipping her coffee.

I gave her a grin, content to sit here. It felt nice. It felt settled. Peaceful.

"How you doing?" She used her low voice, her serious voice for when she was checking in with me and wanted the truth.

Vicky had never been a helicopter foster mom, but she was there. She'd watch, and she didn't miss much, but she also gave me space. I was someone who needed space. Howard was similar, though he was quicker with a joke and more eager to have a beer. He was a one beer at night kind of guy. Just one. If they went to social gatherings or had friends over, he might indulge in two, but that was the limit. Vicky wasn't a drinker. She said she'd never understood the appeal. She liked having all her faculties operational, but she always made sure she had the kind of beer Howard liked stocked. They were a team, a tight unit. They took their jobs raising children very seriously, like it was their purpose in life to raise kind, smart, assertive, and healthily balanced kids.

If I hadn't met them, I didn't know if I'd believe people like them existed. I was grateful.

Because of all of that, and maybe because I had Miss Sylvia Rivera in my arms, I told Vicky about the date. I told her about Brett. I told her about how I'd reacted to him, how I wasn't myself with him.

She sat for a beat, listening. "You're picky about who you let into your life. You were in a rough situation until you came to us, but I always knew your soul was good. You were kind. You were thoughtful. You were smart. But you'd been hurt. Your soul was wounded, but I knew all I needed to do was love you. So I did. I loved you, and I will always keep loving you. You never wanted to be a problem."

She thought for a moment. "No, no... We fostered a few other kids before you. Sometimes there were behavioral problems, which made sense. It wasn't their fault. Your problem was that I needed to make sure you wanted to live. I'm not saying you had thoughts like that, but your candle was barely flickering. I never wanted it to be snuffed out, and the way I kept it getting brighter and brighter was love. That was it. Some kids need structure. It helps clear out the chaos in their mind. But not you. Just loving you." Her smile was fond. "I know some of what you went through, but I know there has to be more that you've never said a word about. Probably never said a word to anyone. I have to say, sitting here, having coffee with you, seeing you with this glow on your face, with Miss Sylvia Rivera in your lap, and hearing how this Brett guy made you act like not yourself, I can't help but wonder if maybe he's the first one to get the real you out of you?"

My vocal cords froze.

We'd had other heart-to-hearts like this. I was well aware of how Vicky loved me, how she thought of me. And she was right. I'd never wanted to be a bother because I'd learned I was always a bother. No matter the therapy I'd gone through, some of that was always going to be with me. I'd accepted it. But it was minimal, which I was proud of. Maybe because of the nightmare, some of it felt stronger than usual today.

"Thank you, Vicky," I whispered, unable to say anything else.

Her eyes were wet. She nodded, finishing her coffee. "You're going to have to bring him for family dinner, you know." She sighed. "Howard will want to have a beer with him and talk football. Warn your man ahead of time about how Howard can be about sports."

"I will."

"What do you have going on for the rest of the day? Besides communicating with this man of yours."

I told her about some of my clients, about the projects I needed to work on today.

She nodded. "Lo was rooting for Travis, but I think she'll be over the moon about this new one too."

"I gotta call her."

"Call her before she gets done with work, or you know she and Roger will come over for dinner again. Though I wouldn't complain about that." She gave another nod before standing and coming around to my side of the table. She brushed my hair from my forehead, gave me a soft kiss, and bent down to take Miss Sylvia Rivera out of my lap. "I'll switch you, Miss Sylvia Rivera for the coffee cup."

She stepped down and was a few feet away when I called her name.

She turned around.

"You were the best thing that ever happened to me," I told her. "I love you too."

Another soft smile filled her face, her head tilting to the side. "I've always known that, Billie. You love people as soon as you meet them; they just don't realize it. But I knew—took one look at you and felt all the love you wanted to give the world. I consider myself real lucky that I was the one who got to raise you."

Cluck! Cluck! Cluuuuuuuuuck.

"See? Miss Sylvia Rivera agrees with me." She gave me a nod. "Go on. Take the cups in and get to work. Thank you for starting the day with me."

9

BILLIE

I'd not gotten to Lo before she finished work. I made the mistake of checking my email first. An emergency project had come up for an ad campaign that was scheduled to come out in a week. There'd been enough problems with the previous designer that they'd scrapped everything at the last minute and prayed for a Hail Mary.

Those were their actual words.

I'd spent the day doing mock-ups for them, and now, with the afternoon almost gone, the third option had just been approved by their team.

"Thank you so much for this help, Melanie. I don't know what we would've done, and your designs are just brilliant," my client gushed. "You have no idea how you've helped us. Our other option was Ronald's cousin, and I know Ronald's cousin. He lives in Ronald's basement for a reason."

I chuckled, but didn't say a word since I was living in Vicky and Howard's guesthouse. "It's not a problem. I'm glad to help. I'll be sending my invoice, and then I'll send the final files once that's paid."

"Of course, of course. Thank you again. Have a great week, Melanie."

We hung up.

I was Melanie Morning to them. There were no pictures of me on my website. I allowed my designs to represent my brand. Word of mouth drove business to me, and I did good work to keep it. I worked fast, professionally, and I always finished on time. That was vital, and after the first few projects, I made sure to receive payment before I sent the final files. Some balked, but that was my policy stated on my website.

When I looked up after finishing that transaction, it was nearing dinner time. I'd not made my call to Lo. So, thirty minutes later, I wasn't surprised when their car came down the two-mile driveway.

I hadn't even had time to check messages today, but Lo had sent a couple texts. I'd thought I might hear from Brett. But I hadn't. He'd said he was going to call, so maybe it would be this evening?

I ignored the little trickle of fear in my stomach.

Lo and Roger parked, and as soon as their SUV stopped, the passenger door swung open and Lo was coming in fast.

That wasn't good.

I'd learned over the years to stall when Lo got in these moods. It meant she had an opinion, a strong one, and she was going to share it whether I wanted it or not. She'd do a lecture that would somehow end on a motivational quote.

I didn't think I had the energy for any of that, so I did what any mature, responsible, courageous adult would do.

I ran.

Though, to give myself credit, as she knocked briefly on the front door, I was slipping out the back. Because, you know, the trail that cut through the woods and went around to the side of the main house, it needed to be checked. Weeds or trees might've fallen over it and would need to be cleaned up. Plus, it was good to check for any signs of a fox, or coyotes, or hogs, or bobcats, or snakes, you know. Just in case.

Totally being responsible here. I needed to protect the hens.

"Where'd she go?" Lo asked, the screen door slamming behind her.

"I don't know. She's not there?" Roger said.

I picked up my pace. They'd check the chickens next.

"Maybe she's in the coop."

I broke out of the treeline right as they ducked inside, a flurry of clucks filling the air. I went into the main house through the side door.

"Give me a job. I've been here this whole time," I said in a rush, grabbing an apron and tying it on as I went into the kitchen.

Vicky was at the counter, and she didn't break stride. "They called thirty minutes ago, asked if you were here. The girls are at gymnastics, so I invited them for dinner." She picked up the pot of potatoes and met my gaze. Her eyes were blank, but I sensed the dark humor swirling behind that wall.

"Uh-huh. Sure you did." My tone was dry, but we both knew I was teasing.

Vicky broke first, a slight grin showing. "You didn't call her in time, huh?"

I sighed, pulling out the silverware. "I got busy with work. Had a last-minute emergency, that type of thing."

"Anything you need to talk about?" She stopped at the screen door, her back to it, still holding the potatoes.

I shook my head. "Nope. It's all good."

"Grab the paper plates and plastic cups. We'll eat out here tonight."

That meant my whole sneak-around was for nothing. When we had dinner outside, no one moved. It was too comfortable and sitting around the patio table meant drinks and loose tongues. The lecture I thought I'd escaped would still happen. I'd just have an audience.

I didn't know why I was hiding from Lo.

She would've talked to Travis, gotten his side of the night. By now she'd heard all about Brett, the same Brett who'd come on strong, texted me, made me feel all sweet and warm, and who I'd not heard a word from today. That Brett.

He should be doing the courting. That was the word Vicky and Howard used, and it stuck because it was the truth. The getting-to-know-you stage in the beginning was supposed to be the guy's job. If he was willing to do that work, it showed how important you were to him.

Therefore, I felt it was important to wait for him to text.

I wanted to see if he followed through on what he promised, another thing that said a lot about a guy. But who knew if I was right to wait or not. The two relationships I'd been in had been good. Safe. I'd felt pleasant enough around them, but the spark hadn't stayed, and both had ended because we were better friends than lovers. So maybe it was me? Maybe I was doing something wrong?

But that wasn't really true.

I didn't date because I hadn't wanted to. My life's purpose wasn't to get married, have kids, get a certain type of house. I'd seen too much already, and knew that vision could be bullshit. My life's purpose was to feel safe, and I did at Vicky and Howard's, with the hens close by. That was good enough for me.

"Mom—" Lo shouted, from the coop, by the sound of it.

Vicky cut her off, shouting back, "She's in the kitchen." A beat later, she spoke normally, "You would've known that if you'd checked the house first. She's been here all afternoon, helping me out."

Vicky totally had my back. Go Vicky. I loved Vicky.

"Uh-huh. I'm sure." Lo's tone was dry, like mine had been earlier.

I chuckled.

The screen door opened and shut.

"She's in a tizzy." Roger came up next to me and bent over to wash his hands in the sink. He swung his hips to bump mine gently. "Heyahowyadoing?" He always said it as one word.

"She's in a tizzy? Like mad?" I'd not been expecting that. Maybe a stern reminder about the goodness of Travis or "*What are you doing with a celebrity*?" Something like that, but she'd let it go and tell me she would support me no matter who I picked. She had to.

"I think she's hurt you didn't say anything about seeing Brett Broudou again."

Oh, no. A hurt Lo was another beast, and she'd been heading to me, to share, and I ran from her. That probably hurt her feelings because we all knew I'd not been helping Vicky this whole time. If Vicky needed help, she'd wrangle Howard to peel some potatoes. She liked to cook by herself otherwise, but the cleanup was always for the rest of us.

I sighed. I need to fix this. "It wasn't like that. He rejected me—"

The door slammed shut, loud and abrupt enough that I jumped, and then came a low and barely controlled, "*He did what?*"

Lo stood in the doorway, her eyes locked on mine and her jaw tight.

I was *really* messing this up.

10

BILLIE

"It wasn't like I was trying *not* to tell you about him. It's just that our first meeting was a lot, and he was a lot, and then he thought something about me that made him not want to do the coffee, but he explained later that he'd messed up and he was sorry about it and he wanted..." I'd been rambling for the last twenty minutes about why I hadn't told Lo about the coffee date with Brett initially.

In this family, getting rejected was something we shared. I should've told Lo about it. Or not that I got rejected, but that it hurt me. That's what she cared about, and now I was trying to explain myself without giving her a bad first impression of Brett. Because let's face it, rejecting me because he thought I was sent to con him wasn't a stellar beginning.

Even as I scrambled to unhurt Lo's feelings, it was in the back of my mind that Brett still hadn't reached out. I snuck a peek at my phone before we sat down to dinner to make sure I hadn't missed anything before I turned it to silent while we ate. I hadn't. It went back in my pocket. As we ate, I was acutely aware of the vibrations of people shifting in their seats, but none of those movements came from my phone.

"Oh my God, stop," Lo finally said, after several minutes of silent treatment. She gave in, holding up a hand. "You're forgiven, but this guy—I don't know about him, Billie."

Great.

Crap. This was what I'd been worried about, though I still wondered if I needed to worry about it at all.

"I love you. I'm over it. You're back in my bosom, okay?" She grinned, rolling her eyes. "But can we talk about Travis?"

Roger expelled a ragged breath, his big shoulders slumping. "Thank God. Now the rest of us can breathe easier, knowing we won't get a spear between the eyes for making a sound."

"I'm not that bad!"

He grinned. "Darling, I love you..." He let it hang.

She opened her mouth.

Vicky held up a hand. "He's trying to rile you up to help give Billie a breather. You've been hammering at her since you got here."

"I've not said a word."

Vicky reached for her tea, raising one eyebrow. "Darling."

Lo's face got red. "She didn't tell me about him," she hissed. "She met someone she was excited about, and I didn't know. I'm supposed to know. I'm borderline obsessed with my sister. I get to know these things. You probably heard about him before I did." She studied her mom a moment. "You did! You heard about him before me. What the hell?"

"Lowie," Howard had been quiet until now. "We're sans the little ears tonight. Please." He leaned in, a grin spreading. "It should be 'what the fuck' tonight, not 'what the hell'."

Roger burst out laughing.

Vicky sent her husband an admonishing look, but the corner of her mouth curved up.

Lo laughed. "Sorry, Dad." She turned to me. "What the *fuck*, Billie?"

"So much better, Daughter. Don't forget, you're a sailor's little girl. Cursing is one of life's joys for me."

Vicky reached over to pat her husband's hand.

"True. What was I thinking?" She zeroed in on me again. "What'd you think about Travis?"

Travis? I thought about it, about him. "I liked him too."

"Shut up!" She slapped the table. "You did?"

Roger and Vicky shared a look behind Lo's head, which I didn't understand. I nodded. "I did." I shared my thoughts about him. It was true. He'd surprised me.

"Travis wants to ask you out again. What about we do a couple thing like I first suggested? Jack's BBQ has live music playing on Friday. We should go. Do you want to go?" She grasped Roger's hand, squeezing tight.

Oh, boy.

Lo was really rooting for Travis.

I met Roger's gaze. There was a slight plea in his eyes.

This was more about Lo than me. I'd have to explain it to Travis.

I was interested in Brett. I'd be honest with both of them. I'd have to explain it to Brett too, reminding him that he'd not called when this insistent request came in from my best friend. I just hoped both would understand.

"Okay," I said.

Lo squealed, still clenching Roger's hand.

"Agh, Wife! My hand. I still need it for a few more years, you know."

"Oh! Shit." She glanced at Howard. "*Fuck.*"

He held up his drink to her. "That's my daughter."

"So sorry, honey," Lo said. "I was all up in my feels for a minute."

"We're quite aware." He smoothed out the cuts her nails had dug into his skin before leaning over for a kiss. "At least let me keep my hand until the girls are eighteen and out of the house. You're going to need both of them for carrying bags, helping hang up posters, rearranging the furniture. But after they're out of the house, you can have my hand. It's all yours."

"Don't forget when they move after college. For their first job? Their second? When they get their first mortgage..." Howard offered.

"Right." Roger gave Lo a stern look. "I need to keep my hand until our girls get married. Their spouses can take over then."

Lo snorted. "Always such a television sitcom around here."

Everyone shared a laugh at that one, and Vicky changed the subject, giving me a break, which I noted as she looked over the rim of her glass at me. She asked how the girls were doing in gymnastics, and I remembered how I would've killed for a family when I was younger. How this, right here, this meal, the teasing, the laughs, and the real conversation, it wouldn't have been a sitcom for me.

It was the family I always wished for, and I'd gotten my wish.

If Brett didn't call, it'd be okay. It wasn't supposed to work for us. And again, I'd already gotten my wish.

I'd be just fine.

"HE HASN'T CALLED?" Lo asked.

It was ten at night, and she and I were sitting on the patio by my place.

Roger had left to take care of the girls, but everyone knew Lo was staying. She wanted to know more about Brett and the date.

Once we were over here, alone, and I'd indulged in a second glass of wine, I admitted the rest to Lo. She was now fully up to date about Brett.

I swallowed a pang of disappointment. "No. Maybe I knew

he wasn't going to call and that's why I kept thinking about it today."

Lo narrowed her eyes, trying to see me better. She'd had more than two glasses of wine, so things were a little blurry for her. "Like you intuited it?"

I shrugged. "I don't know."

The pang was still in my chest. I hadn't been able to swallow it away.

"I was into him, Lo. I really was."

"Oh, Billie." She reached for my hand, holding it tightly.

I turned it subtly, moving so her nails couldn't squeeze in without her noticing.

"This is strike two."

"What do you mean?" I asked.

She let go of my hand, sitting back in her chair. "Strike one, he asked you for coffee and changed his mind. He got you *so wrong* with that assumption, and I'm not going into why he would think that about you, because you are not that kind of person. Strike two, he said he wanted to see you today. That changed to 'call you,' and it's half past ten and he's not reached out." Her eyes turned shrewd, or as shrewd as they could because she was blitzed. "He's going to call, you know. You're a catch, and he knows it. Are you going to tell him about Travis this Friday night?"

"*...he's going to call, you know.*" That shouldn't have made me feel better, hopeful, but it did. I tried not to show it, giving her a shrug and looked down at my lap. "I don't know."

She gasped, jerking forward. It was one of Lo's favorite reactions. She did it a lot. "No way! You're going to tell him? Screw him. Give Travis a try. I'm telling you. Travis..." She lifted her glass, shaking her head. "Travis is a good one. He can protect you. He's got a four-year degree. He's been through the wringer with his ex. Give him a chance, Billie. I think sometimes the strong lust at first sight fizzles out. It's the slow smoldering embers that can build into a bonfire. You mark my words on that one. I think Travis is an ember for you. He can tear down a forest, just give him enough oxygen."

"Lo." I was a little horrified. "A different metaphor, please."

She winced. "Right. I'm sorry."

"All the animals. You're not thinking about all the animals that could die in a forest fire." I shivered.

"I know. I'm sorry." She glanced over her shoulder to the coop. "All the Miss Sylvia Riveras running around, scared, their little tails smoking."

"Lo!"

She laughed. "Sorry, sorry. I'll stop." She paused. "The Marsha P. Johnsons' little heads bobbing, running around so scared they'd probably run smack into a tree and keel over. The — " She was going to keep going. My growl stopped her. Her grin turned lopsided. "No fire will harm our little hens. Dad made sure, reinforcing the coop with metal. If a fire breaks out here, we'll have to take cover with them. Dad should add another extension, maybe put a couch in there for us."

The serious talking was done, finally.

We chatted more about the hens, then moved on to how Roger wanted to get a dog and whether Lo was going to use getting a dog as collateral for maybe getting the pool she'd always wanted.

After that was sorted, after she'd decided she'd let him get two dogs for the pool, after Harold gave his swearing daughter a ride home and I crawled into bed, I looked at my phone.

Nothing from Brett.

My phone beeped thirty minutes later, flashing in the room.

I rolled over, grabbing it, ignoring the searing hope that filled my body.

Unknown: Hi! This is Travis. I just got off the phone with Lo. I'm supposed to call you tonight and cement my "chances." It's late, so I hope a text is sufficient? If it's not, do me a favor. Don't tell Lo. Just let me know, and I will up my efforts. I promise.

Also, she explained about Friday, and I'd love to catch some live music. We can go as friends, if that's what you want. Give me a call sometime. I'd like to hear more about these hens Lo kept mentioning. Something about a chicken on fire?

I grinned, some of my disappointment easing, but I didn't respond. I'd text him tomorrow.

Lying back down, my phone in my hand, I felt it buzz again.

I lifted it slowly, expecting another text from Travis, or even Lo letting me know she'd talked to Travis, and he might reach out.

Brett: Fuck. I'm sorry it's so late. Are you still awake?

Nope. It wasn't either of them.

I stared at the message, wondering why I cared so much? Why I'd obsessed about whether he was going to call all day? He could hurt me. He already had. Maybe it wasn't a big deal to others if the guy texted the next day or when he texted, but he had time. People could text when they were on the toilet. I knew because that's when I did most of my texting. It was one of my favorite places to text, but he hadn't. He'd texted now, like I was an afterthought.

I don't know. I was probably overthinking it, but for some reason it meant something that his text had come so late. Maybe Lo was right. He'd said he wanted to see me, then he'd said he'd call, and he'd dwindled that down to a text coming in at booty-call time of night.

That meant something.

I needed to go with my gut.

I didn't reply to him either.

11

BRETT

Yesterday was our day off, and though I rarely took it because no one took it off, I was forced to this time. I'd gotten a call at three in the morning, just a few hours after I'd come home from going to drinks with Ole, and found Billie there of all places. I'd been planning my Tuesday differently than the way it happened. I'd wanted to head in, do more weight lifting and training, and go over the tapes for the next team. Then I'd wanted to call Billie on the drive home, maybe talk her into dinner at her place or mine (just easier for privacy reasons) or take her out somewhere to eat if that made her feel more comfortable.

I had also planned on stocking up on everything I needed for the house. Some of my buddies didn't think about that since their wives or girlfriends did that for them. Some of the single guys had assistants who did that sort of thing. One of the guys' husbands handled that too.

Not me.

I'd tried an assistant, but it didn't work for me. I stuck with my agent, Jason, and my manager. Sometimes Callie, one of the team's physical therapists, came over if I needed an early-morning treatment, and because we were friends, she'd stick around. At first my house had been a quiet place for her to study since her place was next to a bar and she was going for a graduate degree, but she started spending more time here. By now, I knew she'd be studying at my house every Wednesday, Thursday, and Saturday night. I barely noticed Saturday because I was always gone for our game the next night. The team stayed at a hotel the night before, no matter where it was. Callie had started taking care of the house, and I'd cleaned out a back section on the other side of my garage for her. It'd been used as a gardening area by the previous owner, but I extended it and renovated it into a guest area. That was now where Callie studied.

But with all she did to help out, I never let her get my groceries. That was my job. I'd been looking forward to picking up a steak, maybe a decent red wine if Billie liked that kind of thing, and some potatoes and vegetables for the grill. If Billie hadn't felt comfortable coming to my place, I'd fire up the grill another night.

But none of that happened.

Instead, I'd gotten a frantic call from my fourteen-year-old niece. "*Uncle Brett, Mom went to the casino, and she's not been back in days. I'm getting worried.*" She'd been crying. "*Can you find her?*"

My niece rarely cried, or rarely let someone know she was crying.

An hour later, after making a call to someone I knew in the bounty-hunting business, I'd been in the car on the way to the airport because my sister was in jail.

It took me all day to get there and get things settled for my sister's kids, but I'd gotten back late last night. I'd sent Billie a text when I landed in Texas and was on the way home. I'd called Wednesday and left a voice message, but still nothing. It was now Thursday, and I was just getting home after being at practice all day.

I'd messed up our first meeting, and she was ghosting me. Had I done something wrong?

I had no idea how else to get ahold of her. That Travis guy. *Fuck.*

I bit back a growl, but I could track him down.

As I pulled into my garage, I could see Callie's little white Camry was in the last slot, so I didn't go inside. More than likely she'd be out in her area, but just in case she was using the kitchen, I wanted to do this in private.

I let loose a growl. I hated owing this guy two favors in a row.

I dialed the phone.

"New Kings Bounties." He was already laughing as he greeted me with that.

I cursed. "This is your personal cell."

He barked out a laugh. "No shit, Sherlock. Gotta raz you. This is the second call in three days. To what do I owe the stupendous honor of getting another call from the superstar Brett Broudou?"

Channing Monroe. I knew this kid from school. He'd been a leader of his own group, which made him usually my enemy back then. I'd been about family loyalty and backed up my twin, who wasn't a good guy. Not that I'd consider Monroe a good guy, but he wasn't in prison, so there was that.

And he'd helped find my sister.

"Your nieces and nephew okay?" His tone got serious.

"Yeah. I got in touch with Will. He agreed to take them in."

He was quiet for a second. "I'm sorry. I thought you were steering clear of your half-brother."

"It was him or bring them all to Texas." My hands fisted around the steering wheel, because I hated having to make that call. Will had grown up mostly away from our family, and because of that, he had a decent job, a good wife, and two beautiful little boys. Taking Shannon's kids to his house was going to put him in her crosshairs, but Will was local, or more local than where I was. Having Shannon's kids come here would be a last resort, but it was something I'd do if necessary.

Channing knew I'd been staying away from Will because he's the one I'd asked to give me updates on Will and his family. Channing had done all of that and more, letting me know my half-brother was on his way to building up a solid nest for his family. He didn't drink. He didn't cheat. He didn't even smoke. The guy was almost a saint, involved in their local church. He'd gotten the white-picket-fence dream, and I was ridiculously proud of him. He'd gotten out. He had his life together.

"That's a hard one," Channing added after a moment. "We could've taken them in."

That suggestion got to me. He meant it. My voice was a little rough as I rasped out, "It's family, you know."

"I get it, but just saying, if your brother can't handle when Shannon gets out, we're a last resort before totally relocating them."

"If it comes to that, it'd be a legal fight."

"Which we'll help with. You know that. You know I can handle your sister."

He could. Him, all the bounty hunters who worked for him, his sister, his wife, and all their friends too. Channing didn't know that while he helped me keep abreast of my family members, I kept abreast of him and his family as well. Monroe was never one to back down from a fight, legal or illegal, and he hadn't changed as he aged.

"I'll keep you in mind," I told him.

"Good. Now can we stop talking about serious shit, because judging by the reluctance I'm hearing in your tone, you got something good and personal for me to do for you."

"Fuck you."

He laughed. "What is it, Broudou?"

"I need you to find a detective for me."

He started laughing all over again. "Oh, this is going to be good. Brett, just call nine-one-one. You'll have all sorts of detectives finding you."

I growled.

He howled louder.

"It's a Detective Travis, homicide."

"The fuck? What do you want with a homicide detective? I track down criminals, not cops."

"That's none of your business. Can you get me his last name or not?"

"Cool down, Mr. Football Star. Give me the morning, and I'll give you his last name, his desk phone, his cell phone, any other private phones he may have. I'll give you his address, his email, anything you want to know. I can do it."

"I thought you just tracked down criminals?"

He swore, but he was amused. "I can find anyone. You know that."

Billie... But no. She was mine to track down.

"Just let me know a good time to find him. The conversation he and I are going to have won't be a pleasant one."

"Anything I should know about?"

"No. It's personal."

"It's about a woman?" I could hear the intrigue in his voice.

I remained quiet.

He hooted. "Are you and a cop tangling over a woman?"

"Fuck off." I started to end the call, but repeated, "Tomorrow, Monroe."

"Yeah, yeah—"

I hung up, a wave of humiliation washing over me.

He was right. Me and a cop? Who the fuck was I? I might dress up in football pads and run after a quarterback, but strip all that away and I was still a criminal who grew up in a trailer park.

I had nothing to lose here, so I dialed Billie's number one more time.

Her voicemail came on, the automated impersonal one, and after it beeped, I said, "This is Brett. It's not lost on me that this is my third time reaching out. I'm not sure if I did something wrong, or maybe I read you wrong and this is your way of letting me know you're not interested. I figure one more time, and I'll pull back from here. If it's the case that I did something wrong, I can only say that after I found you Monday night, I felt like finally I got the luck. In my life, that's not normally been the case. I meant everything I said to you Monday night. Meant what I said in the text. And Tuesday, some things happened that took me out of state, so I'm sorry I wasn't able to reach out until late. I'd been looking forward to maybe talking you into letting me grill a steak for the two of us. I was hoping for that night, but I'm now realizing I was getting ahead of myself. I apologize for that. So, this is me officially scaling back. If you'd like to have a conversation or even share a text message, know that I'll be happy to hear from you, maybe learn more about your chickens. I hope things are good on your end."

I hadn't read Billie wrong. She knew it, and I knew it.

I'd wait for Monroe to get back to me, and then I'd figure out my next step.

Because I wasn't scaling back.

I had lied through my teeth.

12

BILLIE

He called.
  He left a message.
I didn't listen to it.
Nope.
Though I totally wanted to.
I really, really wanted to, but I stuck to my guns, as Lo liked to say.

It was Friday night, and Lo, Roger, and I were on our way to Jack's BBQ. Travis was meeting us there. Lo was dressed to the nines in a little black dress and gorgeous thigh-high boots. Her hair was high on her head in a ponytail with long tendrils curled down to tease her back. She had hoop earrings too.

I couldn't compare, which I knew, so I didn't even try. I wore a black tank top and jean shorts, the kind that stopped just over my thigh, so they weren't mini shorts. They were respectful. I'd kept my hair down, though I always got hot so I'd have it up in a braid or a clip by the end of the night. And I wore little black boots. They were cute, and they fit in. They didn't stand out like Lo's thigh-high ones. Hers were marvelous.

I'd kept my jewelry to a minimum, a chain necklace resting down between my girls. I thought it looked classy.

Roger and Travis wore plaid button-down shirts and Wranglers. Both filled them out nicely, but I was going to focus on Travis since he wasn't my kind-of brother-in-law. Travis was at the bar, a woman next to him with her hand on his arm. His head turned toward the bartender as he leaned forward to talk to him. As the bartender nodded, leaving, Travis reached up and pointedly removed the woman's hand from his arm. His head swung back, his eyes no-nonsense as they slid past her and came to me. They stayed on me, widening a little, until he said something to the bartender and headed our way.

The woman was left behind, and she knew it.

Lo snorted, watching.

"Oh, man. She got denied hardcore," Roger said.

Travis paused before stepping in next to me, and his hand stretched up to touch the small of my back. I gave him a nod, and he closed the distance. He drew me to his side and grazed my cheek with his lips before murmuring in my ear, "You look amazing."

"Thanks." I gave him a smile, surprised to feel a little breathless.

A tingle went through me, standing so close to him. He still hadn't greeted Lo and Roger.

His mouth curved up in a tender smile before he stepped back. "Roger. Lo, you look amazing as well." He left my side, giving her cheek a kiss.

Roger turned in, angling his head. "Me too, buddy."

Everyone laughed.

Travis flashed a smile, returning to my side, his hand going to my back again. But he didn't pull me close. He kept some distance between our bodies, enough to breathe, but his hand stayed. It was a move to claim me, but in a respectful way. He was letting me know he was interested, which I had to admit, had my stomach starting to flutter.

The guys chatted as Lo swept the room. She tended to do that everywhere we went, and she always knew four or five people. People respected her and liked her. No matter her age, she had the popular-girl thing going for her, but she'd been one of the cool athletes who was nice too. She got invited to all the parties, no matter who was throwing them, and if she didn't go, they'd keep inviting her and would keep hoping she'd come. They'd never be mad at her.

Vicky and Howard had the same quality.

The hostess came over, showing us to our picnic table in the back outdoor area. On the way we passed a dance floor and a huge, old-school barbecue grill. There were tables inside, with booths lining the walls. You might think this was one of those places only regulars go, and others might avoid because of the rougher crowd. There were quite a few bikers congregating, but it was a Friday night. A lot of other customers were here too. College students. Twenty-somethings. People in their thirties and forties. Some who were retired. There was no one too good for Jack's BBQ. As we wound to our table outside, three people stood up to greet Roger and Lo.

Travis and I kept on to the table. He waited until I sat before settling in next to me. "Being a cop, no one greets me like that."

I smiled, his joke easing my tension. "Even other cops?"

He laughed. "Touché. We go to a cop bar and they'll be all over us. Everyone would want to know you and try their hand at stealing you away."

My cheeks got warm.

He got quiet before leaning over to speak under his breath. "I know this is a friends-only thing, but I hope it's okay if I admit that I'm still hopeful it might turn into something more. No pressure, though, and I mean that. I can back off if you'd like, treat you like a genuine friend, because I want that as well."

I looked at him and saw he was watching Lo with knowing eyes. I held what I'd been about to say.

"Lo told me you don't socialize much," he added.

The way he said that—my back straightened. "Is this a pity date?"

His eyes widened. "No. God, no, unless it's the other way." His mouth tugged up in a crooked grin.

I flushed because it worked for him—the crooked grin, the self-mocking comment and tone, but his eyes were intense.

I sighed, feeling my tummy flutter. "You have a cop's eyes."

He shrugged, but those eyes never lost their intensity. "Attribute from the job, I'm afraid."

"I've grown up seeing cops' eyes, and for a while, it was every day."

His mouth flattened, but he was still leaning toward me.

I couldn't ignore the tingle I got from him. "I never knew if I liked seeing those eyes or not, because at that time in my life, everything shifted. My dad was barely around when I was growing up, and my mom said it was always better if we didn't have a relationship with him. He showed up at random times. He'd stay a few days and take off. My mom said he preferred it that way so we knew his face, knew the name she called him, knew his voice. That was it. But after surviving the Midwest Butcher, my mom and brother died in a car crash, and because the man whose sperm created me wasn't a father, I went into the foster system. It all happened within a few days. A twist of the universe let it pour when it was already raining. I've always associated seeing a cop's eyes with the worst week of my life."

He straightened up, moving away from me.

I put my hand on his. "But I like yours."

His hand jerked, but didn't move away.

"I'm finding that they're growing on me," I added.

He exhaled slowly, as if he'd been holding his breath, and turned his hand upside down. Just as slowly, he laced our fingers. He moved our hands down to his lap, hidden from the table. "That's good to know."

There it was. Another tingle.

Maybe Lo was right.

Maybe the ember was the way to go.

Maybe I needed to let it grow.

"What'd we miss?" Lo and Roger arrived at the table, sounding out of breath as they sat. Lo nabbed the drink menu. "I need a drink. It's Friday night, and the music is starting. Did you guys already order drinks?"

Roger was slower to sit, his gaze trained on the table, right above where our hands were. "You know," he sounded surprised. "I think we should order a round for the table. Right? I'm right. Where's our server?" He turned, and I caught his quick smile though he coughed, trying to cover it up.

Lo's head snapped up. She frowned at him. "We're already starting?"

He turned back to her, his smile stretched from ear to ear. "It's Friday night, honey. Let's do it right and take an Uber home."

Lo's mouth nearly fell open because they'd had a whole debate about who'd be driving home. It boiled down to Lo being willing to spend for an Uber and Roger wasn't. He wanted his truck home and safely in his garage, because like all the females in his life, that truck was his baby.

I'd pointed out that I could drive, which both of them ignored. I was the one they *wanted* to have a good time.

"What just happened here? What did I miss?" Lo scanned over us, her eyes falling abruptly to the same place Roger's had been.

Travis squeezed my hand before letting go, and he rested his arms on the edge of the table. "No need. I already put in an order. The bartender said they'd find us." His eyes moved to a girl carrying two drinks, followed by another girl with another two. "And I think these are ours."

As they set our drinks down, Lo leaned toward me and mouthed, *What did I miss?*

I grinned and shrugged.

She gave me a sharp look.

I ignored it, accepting my drink with a thank you.

Roger held his glass in the air. "A toast, please." It wasn't a request. It was a command.

We all lifted our drinks and waited.

He raised his higher and said, "To good friendships, to great family, and to always being thankful for the blessings we get each day. Cheers, everyone. Let's enjoy the night as we continue to be blessed by being here with each other."

It was a heartfelt toast, and my throat swelled a little. Lo blinked a few times before each of us clinked our glasses and took a sip. Travis watched me over the brim of his glass the whole time.

I liked it.

I also couldn't stop thinking about Brett's latest voice message on my phone.

13

BRETT

My phone buzzed just as I was walking inside.

Callie had asked the night before if she could use my place tonight instead of Saturday night for studying. I hadn't cared. I never did. She was quiet, but tonight as I opened the garage door and headed for the kitchen, there was music playing. Soft piano music, along with the smell of food, which had my stomach growling. It'd been a decent day of practice, but I'd stayed after for another hour in the gym.

"Hey!" Callie was at the stove, in leggings and a yoga sweater that looked more like a blanket wrapped around her, yet still showing a small stripe of her stomach. Her hair was up in a bun, and her cheeks were rosy. I guessed because of whatever she was cooking.

I lifted my chin in a silent greeting, going to the table and putting my bag down.

I pulled my phone out, reading the text from Channing.

Channing: Talked to a buddy who knew a buddy that's friends with a buddy that's tight with Detective Travis Dove. According to the last buddy, Detective Dove had a date tonight. Jack's BBQ. Hope it's not with your girl.

Another text came through.

Channing: You owe me.

"What?"

I lifted my head. "What?"

Callie had her hands folded in front of her, her eyebrows up in concern. "You just made a sound I've never heard you make before. Like you're disappointed or something. Is everything okay?"

"Yeah."

Callie and I didn't talk about personal stuff. She didn't have family here, and I didn't know her situation with friends, if she had a lot or none. All I knew was that she helped clean my place in exchange for using it to study. It worked because I was barely here, and if I was, I was at my end of the place. It was big enough for an entire family to be here and I'd barely hear them.

"What'd the text say?"

"Huh?"

She'd drifted closer, standing on her tiptoes with her head angled as if she could read my phone from where she stood. She couldn't. She was too far away.

I slid it into my pocket anyway. "It's nothing. Just heard someone I need to talk to is at Jack's BBQ tonight."

"Jack's BBQ?" There was surprise and something else in her tone.

I raised an eyebrow. "You know the place?"

She closed her mouth and nodded. "I know someone who works there."

This right here? This was the most personal conversation we'd ever had.

"A friend?"

Her cheeks colored, and she scratched her head, glancing to the side. "Someone I might... Someone I like."

I didn't know if I liked where this was going.

Her eyes darted back to me. "We could go? You could find your friend—"

"Not a friend."

"—and I could see if my friend is there."

Fuck. If he was on a date with Billie, then... What the hell would I do? *Should* I do?

Then again, if he was there with her, I could try to suss out the situation. I wouldn't have to deal with him because I'd not been looking forward to that conversation. I doubted he'd give me the means to reach Billie the easy way, and he was a cop. I hadn't figured out what hard way I was willing to go with him.

"Brett?"

I'd been staring at her while I thought.

It was the glint in her eyes. Hopeful. Excited. I'd never seen Callie like that. She worked. She was quiet. She was one of the team's best physical therapists, and she was motivated for more. If she had problems, I never heard about them.

I didn't know if I was doing this for her or for me, but I nodded. "I can't stay long."

Her eyes lit up, and her head bobbed up and down quickly. "Uh-huh. Sure. Not a problem."

We took my truck, and we parked at the back end of the place. I'd never been here, which wasn't unusual. I'd barely gone out since joining the team a year ago. But even before that, I didn't do this. Not during the season.

The few nights with Ole were the exception.

The place was packed, and since football was a religion here, I pulled a ballcap low over my head.

Callie snorted, her little lip curling up. "If you don't want to be recognized, you need to wear a fat suit. You're going to be recognized. Prepare yourself."

I grunted, hunching my shoulders. I'd try to be as inconspicuous as possible anyway.

We stepped in the front door, and that idea went up in

smoke. The hostess looked up, and up, and up, and gasped. She dropped the pen in her hand. "Hi—ohmygod—hi. I'm— welcome to Jack's BBQ. Table for two?" She nudged the girl next to her, who wasn't paying attention until she gave her a sharp jab.

"Ouch! What?"

The first girl gave her a pointed look before turning to us.

The second girl clued in, and her eyes got big too. "Oh! Hi. Welcome to Jack's BBQ."

The first one skirted the desk, ignoring the people who'd been waiting, and waved us through. "Come in, come in. Jessica," she hissed to the second girl. "Go tell Brent."

"What? Why—oh! Oh yeah." She scurried off.

Callie ignored all this, back to standing on her tiptoes with her head craned to see the bar. Her head suddenly straightened, and she dropped to her feet, turning to me. "Be right back."

I frowned, but she was off, weaving through the crowd until she got to the end of the bar, where she waved at one of the female bartenders. The first hostess was asking me something, but I watched as the bartender gave Callie a small wave.

Callie stood back, her hands folded in front of her, tugging at the end of her shirt.

She glanced my way and gave me a tentative grin.

I gave her a chin lift, and her cheeks flooded again as she looked back to the woman now making her way over.

"Brett Broudou." A man was heading my way, late twenties. He thought of himself as a smooth operator. This must be the manager. He had a look in his eyes I recognized. An opportunist. Before he could get comfortable and give me whatever spiel he was planning, I grunted. "I'm not staying. Just need to see if someone is here." I moved past him, going faster than he'd expected, and gave him a dip of my head. "It's an impressive place. I can see why it's so busy tonight."

After that, I moved through the crowd, pushing past people before they could see me and get a good look. I'd gotten to the far end before I spotted the detective at a table outside with another couple. Scanning the dance floor and then back around, I didn't see Billie.

Another woman went over to their table and sat down beside him.

I frowned. He was on a date with someone else?

That was fast. He'd seemed just as interested as I was. Billie was one of those who didn't come along every day. She was a once-in-a-lifetime type, but it wasn't her who was sitting next to the detective. I knew his name now. I could have a conversation with him some other time and place, something more private.

I turned to go let Callie know I was leaving when one of the bathroom doors opened.

I stepped out of the person's way and she said, "*Brett?*"

I looked down.

It was Billie, looking cute as fuck, adorable, and stunning all rolled into one. How she did that, I had no idea, but she pulled it off, and every fucking man in the place knew it too. Six guys were clocking her as she stood in front of me, her head tipped up with wonder and something else in her gaze. Guilt? Then it was gone and replaced with...hurt? She bit her lip, taking a step back.

I started to go with her, but held myself back. *Fuck's sake.* What was I doing? I looked over my shoulder and saw the woman leaving their table. Detective Travis was now scanning the room, looking for his real date, who was blocked behind me.

"You're here with the detective."

Guilt flared in her eyes again before she looked away. "I —yes."

I saw it then. She was interested in him.

She wasn't interested in me.

I needed to stop this and get a clue. Any more chasing and I'd be a different category of man, one I never wanted to be.

Still, my tone was gruffer than I intended when I spoke. "Fine. You have my number. You can call me any time. I mean that." I stepped to the side, looking back at their table. The detective was watching, probably two seconds from standing up and heading this way. I dipped my head in his direction, and he frowned, clearly not expecting that.

I took another step, away from Billie. "I hope you have a good night."

Her hand touched my arm. "Wait."

I looked back, but I didn't move toward her. I couldn't. Not anymore. She was on a date with another man, after I'd called her for two days in a row and texted two more before that.

She frowned up at me. "What are you doing here?"

I glanced in Callie's direction. She was now watching me. Her eyebrows were furrowed. Her bartender friend, or whoever she was, was also looking my way with rapt curiosity.

A lesser man might've lied to cover his humiliation. "I came to see if *you* were, and I'm hoping you don't ask me how I knew you might be here, because it's making me look a certain way I don't like."

Her little eyebrows pinched together. "I—I haven't listened to your last message. What did you say in it?"

I shook my head. "Just that I was going to back off because it's apparent you're not interested." With that said, I really did need to go. Three guys at the bar were headed my way, and I didn't want to get stuck talking football for the next hour. I touched a hand to her side, and Billie sucked in her breath. I gently squeezed her there. "It was good seeing you again, Billie. I hope you watch the game on Sunday."

I stepped past her.

She whirled with me. "Brett—"

I paused, looking back, waiting. We were close. Her head

was at my chest level, and she dropped her eyes, staring at my shirt. "Why are you wearing a sweatshirt?"

I fought back a grin. "That's what you wanted to say to me?"

She looked back up, and embarrassment flooded her face, which made her all the more adorable and made my dick stand up straight, like a lapdog hoping to be petted.

"No. I—why didn't you call me the next day?"

I frowned.

"You said you wanted to see me. Then you said you would call. Then I got a text."

My frown deepened. "I'm not following."

"You texted me."

"Yeah, I did." I cocked my head to the side, trying to understand.

"It was late."

"Did I wake you up?"

"No." Her eyes skirted around, and she moved even closer, her chest lifting. "It was *late*, like *late*."

Comprehension flared. She thought—I looked around for a side door or an exit, because I felt those guys behind me. More had joined them, and they were only holding back because it was obvious I was talking to a woman. A guy didn't interrupt those conversations, except they would eventually. Football fan code would override bro code.

I didn't have long.

Callie's friend figured out what I wanted and gestured behind her.

I touched Billie's side again and herded her in front of me, my other hand finding her other side.

"Wha—huh?"

"Let's have this conversation somewhere more private." We rounded a group, and I ignored a few people calling my name as I steered Billie past Callie, who was grinning broadly.

"Back door through the kitchen," her friend said, lifting up a part of their bar so we could step through.

"Thanks."

"No problem. Good luck," she called after us as we went through the kitchen doors.

I moved past the startled kitchen staff until we were out the back door. Once there, I moved Billie around the corner and back against a wall. I had to be close. There was something about her. It felt like I was fighting gravity if I wasn't moving to her side or pulling her to me.

She sucked in her breath, flattening against the wall. Her hands tucked behind her, and she swallowed, looking up at me.

Jesus. Those eyes. A man could get lost in those eyes and never want to come back up for oxygen.

"You thought I only wanted a booty call?" I rasped.

She swallowed again. "Yeah," she whispered. Hurt flared in those dark eyes again.

"Thought I'd made my interest real clear."

"Me too," she whispered again, her gaze falling to my chest. "But you didn't call."

"I didn't call because I was on a flight to California, and I was using my phone to track down a half-brother I've not spoken to in almost twenty years because I had to ask him to wade into family drama he probably never wanted to deal with."

Her head jerked up. "What?"

"I wanted to call and talk you into dinner at my place or yours, and if you didn't want either of those, since it would've been a first date, I would've been happy to take you somewhere else in town. Somewhere private."

"Really?"

I nodded, losing the battle not to touch her. My thumb went to her chin. There was a little dent there, and it was cute as fuck. She drew in a breath at my touch, but I couldn't stop. My hand smoothed down her throat, feeling her pulse, loving how it sped up, how her chest was rising. I knew she felt what I was feeling. My hand slid around to cup the back of her neck, and I struggled to keep from moving even closer.

My head bent, needing to be in her space, in her air. My forehead went to hers, resting there.

We were both trembling.

Her hand went to my stomach, and I sucked in my breath, holding still, not wanting to scare her away. I wanted all of her against me.

"It was a family crisis sort of thing." My voice was still rough.

Her fingers curled around my waistband, taking a firm hold. She was hanging on to me. "I'm sorry."

I raised my head, needing to see her better, but I didn't move, loving the feel of her fingers against my stomach. "It was a day."

Guilt flared over her face, tightening around her mouth. "Didn't say I was rational. My feelings were involved." She mumbled that, her gaze falling back to my chest, and she leaned in. I wasn't sure if she was even aware of what she was doing as she rubbed her cheek against my chest, a contented purr leaving her body. She stepped away from the wall, her arms moving to slide around my waist, and then she was plastered against me, hugging me.

I moved in an instant, hoisting her up and moving her against the wall again so her back was supported. Her legs opened, so I moved in even farther. She gasped as we came in contact. I stilled. My God, she felt good. I closed my eyes, bending down, my cheek resting against hers, just needing to feel her.

She had been holding her breath, but let it go, relaxing into my hold, and her legs lifted, winding around my back.

Jesus.

I was one move away from dry humping her.

A growl left me, and she stiffened. I felt drugged; that was the effect this woman had on me. "We need to go somewhere else."

She felt my dick twitch against her, and a haze fell over her eyes. I watched, as if in slow motion, as her eyes half closed and she tugged her lip between her teeth. She moved against me, her center rubbing over my dick. Which I loved. Which I was already craving. For fuck's sake, I was a minute away from reaching down with my hand, and after that, I couldn't promise what we would or wouldn't do. Her hold over me was uncharted territory.

That's cause she's a once-in-a-lifetime type of woman, a voice told me, laughing.

Right. I was aware, more than aware.

"Billie..." My tone was hoarse, strained. My hands clamped on her thighs, holding her more securely, and that only made her grind over me with more fervor. "Billie."

"Jesus Christ."

Déjà vu because once again, his voice broke through our reverie. And he was pissed.

I would've understood if our roles were reversed. Though, as I stepped back, still holding Billie against me, I glared at the detective. He'd been on another date with my girl.

I growled. "You're interrupting."

Billie went rigid before pushing at my chest until I lowered her back down. Her face went pale, and she scrambled away from me a few steps. Not far. I caught the edge of her shirt, keeping her within touching distance.

His eyes went to that touch, and he growled as well. "We're on a date, Broudou."

"Oh, God." Billie groaned, her head dropping forward.

I smirked. "Doesn't look like it's going well."

She groaned again.

"You're a dick."

I inclined my head. "Well. Yeah. It comes in handy with my job."

Another rumble came from him before he drew in a controlling breath. "Billie..."

Her gaze lifted as she gulped, smoothing some of her hair back. "Travis. I..."

I could see her mind working. Both of us were aware of her situation, but she needed to choose. I'd crashed two of his dates, only one on purpose, but there couldn't be a third time. For him or me.

She let out a soft, defeated sigh, her hand finding mine. "I—"

"I got it," he said immediately. "Since I need to pay, I'll let your sister know you're finding your own way home." He skewered me with a glare. "I'm trusting you won't fuck that up?" He shifted, just slightly, but I caught the edge of his holster clipped to his pants.

I smirked again because fuck, but I couldn't help it. I was still a Broudou. "Got it, Detective."

"Good." He was still glaring.

My phone buzzed.

I pulled it out.

Callie: I'll make my own way home.

I tugged Billie along with me as I turned. "Have a good evening, Detective."

We went around him.

He didn't turn to watch us go, but he called after me. "Fuck off, Broudou."

I couldn't blame him.

14

BILLIE

I had never done that. Ever. Gone on a date and left with a different guy? That wasn't me. I was responsible—overly responsible. Overly cautious. Overly reserved. Overly guarded —overly everything.

"So..." My voice broke. I felt Brett's eyes on me, and I could feel his presence like a heaviness that coated me, a calming blanket. It soothed me, but then I remembered all the other ways he could make me feel. My chest constricted, just remembering how he'd lifted me, how my legs had wound around him like it was the most natural thing to do in the world.

"So?" he prompted.

Right. I'd started thinking. "So..." My voice cracked again. "This isn't usual for me." I gestured to the dashboard.

He was quiet. "You're not used to gloveboxes?"

"What?" I looked at him.

The corner of his mouth curved up before he went back to focusing on the road. "You gestured to my glovebox and said this wasn't usual for you."

Oh! I laughed. "No. I mean, you and me. The way I react to you. It's not normal. For me. And going off with a man I barely know? That's really not normal for me."

He looked my way again.

I couldn't look at him. If I did, I'd get drawn into how it felt when he held me. I'd start feeling all warm and focus on how I wanted to feel that way again. How I *only* wanted to feel that way. "I think this is the first time I've experienced lust at first sight."

He cursed, the wheel pulling to the left before he righted it. "Don't know what to say to that."

"Where are we going?" I'd left Lo and Roger back at Jack's BBQ. Also out of character for me. And if Lo called Vicky? Vicky and Howard. They'd both be worried about me. Oh, well... At least I'd told Vicky about Brett.

"...I can't help but wonder if maybe he's the first one to get the real you out of you."

Maybe she wouldn't be so surprised.

"I was just driving until you sorted out whatever you need to sort out," Brett said. "Then I was hoping we could have a discussion about where you'd like to go."

Gah. He was so sweet, which was surprising because the Brood Machine wasn't known for being friendly to anyone, off or on the field. It was well known that he didn't have a lot of other football players as friends. A few here and there. Olvander was the exception, it seemed, but some of his past teammates had done interviews and when asked about Brett, they admitted no one really knew him.

My mind was already going a mile a minute, and it was exhausting.

"I live with Vicky and Howard," I blurted. "On their farm." He needed to know.

His eyebrows furrowed.

"I mean, I don't live *with* them, but I live on their property. In a house. Their guesthouse. It isn't a guesthouse anymore since I started living in it. They have seventy acres outside of town. They could have lots of houses if they wanted, but they don't. Just mine. Which was theirs." I was rambling. I looked his way at a stop light, and he watched me. His eyes were big and dark and chocolaty and warm, and I felt all the tingly feelings again.

I swallowed, remembering what I'd been saying and why I'd been telling him. "So, you know, I moved there because the reporters were bad. They kept trying to follow me and find out where I lived. But it wasn't just because of the press. There were fanatics too."

His eyes flashed. "Fanatics?"

"You know, the serial killer lunatics. All sorts of them. Serial killer groupies. The ones who want to get close to a serial killer. The ones who are inspired by serial killers. The ones who want to finish his job..." Those were the worst. A cold chill went down my spine.

"Wait." Brett pulled to the side of the road, shifted into park. "That happened?"

His eyes were blazing, his jaw clenched. A wave of anger rolled off him, anger and something worse. Violence. He was fully capable of doing serious harm to another person.

I felt that before and felt it again.

I swallowed a knot.

"Sick fucks try to get to you?" he asked.

"There were a few, back in the day. Mostly it's threatening calls and letters. I only had one email connected to Willow Harm, and I closed that down after the show. It gets worse whenever I'm in the news, or if his lawyers are trying to do an appeal."

One was coming up, another attempt for him. They were never successful, but they always did a press tour trying to gain sympathy.

"Hey." Brett's tone went soft, and he inclined his head.

"What just happened? You were with me, talking to me, and I felt a shift. You distanced yourself."

I laughed abruptly. How could he sense all that from me? The way I reacted to him? It was jarring. I'd spent all my life hiding, and he knew what was going on inside me after three times being in my presence?

I felt exposed.

His eyes narrowed. "What's going on? You're a mile away."

I motioned between us. "This is really sudden." He was quiet, and now I felt him pulling away. I didn't look up. I wasn't sure how to handle any of this. "Don't you think?"

"What do you mean by that?"

I looked up and his eyes were different, a wall had come down.

I didn't like seeing that. "I think—I think we should go slow."

"Slow?"

I nodded. "Yeah. Slow."

"What are we talking about? Am I allowed to drive you home, or you still don't want me to know where you live? That kind of slow?"

The wall had come down completely over him, including his tone. "No. I mean, yes, I want you to drive me home. I'm talking about how you seem to know me already. That's—for someone like me, with my background, that's a lot. That's all I'm saying."

He studied me as I spoke, and some of the tension that'd filled the truck eased. "I can see that."

"Yeah?"

His eyes warmed again. "Yeah. How about I give you a ride home, and we do a call tomorrow?"

I felt warm all over again. "I'd really like that."

He grinned at me, holding my gaze for another few seconds before he put the truck back in drive and pulled away from the curb. "I'm quite content to keep driving around this neighbor-hood, but eventually you'll need to let me know how to drive you home."

A slight laugh escaped me, and I relaxed into my seat. I liked riding around with him. "How about when I'm ready to go home, I'll give you my address?"

He flashed me another grin, which sent my pulse speeding. "One might argue that's not environmentally friendly."

"One might argue that we make an exception for tonight."

"I'm okay with that."

"I'm okay with that too."

We were in agreement, and I relaxed even more knowing the boundaries, knowing he would respect them. I felt safe. I didn't know this man, but some part of me said I already did, and that maybe I was the safest I'd ever been when I was with him.

That meant everything.

He took me into a gated community, one where he said a buddy lived, so he had the code to get in. It was October so the lawns were decorated for the upcoming holiday. Almost every house was decked out.

Ghouls. Ghosts. Goblins.

Grim reapers.

One house had a fake guillotine. I hoped it was fake.

Orange lights. Black lights.

Vampires.

Werewolves.

There were light shows against the side of some of the houses, with bats flying and witches.

It was amazing.

I had fun looking around, and after we were done, Brett drove along the river.

I shook my head. "I've lived here a good portion of my life and had no idea about these places."

"Maybe a benefit of being new. I asked around for local sights to see. These were some of their recommendations."

"Who did you ask?"

He lifted a shoulder. "The other players. Some of the coaches. Mostly people from the team."

Right. The team. The Texas Kings. Because he was a professional football player.

"Wait. Don't you have an early morning walk-through tomorrow?"

"You know my schedule?"

My cheeks warmed. "I watch a lot of football."

"Right. The stats. You know my stats better than I do."

"I like it. I'm weird like that. You've been invited to play in the Pro Bowl three times, and you've had three of your own interceptions. In your whole career, not counting this year, you've had four hundred and thirty-two tackles." My cheeks were now hot. "I could go on."

"You do know my stats." He squeezed my hand gently. "And that's not weird. There are television shows about people talking about our stats."

"But you probably need to get back, right? You need your sleep."

We were on the outskirts of the city, which wasn't far from where I lived, though I'd not told him that yet. He pulled over again. "It's not too late, but yes, I should get back."

"We can't mess up your schedule."

"Right." His eyes were amused.

"Because you have a game on Sunday."

"I do. Yes. Routine is important."

I nodded. "Thank you for this."

His head tilted to the side. "This?"

I shrugged. "This. The car ride. Listening to me freaking out and being okay with, well, everything. My idiosyncrasies."

"Your idiosyncrasies are adorable. They give me a window to you."

My idiosyncrasies are adorable?

I liked hearing that. "We're not far from where I live," I told him, making it sound like a confession as I leaned closer.

"You said a seventy-acre farm, so I guessed." His head inclined toward me. "I figured if I was going the wrong way, you'd correct me."

He was right. "No reason to further waste gas." I scooted over another inch.

"Right. This is as much of an environmentally unfriendly date as we can get."

"Yes. Right."

If I moved another inch, and his head bent to stare straight down at me... If I rolled back my shoulder, tipped my head, his lips would be right there. I could brush them with mine.

But he didn't respond. His eyes were so dark, glittering.

A need rose up through me, intertwined with an ache. I wanted to touch him, kiss him. I wanted to see how he tasted, get swept up in all the dizziness and wonderful sensations.

I hardly dared to breathe, I needed to feel him so badly.

I lifted my hand, his name falling softly from my lips, and he began to inch down to me...

Bang! Bang!

I screamed.

Someone was outside Brett's window, a flashlight shining in.

Someone was outside my window, another flashlight shining over our faces.

Brett cursed.

Then my phone rang, and I screamed all over again.

Jesus Christ. What was happening?

"It's the cops." Brett took my hand, giving it a reassuring squeeze before he rolled his window down. "Can I help you?"

I made no move to roll my window down, and the other cop seemed okay with that, his narrowed eyes studying me intently.

My phone kept ringing, so I pulled it out. *Lo.* "Hello?"

The cop and Brett were conversing, but Travis withstanding, cops made me nervous so I focused on the phone instead.

"Where are you? You've been ignoring my texts. Travis said you took off with Brett Broudou? Are you serious? He came back to the table, all heartbroken and—" Roger said something in the background. She responded, her voice sounding far away, before coming back, more clear. "Roger said he wasn't heartbroken, but his ego was bruised. Oh, come on." That was to Roger again. "This was his second date with her, and the second time Broudou swooped in. Which, by the way," she was louder, talking to me. "You left with him. That means we have to meet him. You know that, right? I left you alone, promised Roger I'd let you have your time with him, but it's almost ten, and no one's heard from you." Roger said something again, and whatever it was made Lo huff, annoyed. "Enough's enough. Where are you? Are you coming home tonight?"

Roger spoke again behind her, laughing.

Lo cursed under her breath. "I mean, to your home. Because we're not there. We're not waiting for you in Mom and Dad's driveway."

They had a babysitter. Lo had wanted to stay out late tonight, dancing. But I left... "You're sitting on my patio, aren't you?"

The conversation happening to my left suddenly paused, and I looked over. Brett, his wallet in hand, and the cop were both looking at me. I couldn't read either of their expressions and told them, "She's like my sister. They're waiting for me. Everything's okay."

"Who are you talking to?" Lo asked. "Also, I *am* your sister. Just freaking accept it, would you?"

Brett blinked, putting his wallet away.

I frowned. "Is something wrong?"

"Who's that? Are you talking to Brett?" Lo demanded.

"The police are here," I told her.

"Police?! Where are you? Are you at Brett's? Why would the police be there?"

"No. We're on a road, not far from home. And I don't know why they're here."

"Who's there?" Roger asked.

Lo told him, and he said something else. "What? Are you serious? You called the cops on them?"

I frowned into the phone. "He did what?"

Roger was speaking, "...didn't know it was them. Parked truck by here? You know how it is."

Lo cursed again before a slight laugh escaped her. "Um... Roger—"

I said it for her. "Roger called them on us?"

"Yeah. Sorry. You know how it is, with you being here and someone stalking the place." She tried to smother a giggle, but didn't succeed. "He didn't know he was calling the cops on you."

I ended the call. "Roger called the police."

Both Brett and the cop were fighting back grins now. I wasn't even going to look at the cop outside my window. The humiliation was enough.

"I heard." Brett's lips were twitching.

"We all heard." The cop by Brett's window placed his hand on the door. "Since everything seems okay, we'll take off. You have a good rest of the evening, and *please* win on Sunday."

"Yes, sir," Brett responded, eyes on me.

The two cops left, and the air felt heavy. I wasn't sure why.

"I'm sorry Roger called the police. He did it for me."

"Who's Roger?"

"Lo's husband."

"Ah. The other guy."

I didn't know what he was talking about. "It's the fanatics," I explained. "He was being careful, just in case we were someone trying to find out where I lived."

His eyes flashed. "How often does that happen?"

My heart sank a little. "Not often, but it's happened."

His eyes went hard again before he softened them. "No one's put it together that you're living in their guesthouse?"

I shrugged. "It's kinda hidden from the road. Trees block it from the other side too. And the chicken coop's not far from it. It doesn't look like a guesthouse by design. Howard put some stall doors on it. You know, to trick people. There are grain bins set in front filled with cement blocks."

"You don't use them for grain?"

"No. Raccoons will get into them. Or other animals."

"Right." He was back to trying to hide his smile. "All the animals around you."

"It's mostly the chicken coop, but I'd love it if they got more animals."

"Yeah." He said the word on a small sigh. "You're there, hiding in plain sight. I don't know if it's genius or a stupid risk."

I frowned. "I like the guesthouse. It was my idea."

He sighed again, this one sounding more annoyed. "I'm sure it was." He started the engine, and I couldn't remember when he'd turned it off.

"Are you upset with me?"

His mouth tightened. "It doesn't matter. Where am I going?"

"Hold up. You're upset?" I turned to him, and my hands balled into fists, pressing down on my legs.

He put the truck back in park. "No. I'm annoyed that you have people who are interested in killing you, and it's so normal to you that you've made up a nickname for them. And you're staying in a guesthouse that's designed to look like an animal shed to hide from these sick fucks. Who's keeping you safe? Do you have a security system in place? Have you taken self-defense? Do you have a gun in your place?" His words came at me hard. "What I'm annoyed about is that some sick fuck could get curious, trek out here, find you, and who's there to protect you?"

I wheeled backwards, pressing against the door. "Howard protects me."

"Who the fuck is Howard?"

I winced. "He's like my dad."

"Great. How old is Howard? Does he have a gun? Does he have a security system in place? You're in the middle of nowhere out here."

My blood heated. "He owns a gun, and he's used it before."

"When?"

"To protect me."

"Against *who*?"

I felt like I was taking blows. "From reporters when they were trying to find where I lived."

"He's already had to use it to protect you from reporters? The press? Who'd *love* to find out where you live so they can share it for more views."

My head was ringing. "They didn't find out because those seventy acres are private property. They can't get close to the house, much less close enough to see the guesthouse, which again, is camouflaged so no one would look twice at it."

"Except some real fuck who doesn't give a shit about trespassing if he's there to *murder* you."

I winced again. "Just because you're surrounded by other houses doesn't mean your place is safer."

"I'm in a gated community inside another gated community. And we have a security car that patrols the area."

"Oh." *Well.* "I've been safe so far."

He smothered a curse.

The throb in my head was going to turn into a migraine

soon. I knew the progression, knew the red flags. "Just take me home."

He growled. "I still need to know where to drive you."

I told him, and we made the short drive in silence. Lo and Roger bypassed us on the road just before we got to the driveway. The main house was dark, which was a relief right now. I didn't want to talk to anyone, much less field questions about Brett, who I wasn't happy with.

He parked behind the house.

"Thank you for the drive." I started to open the door, intending to slide out and run inside to my home, which had made me feel safe for the last decade.

"Wait." He touched my arm lightly. His tone had gentled, and I heard a twinge of regret. "I'm sorry. I—this is fast for me too."

I didn't let go of the door handle, but I didn't slip out either.

"The thought of you out here, and now knowing there are sick fucks who'd like to find you, it's making me a little nuts."

I looked back at him. "A little?"

He gave me a slight grin before grimacing. "I get protective of people I care about."

People he cares about... He cared about me.

The throbbing headache lifted. The warmth came back, soothing it, spreading inside me. I focused on his lips, letting go of the door handle. "I'm sorry I got snippy."

He shook his head, his eyes going to my mouth. "We're just getting to know each other. This is going to happen." His eyes lifted to mine, and the somber look there struck me deep, closing my throat for a second. "I'm not going to push my luck, especially because the light just turned on outside the main house, and I'm pretty sure your Howard has a rifle in his hand inside the door, but I'll call you tomorrow?"

"Or I'll call you."

He flashed me a smile, making me feel all sorts of wonderful things. "Even better."

"'Night."

He nodded. "'Night. And fair warning, I'm not leaving until you're inside your place."

"Okay," I whispered.

I slid out, shutting the door and holding my hand up to Howard before heading to my place. Once there, I peeked back and saw that Howard had turned their outdoor light off, but Brett was still watching. I gave him a small wave before going inside and locking the door.

He drove off after that.

I got ready for bed, my insides all twisted up with different emotions, good and bad. When I laid in bed, my headache was gone, and I held onto my phone, just knowing...

Twenty minutes later, it buzzed.

Brett: You're still safe?

I knew he was going to text.

Me: I am. You got back okay?

Brett: I did. I'll call you tomorrow. I'd love to get together? Maybe eat something?

Me: I'd like that. Have a good day with the team tomorrow. Night.

Brett: Night.

15

BILLIE

We hadn't kissed Friday night.

We couldn't, not with Howard on the other side of the door and after our little tiff.

I'd had a tiff. With Brett Broudou.

Because I was someone he cares about.

I was still trying to wrap my head around that as we got ready to watch the game. Lo, Roger, and the girls had come over for lunch after church, and since the game was at three, they stayed. The girls had a gymnastics competition all day yesterday, so Lo hadn't been over demanding answers, but I knew my time was up. I'd been glad to keep those details for myself, at least for a little while.

Once she grilled me, it wasn't just my secret or my new thing with Brett. It became Lo's business. And she loved me. I knew she did. She only wanted good things for me, but I'd enjoyed having a day without the pressure.

Brett and I hadn't been able to do get together yesterday, but once he was at the hotel with the rest of the team, he'd called from his room and we talked for two hours.

Two hours.

It'd been so long since I was on the phone with someone for two hours, particularly a romantic interest. Thirty minutes was the most Daniel and I had ever talked when we dated. We were not phone people, or even really talk people. I knew about Daniel's job, his family, his shows, and that was it.

Seraphina, before him, had been a bit different. We did talk, but it wasn't over the phone. She just came over to my place during college. Or I went to hers. That'd been new to me. She was my first relationship, so I hadn't totally known what I was doing.

After them, I'd given up, figuring dating wasn't for me. It wasn't going to be in the cards. And now this? With Brett?

I hadn't stopped smiling. I was excited to see him on the field. I was being totally cheesy, but I let myself indulge. There was too much hard shit in life. So yeah, I let myself feel all the sunshine and rainbows right now because who knew what would happen in the future.

"Lo's about to lose her shit." Roger stepped over my feet, which were resting on the coffee table, with a bowl of popcorn. He dropped down next to me on the couch, and I bounced up from the motion. He nodded at the television, where the news-casters were making their predictions for the game. The Kings were playing Minneapolis, and for some reason, since we'd won the Super Bowl last year, everyone was counting the Kings out. They all thought they'd peaked.

I was going to enjoy it when they ate crow.

I sat up, folding my knees under me. "Why's she about to lose her shit?"

"Because of you." He tossed a handful of popcorn in his mouth and grinned.

I narrowed my eyes. "Because why?" I grabbed the remote and turned the volume down.

"Because you haven't told her about you-know-who." He gestured to the television.

Brett. "What? But..." Dread spiked in my chest. "I thought she'd hunt me down, like she always does."

"Nope." He shook his head, throwing more popcorn in his mouth. "Her feelings are hurt."

"What?"

"She gets like this when she's in her feelings. It's on you to figure out what's wrong with her and then say what she wants you to say."

"But..." I sputtered.

"Good luck. It usually takes me two days to figure out what I've done wrong. But you're a girl. She's a girl. You'll probably know what she wants to hear."

He was right about that. She wanted to know about Brett. But man, I'd just wanted a day to keep him to myself. I groaned. "She always hunts me down. I was planning on telling her everything. She usually makes me go on a walk with her."

He paused. "Not this time. You gotta go to her." He glanced at the television. "Make it speedy because we got thirty minutes before kickoff."

"But—"

"If you don't get to her now, it's going to make it worse. She'll ice you out until at least next week sometime, and she'll make all of us leave right when the game ends, and none of us wants that. Howard made ice cream. The girls are playing outside. We're all happy. Everyone's going to want ice cream. For the sake of my family and our love for ice cream, go talk to Lo *now*." He reached over and plucked the television remote from my hands.

I stood and passed Vicky in the kitchen. I paused on the way out. "You need help?"

She shook her head, rolling out some paper at the kitchen table. "Not one bit. You go have a chat with Lo."

"You heard?"

Howard was at the sink, washing a few things. He chuckled, his back to us. "Hard not to hear that boy."

"Hey!" Roger called from the other room. "I'm not loud. It's called charisma. People just pay attention to everything I do and say."

"Yep. That's what we call it. Charisma." Vicky's tone was dry.

"That's right. Charisma. And I'm a man."

Vicky called back, never stopping what she was doing, "You're always going to be our boy."

"That's okay. I love you too, but I'm a man. With charisma."

Howard hung a towel in front of the stove. "Well, would the man in the living room want a beer?"

Roger was quiet, then appeared in the doorway. "I'll grab 'em. You want one, Howard?"

Howard's gaze swept over me as he nodded. "A beer sounds real good today. Perfect to watch the game with."

Roger went around me, heading to the garage where they kept the beer.

"The longer you stall, the madder she's going to be," Vicky said, still pressing her paper out.

She was right, and that made the nerves twist tighter inside me.

Two of the girls were practicing somersaults and hand-springs in the backyard, under the giant willow tree, while Luna, their third, biked up and down the driveway, leaning forward and going as fast as she could.

Lo stood between them, her hand at her forehead, giving her some shade as she watched.

"Hi, Billie!" Cynthia and Charlotte stopped their somer-saults and waved. They almost spoke at the same time.

Lo didn't move.

I waved to the girls and made small talk for a bit, asking about how high they could kick. They were eight, ten, and twelve. Luna was the youngest, and how hard she was trying to crash her bike was a testament to her place as the wild one in the family.

"Luna!" Lo yelled, cursing under her breath. "If you don't stop using the fence to stop your bike, I'm coming over there and taking it away from you. Unless you're going to pay your own hospital bills?"

Luna's bike had veered dramatically to the right, going into the fence, but at her mom's words, she hopped off and turned it around, glaring at Lo as she did.

"I saw that, my child who I love so much but can't protect against your own recklessness. You hear me? I'll love you more if you're all in one piece!"

Luna moved the bike to the gravel and hopped on it. She yelled over her shoulder, just before she tore off down the road, "Love you, Mom!"

I was at Lo's side now, and she lowered her arm, sighing, "It's karma coming back to kick me in the ass. I was just like her. Mom was ready to wring my neck at the same age."

"*Just* at that age?"

Her eyes shifted to me, and she gave me a slight grin. "Touché." She smoothed her hand down her pants. "Walk and talk?"

"Walk and talk."

I dove right in as we started. "Friday night was a whirlwind. I should've texted you, let you know I was leaving, but Travis said he would tell you. I apologize for that, though I'm aware you checked my tracker four times, the last time after I got home."

Her mouth tightened.

"And I didn't call yesterday because I wanted a day of him to myself. I knew you'd be coming here today, and I was planning on telling you. I wasn't trying to keep you out. I just wanted some time to myself. It wasn't about you."

That was my spiel, though I wasn't apologizing. I was explaining. I eyed her as she was quiet for a few seconds.

A few more seconds.

And still more.

We'd walked a quarter of a mile, with Luna speeding past us twice, before Lo griped, "Goddammit. I can't even be mad at you because you've twisted it to where now I have to apologize."

She gave me the side-eye. "I'm sorry for being self-centered."

Luna chose that moment to zoom past us and overheard. "Mom! You're self-centered? I'm telling Dad."

Lo groaned. "That's going to bite me in the ass too. Karma. Just karma."

Luna was doing a circle around us and caught the tail end. "What's karma, Mom?"

"It's where everything you do will be done back to you."

Luna braked suddenly and stood, lifting herself off the bike seat. "What?"

"Yeah." Lo laughed. "Think on that, my beautiful one. How you treat others is the way others will treat you."

She considered that before starting to pedal again. "Dad must've been a real good kid because everyone loves him."

"Hey! What about your mother?"

Luna's eyes twinkled. She had a little smirk on her face. "Everyone's scared of you, so you must've been a scary kid. You know, back in the day. Like, a looong time ago."

"Okay. We don't need to talk about your mother's age. I'm young at heart," Lo countered. "You got that? I'm always young at heart. That's the only age that matters."

"Except when you're telling us how 'we're going to understand when we're older'," Luna noted. "Then you're all about how old you are, Mom."

Some laughter escaped me as Luna used that as her parting shot and sped back to her sisters.

"We should've waited to take off her training wheels. She

got her smart-aleck attitude when she got her freedom." Lo gave me another side-eye glance, seeming to deflate. "You must like him."

We were back to Brett. I nodded, smiling. "I do."

She let out a dramatic sigh, shaking her head. "Then I'm going to have to give him a chance."

"I mean, to keep this in perspective, we've not even gone on a first date."

"I know, but you walked out on Travis twice. Travis. He's, like, *the* catch."

"I know, but—"

"But you must have some intense chemistry with this other guy."

"I do." I widened my eyes. "It's a lot sometimes."

She bumped her shoulder into mine before stepping away. "You have no idea how much I was going to enjoy rubbing it in Missy Smith's face that Travis was seeing my sister. She's been after him for years."

I knew all about Missy Smith, Lo's arch nemesis from the parents' circle at the church and also the planner for most of their fundraisers and events. She'd been single for two years since her husband cheated on her with a waitress at their country club. He was now married to that waitress, and according to the church gossip chain, she'd gotten a boob job.

When Lo told me things like that, I was glad I chose not to attend their church.

I shrugged. "You can tell her we went on a couple dates. She doesn't need to know anything else."

Lo considered that, her head lifting. "I can stretch it out. Technically, you went on two dates. I'll drop one date at a time on her, let her stew on that."

"You're a bit sadistic."

"Yep." She threw an arm around my shoulders, pulling me into her side. "That's why if anyone comes for you, they'll turn tail and run because they won't be ready for me." An evil laugh came out of her before it subsided into a genuine chuckle. She squeezed me one more time, then let me go. "I know Travis. He's steady. He can protect you, and he's a good guy. I don't know this Brett Broudou except that he's a professional foot-baller, and he got on Travis' nerves like I've never seen."

That explained things a bit more.

"I'm sure Trav gets mad, but I've only seen him mad once," she continued. "A guy got drunk and was trying to drive home from a charity function at the country club until Travis stopped him. He got real pissed." She flashed me a grin. "And it was hot. I got permission from Roger to say that. He thought Travis was hot in that moment too."

I snorted. We were cresting the hill where we could see the end of the driveway. "Do me a favor? Give me some space so I can get to know Brett? I want to try."

We both paused because this was as far as we usually went. If we went farther, we wouldn't be able to see the girls. The game was starting soon as well.

"Define space?"

I growled.

She laughed, giving me a hug. "I'm kidding. I'll back off. I promise." She stepped away. "I'll try to back off. I will attempt to try to back off."

I growled again.

"I'll back off." She held her hands up in surrender before gazing back at the girls. She groaned. "Right there. I don't understand why she just doesn't squeeze the brake. It's like she forgets and decides to use the fence post instead. We're going to end up in the emergency room today, I'm telling you." She started back, grumbling.

I began to go after her but paused.

A truck was parked on the road, not too far away. It was tucked off to the side.

Parked trucks weren't uncommon. Hunters liked to scope out the land, and sometimes they'd track down Howard to ask if they could hunt around here. His response was always no. Howard liked to say he was keeping the land for himself and his son-in-law, but the truth was that neither Howard nor Roger hunted, though I'd never asked why not. I liked that they weren't hunters.

Seeing a truck there shouldn't have given me a pause, but Brett's words were still in my head from Friday night.

"...*some sick fuck could get curious, trek out here, and find you.*"

That's why a cold tingle formed at the bottom of my spine.

Brett put the thought in my head.

It was only because of that.

16

BILLIE

M inneapolis was up, twenty-seven to twenty-four. There was a minute left on the clock, and they had the ball, hoping to score to make that lead even bigger. It was third and goal. I held my breath because Brett was giving it everything he had. He kept fighting against the guy guarding him, grappling to see if he could get an inch of an opening to rush the quarterback.

"Broudou's been going hard at Leroy the whole game," one commentator said.

"You're right," the other agreed. "What a great player we got in him. The Kings' defense coordinator must've leapt for joy when he got a player of his caliber. He knows what he's doing. All the little touches, the holds he's doing on the quarterback? That's what a top-notch defensive lineman does. He's getting in the quarterback's head. It's his job to do anything to mess up his game."

"Anything within the rulebook."

"Of course within the rulebook, but Broudou is a treat to watch."

For most of the game, they'd been talking about the two

quarterbacks—Doubard's game versus Leroy's, though for a few moments they'd raved about Stone Reeves, the Kings' wide receiver who'd run in two of the touchdowns. But for the last ten minutes, they'd been focused on Brett. He'd sacked Leroy twice and was pushing to get a third. If there was any time that it was needed, it was now.

The players lined up.

"Let's see if they can pull off the money play."

"Yeah, let's see what Broudou is going to do here."

The quarterback called the play, and I was on my feet.

Lo was on the couch, frowning at her phone with one of the girls trying to get her attention. Roger and Howard had ceased talking.

"He's open! He's totally open—" Roger yelled, pointing at the television.

The guy who'd been guarding Brett had turned to block the other defensive lineman, which gave Brett a wide-open shot to rush Leroy.

Leroy shifted back to let the ball loose, but Brett was there. His hand was up, just as Leroy threw the ball, and he got a finger on it, tipping it up.

Roger and Howard were yelling.

I couldn't breathe.

Brett finished the sack, grabbing Leroy around the chest and taking him down in a very clean tackle. The ball was intercepted by one of the Kings' players, and he ran for their endzone. Because most of the Minneapolis team had been positioned behind him, he had an almost open field. He got to the Kings' fifty-yard line before getting caught and pushed out of bounds.

I whooped. The guys were going crazy.

Lo frowned. "What happened?"

The announcers were going crazy as well.

"What happened?" Roger repeated his wife's question,

wrapping his arms around me and lifting me off my feet. "This one's man just gave us a chance to freaking win this bitch."

Luna started giggling.

Lo scowled. "Roger, language."

"Oh. Sorry." His wide grin said he was having a hard time meaning it. He let me go and ran a hand through his hair. "Man. This is great fu—errr, great—er, football to watch. What a game."

"You stop talking as if it's done." Howard's tone was no-nonsense. "We ain't done. We still gotta score."

Right. His words doused us in reality, and we all quieted, though I was pretty sure Roger was praying under his breath.

The Kings ran off the field, and the camera lingered on Brett as his teammates pounded him on the shoulder pads in congratulations. A few of the coaches went over, showing their thanks, as the offense took the field.

Roger sat on the couch, but scooted all the way to the edge, his elbows on his restless legs as he breathed into his palms. "We need to get closer. Just a little closer and we can do a field goal, tie the game."

"Forget a field goal." Howard grunted, gripping his second beer. "We're going for a touchdown. We're going to win this thing."

He was right. They got up to the thirty-second-yard line, and it was first and six.

"First down, first down..." Roger was on repeat.

The announcers were back to talking about Brett's play, showing it several times before going back to the game. The camera panned over to him on the sidelines, as he stood with his helmet off, all his fierceness directed to the game.

I got a little lost, watching him, because I knew he was going to call after the game. He'd mentioned maybe trying to get some food together. This big guy—who wasn't as big as the big-big guys in the middle of their line, but was still big to me—wanted to see me, talk to me, spend time with me.

I remembered the feeling of him holding me Friday night, like I weighed nothing.

A shiver went through me, a delicious sensation filling me right up.

The camera kept panning over to Brett in between the plays, and Colby Doubard kept throwing for a first down until the Kings were at the ten. Then, while Reeves was covered by three guys, Doubard tossed the ball to another of their wide receivers.

They scored.

The kicker came out, and they *still* kept showing the play that had changed the game. Then the kick was good.

Kings were ahead.

Minnesota got three plays in before the clock ran out, and Leroy reared back, throwing as hard as he could to their end. But no one was there.

"Ahhhhh! Hell yes! Hell yes!" Roger nearly exploded.

"Dad, you're loud," Cynthia grumbled.

"Yeah, Dad! Stop being so loud," Charlotte echoed.

"You're right, kiddo." He ruffled the top of Cynthia's hair as she tried ducking out of the way, giggling. "But your pops is happy." His beaming eyes found me. "We're going after that Lombardi again. I can feel it. I can just feel it."

He and Howard launched into a conversation about the team's real chances of getting back to the Super Bowl as Lo caught my attention. She motioned her head to the side. As I nodded, she stood and announced, "You're up, honey."

She followed me out of the room.

"What? Why? What's going on?" Roger asked.

"I need some sister time."

"What? But—"

"But nothing. I love you, but I've been watching the girls all afternoon. You're up."

"Howard was going to show me some new beer he bought."

"He can show the girls as well and make it an educational talk. Just make sure Luna doesn't kill anyone. That's really your only responsibility."

We moved through the kitchen, and Vicky called my name.

I paused. She turned around, her arms deep in the ice cream machine. "If you'd like, invite your man out for some dessert. But only if you want." She smiled. "Tell him he did a great job."

I smiled back as I nodded and pushed out the door, going with Lo to my place.

I texted Brett as Lo pushed open the door and went to sit on the couch in the living room.

"Go on." She motioned to me. "Finish texting your man."

"Some privacy, please?"

She studied me before crossing her arms over her chest and leaning back. "No."

I lowered my phone. "No?"

"I don't think so."

I raised an eyebrow. "You don't think so?"

"You heard me." She nodded. "Text him. I want to see this special magical effect he has over you."

"We just had a conversation about how you were going to give me space."

"I did, all afternoon until I saw how you were looking at the TV when your man was running around in those tight pants." She shook her head. "Straight up eye candy. Come on. I'll give you space, but I want to be here. That's it." She let out a frustrated sigh. "It's texting. It's not like I'm going to overhear you."

I scowled. "Still want my privacy."

"Billie—"

"It's too new."

She rolled her eyes and gave in. I felt it as she pushed herself back up from the couch. "Okay, okay. Text him. I'll be out on your side patio thing."

"I will be right out." My tone was stern, which earned me another eye roll and a twitch of her lips as she passed behind me, making a show of shutting the door.

I'd just started to text again when the phone came alive, ringing in my hand.

Brett calling.

I answered. "Hi. I was just going to text you."

The noise on his end was deafening. "You were? What were you going to say?"

"Where are you?"

"I'm still on the field. I need to do some interviews, but listen, I'll be able to get out of here in like an hour or so. Maybe shorter. What are you doing for dinner?"

"Brett," I started.

"Hold on." He must've done something because the background noise faded dramatically. His voice was clearer. "This is better. Did you say something?"

"Congratulations on the win."

"Hey!" I swore I could hear his smile. "You watched?" He laughed. "Of course you did. I forgot for a second how much you like football."

"I can safely say that I'm speaking on behalf of most of Texas in saying thank you. You were phenomenal."

He laughed again, the warm sound washing over me. "Thank you. I mean that. But it wasn't just me. The whole team got the W."

"You helped *a lot*."

"Brett!" someone called on his end.

A static sound took over, the drone of his voice sounding next, but I couldn't make out what he was saying or who he was talking to. The static left, and he said clearly, to someone else, "Okay. Give me a second. I'll be right there." Then he spoke to me. "I have to go, but do you want to do dinner? I'll do whatever you want. Can you let me know what you want? I want to see you. My place, your place, or somewhere else, just text me. I can pick you up too. I'm easy. You pick. Is that okay?"

"Yeah. I'll text you."

"Awesome, and it's fucking phenomenal to hear your voice. Thank you, baby."

He ended the call.

I was left speechless.

Baby.

He'd called me baby. He'd said it so quickly, easily, as if he'd been calling me baby for years. Had he called other women that? Was that his term of endearment for the women he dated?

"Oh, for the love of Jesus Christ from church this morning!" Lo's voice came through the door. "I'm dying here. Please tell me what's going on!"

I laughed and let out a sigh, releasing any negativity that lingered in me.

Me: There's homemade ice cream here, and Howard is showing Roger some new beer he bought. I was asked to relay an invitation to you. By the time you get here, I'm sure we'll be sitting down for dinner. One more plate is easily added to the table.

Brett: Awesome! I'll let you know when I'm headed your way.

Lo had a peculiar look in her eye when I took a seat beside her. She'd pulled her chair over so she could still see the front yard since the girls were back to playing. They were riding around on their bikes. Luna kept trying to pedal away, but Roger was there, talking with Howard, and he had a hand on the back of Luna's bike. She was pedaling, but not moving forward. She kept glaring, but Roger was ignoring her, listening to Howard.

Lo's eyes shifted to me as I put my phone on the table. "You're quiet. Why are you quiet?"

I gave her a look. "I'm always quiet."

"True, but this quiet is different. Why's it different? Did you sext with Broudou?"

"What?"

She laughed. "Never mind. You didn't sext. I'd be able to tell."

I frowned. "He's coming for ice cream and dinner."

She froze, her eyes latched on me.

My frown deepened. "Was that the right move? I could cancel, tell him we should go somewhere else."

She jerked forward in her seat. "No! I mean, that's great." She coughed, her voice more normal. "He'll be here? I can finally meet this guy."

Crap. I'd messed up.

It was too soon.

And after I told him I wanted to go slow too.

I'd totally messed up.

As if reading my mind, Lo's hand shot out. "No. Whatever you're thinking, stop. This is good. Great. Fabulous. Roger can have his fangirl moment."

Luna was shouting now, so Lo's attention was divided. "Especially if this fizzles out fast. Roger will always have his memory of having dinner with Brett Broudou."

Fizzles out fast? I groaned, reaching for my phone. "This was a mistake. We should go somewhere else."

"No!" She plucked my phone from my hands. "Sorry. I'm being—we've already covered this, but I'm just protective of you. You hardly ever date. And other than Seraphina and Daniel, they were creeps. I'm not counting Travis."

Yeah. I'd really messed up. "You can't tell him about them. I barely even count them."

"Why not?"

I cringed.

"Why *not*?"

"He got upset on Friday."

"At you?"

"No. Oh, no. Not like that. He was worried about me being out here with, you know, the weirdos who are infatuated with the Midwest Butcher."

She visibly deflated, a solemn expression coming over her face. Luna was yelling again, but Lo didn't look. Her eyes remained on me.

"What?" I almost squirmed, she was staring so hard.

"He likes you." Her tone filled with wonder. "Guys get upset about that if they care. He already cares about you."

Oh. Now I did squirm a little. I also shrugged.

"Or that's bad, and he's going to be a controlling asshole and we have to make sure he doesn't brainwash you away from us."

I rolled my eyes. That too. "Don't take this personally, but I think it's best if I don't talk to you about Brett for a bit."

She frowned. "Why? What'd I say?"

BILLIE

B rett rolled in two hours later, the dust coming up in a cloud behind his truck. I'd been waiting at my place for him to show, knowing everyone would be at the window in the other house to watch him drive up. The guys would probably be the worst, so my nerves were very real when I went outside to meet him.

He pulled over to park in front of my place, taking a second before stepping out of his truck. He stuffed his phone in his pocket at the same time his other hand ran over his beard. His eyes trained on me and warming as I approached. God. He seemed bigger than he had Friday, and he smelled even better. Freshly showered. He held his arms open, sweeping me up before I could even get to him, and lifting me all the way in the air. His head buried in my neck, inhaling me as I got another good whiff of his scent. Pine, soap, and leather. I loved it.

His hand swept down my back, and he lifted his head, still holding me in the air. "Your whole fam is watching us?"

My grin stretched, a lazy feeling coming over me, and not one I'd experienced before. I felt safe. I felt secure. I knew he wanted me, knew the reason he was asking, and that filled me with supreme confidence. "Yeah," I whispered.

His eyes darkened. "Right." The regret was clear. His hand flexed on my hip as he lowered me down. "A man could get addicted to a greeting like that."

My cheeks got warm.

He chuckled, the sound smooth. "Just saying." He grinned down at me, not stepping away. "I liked how you say hello."

Man, oh man. I reached forward and fisted my hands in his shirt, tugging him closer until I could rest my forehead to his chest.

His hand cupped the back of my head, and he lifted me up again. "Damn," he whispered, carrying me around the guesthouse so we had some privacy.

I already knew where he was going because it was becoming his signature move. My arms went around his neck, and my legs went around his hips as my back went to the wall. He held me in place. "Is this your tradition with the women before me?" I traced my fingers through his hair.

"Fuck, no. I only act like this with you." He closed his eyes, as if savoring my touch. "You have magic in your fingers, Little Billie." He looked a bit drugged as he gazed at me.

I went still, seeing how I affected him, hearing that name come from him. An addictive power swept through me, making me want to move my lips over his, which were turned up to me.

No one could see us.

They'd wait and let us come inside.

But... Why was I waiting?

I'd just started to lower my head, sighing his name when...

"Is she really showing him the chickens—OHMYGOD! I'm so sorry!" Lo reeled back, hands over her eyes, and her face flaming red. "I'm so sorry. How—just...forget I was here. Please, er, resume?"

She stumbled back around the corner, her elbow hitting the wall before she was out of sight, cursing.

I was too floored to move.

Embarrassment flooded me until I registered that Brett's chest was shaking. He was laughing.

I rested my forehead to his. "I'm so sorry. I never thought they'd come out here."

"That's the sister?" Brett lowered me, his hands going to my hips. His fingers flexed against me.

"That's Lo. She's, uh..."

"She's a Travis fan?"

I looked up, frowning. "How do you know that?"

There was amusement in his gaze as he gestured toward the house. "Glimpsed the whole gang before you came out. They were clocking me all the way in. She was the only one not liking this. The rest looked okay with it. The little girls were confused. They were on the other side of the house, so I hope they didn't see our greeting."

"Oh." It made sense why Lo would come out then.

"She thought you were introducing me to Miss Sylvia Rivera?"

As if hearing her name, a loud *cluck cluck cluuuck* sounded from the coop. The rest of my embarrassment melted away, and I stepped back, taking his hand. "I'll introduce you another time, when it's right."

"It's not the right moment now to meet your chickens?"

I huffed lightly. "Not for Miss Sylvia Rivera or Marsha P. Johnson. It has to be a whole experience. Plus, I've not even told you about the rest of them."

His fingers laced through mine, squeezing my hand. "Then I can't wait. It'll be magical."

I huffed again, louder and with some indignation. "Damn straight it will be."

He laughed. "Oh, you're serious."

I shot him a look, leading him back around to the house. As we came into sight, the curtain on the back door swished closed, and I caught movement in the other back window. They were hurrying to the kitchen.

When we stepped inside, everyone had arranged themselves. The girls were standing ramrod straight in front of the kitchen counter, where the ice cream was sitting. They were staring at us, but their heads lifted as they took in Brett.

Howard and Vicky were by the sink, pretending to be leaning back against it. As I looked their way, both cleared their throats, a flash of guilt flooding their faces before Vicky came forward with a polite smile.

"You must be Brett." She held her hand out. "It's so nice to meet you."

Brett transferred me to his left side so he could hold my hand and shake Vicky's at the same time. He said something to her, but I was distracted by Lo and Roger in the dining room. Roger was openly gaping at Brett while Lo's eyes were fixed on our hands.

I cleared my throat—had to do it twice before her gaze jerked up to mine. Howard now came forward and introduced himself to Brett. Lo and I were in an unspoken conversation.

My eyebrows went up to say, *What were you doing?*

She shrugged, looking away, but the color was high on her cheeks.

I growled low in my throat before stepping out of the way as Roger bulldozed past his wife and past me, his hand in the air, waiting for Howard to finish shaking Brett's hand.

""Heyahowyadoing? I'm Roger. I know this one here." His head dipped toward me, but he kept talking. "Can I just say how awesome and amazing it is to meet you? When you broke free from Hawkins' hold last year in the AFC championship and you slammed Bent to the ground on their fourth and one, I went hoarse from yelling so loud. It was awe-some! And you kept going after him. He was so frustrated with you by the end of the first half. All the announcers were talking about it. Quarterbacks *fear* you, and it's the *best thing ever* to have you on our side, finally. You were a *nightmare* to play against." He had to stop to take a breath, his hand had taken hold of Brett's and was still pumping it in the air.

"Uh..." We all spoke up at once—Lo, myself, and Vicky.

Vicky laughed as Lo and I quieted, and she gestured behind her. "Brett, can I call you Brett?"

"Please." He was laughing, trying to hold it back, and I reached forward to pry Roger's hand away from his. I had to let go of Brett's other hand to do so, but he caught my side.

Lo sucked in her breath, her eyes now transfixed at that.

"Lo, dear, why don't you take your husband outside so he can get ahold of himself? He's fanboying a bit too much. His girls don't know what's happened to their father."

Luna snorted, giggling.

Cynthia and Charlotte both started laughing too, hiding their heads in their hands.

Roger blinked, as if coming out of a trance. "Huh?"

His girls laughed louder.

"Daddy, you're acting weird."

"Weird?" Roger blinked some more, focusing on Charlotte as he swept her up. She shrieked, laughing as he flung her in the air, letting her go and then catching her.

Lo gasped as her head came an inch from the ceiling. "Roger!"

"Relax. I know what I'm doing." But he took her outside, and we could hear another shriek. The other girls scrambled to join in.

Vicky motioned to the food sitting across the stovetop. "I figure you're famished after helping us win that game today. We're going to do buffet style. You're the guest of honor, so you can go first, or you can have Billie lead the way. Whichever you feel the most comfortable with. You can sit wherever you'd like. We already had the more formal meal today, so this one is more relaxed."

He nodded. "Appreciate it, ma'am."

Vicky's eyes widened. A soft laugh left her. "Vicky. Call me Vicky."

"And you call me Howard," Howard's voice boomed.

The corner of Brett's mouth curved up. "Appreciate that also."

"Good." Howard was smiling broadly, standing close behind Vicky.

Brett glanced to me, a question in his eyes, but Lo cleared her throat, moving past me. Her hand extended toward him. "Hello. I'm Elowin, Vicky and Howard's daughter. Uh..."

Brett caught her hand, giving it a shake as she paused in her introduction, looking down at their hands as if she'd forgotten what she was saying. "Uh. Yeah. Hi. Billie's still tentative in claiming us as her family, but we are. She's my sister. I love her like a sister. So, yeah..." She trailed off, staring at me a moment before shaking her head. "It's nice to meet you. My mom's chili is the absolute best. She's won the tri-county chili cook-off three years in a row."

"Uh, Lo."

Lo looked at the dishes behind us. "When she makes it, you'll have to come back and try it." She remembered me, and added quickly, "If you and Billie are still seeing each other by then, I mean."

"Lo!" Vicky snapped.

"What? He won't be coming if they're not still seeing each other, obviously."

Brett had reached around me, slowly pushing me in front of him until we were turned to the food. "I'd love to, either way. I've not had chili in a long while."

Vicky continued glaring at her daughter.

I could hear Lo muttering under her breath. "I was just saying. I'm not trying to be rude."

Brett's chest shook again in silent laughter behind me, which settled some of my irritation. He wanted me to take the lead, so I picked up a plate and glanced over my shoulder to him. That stopped me in my tracks.

A sense of wonderment had washed over his features as he looked at the food. I caught a brief glimpse of a little boy before he blinked and pushed it away. He flashed me a grin. "It looks amazing."

His tone sounded fine. Warm even. But his smile didn't reach his eyes. Why was he faking? Had it been Lo?

"Billie, the man's probably starving, honey."

I started forward at Vicky's gentle prompt, reaching for the mashed potatoes first.

18

BILLIE

Brett didn't look tense. He didn't sound tense either.

We sat at the picnic table he and Roger had brought over so everyone could sit outside together while the girls went back to riding bikes around the yard. He straddled the seat, and I leaned back in his arms, which held me loosely.

Roger and Howard dominated the conversation, asking him questions about football and listening to him tell a story about the night he'd hung out with another player who retired ten years ago but would always be considered one of the greats.

The guys hung on his every word.

Even Vicky and Lo were enjoying this. Vicky would normally have gotten up thirty minutes ago to do something because she didn't like sitting around. She was perched on the end of the seat as if her body wanted to go, but the story was keeping her in place. And Lo had slowly defrosted toward Brett over dinner. He and Luna had a moment where she was struggling to eat her hot dog. He reached over to cut it into the pieces, the same way Lo had cut her green beans. Right after, he pretended to try to eat those pieces.

Lo's mouth fell open, watching as Luna perked up, giggling,

but ate the rest of that hot dog in no time flat. It was always a struggle getting Luna to eat her meat. She could be picky at times.

To Brett's credit, he wasn't trying to impress them. He was just remembering that night because it was memorable—and hilarious at times.

But while he sounded and looked the epitome of relaxed and cool, he was not.

I could feel his chest behind me. He was rock solid and rigid.

My hair fell forward, and I snuck a look at his eyes, my hair covering my glance.

He caught my look as he finished telling his story. His grin faded a little as he focused on me.

"Are you serious? Kerkumpor left it like that?" Roger pounded the table, his laughter bellowing out of him. Howard shook his head, grinning and chuckling as well.

Vicky stood, her serene smile on her face, the one she used when announcing that we were left to our own devices because she was heading to bed. It'd gotten dark. It was past nine, so that made sense. The girls had moved inside with a movie playing in the living room, but they were still up.

"To his credit, Manion didn't see the alligator on the golf course. It just happened to be there."

"Still." Roger kept laughing. "Oh man. That's legendary. Thinking you're going just for a drink at a bar in Denver and ending up running from a gator on a golf course in Florida the same night?"

"Technically it was five in the morning by then."

"Even better." Roger sighed as he caught his breath from laughing so much.

Howard laid a hand on the table and stood. "Well, every-one..." That was the beginning of his "I'm following my wife to bed, so clean up after yourselves or you'll hear from me" speech. Lo and Roger stood right away, reaching for the rest of the plates in front of us.

Brett started to rise.

"No, no. You stay." Lo gestured with a soft smile. "You're the guest. We'll take these in and help clear everything before taking the girls home. You two stay, talk. Enjoy the night."

Brett looked my way before he stood anyway. "Always enjoyed doing dishes when I grew up. Got no problem helping clear, especially after a meal like that."

Roger shook his head, muttering to himself as he headed inside. "Just legendary. Legendary."

Lo snorted, watching her husband. "You know, I'll take you up on that offer. I'm thinking with all the sugar the girls had today, we're going to have a struggle getting them to bed. It'll sound like someone's committing murder." She walked off with a pile of plates in hand, so she didn't see me flinch.

Brett caught it. "You okay?" He shifted all his dishes to one hand and touched my arm with the other. "She didn't think."

"I know."

It wasn't the first time Lo had made a comment like that, an off-the-cuff phrase. Roger did it too, and Howard once or twice. Vicky almost did once, but she caught herself and changed the topic.

Maybe Vicky realized more than the others.

"I'm grateful that they don't think about it when they say things like that," I told him. "I know they worry about the fanatics and the reporters, but they don't think about that actual day. Not anymore. Vicky... She remembers sometimes, and she gets this sad look on her face when she looks at me."

I wasn't back there, not totally. I wouldn't let myself go all the way there, but there were flashes I couldn't stop from coming.

An image from under the bed where I'd been hiding, with the sheet hanging down.

From that angle, I'd seen the door slowly opening, his boot as he stepped inside.

I blinked, pulling myself out of the memory. I couldn't think of it anymore. I couldn't let myself remember what I'd heard... *The screams.*

"Hey." A firm hand touched under my chin, moving to the side of my throat and resting right over my pulse. His thumb smoothed over my cheek.

I blinked again, coming more fully to the present, leaving the past behind. "Sorry," I rasped.

His eyes had clouded over. "You were starting to shake."

"I was?" As if on cue, I hugged myself, suddenly cold.

I bit out a laugh, then bent and grabbed the rest of the dishes on the table.

Brett watched, studying me.

I moved around him, looking over my shoulder as he began to follow. "Hope you don't mind drying because I'm always the washer."

"Are you now?" His face lit up, but the shadows were still there. I hated that I was the reason for them.

The screen door squeaked open, and I stepped into the kitchen. "Yep. Every time. It's a rule around these parts. If I'm doing dishes, I'm washing."

Lo moved past, carrying the girls' backpacks. "Good luck wrestling that dishrag from her. I think it's the water. It's like she plays in it. Try to make her dry the dishes and you'll find yourself doing the dishes alone. I eventually just gave up and let her wash every time."

"Now, me," Roger added, carrying a sleeping Luna in his arms. "I load up the dishwasher as much as possible. But it's some foreign invention to them. If they have time and a choice, they'll wash the dishes. Took me three years of persuading Vicky before they finally indulged. And that's what they call it. An *indulgence.*"

Brett's mouth curved up, taking the plate I'd washed as Roger was speaking. "Yeah?"

Lo disappeared into the living room and returned herding Cynthia and Charlotte in front of her. Both girls were sleepy, dragging their feet. "Tell Billie and Brett goodnight. Okay, girls?"

They did one better, coming over and giving us tired hugs and mumbling goodnights. Then they trudged out the door, giving one last wave.

Roger had ducked out with Luna, so Lo was the last one. She held up her phone in a wave. "'Night. It was good to meet you, Brett. Billie, love you. Call me tomorrow." She left with no more fanfare, so I knew she was tired as well. Or distracted.

I picked the latter because she hadn't hugged me goodbye. She always hugged me when she left.

I felt Brett's attention as I watched through the kitchen window. They went to their SUV and headed down the driveway.

What was she distracted about? It couldn't have been Brett. Or maybe it was?

"You okay?"

I answered without thinking. "She just worries about me."

Brett's eyebrows lowered, but he kept drying the dishes I put on the rack. "About me?"

"It's not just you. I think..." Understanding dawned. "It's because of me."

"You?" Brett took a pan from my hands.

"Because of you." I turned sharply, angling my head back to see him.

"Not following you."

I flushed and went back to washing. "It's because I'm different with you. She's never seen this side of me." I considered it. "I've never seen this side of me either."

"How's the side of this you different than the other yous?"

"I'm..." I paused with my hands in the water. "I'm more me with you than I am with anyone else."

His eyebrows lifted.

I returned to washing, sliding the washcloth over a bowl. "I'm more carefree, more relaxed. I feel safe with you."

He stepped back from the counter, setting the plate down. "You don't feel safe with other people?"

"Other guys. Other people I might've dated. I'm always cautious. Always. That's why. She's worried because she thinks I'm not being myself." It made so much more sense now. I went back to washing, moving faster, now wanting to be done. "That's also probably why she was rooting for Travis so much, 'cause he's a cop."

A shadow flashed over his face before he straightened. "Right. And I'm a big guy."

"Big and athletic. You're not *big* big. You're strong big." I dried my hands and reached over, touching his stomach, feeling him still. "You're all muscle. And fast. Threatening." His stomach twitched. "You're not the biggest guy on the team, but you're not wide-receiver size either."

"Yeah?" His voice was low, guttural.

I glanced up, and my train of thought vanished. His eyes were blazing. I knew he wanted to back me up against a wall.

My breath caught and held in my throat because that feeling was spreading inside me too. Fast. Frenzied.

It overpowered everything else.

I forgot what we were doing completely, the room melting away.

My hand flattened against his stomach. I moved closer, feeling his heat, feeling his jeans, my fingers slid under his sweatshirt until they touched skin.

He groaned, but I was focused on his chest. I moved my hand up, smoothing over his very flat stomach, over all the dips and rises, all the way up, as if I could tunnel my way to his heart. Then he backed me against the counter and stood right in front of me.

His front pressed against my front, and it felt so good. I wanted to feel more of him, and my hand moved south, between us—over his stomach to his jeans. My fingers curled over the waistband, brushing inside.

"Billie," he rasped out on an exhale.

My hand went to the top of his jeans, outlining the button. I tipped my head up to see his face in shadow, rimmed by the light behind him. I took inventory, putting all that data away so I could remember it later. I never wanted to forget the way my pulse sped up, knowing he was about to kiss me.

I lifted my mouth up, drawing him in at the same time.

He moaned, his hand catching the side of my face, and his lips were on mine.

I surged up.

Yes!

19

BRETT

I wanted to press her against the counter, destroy those lips of hers, rip her clothes off, and surge inside. But I needed to curtail everything because it wasn't right. Not for her. Not yet. I needed to go slow. I needed to savor this, be respectable.

She deserved the world.

It took every ounce of willpower, but I ripped my mouth from hers.

"No," she whimpered, leaning forward, chasing me.

I was breathing hard, my chest rising and falling. "Babe." I panted, my forehead to hers.

Jesus. I was standing between her legs, my hands half down her pants, and we were in the kitchen of the family who'd taken her in and loved her. Jesus Christ. The same people who'd welcomed me, fed me, and showed me a glimpse of what a normal family might've looked like, a tease of paradise.

Screwing Billie on their counter wasn't any way to thank them.

She pulled me back, lust blinding her.

"Billie," I said, my voice low. It took everything in me to step away from her, especially as she tried to pull me back, back to her warm honey. That's how she tasted, how she smelled, how she felt. Pure fucking honey. Men everywhere would salivate for just one taste of it. That was Billie.

"We can't."

Her eyes flashed, and I stepped even farther away, my body peeling off hers as some clear thinking settled back in. She remembered where we were, and her mouth clenched as she hopped down from the counter. I didn't move out of the way. The dick in me couldn't make myself move because I still wanted to feel her as she brushed against me.

She trembled slightly before raking a hand through her hair and moving to the door.

I followed silently.

She turned off the outside light, locking the door before pulling it closed behind us.

Her hand caught mine, and she took me to her guesthouse. We stepped around a partition, over a hidden patio, and through her door. She flipped on the light. If I'd had a predisposed idea of what the inside would look like based on the outside, I would've been vastly wrong. The inside was cozy and chic. It was her.

There was a small table set against the wall with a laptop on it. I could immediately envision her sitting to work where she could see the back area by the chickens and the driveway. The window must also be disguised, because from the outside, I hadn't noticed it.

Her small living room had two super comfy-looking loveseats with blankets thrown over them. A small television had been mounted on the far wall so no matter where you sat, you had a good view of it. The kitchen was tiny—fridge in the corner, sink, not much counter space, cupboards, and a tiny dishwasher. She had a wall of mugs hanging from nails.

I looked toward the back and saw a bathroom and a

bedroom. There was also a loft area above. The place smelled of her. Like honey and lilac.

"This is where you live?"

I could sleep here. The second I'd stepped inside, my body relaxed. That was Billie. She did that on purpose, designing everything so you had no choice but to destress.

She leaned back against the kitchen counter, her hands behind her. Her little shoulders lifted. "It's enough for me." She glanced around, maybe trying to decipher what I was seeing. "It's home." Her eyes found mine, and there was a message there for me. "I feel safe here."

That was it.

I nodded, taking a step back. "Howard was in the military?" I recognized the way he held himself.

She nodded. "He was in the Navy. Were you?"

"Almost. My brother went to prison our last year of high school, and I wanted to get as far away from him as possible."

"But you didn't?"

"The weekend I was going to decide, a coach saw me, asked me to try out for his team instead. The school was far enough away—a whole different world. It felt good enough for me... My dad used to be in the military. He came back fucked up, and he never unfucked himself. Howard's not the same."

"No," she said lightly. "He's not."

"Roger's no fighter though."

Her eyes flashed to mine.

"He's not a killer either, and he knows it," I added.

Her lips opened. "How do you know that?"

"I grew up with people who could hurt. You know who they are for the rest of your life." A shadow crossed her eyes. "You know that too."

The air grew heavy, more intense. I could feel the ghosts from the past making themselves comfortable around us. I looked over her body, seeing everything I wanted to make mine.

But I still needed to go slow. I would fuck it up if I went too fast. She was precious and needed to be handled with care.

"If I start touching you now..." I stopped talking as a determined expression settled over her face and she pushed away from the counter, her head tilted to the side as she came to me.

"What?" Her hands moved over my chest, sliding around to my back as she hugged me. "What will happen then?"

I couldn't answer. The need to touch her, taste her, make her mine was almost too much.

She tipped her head back, her chin resting against my chest. "What are you going to do? Because I'm the one touching you."

Fuck.

Those lips. I wanted to explore them, see what all they could do, see what sounds I could make come out of them. I reached to touch the bottom one, feeling her tense against me, waiting to see what I'd do. I pulled her lip down, playing with it before my eyes caught hers again.

They were wide, watching me. Excited. That shadow was still there, though, as if waiting for the pain to come too.

"I met your family tonight," I murmured huskily.

She flinched, just barely, but it was there. I felt her starting to withdraw and clamped a hand on her back, holding her in place.

"When I explore you, I don't want to stop, and it doesn't feel right just after having a meal from your mother's hands."

She suppressed a shiver. "You're assuming I'd let you," she whispered, looking away and pulling her lip out of my touch.

I tilted her head back up, loving the way she reacted to my touch. Her whole body was trembling. I didn't think she was aware. "I'm not alone here, little one. This?" I moved against her, letting her feel me, really feel me. Her eyes glazed over. "That goes both ways."

She bit her lip, the same one I'd been touching.

I moved with her until she was against her kitchen counter, and we were back in our favored position. I closed the distance, my arms trapping her in place. Her eyes closed. Her hands went to my chest, sliding down until she'd again curled her fingers over the waistband of my pants. Her fingers rubbed against my stomach, her little move.

I bent down, and whispered, "Hey."

She lifted her mouth, and there I was, closing the distance. Finally.

20

BILLIE

I'd kissed Brett last night in my kitchen with everything I had, climbing up his body like a squirrel. The way he'd engulfed me when his lips met mine, I knew everything was going to be different from that moment on—like he was changing me from the inside out.

I was swept up. We'd made out for...I didn't know how long. I could've kissed him for the rest of my life and not needed to come up for food and water. Air and him were all I needed.

"Miss Billie." A warm and friendly voice pulled me out of my reverie. A woman was coming my way in the grocery store. "What are you doing here?" She looked over my cart. "Ah. Doing some legwork for Miss Vicky?"

I had just entered Central Grocery, and Deandra Walkins had caught me fantasizing in real time about last night. I was flushed from the memory, and coughed, trying to cover what I'd been thinking about. Deandra was sharp. She didn't miss a lot.

"Yes." My cart was full of eggs in cartons. "She's wondering if Martell wanted to buy these from her? Put them in the local organic section?"

Deandra was from Hawaii, her hair kept short and natural. Sometimes she wrapped a silk scarf around it, and she wore no makeup. Kept herself in shape, though she was a little thing like me. She was even a little smaller. Today she had on her usual outfit for when she worked as a manager for her fiancé, Martell Hibbley—khaki pants, sneakers, and a white dress shirt on top. No jewelry, though I'd always thought that was Deandra's personal policy since some of the other workers were decked out in jewelry. All sorts. Nose rings. Eyebrow rings. The big hoops that stretched the earlobe. As long as they wore a blue vest, were clothed, showed up on time, and were kind to the customers, they could dress as themselves. Martell didn't care.

I knew this because I used to work here as well. Central's was a small grocery store not far from where we lived. Martell had good relationships with local farmers like Vicky and Howard. We had a surplus of eggs sometimes, which was how I'd found out about Central Grocery in the first place. When I'd realized they had a little community within the store and its customers, I got a job here.

I'd left two years ago because my design clients paid enough, and my shifts began interfering with my design work. Otherwise—I looked around fondly—I would've stayed here forever.

I also missed Deandra. We'd only worked together for six months, but she'd warmed up to me, and we'd met for coffee a few times.

"How are you, Billie?"

I frowned, catching a note in her tone. She had a reason for asking. "You saw the clip of me tripping?"

She smiled wide, showing her white teeth, and rested a hand on my cart. "It was hilarious, adorable, and had women everywhere melting. Brett Broudou? Are you kidding me?"

A little ball of tension inside of me eased. "I've been working and hibernating. You know how I am."

She nodded.

"I'd kinda forgotten about the clip. It's still trending?"

She hesitated before nodding. "Martell sees it on ESPN. After Broudou's last game, the way he helped us so much, they keep playing it. It's more about him than you."

Crap. "Yeah."

She gave me a reassuring smile, but I still caught some pity in her eyes as she touched my arm, giving it a gentle squeeze. "It doesn't make you look bad at all. Women are jealous. They'd love for a chance to be saved by Brett Broudou. Tell me you and he exchanged numbers after meeting that way?"

My eyebrows shot all the way up.

Reading me wrong, she let me go, laughing. "Next time, Billie. If the universe brings a man like that to rescue you, you get his number. I secretly hoped he got yours, but knowing you, you probably snuck out of there as soon as possible."

She'd not seen the other clip then, the one with those guys on the street. I ducked my head down. "Next time maybe I'll have you come with me."

"I'd love that." She nodded to someone behind me. "Miss Vicky sent her in with a whole cart full of eggs."

I turned, but already knew Martell was coming our way.

He perused the cart. "Bring 'em on back. We'll look them over, but Vicky's good with sorting out the bad from the good ones."

She was indeed, but I still pushed the cart to the back of the store.

I found Deandra again after that, talking with one of their checkers. "I need to run some errands for Vicky, but I have a few things to grab here," I told her. "I'll get them when I come back. Is that okay?"

She held up a hand in a wave. "For sure. We'll have the tally for you."

I nodded, heading out to my car. I was crossing the lot, my keys in hand, when a shadow fell over me. My chest constricted, and I whirled, but it was only a man going to his vehicle.

He paused, startled by my reaction, before continuing, holding his grocery bag in hand. His tie flapped over his shoulder, and he smoothed it down, looking harried and in a rush.

"Oh. Sorry."

He gave me a distracted frown, getting in his vehicle and pulling out.

Why had I reacted like that?

I remembered the parked truck from yesterday. And Brett's comment the night before.

That was it. That was all.

Brett was new to my life, and he worried with reason, but *he* was the new factor. He had stirred things up inside me. I was fine. Though, as I got in my car and put the key in the ignition, I realized there hadn't been the usual calls or letters this time.

Whenever I made a public appearance, that stirred the fanatics up. Vicky and Howard would normally have gotten at least a few calls, a few hang-ups.

But nothing this time.

Why was that?

And if that clip was still trending...

It didn't make sense. Society was obsessed with serial killers. I was connected—and would always be—to a serial killer. The interest wouldn't die down. It wasn't that. I'd lived this life for so long that I'd accepted the attention from people, but it hadn't happened this time.

Unless... I called Howard at his office.

"Mitchell here."

"There's been no calls from the fanatics," I blurted. "Did you guys do something?"

He hesitated before sighing out my name.

I cursed silently. "You did."

"We, uh, yes. We added another layer of security filters, and it's helping, but we're still getting the calls."

So there *were* calls.

I didn't have social media, except for my design business. I needed it for my clients, but they knew to email me if they needed to get in touch. I'd purposely not checked there since my appearance, but there should've been nothing anyway. That wasn't affiliated with Willow Harm at all, only Melissa Morning.

Howard had told me he'd be getting the mail for the next month. He'd said that the morning before I went on the news for that segment...

"Have there been letters?" I asked.

"Billie..." Another hesitation.

"How many?" I croaked.

"Some."

I still heard hesitation in his voice. I cursed softly to myself. "How many?"

"Billie, it'll fade out. It always does. It's just going on longer because of that clip."

My chest had tightened. It was getting tighter and tighter. "Brett is a new star on our football team, and we went to the Super Bowl last year. That could mean months. Months of attention could stir up..." I sighed. I didn't want to think what prolonged attention could stir up.

It was its own tsunami. He was a monster, the Midwest Butcher, and there were always others. The documentaries. The shows. The *Datelines*. He was up there with Manson.

My hands began shaking. "Are you reading the letters?"

"Billie..." Another sigh.

"Goddammit, Howard."

He was quiet. I never swore, never, and I'd just sworn *at him*.

"You've always let us handle this before," he said. "Why is this time different?"

"Because before it's always been brief. This isn't brief. This might not slow down, and if Brett..." I had to stop because I didn't know. If we got together? If we stayed together? If he remained a football player?

If he remained being a football star?

"This is so not good."

Howard let out another sigh. "Maybe Brett could talk to ESPN, see if they'd stop airing the clip? That's where it's getting most of its airtime."

"Yeah. Maybe."

"You and Brett need to be a secret because of all of this."

A slightly panicked laugh burst from me. "You think?" I immediately regretted that. "I'm sorry, Howard. I—" I just wished this would go away, but it wouldn't. It'd never go away. I'd always be connected to the Midwest Butcher.

"Where are you?"

"Running errands for Vicky." My heart blasted against my chest. I was also trying not to have a heart attack, but I didn't share that.

"Come home. I can get all that for her."

"No. She said you needed to go to Cascade for an auction. That's why I went today."

"I canceled that. I'm going later in the week. I'll come into town and finish everything else up. You just come back. You'll feel better."

"No." I winced as I heard that because it was weak. I sounded weak. "No." That was better. My head started to pound. "This isn't the first time I've panicked. I'll be fine. It's a twenty-minute drive. It'll be fine."

"Tell me your contingency plans," he prompted. We'd done this so many times before.

"I have my GPS linked to my voicemail," I started.

"That's right because if—"

"If my phone shuts down, my voicemail will automatically give my location."

"What else?"

"I have a panic button in my car that goes to the nearest police station."

"Yes," he confirmed. "And what else?"

"I have pepper spray on my keychain, a taser gun hidden in the back, and my gun is in its case in my trunk."

"And?"

I recited the rest, which was a reminder that I wasn't out of control. I knew ways to defend myself. I had more control than anyone might think. I knew self-defense. I knew how to shoot a gun. I knew how to wield a knife. I wasn't weak. I wasn't helpless. I wasn't defenseless.

I *could* protect myself.

And the best weapon I had? I was a woman, and he would underestimate me. Everyone did.

"Good. Good. How are you feeling?" Howard asked when I was done.

I was breathing evenly again. My pulse had steadied. "I'm better. Thank you."

"I'm not wanting to stir up anything more here, but we got a call earlier today from the Kings."

Stir up anything more? "Brett's team?"

"I guess those kids who were hassling you and Brett on the street are trying to say he was aggressive with you. They doctored a clip to show that, but the team got their hands on it."

"They're what?" I barked out.

"I figured you wouldn't be happy about that, but I gotta ask, because I love you and see you as my daughter... He didn't grab you in any way that made you uncomfortable, did he?"

My heart sank. For Brett to even be questioned about that? "No. Those kids were the assholes."

"Good to hear. Not that I expected otherwise, but I needed to ask. Anyway, they sent over some legal papers they want you to sign, just saying Broudou wasn't aggressive with you. You feel comfortable signing them?"

"Of course I will."

"I'll let Vick know. She's got them printed and ready for you here. She'll fax them back in. Are you going to finish Vicky's errands? My offer still stands."

I was already shaking my head before he finished. "No. I'll do it. I'll be back within an hour or two."

"Travis' precinct isn't far from you. You could give him a call?"

"I'm good."

"Text when you're heading back. Alright?"

"I will," I noted softly before ending the call. I looked over to the parking lot across the street, automatically scanning it, because it was a habit—or it used to be. I'd gone soft over the last few years, getting comfortable, feeling familiar, not remembering what else was out there.

I couldn't forget.

After scanning that one, I scanned the one behind it. To the side. To the next side.

I scanned all the parking lots, mentally cataloging as much as I could about all of the different vehicles—makes and models and the letters of the license plates. We'd figured out a trick when I was younger to remember them, and I began chanting the vehicles into a song in my head.

I was rusty, but I'd need to get sharp again.

21

BRETT

I was on my way out of the physical therapy room when Callie approached. She'd spent a good hour on my knee earlier and was usually gone for the day by now, so I paused, waiting to see what she had to say.

She crossed her arms, her eyes shifting to the ceiling. "Just got a call from PR. You're wanted up there."

Shit. Kim.

But Callie was avoiding my eyes, and she didn't do that. Usually, if she had something to say, she said it and moved on.

"What's going on with you?" I asked.

Her eyes flicked to mine, her expression wary. Her hands slid into her pockets. "Nothing..."

I grunted. "Out with it."

A grin flickered over her face before she shook her head, rolling her eyes. "It's nothing, honestly. Just...who was that woman at Jack's?"

I raised my eyebrows. "We're that type of friends?"

She swore, laughing. "I was only wondering. That's all."

"Who was *your* friend?"

She pressed her lips together, shifting back on her feet.

I laughed, moving past her. "That's right. That's what I thought. You want a gossip session, you gotta 'fess up too."

Stone Reeves and Colby Doubard were leaving the next room, and Stone called my name.

I lifted my chin. "PR called me up."

Colby winced. "I, uh, I'm not here." He darted around me, going into the locker area.

Stone started laughing.

"What's that about?"

"Uh..." Stone grimaced, still trying not to laugh. "He got himself in a situation. The PR heads weren't happy. He's still smarting from it, I think."

I remembered Kim mentioning something about a Colby-sized hole.

"But hey..." Now he officially looked uncomfortable, even a bit green. "Listen, I promised Dust I'd bring this up to you. Since we had dinner last year with the Kades, she's been on a mission to find you a wife. She doesn't approve of the friends of the other players' girlfriends, and she's been looking for someone to set you up with. That's why I'm here."

"Ah..." It was obvious to everyone with eyes that Stone would've rather run a marathon than have this conversation with me, but I knew his wife. Dusty Reeves had a good heart. She was happy and wanted everyone else to be happy. I'd gone over to their place for dinner a couple times, but nothing beyond that. Dusty had a mission to bring me into their group of friends, and she meant well, but I operated better on my own. Always had.

She also had a mission in life to rescue every sea creature there was in the world, and I wondered if she thought of me as a broken sea turtle in some way.

"She found someone, and she wants you to come over for dinner tomorrow night." Stone scrubbed a hand over his face. "Please tell me you've met someone, because that's the only excuse she'll take for you not coming to dinner. Colby and Jake are coming, so you won't be alone. Dusty's set them all up too."

There had to be some good stories there. "Actually, I have met someone."

The relief on our star wide receiver's face was comical. "Thank God," he muttered.

"Let your wife know I appreciate the thought, but I'll be passing on dinner tomorrow night."

He gave me a nod, starting for the locker area. "Have a good one. I'll pass the message along."

I continued down the hall to the elevator, and when I stepped off on the PR floor, the secretary waved me on. "She's been waiting for you."

Kim came to the hallway, her eyes set on me, and she wasn't happy. "Get in here." She stepped back, closing the door as I sat in the chair in front of her desk. She settled behind her desk and leaned back. "I wanted to update you."

Right.

"We hired a guy—"

"What?"

She frowned at me and continued, speaking a little slower. "Like I said, we hired a guy, and he found out that Billie's in contact with a couple, Howard and Vicky Mitchell." She watched me like a hawk. "We reached out to Howard. He referred us to his wife, and according to them, Willow Harm has officially cleared you of any wrongdoing in the video where it looks as if you're being aggressive with her."

I waited. Knowing Kim, she had another shoe to drop.

"Our lawyers sent something over to them. They expect Willow will sign it at her earliest convenience. You're in the clear. I wanted to let you know."

"That's good. Thanks."

She narrowed her eyes. "That's all you have to say?"

I leaned back in my seat. "The clip was bullshit."

"Right." She paused a moment. "I also wanted to let you know that our guy got ahold of the clip in its entirety, and you were right. It shows you protecting Miss Harm, but you were aggressive to those guys."

Fuck th—

"I'm sure you're currently thinking, *fuck that*, but it's still a bad look. As soon as we receive Miss Harm's signature, our legal department will be hitting those kids with the threat of a defamation suit if they continue in their pursuits. You shouldn't have to worry about this anymore."

I frowned.

"And I'm sure you never were worried, so I'm doing all of this for no reason, aren't I?" She sighed, leaning back in her chair.

She'd read me right. "I appreciate it."

She nodded. "Okay. You can head out." She waited until I was at the door before adding, "Be smart in your future endeavors with Miss Harm, Brett."

She *knew*. I stopped and turned back around.

Yep. She knew. "My personal business is my personal business."

She pursed her lips, and her eyes got almost mean. "The NFL does *not* do scandals. Willow Harm is a scandal in herself."

I opened my mouth.

"I have sympathy for her. Everyone has sympathy for her, but she is the only survivor of the Midwest Butcher, and everyone goes fucking insane about serial killers. Miss Harm keeps a low profile intentionally, and possibly for very sad reasons, so you might want to think about what being linked to a professional football player would do to her. When you get that answer, then think about what it'll do to her when it comes out that she's fucking you."

"You go too far," I snarled.

Her face showed no emotion. No remorse. No sympathy.

Despite her words, just a coldness. "I am very good at my job, and you and Willow Harm being in a relationship, no matter how brief or how long, spells disaster. If you've already fucked her, let her go. If you haven't, *let her go*. You will bring a spotlight to her life that will not benefit her. At the very least, think of it that way."

"No one's cared about who I'm seeing before."

She made a frustrated sound. "Everyone cares. Blogs and social media care. You're discreet. You're very, very discreet, and there have only been two women linked to you over the years. When we won the Lombardi last year, all your perceived anonymity went away. Yes, it was a team effort, and yes, we have other players we wouldn't have won without, but you helped. I've already laid out all the reasons people are intrigued by you, and that interest has gone up since everyone saw you rescue Willow Harm not once, but twice. They like the look of you and her, and they want more. But I'm telling you, *don't* give them more."

I stared at her.

A slow smile spread over her face, not making its way to her eyes. "You risk your own past becoming an issue again. You won't like the headlines: *The Twin of a Rapist with the Survivor of a Killer*."

My stomach sank. "My brother was convicted of attempted rape. I've never hidden that."

"Does that really matter?" she volleyed right back.

"Anything else?" I clipped out.

"I've said what I needed to say." To her credit, she didn't sound like she'd enjoyed it.

I didn't like it, but I'd heard her.

But fuck.

Fuck.

Billie.

22

BILLIE

Something was wrong. I knew it. I just didn't know how to bring it up.

Brett had come over, bringing food with him, and we'd eaten in my little home. We were now curled up on the couch, a movie on the television screen, and though I sat right next to him, touching his leg, his arm, his side, he couldn't have felt more far away.

I had no idea what we were even watching.

What was going on with him?

Was it me? Had he realized I wasn't worth it?

I reached for the remote and turned everything off—not just the movie. I turned off the entire television and tossed the remote to the side. Brett looked my way, waiting. I shifted so I could face him, one of my legs pulled up and resting on the couch between us. "What's going on with you?"

His eyebrows dipped. "We were watching a movie."

I made a frustrated sound. "You're here, but you're not here. I've been around you enough to know when you're present, and you are very much not present with me." My heart pounded against my sternum, because in a way, this was a test. Would he own up to it and let me in, or would he pull a typical guy move and pretend nothing was wrong, that I was the problem. He could try to make me think I was imagining all of this, but I wasn't.

His eyes grew pensive before he sat up, taking my hand and pulling me with him. "Let's go for a drive."

I hadn't expected that. I frowned and stood there as he looked around, finding my phone, keys, and purse. He looked me over. "Are you cold?"

He didn't wait for a response. He opened my closet and pulled out a sweater, then grabbed one of my blankets. Taking my hand, he led me to his truck. "Do you need to lock up?"

I was about to say no, because that was the truth, but remembering my call with Howard today, I took my keys and locked the door.

A moment later, we were in his truck, the heat blasting since we were having a rare cold front as we headed down the driveway.

We got on the interstate, going south of the city, and then got off to wind around in neighborhoods until the spaces between the houses started growing larger.

Eventually we went through a gate and into another neighborhood. I'd only seen houses like this in movies. Never in person. We passed through another gate and there was a whole different vibe. Each of these homes had their own gates with driveways I couldn't see. The houses were completely hidden.

Brett drove a few more blocks before pulling up to a large gray wall. He hit a button and that wall slid away, revealing a cobblestone driveway. He pulled in, following it around a hill and into a round courtyard.

The house that rose up in front of us was giant. Very modern. White and gray color scheme.

He had a five-car garage, and he pulled into the second slot. The rest were empty.

Turning off the engine, he got out without saying a word. I followed.

He waited to take my hand again as I rounded the truck, and he opened the door into the house for me, hitting the button to close the garage as we went inside. We entered through the kitchen.

"Do you want anything to eat? Drink?"

I shook my head.

"Bathroom?"

I hesitated, and he went into a room from the hallway and flipped on the light.

I nodded and went in. When I came back out, he was waiting for me.

He took my hand, leading me up the stairs and back through another set of hallways. We continued to the far back end of the house, which was connected by a lone hallway. Once there, he flipped a switch, and the roof of the room slid away.

"What?" I moved ahead, staring up at the sky. We were far enough from the other houses that it almost seemed like it was only us and the sky, the stars above.

Brett stepped up behind me, his hands coming to my sides. "Had this built because..." He hesitated. His fingers flexed over my hips. "I like to sleep here sometimes. There's a screen up there, so no bugs will get in, and if it starts raining and we still want to see, there's a glass closure too. It's over the top, but it's my favorite room, and being in Texas, I use it more than I did at my other place."

"You had something like this before?"

"A much smaller scale and not so comfortable." He turned me around to where there was a giant spread of cushions. Almost the whole side of the room was full of them, complete with a pile of blankets.

Brett let me go, separating. I bit my lip from the disappointment. He reached over, grabbing a blanket, and stepped back.

"Will you stay with me tonight? Stay here unless it gets too cold?"

This was the opposite of what I'd thought was going to happen.

"Of course." I climbed onto the cushions, going to the middle.

Brett disappeared for a second, then settled in next to me, his body heat blanketing me even before he pulled the actual blankets over us. I curled into him, my cheek to his chest and my hand on his stomach.

"I slept outside a lot," he said. "Most nights, to be honest, until I got older, and then I'd crash with some buddies. We didn't have a great home life, but I was able to get this view, so I preferred being outside as much as I could."

I remembered what he'd said when I first met him. "...*My dad was a drunk all my life.*"

"What did you mean when you said your mom never left the trailer park?" I asked.

His arm tightened around me. "Some parks are great. Depending on who lives there, they can be a great way of living. But the one I lived in wasn't. It was the stereotypical way of trailer-park life. Drugs. Drinking. No hope. Misery. I never knew my grandfather and grandmother, my mom's folks, so I can't say what her childhood was like, but I think maybe, looking back, that either my dad broke her down or she'd been torn down before him. She was never able to leave that way of life. She only stayed in the house I bought her for a year before she moved back in with a new guy. Different trailer park, but it was the same kind of living. She went back to where she was comfortable. I don't know if she was even aware of it, to tell you the truth, but after trying a few more times to get her back in my house, I gave up. That was the last time I spoke to her."

"Do you still have the house?"

"I do, yeah. I'm renting it out to a nice family. They take good care of it."

"What about your place in Kansas City? Where you used to play?"

"I sold that place." He tipped his head down to see me. "Knew I wouldn't be going back."

"Why are you telling me this? Why'd you bring me here tonight?"

His eyes got a distant look, and he lifted his gaze back to the sky. "I know it's only our second date, but maybe I wanted to bring you to my happy place? That okay with you?"

He wasn't answering me.

"Brett." I shifted to sit up.

His eyes closed, and he shut down. I could feel him putting a wall between us. Pain pierced me. "Your team called about that video clip. Is this about that? Do you think I thought you were manhandling me that day?"

"Billie," he said softly.

I placed a hand on his chest, feeling his heart beat so fast. "You've always been forthright with me. Don't stop now. What's going on? I deserve to know too."

He drew in a deep breath, his chest rising under my hand. His eyes opened. There was a haunted expression there, one I barely registered because I knew it so well. It was in me too. His hand curled around my hip, burrowing under my shirt to touch skin.

His touch burned me like always, but whatever was going on smothered some of the fire.

"I don't know much about your life except what happened to you," he said.

Now I burned from a different sensation. "You want to know about the Midwest Butcher?"

"No." That word came out strangled before he cleared his throat. "But I'm thinking I need to. You told me fanatics come out of the woodwork when you do anything in the news."

Dread sank into my bones. "You've been talking to Howard?"

A frown flitted over his face. "Should I be?"

I pulled away, getting enough space so I could cross my legs in front of me. "You're worried about the trending clip of you and me?"

His hand moved to my knee. "I'm worried about the continuous attention you'll get if you're linked to me."

My heart sank. This was what I'd feared. "Why are you worried about that now?"

"Just tell me. What would your life look like if there was press about you and me? And it wouldn't di—fade away?"

"That hasn't happened yet."

"It could. What if it did?"

I lifted my head, finding his eyes on mine.

"I'm not used to people caring about me," he said. "Never happened when I grew up, and it rarely happened when I got older—until football. The attention grew, but it was still not a lot. Defensive ends usually don't get a lot of attention, but yeah, sometimes we do. I've had five relationships in my life, and only two of those women were publicly identified. I didn't think about you and me, about the ramifications for you, until it was pointed out to me that there's been a new spotlight on me since last year."

The dread grew in me, lining all my organs. "Worst-case scenario for you and me? There are serial killers out there, and new ones starting every year. They're all sick, and they all have egos, but they fixate sometimes on the ones who came before them. The worst-case scenario is if someone who wanted to make a name for himself considered finishing what the Midwest Butcher hadn't finished. It's out there that he didn't kill me, so as a present, someone could do it for him and do it in the way he used to kill. They'd slice and dice me up, and they'd do it in my home, because that's how he did it. He always killed people in their homes. There were other things he'd do, but that was the main gist. Worst-case scenario is if someone decided to make me the 'starting point' for their own career."

His lips thinned. "Starting them off to become a serial killer themselves?"

I nodded.

"That's the worst-case scenario? Footage of you could entice them to finish what the Midwest Butcher hadn't been able to?"

"That's what they think, yes."

He was quiet a moment. "Jesus Christ, Billie. Being with me could potentially get you killed?"

"If it helps, this could happen anyway. This does happen. The Midwest Butcher has ambitious lawyers. He was supposed to get the death sentence. They got that shifted to life. He was never supposed to get an appeal, and now they've fought so he gets to try for one. Every year they do a big press splash and swear he's not the Midwest Butcher. They keep saying they've found new evidence that it's someone else. Every time that happens, my picture, my name, it's always in the news, and it could happen just from that. Nothing to do with you."

He fell quiet again. "How are you okay with this? Why aren't you angry?"

This was my life. I'd dealt with this since I was twelve. I'd always deal with this. "Because I can't change anything. Only thing I can do is change me. Maybe my name? Leave a family that took me in? I lost my friend, and then my mom and my brother in the same week."

"You said your dad wasn't worth reaching out to?"

My chest got tight, and I balled my hands into fists, pressing them into my lap. "No, he's not. There was a reason my mom didn't want us to have a relationship with him, though that was ultimately more his decision. She never fought him when he stopped in to see us. It was always at random times. He traveled a lot, but he wasn't a good person. I didn't even know his name to give the police, and it was better that way. He never came forward when I was in the news."

Brett went back to rubbing my knee. "If I'm a danger to you just because of who I am? What I do? I can't carry that. I can't be the reason you—"

I covered his hand with mine. "I've lived, okay? I've lived through nightmares. I've lived through loneliness. I don't know where you and I might go, what could happen, but I feel like I have a chance at living in the sun. Don't take that away."

His eyes darkened, and his hand gripped my knee. Holding on tight. "Your safety isn't wor—"

"That's my decision. *Mine*. Not yours. We're adults here. I've lived long enough to know what I want to try for and what I can't risk. So have you. We'll be safe. We can be discreet. We can..." I paused, not sure he was hearing me. "Don't make a decision like this for me. Let *me* make it."

Why did I feel like I was pleading for my life?

Everything in me felt squeezed, taut, waiting.

He expelled a ragged breath. "Fuck." He shook his head, scooping me up and shifting so I lay on top of him, propped on the pillows. My legs fell to the sides of his, first from surprise at the sudden change, and then hunger lit up inside me.

I was starving for him.

The need erupted.

But I held back, even as his hands went to my thighs and began kneading. I placed a hand on his chest, finding that I loved feeling his heart, knowing how he was affected. It was racing right now. "What does this mean?"

He shook his head, his gaze lingering on my lips. "It's your decision." His voice was rough. "But if anything happens to you—"

I leaned in, my mouth touching his to quiet him. "We have contingencies in place," I whispered. "We'll set new ones."

I'd moved to kiss him again when his hand went to the

middle of my chest and pushed me upright. "You have what in place?" he asked.

I sighed. "Do we need to get into this now?"

His eyes grew sharp, and I was in the air again as he lifted me, carrying me out of the room and into a different one. The lights flipped on in his bedroom. He set me on his mattress and backed up, his hands at his hips. He clipped out, "Explain them. All of them. Don't leave anything out."

Disappointment weighed on my shoulders. This was going to take us a whole different direction than I'd hoped for.

But there was no way around it, so I told him everything.

"You know how to shoot a gun?"

I nodded.

His nostrils flared. "And what do you mean you know how to use a knife?"

"I've taken lessons in Arnis martial arts. It specializes in—"

"Knife fighting. I'm familiar." His eyes were still so sharp. "You have a gun in your car?"

I nodded. "I don't carry it on my person. I don't feel comfortable doing that. If a gun is pulled, no matter the situation, it's usually perceived as a threat." I stood, going to him.

He backed away more. "Don't. I still need to think."

I paused, feeling completely vulnerable and exposed. "What is there to think about?"

"I have enemies in my life. My sister, for one. If she finds out about you, she'll use it somehow. I don't know what she'll do, but she'll weaponize you. That will happen. There's no if there. My sister is a calculating bitch. The only thing that's stopped her from really wrecking my life is that she can't afford to get the fuck out of California."

I nodded, accepting that.

He scowled. "That should terrify you."

I shrugged. "I mean, look at my baggage...?"

He barked out a short laugh before cursing under his

breath. "I'm terrified of hurting you. I couldn't—I don't know how to protect you against some sick fuck out there."

"You can't. That's why we have all the contingencies. And if it gets out about you and me, we'll make more." I chanced it, going to him again. This time, he held still, watching me come with lidded eyes. He watched my hand move toward his chest, and as soon I made contact, he yanked me against him.

I squeaked as his hands slid down my ass, smoothing to the backs of my legs as he lifted me up. So easily.

I wound my legs around him and looped my arms around his neck. I was flush against him. Eye to eye. Mouth to mouth.

He searched my gaze before falling to my mouth. He walked me to his bed and shook his head as he lay with me. He started to roll to the side, but I wouldn't let go, my legs squeezing until he had to stay where he was, right on top of me.

He shifted to balance his head in his hand. He gazed down at me. "If you get hurt..."

I slid a hand to the back of his neck, pulling him close, and I whispered, "Then you can say 'I told you so.'"

"This isn't fu—"

My mouth touched his. There was no more talking.

No matter what, I was going to have my moment in the sun. I hoped it would last.

23

BILLIE

I could kiss Brett like this forever.

His lips skimmed mine, tentative, and then it hardened, almost punishing. Brett took control, demanding more. More access. More taste. His hand slid down my throat, between my breasts, to my stomach. I squirmed, wanting it to go farther. I wanted to feel him completely against me, but he held himself back.

His massive shoulders. His rock hard chest.

My hands slipped under his shirt, stroking his skin, and he groaned deep in his throat as he changed the angle of our kiss, his hand moving to the back of my neck. He anchored my head, somehow getting an even better position to explore my mouth.

I panted, burning up.

I lifted myself toward him. If he wouldn't come to me, I'd go to him. He wrapped his arm around me and turned so I was sprawled on top of him. I was lost in him, in the push and pull of kissing him, tasting him. It was so natural to be here, with him. Pleasure pulsated through me, rising, and I wanted more.

Growling, Brett shifted, and I gasped, straddling him. I

could feel him against me, where I needed him, and I grinded against him, slow, savoring.

"Jesus," he groaned, his head falling back, his eyes closing for a second. His hands went to my thighs, at first clamping me against him, and then guiding me forward, holding, and back again, before he cursed. His hands became fists. "Billie, we need to stop."

His words didn't penetrate. Carnal need raced through me, making me blind to everything else going on. I was in a state of raw ache, and it was the most natural act in the world to move over him like this, as if I should've been here all along.

He touched my legs again. "Billie." His voice was more clear.

It started to pierce through my haze, but I frowned, not wanting that.

I bent to him, my forehead finding his shoulder. His arms wrapped around me and set me to the side of him.

I moaned in protest, reaching for him.

"I know. I know." His hand caught mine, and that finally woke me up.

"What?" I sat straight, panic bolting through me. "What's wrong? Why did you stop?"

"Nothing." He shook his head, tucking hair behind my ear. "I needed to stop us. If I didn't..." He grimaced. "It's our second date. I didn't bring you here for this. I wanted to talk, share a night with you in that room."

Right. The room. With the stars.

He'd been distant, and then we'd talked about it.

I frowned, not sure where to go from here. I mean, I wanted him. I wanted to touch him, and more. A lot more. Why was he stopping?

I groaned and flopped back on the bed. "You're still having second thoughts about us?"

"What?" He looked down at me. "No."

"Then why?" Some irritation slipped out.

He laughed softly. "Honestly, I don't want to go too fast."

"*Why?*"

He laughed again, louder this time. "Because...fuck. I don't know. I'm starting not to remember with you looking at me like that."

I paused a second. "How do I look?" I ran a hand through my hair. It was probably all messed up.

He caught my hand, using it to pull me back up to him. His voice dropped low. "You look like sex. You look amazing."

But he wasn't closing the distance. He held there, in my breathing space, his gaze skirting from my eyes to my mouth.

"Since I met you, we've been on the fast track," he murmured. "I don't want to fast track being with you. Kissing you. Touching you. Spending time with you. Finding out what makes you laugh, what makes your eyes soften—those are the things I want to learn along the way. Having sex..." He hesitated. "I just worry. I don't want to fuck up with you."

My irritation faded...slightly. "You don't want to fuck it up by having sex with me?"

"In a nutshell." The corner of his mouth lifted. He reached up, touching the side of my mouth with his thumb. "Will you stay with me?"

I really wanted to kiss him, but I nodded and murmured, "Yes."

He flashed me a grin before getting up.

He showed me the bathroom I could use and brought in what I'd need—toothpaste and everything else. He brought me one of his shirts, which I *loved*. It was a Kings shirt with his number. It smelled like him. This shirt wasn't ever making it back to him. It was going with me when I left in the morning.

In the bathroom, I took a moment.

Is this real?

Everything that had happened? We'd had a meet-cute, an

actual meet-cute. He'd crashed two of my dates. He'd met the closest people I had to family, and our second official date was him asking me to sleep under the stars with him.

This wasn't real.

There was going to be a universal joke pretty soon, on me.

This stuff didn't happen to me.

Losing people, that happened to me.

People left me.

That's why I was scared to call Vicky and Howard my parents, Lo my sister. Her girls, my nieces. Roger, my brother-in-law. It was safer to keep myself apart.

I was scared of losing them.

Or worse...

A shiver worked its way down my spine.

The universe. It was magical and powerful and scary, and yeah, it could happen.

"I'm going to go see Jojo."

My mom's eyes had widened, and she'd paled. She'd reached for me, her blond hair sweaty and dirty from not showering. *"No, honey. You can't. We have to get ready for dinner. We have—"*

I'd shaken my head, sticking out my bottom lip. *"No. I'm going."*

Ben had come to the doorway. He didn't say a word, but I'd seen the hope in his eyes. He wanted me to go. He wanted to hear about it afterwards.

Mom hadn't wanted us to make friends. We'd moved from place to place wherever she could get a job. But in every town, her boss was mean, her boss was a bitch, her boss tried to steal from her, set her up. She'd had a different story every time she was fired. Then onto to the next place. Eventually she'd just said we couldn't get to know people. We'd have to leave again anyway, so it was easier.

I sucked in my breath, pulling out of the memory.

It hadn't been easier that way. It'd just been lonelier.

That'd been the first time I went to Jojo's over the summer.

This wasn't the same. Vicky, Howard, Lo, Roger, Cynthia, Charlotte, Luna—they weren't the same.

I looked at my face in the bathroom mirror. I could be someone worth not fucking it up with. I could. I'd come so far from being that twelve-year-old who'd dared to defy my mom and make a friend.

But I was still that person too.

My hair had been more blond back then, longer too. I swept it back and drew in a breath, seeing the fullness of my face. I was a woman now. I'd lived back then. I'd smiled. I'd laughed. I'd felt I could be happy and knew no reason why I couldn't.

Life had shown me different.

It wasn't all gone, though. I was strong. In mind and body, but not in my heart. That'd been shut off for so long.

Was I going to turn my heart back on?

"You gotta always make sure that light in there is shining and bright, as bright as you can make it. The world needs it." My mom had pointed to my heart, her face lit up because my face was lit up when I told her about Jojo's uncle, who told stories about trying to fire his newest employee who refused to be fired. Jojo's uncle had said that by the end of his employee's speech, he'd ended up hiring him back, only to fire him again the next day because he was four hours late.

I looked at where my heart was and touched there.

I sucked in a breath. I hadn't thought about a light in there for so long.

There was a soft knock on the door. "You need anything else?"

It hurt right now, to feel my heart bursting because Brett could make me want to put the light back in there. But I knew this was a good pain to have.

I opened the door and found him waiting, his gruff eyes concerned. I smiled. "I'm ready."

The universe wasn't going to punish me because I let anyone in too close.

At least I hoped not, because I was already too far gone.

24

BRETT

My phone rang out through the room, and cursing, I checked the time before answering. Six in the morning. I muffled another curse before answering. "One second." I slipped out of bed, glancing back, and then froze because Billie was awake.

She looked terrified.

"It's someone from back home. This is probably about my sister, that's all."

She expelled a ragged breath, her eyes closing.

I frowned. "Babe."

She blinked a few times before shaking her head. "I'm okay. Honestly. I'm okay." Her eyes moved to my phone. "I hope everything is okay there too."

Right. Home. My sister. I jerked out of my—whatever that had been. I was unsure, just knew I didn't like my woman seeming like she'd seen a ghost. "I'll be back. You want coffee or want to sleep some more?"

She grinned ruefully. "Coffee probably."

"Okay." I shut the door and brought the phone back up to my ear. "What the fuck, Monroe?"

He was laughing. "You crashed the date and you got the girl. That's the Broudou I know."

"Fuck you. You don't know shit about me." My lip twitched as I made my way downstairs and to the bathroom. "I'm muting myself for a second, but I can hear you just fine. Why are you calling?"

"Christ, you're taking a piss, aren't you?"

I laughed, but just waited until he sighed and started in. "I got a call ten minutes ago. Your sister's being released from county in an hour."

I cursed, finishing exactly what he thought I was doing and washing up before unmuting myself. "I didn't think about the time difference. She's being released at five?"

"They start the discharges then. It'll depend on how many others are being released and where she falls in the line."

I'd known this day was coming. It'd just come sooner than I wanted.

He read my silence right. "Sorry, man. Have you talked to Will? How are the kids doing with him?"

"Oh, you know. He's a Broudou. He's a fucking chatterbox."

Channing snorted. "What? It's your day off there, right? So you're going in at nine?"

"Watch yourself, Monroe. You almost made me smile there."

"Wouldn't want that." He got serious. "I got time today. I can run by your brother's and check in with him, see what he's thinking of doing moving forward."

I considered it. "I'll call him and piss him off. Then you go in—"

"I'll offer a sympathetic shoulder where he can unload what an asshole his big pro-football brother is and always has been, who doesn't have the decency to reach out after he's hit the big leagues. What a dick, right?"

"You're quick to this role."

"That's me. Actor extraordinaire."

I fought against rolling my eyes.

"Yeah," I grunted, heading out to the kitchen and starting the coffee. "He might be willing to be up front with you about what he needs."

"I gotta ask. If the kids want to go back with her—"

"They don't. I know my niece well enough. If she did, she wouldn't have called. Stevie's tough as nails."

He was quiet for a beat. "And if Will doesn't want to fight your sister?"

"They come here." It wasn't the best answer for the situation, but the kids weren't going into the system, and fuck my sister, because a week ago she'd stopped being able to keep the kids clothed, fed, watered, and with a shelter over their heads.

"Give me a rundown on the kids. You've never asked me to watch them for you."

"Stevie's the oldest. She watches over the two younger ones. She's fourteen and total opposite her mother. She hates Shannon, but loves her mother, if that makes sense. The other two are eleven and eight. George and Sammy. He's sensitive, and Sammy's, she's a sweet, wild one."

He was quiet again. "Sammy?"

I bit out a laugh. "That's how it's spelled on the birth certificate."

"Jesus Christ."

There was a creak from the stairs, and I watched as Billie appeared, all tentative like. My shirt fell to the tops of her thighs, and she had one arm across herself, her other hand tugging at the end of my shirt. Her eyes still had their softness from sleep.

She looked good enough to be my breakfast.

I settled back against the counter and held out an arm, waiting as she fit herself against me, right where she was always supposed to be. The perfect fit. "My woman's here," I told Channing. "Can you wrap this up?"

He laughed. "Are *you* wrapping it up? That's the more pertinent questi—"

"I'll give Will a call and signal you when to sweep in." I ended the call, ignoring his laughter and dropped the phone on the kitchen island. "Morning." I shifted, bending down to pick Billie up.

She squeaked before catching herself, her arms on my shoulders as I placed her on the counter. I slid my hands down her legs, moving them apart and stepped between them. She was at the edge of the counter.

That's when I realized my mistake.

My dick was right at her entrance. The only thing keeping him back was my boxer briefs and her underwear, and both could be easily discarded.

I ran my nose down her throat before nuzzling on the other side, and shit. *Shit.* I was in trouble. My hand moved under her ass, groping her. My cock strained to get inside. He knew exactly where he wanted to be.

She moaned. Her hand moved to my chest, as if she was going to push me away. Instead, she slid it up to my shoulders and pulled me in.

Fuck yeah. That's what I wanted.

I lifted my head, and her lips were right there, ready for me. Her mouth opened, and I was in there, exploring, claiming, tasting.

This was my woman.

Mine.

She tasted like honey on top of strawberries. I swept my hand up, tipping her head back.

"Wait." Billie's hand went to my chest. "Wait. Your phone."

I growled. "Fuck my phone."

"No." She gasped, pulling away from me. "Will. You were going to call him."

Reality came in, and it wasn't welcomed. But dammit, she was right. I leaned against her, my head on her shoulder as I pushed up and reached for my phone. I was tempted to stay here, standing between her legs to do this call, but I couldn't. I'd want to get off the phone so I could get off in a different way, and that wasn't fair to Will or Billie.

I hit dial on his number and pressed a kiss to her forehead. "Coffee's brewing. There's cream or milk in the fridge. If you want sugar, it's in this cupboard." I motioned to it as I headed out.

I was entering my office when Will answered. "Thefuck-youwant?"

I checked the time. It was four thirty there. "Shannon's getting sprung in half an hour."

"What?" He roared to life, and I imagined him bolting upright.

Right on cue, I heard grumbling in the background, followed by a quick muffled conversation before Will was back to the phone. "Fuck you, Brett. Just fuck you."

"I only got the call thirty minutes ago myself."

"Still. Fuck you."

A door opened on his end, then closed. Then a soft steady buzz. I was guessing the bathroom fan? And yep. Now came the other sounds that happened when a guy got a rude wake-up call. The bladder needed to be emptied. There was some family resemblance here.

"She's getting out of jail? Do you know anything else?"

"I called her lawyer a couple days ago, but he wouldn't talk to me," I said. "I'm guessing Shannon put him on ice, but she knows you have the kids, and she knows I'm the reason you have the kids."

"Jesus Christ. Fuck. My life's been normal. Normal and steady. We go to fucking little league, Brett. I know your mom never took you to little league. You have no idea what I'm talking about, but it's something we do. We're in 4-H, and we do the club *all year* round. We're not just summer 4-H people. We're year-round 4-H-ers. That's us. Fuck you. Are you getting a picture here? I'm the guy who mans the door when our church does an overnight at the Fallen Crest Country Club. Me. My wife doesn't just chaperone, she's the one making fucking popcorn balls. Popcorn balls, Brett. This is the shit you never got growing up. Fuck, neither did I, but my childhood was a lot more normal than yours. That's my life now. Are you getting the picture here?"

I gripped my phone. "I'm trying so you don't hear my smile."

He exploded on a litany of curses, which impressed me.

"Shit, Will. For a moment there, I thought maybe you didn't share my genes. It's nice to hear some familiarity."

"Jesus—" and he was off with another slew of swear words. After a moment he reined himself in enough to say, "Stevie was using rolled-up toilet paper for when she got her period."

"What? Why would you tell me something like that? I don't need to know that stuff."

He kept on, ignoring me. "She got her period for the first time a year ago."

"I know nothing about women's menstrual cycles, and I don't *want* to learn this morning."

"Well, you woke me up, so I'm going to include you in some of our finding-outs here. Girls usually start their periods when they're twelve or thirteen. Some get it when they're eleven. Our niece got it when she was thirteen, and she's only had it three times, so to her, it just made sense to roll up a bunch of toilet paper. She didn't know about tampons and pads. Do you know that I now know eight different brands of tampons? And sizes. They have different sizes. And different colors. And the colors don't coordinate with the same sizes. A regular on one brand might be blue when a regular on another brand might be pink. They have super size and super-plus sizes. Super fucking plus sizes, for my niece. At first, that made me think it was the size of—"

"Oh my God! Shut up."

"—something else. I didn't want to be educated that it's about her *flow*, which is how much—"

"Shut the *fuck* up!"

His voice was rising and cracking, and so was mine.

I had to get him to stop talking. "I'm going to hang up," I threatened.

"No, you're not. You're not going to hang up, because the reason you called me, and the reason you have Channing Monroe showing up at odd times and places, is because you're checking up on us. And now that I've clued in to him, I'm realizing you've had him checking up on me for a long time, so no, Brett. *Brother.* You're not going to hang up, because you're in this whether you want me to know or not."

He stopped talking, finally, and it was my turn to let out a bunch of threats and curses and ominous promises about what would happen if he didn't stop talking about women things.

"Things?"

"You know what I mean," I said hotly. "You're saying you're in?"

"I'm in. We're in. Fuck you for bringing this fight to my doorstep, but we're all the way in. Harmony's talked to a lawyer. With your permission, I'd like Monroe to share everything he has on our sister. I know she's got a record, but she's had the kids this long, so there's a reason. I'm going to find that reason, and I'm going to obliterate it. Sammy had no idea what broccoli was, or green beans, or lettuce. Apparently at school, she gets chicken nuggets and brownies. She had no idea that we're supposed to get three full meals a day, and the last meal isn't a box of Pop-Tarts being shared on the couch." He stopped, and when he started again, his voice broke. "We found her hiding under the bed, because apparently that's where she was told to sleep so she was always hiding if the 'bad guy' came into her room. And when I asked who the bad guy was, she didn't know because they always changed. We caught Stevie two seconds from leaving to do something stupid so she could get arrested and go to jail, because she thought she'd go to the same one where her mom is, or *was*, to hurt Shannon. Apparently, Shannon is the one who had the foresight to look out for her eight-year-old daughter by telling her to hide from the men she brings home at night. Yeah, we're in. She's not getting these children until they're of age and of mind to decide they want to have a one-on-one relationship with her. And I will do my *damndest* to make sure that when and if that happens, they are equipped with all the skills they need to handle her."

He ran out of breath, or he was trying to calm himself. Either way, he went quiet.

"If you need anything—"

"Don't take this the wrong way, because I don't mean this as an insult, but I'll be *damned* if I take money for this fight," he said. "We do well. We can financially handle this battle, and if we need to dip into emergency funds, Harmony's parents are wealthy. They are also in absolute love with Stevie, Georgie, and Sammy."

"Georgie?"

"It's his preferred name. He wants to go with the status quo of a name ending in an -ie or -y."

I snorted. "That mean I can call you Will—"

"When Channing Monroe calls or conveniently shows up where I've stopped to fill my vehicle with gas, or get food at a grocery store that's forty minutes out of his way, or who knows what excuse he'll have—am I right in requesting that he send me all the information he's obtained on our sister over the years?"

I fought back a smile. "Think I liked you better when you didn't talk to me."

"Brett."

"Yeah. I'll shoot him a text. When he checks in on you today, knowing him, he'll probably have everything ready for you."

"That would be appreciated. Now, is there anything else to talk about? Because I'd *really* like to try to get thirty more minutes of sleep so I can round my sleep tally up to three hours before tackling the shitstorm the rest of the day will be."

"No. There's nothing el—"

He ended the call.

I stared at the phone, a sense of wonder coming over me. Who had that been? That'd not been the half-brother I remembered from school, getting a glimpse of him at sporting events when Roussou played Fallen Crest or from the very, very few holidays when our dad got a hankering for all his kids to be under the same roof. That hadn't lasted long. Will stopped coming after three holidays.

"Was it a good phone call?"

Billie was in the doorway, still looking delectable and holding a coffee.

"Yeah." That surprised me. "I think it was."

"Good."

She still had sleepy eyes, and there were lines over her cheek from where she'd been hugging my pillow. But it was her smile that forced me to draw in some air, feeling a crack inside of me.

Goddamn.

I didn't want to think about what that meant, so I walked toward her.

Her eyes grew big, and alarm flashed on her face, but she only had time to back up one step.

I snagged the coffee, putting it aside, and hoisted her up.

"Brett!"

I tossed her over my shoulder.

"What are you doing?"

"We're going to bed."

"To sleep?" There was a hopeful hitch in her tone.

I had no intention of sleeping.

25

BILLIE

I t was date night tonight. We were going on an official date. I wasn't nervous. My armpits weren't sweaty. They were so sweaty. Gah. I was freaking out. I'd met Dee for coffee yesterday and we caught up. Their wedding planning was starting to look like it'd be an elopement in Vegas. She was more than happy for that since Martell's daughter was happy with that choice as well. Dee had been mostly worried about if Kindra would be upset about that or not.

Then the tables turned and she asked about my love life. If I had a love life.

I wasn't going to say anything, but it was Dee and Lo was still not quite off the Travis hill, even though she said she'd give Brett a chance. So, well...

Dee spewed out her coffee when I told her who I was dating.

"Girl." She sat back, shook her head, and sighed. "You did get his number! You gotta tell me e-very-*thing*."

I spilled. Not all of it, but most of it.

Her eyebrow was so high by the end, and she hunched farther over the table. "And you're taking it slow?"

"Trying."

But it'd been hard, so hard. Pun very much intended.

Over the last week and a half, Brett and I had spent almost every night together, alternating between my place or his. Tonight was Friday night so we'd end at his place, and we'd torture ourselves. Brett needed to get good sleep for football, so it wasn't unusual if we headed to bed around eight. That was just the beginning of the torture sessions.

I was damn near combusting, just thinking about it. I shifted in my seat, readjusting my shirt. Was it hot in here? It felt hot.

"You've got it bad, Billie."

I groaned. "I do. I really do."

"What are you two doing for date night tonight?"

"I have no idea. He said it'd be a surprise."

It'd be nice to talk with Dee, catch up, but now I was back at the farm and getting ready for Brett to pick me up.

I was in the sweating phase. Sweating like a penguin that swam too far north and ended up on an embankment with crocodiles. One thing did not fit in and was definitely not supposed to be there. That was me. That's how I felt.

Brett said athletic cute for the first part of the date—which I had internally freaked out that there were two parts of the date? Two? And what was athletic cute? The second part of the date was casual date. Again, what was casual date? No pants and an oversized hoodie? No. That was lounging Netflix date attire.

I'd gone with black leggings, those were always appreciated by men and a black racerback tank. They were my favorite because they made my boobs look magnificent, and I wasn't usually someone obsessed with her boobs. Except I was when I wore a racerback tank, which note to self, I needed to wear them more because they were awesome.

Brett wore black sweatpants and a T-shirt. Both casual, athletic, and comfortable, but on him, they looked good. The shirt molded over his big shoulders, those nice strong pectorals, hugged over his very firm and ripped stomach, the same stomach that wasn't lean because there were muscles over muscles over muscles, and I was drooling.

Grabbing my purse, I opened the door and left. My second outfit was in the bag strapped on my back.

Brett stopped, seeing me, and his eyes warmed, darkening as they slid over me, feeling like a caress.

I was already heated, the sweat was still there, and at that look, my body sprang from warm to hot. I flushed all over, knowing that was going to show on my chest and neck. Red cleavage, that was me.

His mouth curved up. "Thinking this first part of the date was a bad choice." As I got closer, he drew me in, pulling me to his chest as he wrapped his arms around me. His head turned down, looking at me, so I did the same, but my nips were out saying hello. Then, purposely, he slid a hand to the small of my back and pulled me the rest of the way to him, so I could feel just how excited he was in return. His cock was up and hardening as I pressed in against him.

His eyes heated, and he sighed a curse. His head fell down, and he met my lips with his, a soft graze before he whispered, "Definitely backfired on me."

Some of my sweaty nerves were standing down, and I melted more against him. My head fell back and I grinned up at him. "We could skip?"

He was considering it, really considering it. The blatant hunger was all over his face before he let out another sigh and released me. "I can't or I can never let you know what we're going to be doing. You'll have my balls if I do."

My hand jerked forward, a reflex, and brushed over his dick.

We both paused.

Brett closed his eyes. "Do it again."

I shifted so if anyone was watching from the main house, they wouldn't be able to see as I slowly rubbed over his dick, and then I rubbed it again. Up. Down. It jerked under my touch, and my hand moved to grasp it, my whole hand wrapped around him through his sweats. I began stroking him, squeezing gently, then stroking again, a little harder.

I glanced up.

Brett's eyes were lidded and heavy, and molten. "Keep going."

I looked over my shoulder, but no Vicky or Howard in the windows.

Brett cursed, taking hold of my hips and began walking us backwards.

I started to let go of him— "Do not," he said through gritted teeth. "Do not let go of my cock. Keep your hand on me."

I kept my hand on him.

Then we were inside my place, and the door was slammed, and fuck it.

As soon as that door shut, I fell to my knees.

"Oh, God," Brett moaned.

I yanked down his sweats and boxer briefs and wrapped my hand around his cock all over again. I began stroking him.

"Jesus," he breathed out, almost hissing.

He was watching me, his eyes almost black they were so dark, so hungry.

I began to ache for him myself, getting wet, so I moved forward, replacing my hand with my mouth, and Brett pushed his hips forward, his cock slipping deeper inside my mouth.

I started sucking, bobbing my head.

As I kept going, Brett's hips were rocking into me until his hands went to the side of my head and he began guiding me. Feeling me relax, he gripped me harder, holding my head steady, he began to fuck my mouth.

Fuck.

He pushed so far in.

I widened my throat, welcoming him even farther.

"Shit, you feel so fucking good. Your lips wrapped around my cock. Your mouth fucking warm and wet, so tight around me." He grunted, his speed increasing.

I shifted on my knees, getting a stronger stance, and I reached around him, my hand splayed out on his ass. I yanked him closer, and he ground against me, his cock swelling and then unloading inside of my mouth.

I waited until he was all done, and as he pulled back out, I swallowed, then tilted my head up, a sated smile on my face. His eyes darkened all over again, the lust was still there, and we shared a look for a moment. An intimate shiver went through my body. I wasn't sure what that look was for him on his end, but all the nerves I'd had earlier ceased away. I felt our connection flare between us, almost vibrating.

I loved that feeling. This connection.

He ran his thumb over my mouth tenderly. "It's like this mouth was made just for me." He leaned down, capturing it with his as he lifted me up and placed me on my table, moving between my legs, never breaking contact with my mouth. His tongue slid inside, and soon I was clinging to him.

He pulled back, cursing. "We're supposed to be going slow."

I gave him a wry look. "We can try again on the next date."

He barked out a laugh, his thumb grazing my bottom lip again, as his eyes gave me once-over. "If that's the case, let's get this date done so I can take you home and you're going to feel my tongue slide so deep in your other lips, that your legs are going to wrap around my neck and squeeze long, and hard, and slow until you forget you even have legs, and that's when I'll make you scream, and I'll lick you clean, taking all the cream you give me." His voice dropped, throatily. "You're my dessert tonight, Billie."

My body trembled. Holy shit. I asked, not really joking, my

legs wavering already, "What's our first activity again? Can we skip it?"

He was tucking himself back in, readjusting his pants as he shot me a rueful expression. "I wish, but I meant it. You'd be pissed if we missed. We're going to goat yoga."

My mouth dropped and I shouted, jumping off the table, "Goat yoga? We're going to be late. Come *on*."

———

I WAS IN HEAVEN.

Little baby goat, kiddie goat heaven with their little neatly trimmed hooves, and their little heads, and their little ears, and their little adorable black noses. And their tiny jumps like a hee-yah and a yaw-whoo as they jumped around and then bounced on our backs.

So in goat heaven.

And the mamas.

I'd not even gotten over to the one big mama, all white, who was lying on the ground. Her milk so full and needing to be eaten by the little babies, but she seemed content as her head was lying in a girl's lap. She was petting the mama as the mama's jaw was chewing over her cud. The owners who hosted the goat yoga had it set up in their barn on their farm. The barn was adorable, freshly painted. Clean stalls. They had cleared out the main room in the barn and added blankets and large pillows on the floor. People brought their own yoga mats, or like Brett and me, used some mats that were offered from the business.

When we first arrived, as we drove down their driveway, there was a line of vehicles already parked. Brett pulled in at the end. There were other couples walking just ahead of us. A few holding hands. For a yoga class, there were a decent amount of men in the class. The majority were woman, but that was the norm when I'd been to a class, so I wasn't surprised.

A few of the guys came solo, or with friends, and it was obvious they were there to meet women. Or was somewhat obvious. A few guys played it cool, or they genuinely were only interested in yoga while their friends were eyeing up anyone who was eyeing them back. Three other guys were there on dates, but all the guys did double-takes when they saw Brett joining the group.

Everyone congregated outside the barn until the yoga instructor and the owner of the place gave a talk, introducing themselves and explaining more about the farm. About the goats. Giving the rules of how to handle the goats, which was basically to be aware the kid goats would jump on them. The older mama goats would love to be petted, which was happening right now.

The owner came over, seeing I was obsessed with the mama goat because she was my next target to go and love all over her. She sat down, crossing her legs. "That's Ruby. She's a Saanen. They're all white and their ears point upwards. Ruby's the big mama around here."

Most of the baby goats, or kids, were all different colors with floppy ears.

She saw me watching them and added, "They're Nubian goats. They're spotted all over, all different colors, and you can see their ears hang down, not like the Saanens. You're an animal lover, huh?"

"Yes," I breathed out, feeling high and giddy as three of the baby goats chased each other, going past us. One tripped and would've fallen into Brett's lap, but he caught it, sitting up from his pose.

The owner laughed, reaching over and picking up the baby from him, setting her back on her feet. The goat was off, like a race car, careening back out of the barn where the other two had gone. She leaned back on her hands, resting them behind her and lifted her chin toward the opposite end of the barn. "We have all sorts of goats. A few sheep."

My eyes were just getting bigger and bigger. "Any other animals?"

"A few alpacas—"

"Alpacas?" Say it ain't so. Alpacas? I was in goat heaven, sitting near an alpaca heaven, and I had *no idea*?

Brett snorted, shaking his head and grinning as he resumed to his next pose, following with the class.

I'd given up as soon as we laid out on our mats and they released the goats. Once that happened, there was no pretense here. I was only about the goats.

The owner chuckled, her eyes warmed. "Latice usually lets each class have fun with the goats a little bit at the end before she starts herding everyone out of here, but if you stay, I can give you a tour? Show you the rest of the animals? We have some horses, a couple donkeys. And a mini-donkey."

"A mini-donkey?" I was becoming annoying, but I couldn't help it. I asked, breathless, "Do you have chickens?"

"Oh yeah. And geese. And ducks."

Literal drool was falling out of my mouth.

The owner noticed and laughed again before leaning in, lowering her voice, "You know, you're drooling about my animals the same way most of the women in here are drooling over your date." She eyed me, the end of her mouth folding down. "You're okay with that?"

I swallowed and grabbed the end of my tank to wipe off my mouth.

Brett groaned quietly from next to me, flipping into the next pose and shooting me a heated look, one smoldering with promises of what we'd be doing after this.

A zing traveled through me, all the way between my legs, and while I was giddy in the heart for the animals, my body was still throbbing for Brett. After we left Vicky and Howard's farm, it'd been there, brewing, building the whole time. A good decent simmer.

"Oh." The owner readjusted her legs. Her voice was a little hoarse. "I see how it is. Yeah, you're good. You don't have to be worried about the other women."

I bent forward, half-heartedly joining the class, and I started to raise my leg up as my head went down. I sent her a furtive grin but didn't comment. Most of the class was buzzing that Brett was here. Earlier, I'd noticed that the owner herself had started to head back to her house at the end of the introduction talk, but she caught sight of Brett, paused and went with us inside. Latice, the instructor, shot her a brief quizzical look at that time but hadn't said anything.

We got through one more pose before the same three kiddies raced back inside, and one ran past me. I reached out, scooping it up, but it didn't want to climb on me. It wanted to play, balking. I let it go, smiling so happily and knowing I looked silly. I didn't care, but I gave up on the class totally and left my mat to go and sit next between two of the mama goats, a Nubian and Ruby, the Saanen. Both mamas swung their heads my way, tilting them so I'd give them all the pets as they stayed in place. Both were chewing their cud, as the owner already explained before the class.

Cud was some food that the goats kept tucked away to chew and rechew later on, or that's how the owner explained it. I was thinking there was more involved, but it made sense to me. Little cheek pockets where they stored their food, like squirrels. They were efficient snackers.

When the class was done, I was resting against a stall door behind me, and was so relaxed that I jerked up, but I hadn't fallen asleep. That would've been rude. Snoozing during a yoga class.

Brett stood over me, a crooked smirk on his face. The class

was obviously done, with the people standing in groups. Some were talking. Some were petting the goats. A few mats were left on the ground, but most had already rolled theirs up and were tucked under their arms.

"Hi." I blanched. My voice was crusty. I swallowed, clearing it and tried again, "Hey. Hi. I was just..." The Nubian was still by me and so was Ruby. I needed to find out the Nubian's name. Both swung their heads my way and my hands went to petting them, as if they'd conditioned me to do this.

I was happy and curled my hands, scratching under their jaws.

They loved that, stretching out their necks and heads, their mouths moving and their tongues started coming out. Oh my word. My heart flipped over. That was so cute. Their little pink tongues.

Brett coughed, clearing his throat.

My gaze lifted to his, and my body warmed, as if I'd been caught doing something wrong.

His eyes were laughing as he knelt in front of me. He reached over, his hand circling one of my ankles. "You, uh, have some drool." He motioned to the side of his mouth. "Right there, if you want to wipe it away."

Shit.

I jerked my shoulder up, ducking down to erase that.

My face flooded again. "I told you I like animals."

"Yes, you did," he noted, softly, his face growing somber, studying me quietly. "I need to remember this for future dates. If I want your attention, don't take you near animals. There's no competition."

Well, that was embarrassing.

He caught my train of thought and tugged on my ankle, scooting me closer to him. His head lowered even more, his eyes so dark and intense, taking in everything about me. "Don't be embarrassed about that. I like that about you." He cleared his throat again and readjusted on his feet. "I really like that about you. It's you. It's genuine." And his gaze fell to my lips. "While I'm glad we didn't skip, I'm remembering a certain promise I made you before we came here."

"Hey, man." A guy came over, standing. He'd been one of the guys eyeing up all the women, or most of the women. He and his friends. He wasn't adhering to the unspoken dynamics going on between Brett and me, that this was a Brett and me moment, with Ruby and Joy.

I'd just named the Nubian mama until I knew her real name.

I checked. She wasn't wearing a cute little necklace with her name on it.

Brett stood back up, towering over the guy, who wasn't fazed and was still interrupting our moment. He was big and muscly, looking like he spent lots of hours in the gym. He smirked. "Don't know if you two have plans, but there's a little pub and eatery not far from here. Called Rinascita. They're known for their organic food and they brew their own beer. All of it's grown and made by the owners. A group of us is going to go over for a drink. Would you like to join?"

I was reluctant to move away from Joy and Ruby, but I stood, brushing some straw that'd gotten on me. Brett curved an arm around me as I went to his side, resting against him.

The guy didn't move back, looking down at me, and his smirk grew. "What do you say? A quick brew?"

I tilted my head backwards, looking up at Brett without moving away from him. I was looking at him upside down.

His eyes flashed, and his mouth curved as his hand pressed flat on my hip, hugging me closer. "What do you say?"

I studied him.

There was a second part of our date, but he wasn't saying it was something we'd miss if we didn't leave now, like this class.

I confessed, "I didn't know this place existed and a little pub and eatery that uses their own organic products? I'm kinda curious about them, and why I haven't heard of them before now."

"Okay." Brett jerked up his chin to the guy. "What's the name of the place again?"

I EXCHANGED numbers with the owner, wanting, no—needing to go back another time for our tour. I wanted all the time I could get with those alpacas, and the horses, and the mini-donkey, and the ducks—all of the animals. Every single one.

I was going to bring Miss Sylvia Rivera with me, but she'd stay in my arms so she wouldn't be scared. We used to go on more adventures, but it'd been a long time since our last one.

The rest of the yogis went straight to Rinascita so we didn't change outfits. We were parked there, and this wasn't what I expected.

Brett's eyebrows were furrowed together, also taking note of the place. He grunted. "Fuck. What do you want to do?"

I expected something small. Quaint. A few people here and there. A low murmur of conversation and maybe coffee shop music in the background. The building was small, seeming where it was only big enough for the kitchen and bathrooms. People went to the counter to order, and the food was brought to them.

That was the only thing that aligned with my expectation.

Techno music blared from their speakers. There was a dance floor among a group of picnic tables where a bunch of people were dancing. There were college students. It looked like a family reunion was in attendance, all wearing the same pink and purple T-shirts. There were a couple grandmas dancing, their grandbabies being held up in the air by younger people. In the back corner was a group of tables pulled together, board games spread out, and there were young people, middle aged, older adults all there. A few elderly.

And there were bikers. Quite a few bikers. Maybe twenty, maybe slightly more. Some were mingling with the crowd. Some were dancing. Two were standing near the board table, watching the games, holding a beer in one hand. The rest were amongst themselves, taking up a large table in the corner of Rinascita, around the corner from the dancing.

Brett sighed. "It's up to you."

"What was the second part of our date?"

"Honestly?" He grinned at me. "Something similar. I wanted to take you to Jack's BBQ. I talked to a friend of mine, that girl who showed up with me, and her bartender friend said we could use a back table if we ever wanted to go somewhere new. She said the back section could be roped off so we'd get some privacy. But this..." He went back to the crowd. "This is either a seriously bad idea or we're going to have the best night ever."

"Then we have to find out which one."

"Right." He didn't sound convinced, but as if we were one being, we opened our doors, getting out at the same time.

Brett fell in step to my side, but slightly behind me, his hand to the small of my back.

"Hey ho! You made it." The guy held his arms out, a fruity looking drink in one hand, and walked right to us, throwing both his arms around us. I twisted, catching his drink before he poured it down my back. Brett growled and shoved him back before he could completely close the distance. "No."

The guy frowned. "Dude." His head went to the side.

"No." That was a firm no too.

The guy shifted to the side, taking me in, and he raised an eyebrow, his interest evident.

A creepy sensation slithered through me, and I began to step back from instinct.

Brett moved, stepping into the guy and forcing him back from me as Brett took my hand, lacing our fingers, He moved me away from the guy, turning so he was in the guy's face, and he was looking down since he was taller. There was no growl this time. Just an edgy calm that had my blood spiking as he said, "Don't know you. Don't want to know you. And if I see you breathing the same air as my woman, I'll break your dick."

The guy turned red, sputtering.

"Touch her and die. Do *not* test me."

The threats were delivered smoothly, succinctly, and Brett led me forward, leaning over to say, "He's the kind of guy that needed to be put in his place or we'd have problems with him later on."

I squeezed his hand, trusting him.

When we passed the first set of picnic tables, there were two empty ones on our right. The left was where all the bikers were lounging, and we got two steps before one of them shoved up to his feet. "Hey!"

Brett stopped, facing away. His hand tightened on mine, just briefly.

"Hey, man. He—"

Brett's jaw clenched once before he swiftly faced the guy, and as he did, the biker stopped in his tracks, surprised by suddenly how in-his-face Brett was being. The biker was tall, but he still came one or two inches below Brett. Lean. Golden tan skin that glistened with a small amount of sweat. He wore a leather cut, nothing underneath showing a smooth and slightly ripped stomach with a few tattoos on his chest. His jeans looked well-worn and hung from his hips. Dark hair that was messily rumpled. A thick barbell pierced through one of his eyebrows. Dark eyes that were squinting as he held a beer up, a finger pointing toward Brett.

"That guy was a friend of yours?" Brett's question threw him off.

The finger and beer dropped, and he raked a hand up the back of his head, bringing it toward the front through his hair. "Huh?"

Most of the bikers were watching our exchange, but I skimmed their faces. None looked disturbed. Most seemed curious.

Another biker got up from their table, an inch shorter than the first one, but thicker. He was solid.

Though, not as solid as Brett.

This one wore a white T-shirt under his cut. Baggy jeans. Chains hung down over the sides. This one had greasy blond hair and laughing brown eyes. He was white, but with a golden tan. His face was slightly too flat across the front to be considered handsome, but he had an arresting quality to him.

Also, the bad boy vibe was thick with both of these men.

Their entire table, even the women that were with them.

The guy who joined us slapped his buddy on the back, his hand staying and resting on his shoulder. "Shark, you don't know this man." He tipped his other hand toward Brett, the one also holding onto a beer bottle. He gave Brett the slightest bit of a nod, a coy smile tugging at his mouth. His eyes were sober, amusing.

Shark tensed, his chest drawing up. "I do too. I know I do. What's your name? How do I know you?" A sudden short and menacing growl burst out of him. "I don't like not knowing how I know you. Makes me think we're enemies." He began to shift his weight, his free hand reaching to his pocket.

"Oh! Whoa there, buddy." The other one grabbed his hand, then stepped in front of him, eyes on Brett, but said to the man now somewhat behind him, "You know him because he's a football player."

"A football player?"

He clapped his hand on Shark's shoulder, relaxing a little as the tension left his friend. He moved so he was sideways, indicating Brett again with his beer. "This here is the reason we won the Lombardi last year. Brett motherfucking Broudou. The Brood Machine himself. He's here. At our humble abode."

Shark's eyes got big, and he was all smiles after that. "Whoa, boy—" He began to stick his hand out.

His friend now shouldered him out of the way, speaking straight to Brett. "It's a damn kick in the pants to see you here. What brings you here? This is my sister's business. We're having a little party. Goddamn tickled pink having a bonafide celebrity among us." He held his hand out. "I'm Rowdy."

Brett removed his hand from behind me but nabbed my shirt and yanked me against him so my entire side was plastered to him. Then he shook the man's hand. "It's nice to meet you."

Shark whooped, jumping up. "Goddamn! Goddammit. This is something else. Buck! Buck! Do you know who this is?"

My eyebrows drew low because it was a sight to see as this biker had been snarling one second, about to draw some kind of weapon on us, and within three seconds, he'd transformed to Will Ferrell's character in *Elf* the day they announced Santa was at the store.

He was pointing at Buck, his hand raised as high in the air as he could get, still bouncing. "This is Brett Broudou. He's that tackle guy. The one who smashes quarterbacks for a living." His smile stretched from ear to ear. "It's a fucking honor to have you here. You drink? You like beer? What do you like?" His eyes fell to me. "What does your woman like?" He rounded again, his hand cupping around his mouth. "Hey, Tina! Tina! Woman."

We couldn't see her, but we heard from the side of the building, the side that faced the dancing area. "WHAT? GODDAMN, SHARK. SHUT THE FUCK UP! I'm working here and this is my business, and..." A very small and petite woman came around the corner, wiping her hands on a towel. She wasn't looking up, but snarling as she finally did, saying, "...this ain't the clubhouse. We're not here to serve you—" And she stopped, taking in the scene as Shark had gone back to bouncing, jerking his finger in Brett's direction. Her eyebrows slammed down. Her snarl never left. "Fucking wha—" Her eyes went to Brett, skimmed over, went to me, and she did a double take. She gasped, her body flinching as if she'd been slapped. "Holy fucking shit balls of all hair balls. You're Willow Harm."

Shark stopped bouncing. "She's what?" He pivoted on his feet, studying me again.

Rowdy said under his breath, "Goddamn, she is." His voice was quiet.

I flicked him a look, and he gave me a slight grin and another nod.

His sister was rooted in place, her eyes blinking as if she thought I was a mirage.

There was a brief moment where no one said anything more.

Shark's head was jerking from Rowdy to Tina, to me, to Brett, to me, and back to his friends. He scowled. "I don't know you."

Tina cleared her throat, and she took a long jerking step toward me, saying softly, "This here's—"

"I'm a cheerleader for the Kings football team," I said quickly.

Shark continued to look at me as if I told him I had three breasts. Oddly intrigued, but he cast Brett a nervous look.

"And cheerleaders aren't supposed to date the players. It's against policy so I could get fired. That's why we're here. We're dating in secret." I didn't want to see the weirdness that came over people when they found out the truth, just like how Rowdy and Tina reacted. I caught the sympathy in both of their gazes. Sympathy or pity, sometimes I couldn't decipher between them, and I got tired of it. It was easier this way.

I sent both a silent pleading look, just one, and it was short.

Shark had to ponder on my statement before he burst out, "Well, what the fuck do they know? They can't tell you who you can fuck or not fuck—"

Rowdy added, "They're dating."

"—date, fuck, it's all the same. It's none of their goddamn fucking shitting damn business." He loped to me and threw an arm around my shoulders. He squeezed me to him in a half hug. "You and your man can party here any time you want. Drinks are on the house—"

"They are not." Tina gave him a scathing glare.

"—tonight, drinks are on the house—"

"They are also not." Tina yanked him off me, shoving him back, that glare still in force. It changed to a polite smile as she said to me, "But for you and your date tonight, that *is* on me."

"Tina," Shark leaned forward.

Her voice rose sharply, "—and they're only for our two surprise guests of honor. Anything you'd like for drinks? And I would love the opportunity to make you dinner of my choosing. If you'd like, of course?"

Rowdy said, his voice proud, "My sister studied under a Michelin chef. She was overseas and working on giant yachts for the one percent in the world before she decided to come back and try her hand with this little gem." He gestured to the sign that had the title of the eatery. "Rinascita. That's Italian for rebirth." His eyes fell back to his sister, warming. "That's our little Tina. We're real proud of her."

The two shared a look before Tina flicked at something on her cheek, clearing her throat again. "And enough of the sappy moments, your dinner? Would you like to trust me?"

Brett's arm went back around me, anchoring me to him. "We'd love that."

Shark's chin lifted all the way up, as far as he could go. "You want anything else? It's our pleasure having you both here."

Brett glanced over my head, hardening. I didn't need to guess to know who he was looking at.

He answered, his tone hard, "I'd like that guy kept away. He's going to be trouble later on."

"Consider him out of here. Let's go, boys!" Shark flew a hand in the air, and at the motion, a bunch of the bikers converged with him. The two who'd been overlooking the board games came over as well, all disappearing around the other side of Rinascita. We heard raised voices not long after, and the bikers escorted that guy and a couple of his other friends from the premises.

Rowdy laughed before raising his beer to his mouth. "That was more for us. We've been wanting an excuse to kick those fuckers out of here. It would've been now or later, and later it would've been a lot bloodier. You did us a favor." He tipped his beer back, taking a drag from it before jerking his head to the tables behind him. "You're more than welcome to join us or go ahead and grab your own table. We won't bother you. More just excited that you're here at my sister's place of business. And thank you for letting her choose the dish for you. She's going to go all out. It'll be the best you've had, and Shark's invitation stands. You're always welcome here. You won't be bothered by jerkfaces like us. It's out of Shark's system. He's like a bulldog. Once he decides he likes you, he's all happy and giddy around you, but make no doubt, he'll turn rottweiler real fucking quick to have your back." He gave us both a wink. "He's going to be worked up about the injustice of cheerleaders and football players not being able to date for the next week. I'll fill everyone in. We'll all enjoy while he gets himself riled up about it. Have a good night."

He returned to their table.

A few of the others gave polite nods, smiles, or a couple held up a hand in wave.

We were left to ourselves after that. Though Shark circled

around us a few times when the dancers migrated closer to our table than he would've wanted. Once they dispersed, he wandered back to where the rest of their group partied the rest of the night.

The food Tina prepared was some of the best I'd ever experienced, and it *was* an experience. Four courses. I was blown away.

The first was a butternut squash ravioli with some type of butter drizzled over it. My mouth was watering as she did the drizzling in front of us. I also blanked at listening to her because I was that hungry.

The second course was a kale salad with candied walnuts and a dressing she made herself. The third was the main meal. Chicken marsala and roasted potatoes. The dessert was lemon sorbet.

All of it was superb.

Brett had been right.

By the end of the night, as we sat under the stars, at a four-course meal that came from a gourmet chef, as the dancing crowd left, the music changed, slowing to indie folk songs, this was one of the best nights ever.

There was slow dancing.

Three seconds after we hit the floor, the space around us filled up with bikers also swaying in rhythm with the music, all pairing off.

I felt safe, and I felt safe in a way where Brett could relax and enjoy himself too. I think that was a big part of the reason we stayed as long as we did, but when it started getting dark, we said our goodbyes and our thank yous, and headed back to the car. Brett caught my hand, lacing our fingers, a tingle went through me.

Not a normal one, one that was sexual.

This one was special. Different.

It was unique, and it wound its way deep into me, giving me

an extra buzz because tonight had been a dream. I felt like I'd spent the whole day basking in sunshine.

Like this whole date, these experiences, meeting those bikers, had been a part of a different reality. A break in our regularly scheduled programming. I didn't know if we'd ever go back to Rinascita, but I would savor the memory at least.

When we got to Brett's house, I didn't want to keep going slow.

I wanted to let go.

I wanted to let the fast speed back in.

I wanted to have more nights like we just did.

Over another week and a half, we did.

There were dreamy moments.

I took Brett back to the farm and introduced him to the ladies.

Miss Sylvia Rivera stood on his knee and cocked her head back, as if inspecting him for a minute before she jumped down and darted over to me. Marsha P. Johnson was more welcoming, staying on Brett's lap for ten minutes, her contented cluck almost purring out of her.

But none competed with Nellie Bly. She was a dark chestnut hen with a few black splotches at the top of her hind legs. Usually she'd keep to the back. Clucking to herself, but she took one look at Brett and off she went, running over to him.

Where he went, she followed.

He had no idea what to do. He began speaking to her as if she could understand. Sometimes, she rotated her head around and I wasn't sure that she didn't understand. When he tried to pet her before we left, she flapped her wings and took off.

My sides hurt from holding in my laughter. I couldn't wait for his second visit.

When that happened, Nellie Bly was the first one running toward him. Once she got to him, she began poking at the ground around his feet. Eventually, she settled down, sitting a few feet away, but always near Brett.

It'd been three weeks of happiness. Three weeks of smiling. Laughing.

Holding hands.

Cuddling.

Three weeks where Brett made me pant for him, curse at him, and groan as he slid down my body, where his mouth showed me all the different ways he could suck on my clit, lick between my folds, sliding inside, tasting me, and making me scream for him more than once, always more than once, before he'd let me return the favor.

We were going slow, but we weren't at the same time.

I usually railed at Brett as he pinned me down with either his hand between my legs or his mouth or both. But he was the one who always held back.

I was considering picking a fight, just to make him snap and he'd have to tear down that iron-clad discipline he kept over both of us, but there was also an itch. A small one that settled between my shoulder blades. That itch was telling me we were running out of time.

That all the dreaminess, the warm sunshine Brett was letting me experience, was going to come to a close. The shadows were done waiting. I felt them drawing nearer until one morning I woke. Brett had already gone to the stadium. I'd slept over at his house and had decided to work from here for the day.

The itch was gone.

I didn't think about it.

Then my phone buzzed that afternoon, as I was finishing up a meeting with a client.

Vicky: Could you and Brett come out for dinner?

26

BILLIE

B rett's garage door opened at seven that night. I'd texted him that Vicky had asked us to come over for dinner. When he came in, he took stock of me in the kitchen nook with my laptop in front of me, and his eyes changed. His head tilted to the side and he went all dark and smoldering, and oh boy. I knew what that look meant.

He was either going to torture me or he was done torturing himself.

My vagina instantly clenched, already wet because he'd primed me for so long that a fucking look from him and I was ready to explode.

I began backing up, not knowing if I could handle him stopping just short of what I wanted, what he wanted, what both of our bodies wanted.

His dick. Inside of me.

All the way inside of me.

And doing it over and over again.

I broke out in a sweat just envisioning the feel of him in me, but I said, "Vicky asked—"

He started for me.

My pulse spiked, while I was already starting to pant. "It'd be rude to be late—"

That's when he dropped his bag, grabbed me, and threw me over his shoulder.

I shrieked before groaning. "Brett."

His hand came up to my ass, patting me and then caressing me. "Yeah, baby?"

Baby.

Oooh.

I really liked that.

"Wha–what are you doing?"

He carried me upstairs to his bathroom and turned the shower on.

"Brett!"

He ignored me, setting me down and tugging at my clothes.

"I already showered."

He still ignored me, digging into my jeans pockets to pull out my phone, a pen, a Chapstick, and a paper clip. He frowned at the paper clip. All of that went on the counter. He hoisted me up.

I'd fallen silent by this time, enjoying his touch. On the inside of my leg. My back. Down my arm. His chest against mine. All the little points of contact. I was quickly getting distracted.

He pulled off my sandals and straightened, sliding his hands along the inside of my thighs. He held there, his eyes meeting mine, darkening. His finger pressed against me, rubbing in a circle.

My lips parted and swirls of pleasure climbed through me, my ache growing, starting to throb.

His lips found my shoulder, tasting me as he yanked me against him, his hand still between my legs.

I grabbed for his shoulders, my eyes closed as I groaned. "That feels so good."

"Good," he whispered. Then his mouth was on mine, and I sighed into his kiss. So good. So delicious.

The kiss grew harder, more demanding.

I opened for him.

His tongue slid inside, tasting me. He undid my jeans and moved them down—or tried. He pulled away, looking between us. My pants were too tight, so he grunted, wrapped an arm around me and held me up so he could peel them down. Then he set me back down and yanked my jeans the rest of the way, kicking them to the side.

His mouth found mine, reclaiming me as his beard teased at the same time.

He tore my top off, only lifting his head long enough to whisk it over me. My bra came next. He had it off in one second, which was impressive, and I smiled at how good he was at that.

His hands were everywhere, his body against mine. His heat engulfed me, and I wound my legs around his waist, feeling him against my center. I moved over him, grinding, biting my lip as a moan shuddered through me.

He ripped his mouth away. "Fuck." His forehead rested against mine as he breathed hard, fighting for control. "Fuck. Dinner."

I frowned. *What is he talking about?*

He groaned and started to pick me up.

"No." I tugged at his shirt, needing that off. I wanted skin against skin.

The rest of his clothes disappeared in record time. He stroked himself once as he looked me over. The connection between us was pulsating, an actual throb I could feel in the room.

"Babe," he whispered, his dick pressing against me, through my panties.

We paused at the contact, breathing each other in. I clung

to him, my legs lifting to his hips, and he ran a hand down one of them, catching my knee and tugging me tighter against him. The barrier was still there, but it was so slight.

He could move it aside, and he'd be in there. That's what I wanted. What he wanted.

Nothing else existed. It all faded away.

It was just him and me, and the feel of him right where I needed him.

We'd had a conversation about protection. I was very much clean since I'd been abstinent for so long, and he'd had regular check-ups, the last one being right before we'd met at the show.

My hand moved down, sliding over him, curling around his dick.

He went still, his forehead falling to my shoulder. He was trying to regain control, but no. That's not what I wanted. I made a decision, and it felt good. It felt right. It felt powerful.

A sensual and almost lazy feeling of good spread through me as I moved, taking my panties off —then the phone rang.

We both froze, but no. No way. No one was going to interrupt this.

I clasped him tighter to me, needing him to be inside me.

The phone rang again.

"Shit!" Brett growled, ripping himself away from me. He snatched up his phone and answered without looking at the screen. *"What?"*

27

BRETT

"**B**rett?"

    I had no idea who this woman was, whoever was on the other side, and who wasn't sounding happy to be calling me in the first place. Jesus Christ. I was struggling for some control. Billie was here. She was waiting, fucking dripping, and she was the type of woman a guy waits an entire lifetime for. And she was in my arms *right now*.

"Who is this?" I growled again, raking a hand through my hair, breathing harshly.

Why the fuck had I answered the phone?

Right. To make the ringing stop. I should've tossed it out the window.

"This is Vicky. Billie's—"

Her mom.

Shit. "Vicky. Sorry—"

I looked at the screen, seeing a number I didn't recognize. Billie said something about Vicky and I was struggling with coherent thoughts at this moment.

"You guys are still coming?"

Dinner.

I forgot. And we'd be late if we didn't get going. "Yes. We're running a little behind."

Billie's eyes bulged out, and she paled, realizing who was on the phone. She scrambled away from me, squealing, and raced into the bedroom.

She sounded suspicious. "Is everything okay?"

"Yes. I—yes." I reached into the shower, turned it off, then headed into the laundry room. Billie was frantic, trying to get dressed as she yanked a shirt whose back was now on her front. She cursed as I kept going and reached for the dryer. I pulled out some clothes and tugging them on until I realized we'd both have to shower. Or I'd need to shower. I tossed the clothes aside, and leaned against the machine. Still buck naked. My dick was hanging out. "Billie and I lost track of time. I—"

"Yes." There was an odd ring to her voice.

I frowned, trying to place it. "Yes?"

"I was calling to make sure you're still coming. It's important."

I straightened, growing more alert. Something was going on, something real. Something that concerned Vicky. "We'll be out the door in ten minutes. I apologize again, Mrs. Mitchell."

"It's Vicky, and that's okay. Just, just come, and tell her not to be alarmed when you come down the driveway. No one's hurt. They're just here as a precaution."

"A precaution?"

She ended the call.

"What was that about?"

Billie was in the doorway, her shirt still on backwards. Her hair was a mess and her lips were swollen. She was naked from the waist down, and I got distracted for a minute.

Like, a full minute.

"Brett?"

Her pussy, her very sweet, sweet pussy, how I'd just about

had her clenched around me—my dick was at full attention and getting harder by the second. I bit back a groan.

"Wha—" Billie started laughing.

It was a little worrisome how that sound from her made me want to move mountains to keep her from whatever had her mom worried. But I sighed, knowing this was probably something we needed to tackle sooner than later, whatever it was.

Still, though, I went and lifted her up.

"Brett." She laughed again, her voice a little breathless.

She wrapped her arms around me and wound her legs around my waist.

My hand fell to her ass, cupping her, holding her up that way as I went back into the bathroom and opened the shower door.

"What? No. Not again. We have to go."

I turned the shower on, set her on her feet, and rubbed a hand down her arm. "I can't speak for you, but I didn't shower after practice. At least one of us needs to get clean before heading out there."

"Wha—"

I tested the water. It was warm, so I stepped inside.

She squealed, shoving off me and jumping back.

She stood on the other side of the door, dumbfounded.

"In or out, Billie." I held both of my hands up. "I'll behave. I promise."

Something was going on that waited for us when we got to the farm, and a part of me wanted to stall. I wanted to prolong the time before Billie would have to face whatever it was, just for a little bit.

Her eyes darkened, and she toyed with her bottom lip, her hand playing with the bottom of her shirt. She groaned, then whisked it off and stepped inside with me.

We were going to be a little bit more late.

Good.

28

BILLIE

There was a squad car at Vicky and Howard's house when we arrived.

My heart dropped.

Brett held my hand, rubbing his thumb over my knuckles.

"Why's a cop here?" I asked, but I knew Brett couldn't answer. I wanted to think it was Travis, that he was here for a surprise party and hadn't hidden his car well enough. That wasn't true, though. Travis was a detective. He wouldn't be arriving in a squad car.

We pulled in, and the front door opened as I rounded Brett's truck.

Vicky came out first, followed by their lawyer. I stopped in my tracks. What was she doing here?

Brett was behind me. I wanted to step back, lean all my weight on him, knowing he would hold me up, but I couldn't. Whatever this was, it was the beginning of the universe taking away all the good in my life. I knew it. I felt it.

Me being with Brett—me *letting* myself be with Brett—had tipped the scales.

It was too much good. I wasn't allowed too much good.

I started to tremble, and Brett's hand came to the small of my back. That touch centered me, and I drew in a breath.

"Willow." Their lawyer was a woman, with dark red hair that looked like burnt amber. I'd always been jealous. She was so beautiful. Pale, but clear skin with a light smattering of freckles. Green eyes. She wasn't a petite woman. She had big bones and some weight on her, but it worked for her. Towering over me by a couple inches, she wore a business skirt and silk top that matched the color of her skin. She was one of those women who knew how to exude power and use her sensuality as a weapon.

She held out a hand, her eyes flicking to Brett behind me. "I don't know if you remember me. Mallory Christening."

I gave her a nod, but I didn't shake her hand.

Vicky stepped between us. "Billie's not keen on touch with most people. I hope you'll understand."

"Of course." Mallory folded her hands in front of her, but her eyes kept flickering to Brett again. She let them stay this time, and she cleared her throat. "You're Brett Broudou."

"Yes. We, uh..." Vicky looked between us.

I glanced at him over my shoulder.

Brett didn't respond, and judging from the harshness on his face, he had no intention of responding to her. Surprise flickered in Mallory's gaze, along with something I couldn't place. Respect? Challenge?

"It's new, and we'd like their relationship to remain a secret," Vicky finally managed. "They've been discreet for a reason."

"Yes." Mallory pasted a professional smile on her face. "I fully understand that, and Willow, anything we discuss is confidential as well. Of course."

I frowned, glancing at Vicky, who rolled back her thin

shoulders. Those same shoulders that could and would hold the weight of the world if it was needed. She said, "His lawyers are here."

His. He. As in the Midwest Butcher.

Panic speared me, and I swayed backwards on my feet.

Brett closed the distance, a hand to my hip, and cursed under his breath. "They're here?"

Vicky pulled her gaze from me to him. Her lips parted as she took an involuntary step backwards. I could imagine what she saw on his face. "We also needed to be discreet."

"This should've been done in a hotel room, whatever it is," he clipped.

She blinked, as if the thought hadn't occurred to her. Her hand lifted to her hair, but fell halfway through the motion. "I, uh, next time, if there's a next time. But since Billie doesn't live here, we thought a location familiar to her might bring her comfort."

So he wouldn't know where I lived, that's what she was saying.

They were still keeping my home location a lie. Vicky and Howard had once purposely invited a camera crew into their home to show I wasn't living there, and they never asked to tour the remaining buildings. The outsides looked too decrepit to house anyone else. Sometimes it seemed ridiculous that I was living in plain sight on their land, but no one questioned my home not being a shed for their animals or for the animal's food. The back of the guesthouse looked ready to fall down.

Mallory smoothed her shirt. "Fowler's attorneys are the ones who asked for a police escort. They've learned having one with them is a good idea, as a precaution. They're here because they've found new DNA on one of the murder weapons. Their own team did a test."

I winced before I could hide it.

Brett's hand flexed on my hip.

Mallory noted his hold on me. "It doesn't match Cameron Fowler."

It was easier to think of him as the Midwest Butcher. Hearing his real name was worse somehow, more personal.

"Or any of the Braatens."

That was Jojo's family.

"They'd like to take a sample of your DNA to rule you out."

Vicky jerked in Mallory's direction. "You never told me that. They should have that on file somewhere. In evidence somewhere?"

Mallory replied without looking away from me. "She was a minor then. They need permission from her now since she's an adult. Also..." Her lips curved in a sneer. "Some of the evidence has gone missing."

"Missing?" Vicky's tone was sharp.

"It happens sometimes."

Vicky drew in a sharp breath.

"They're waiting inside while I talk to you about what they want," Mallory continued. "They're prepared to compensate you, of course, and it would help them if your DNA was ruled out. Having said that, as your family's lawyer, I must tell you that it's generally considered not a good idea to give them your DNA unless they obtain a court order. Cross-contamination can happen. It's been proven in multiple cases."

Cross-contamination? "Are they thinking I did something?" I shrank against Brett.

"Jesus Christ," Brett spat.

Mallory's eyes flicked to Brett, almost as if she were having a hard time not paying attention to him. She shook her head, focusing on me. "Of course not. I'm just saying worst-case scenario."

"Uh..." Vicky gestured to Mallory. "Mallory was saying

earlier that if these lawyers keep pushing things, it might be a good idea to bring in another lawyer who specializes in cases like this."

"In serial-killer cases?" *There are lawyers who specialize in that?*

"In forensic cases," Mallory explained. "I'd stay on as well. They would be my co-counsel."

More lawyers. I looked over at Vicky. More bills.

I'd had my own lawyer when I was a child, who was more a child advocate. He'd been assigned to me.

"I'm not giving them my DNA. I'm not doing it. I don't care."

Mallory cleared her throat. "I'll be blunt here since I'm sensing you're about to shut everything down, which is your right to do and what I would do as well. I need to advise you that these lawyers are ambitious. Vicky informed me that they've tried to reach out to you before."

I looked over at Vicky, not knowing this.

She looked away.

I didn't like that. Vicky and Howard hadn't told me.

"They've been in the news lately," Mallory continued, "promising their latest attempt at an appeal will be successful."

I went back to watching Mallory.

Her mouth went flat. "I think they're full of shit, but lawyers can sometimes pull a rabbit out of a hat. With the new DNA, they want to rule yours out so they can say it's another unidentified person at the crime scene. They'll argue that could've been the real killer."

"What the fuck are they saying is their client asshole's reason for being there then?"

She lifted her eyes to Brett. "They've not made their argument official, but my guess is that they're going to claim Cameron Fowler *happened* to be in the area, heard a scream, and came in to help." Her eyes flickered to me before returning to him. "According to Miss Harm's statement, she didn't actually see him murder anyone."

God. I was back there.

The screams.

"I saw him entering the house, and I hid," I told her. "They were alive when he came in and dead when he left. There was no one else there."

Silence fell over the group.

Mallory's shoulders stiffened. "Yes. They'll pick that apart."

I rocked back against Brett.

This was a nightmare. My nightmare.

It was going to work—everything she'd said they were going to do, and he was going to be released.

Then he'd come for me.

This was it. This was how the universe was going to take everyone away from me.

Panic built in my chest. Slowly. It had grown with each word Mallory Christening said, and now I couldn't move. I couldn't breathe.

I could only think of one word.

Run.

I tore myself away from Brett. "I'm not giving consent. I don't give a shit what they say."

Mallory frowned. "Willow—"

"Do whatever you need to do. Send me the bill, but I'm not giving my DNA, and they need to get the fuck off this land. It's private property. They no longer have permission to be here." I swung around, blinded by my need to get away.

I started for Brett's vehicle but stopped just as quickly because coming over the hill, red and blue lights flashing, was a caravan of cops.

The first was a black truck, one that I recognized.

I was aware in the back of my mind of the screen door

opening and people coming outside, but I was locked on the first truck's driver as he parked and got out.

Travis.

His badge hung from his neck.

His face was grim.

He was here on official business.

29

BRETT

"Who died?"

Billie was the first to ask, and her voice was hoarse. She was standing by herself now, and my God, the sight of her, facing the onslaught of law enforcement vehicles. Tiny. Petite. Those lights swallowed her whole.

But she stood there. Fierce and firm, except for a slight tremble in one of her arms.

She tucked it behind her and raised her chin, as if she could defy whatever bad news was coming.

I was punched in the gut. This woman was mine and was going to be mine for the rest of forever. *She is mine.*

A wave of possessiveness and protection surged up in me. I moved to her as Detective Dickhead approached. I'd been fine standing behind her earlier, but this shit was different.

He stopped just short of her and looked her over, a bleakness on his face before he blinked and it was gone. His gaze moved to Vicky, who had migrated forward. Howard now stood behind her, a hand resting on her shoulder. She covered his hand with hers. They were both there, as a unit, for Billie.

Billie knew it. She pulled in a breath like she was reaching out to them, drawing some of their strength.

My fingers curled around her arm before falling to her wrist, then sliding to her hand. She laced our fingers and moved to my side, her forehead resting against my bicep.

I still felt a slight tremble from her, and I squeezed her hand gently. She drew in another breath, her mouth moving so her lips could graze my skin.

My bicep flexed, all by itself, among other body parts. He liked that touch.

I liked that touch.

She burrowed closer to me.

"Travis?" Vicky spoke up, alarmed. "Not Lo?"

He blinked, startled. "No! God, no. I'm sorry. I didn't think you'd jump there." He spoke to her, but his gaze kept going to Billie.

"Why are you here?"

His eyes found mine. He could see I wasn't happy about any of this.

About him coming here.

About us needing to be here for those fucking lawyers.

About how he kept glancing Billie's way as if she were his to take care of, but he couldn't so he had to stand away from her and do his job, because *that* was why he was here.

I hated all of this, but mostly that I couldn't make any of it go away.

I was the one who fixed everything. I protected. But with this shit, I was just another fucking helpless bystander.

Travis opened his mouth.

Here we go.

"Who are you?" he asked, looking at the lawyer.

Billie's fingers tucked into the back of my jeans.

"I'm Mallory Christening, from Jacobson and Jacobson."

His mouth turned down in derision. "You're a lawyer."

"Yes." Vicky's voice rose, taking over. "And the lawyers who came out of the house behind my husband are the lawyers for Cameron Fowler."

I could tell Detective Dickhead disliked their presence even more than the first lawyer. "Why are they here?"

I had a feeling if it'd been at all professional for him to curse in the middle of that question, he would've.

They didn't respond right away, so I did, letting him know that I was right there with him in his assessment. "They're asking for DNA from Billie to help support their new scheme to say the Midwest Butcher was a Good *fucking* Samaritan, who just happened to be in the neighborhood, heard the screams, and came to help. They're saying another person was there, based on some new DNA found on one of the murder weapons." My sarcasm was savage.

This was a fucking shitshow.

He and I read each other before his eyes flashed. "I want all the lawyers out of here," he ordered, his hand going up in the air as a signal to his co-workers.

I liked hearing that.

All the lawyers started protesting.

"But wouldn't it be a precaution if—" Vicky began.

"No. I'm sorry." He shut her down. "I'm not here to question Billi—Miss Harm. I'm here to let her know about an incident that occurred, and to ask if my men could search the premises."

Howard spoke up, "On what basis?"

"To make sure no one is here. To make sure you're safe, that Miss Harm is safe."

"And your reasoning for that?"

Detective Dickhead hesitated, as the lawyers were still protesting their removal. "Could we have a word inside?"

Mallory started marching for the house.

"Family only," he clipped out. "That doesn't include you, Ms. Christening."

"I'm their lawyer." She harrumphed, her nostrils flaring.

He moved past her, giving her his back as he went for the house. "When they've decided you need to know, they'll let you know. Until then, get the fuck off these premises."

Her eyes bore a hole in his back. "You'll be hearing from me, Detective..."

He didn't respond, just followed Howard, who'd led the way inside.

Billie hadn't said a word. She was still pressed against me, and I didn't move, not even as their lawyer turned, taking us in. A thought passed over her face, but her mouth stayed in a flat line.

"We'll...we'll be in touch, Mallory. Thank you for coming out." Vicky watched as the other lawyers were escorted to their vehicles. They were still arguing, but one by one, they got in and left. The squad cars moved so they could proceed down the driveway.

"I strongly advise that you have a lawyer present for what-ever this detective has to tell you. And do *not*, under any circumstances, let them search your premises," Mallory said. "They don't need an entire arsenal of police here to make sure no one is lurking. A handful would suffice for that."

"Yes. Well..." It was apparent that Vicky wasn't thinking about that at the moment. She wanted Ms. Christening to leave so she could go inside and find out why the detective was here. "We know Travis. He's a family acquaintance. If he's here for any reason other than what he's stated, we'll call you."

"Don't let them search—" she ground out again.

"I'm aware of that as well. Thank you. Goodnight, Mallory," Vicky said firmly, as she came over, touching Billie's arm. "Come on, Billie. Let's go handle this, whatever it is."

Handle this.

She was going to go in, hear him out, discover the new

battle, and then proceed to do what was needed to protect her daughter.

I liked that plan. I liked it a lot.

I started after them.

"Mr. Broudou," the lawyer's chilled voice halted me.

I looked her way, not saying a word. She was watching all the cops who had spread out, waiting for their command to get searching.

"Cops sell information too." Her eyes held a warning. "Just so you're aware."

Right. Our relationship.

That would be handled when and if it needed to be handled. Until then, she was a lawyer.

I didn't like lawyers.

I smirked at her. "Leave."

30

BILLIE

The room felt different.

It wasn't normal anymore.

It was cold now. Alien.

I drew in a breath, knowing it was me, not the room. The room was fine.

Travis was waiting. Howard too.

Vicky came right behind me. She'd left the door open.

I didn't like this. I didn't want to hear that someone else was dead. Because even though Travis hadn't said it, I knew that's why he was here.

It wasn't Lo. At least we knew that.

"Can we...can we just get to this? Who's dead, Travis?" Howard asked, a break in his voice.

Travis looked to the door. "Is Brett coming..." He trailed off because the door opened.

Brett came inside, scanned the room, and shut the door before he moved to lean against the wall behind me. Vicky had taken the seat beside me, and the other chair was at the end of the table. Brett wouldn't have been happy that far from me. I knew by now that he wanted to be near. No, needed to be.

Travis shot me a look. "Did you know a Deandra Walkins and a Martell Hibbley?"

Oh no. Pain rose up in me.

"You're mistaken," Howard choked out.

Travis' mouth turned down. "You do, then."

"Oh—no, no. This... There's a mistake. Travis, there's a mistake. There has to be." Vicky's voice began to tremble.

There wasn't.

"They're dead?" I asked quietly.

Brett was right behind me. He wasn't touching me, but I felt him. Could feel his heat. Could smell him. Pine and leather drifted over me. I sucked it in, needing it because, my God, what did this mean?

"They were murdered, yes." Travis hesitated again, just briefly, before the cop in him took over. He grew cold. Distant. "They were found in their home."

"The kids?" I asked, my heart pounding as I remembered. "They—Martell has a daughter. Deandra used to watch some neighbor's kids."

"No children were in the home. And there was no indication any had been present. We've sent units to the home of Kindra Hibbley. She's his daughter, right?"

I nodded.

This was all wrong. All a mistake.

"He had her when he was young," I said. "She's an adult now. I think she has her own kid." I shook my head, feeling completely untethered. "I think. I don't know. I'm sorry."

"Listen." Travis pulled out a chair, scraping it over the floor. He leaned forward, his arms on the table. "I'm here because the case was assigned to me. But, Billie, I would've asked for it anyway. They were killed the way the Midwest Butcher murdered his victims."

I nodded. I'd known that was coming. A sick feeling grew in me. "A copycat?"

"Maybe." He raked a hand down the side of his face. "But there were things...things the Midwest Butcher did with his victims that were never shared with the media. No one knows. This killer, he did the same things. The *exact* same things."

"What are you saying?" Howard jerked toward the table, grabbing the back of the chair on the end, unsteady on his feet. "What are you saying, Travis?"

"Did you request the prison logs for visitors?" Brett asked behind me.

Travis cleared his throat, leaning back in his seat. "We did, yes. If Cameron Fowler was in contact with anyone other than his lawyers, we'll find out."

"He's smart," I said before I even realized I'd opened my mouth.

I felt their attention come back to me, but I couldn't look at anyone. I fixed my gaze on the table, seeing the past. "The Midwest Butcher came through the back because he knew it was unlocked. Jojo's brother had just come in. The door didn't even shut. He caught it and was inside before anyone could react. He's smart. With how fast he... He was so fast." I closed my eyes, their screams now deafening. "Jojo's mom started screaming. Then Jojo. Her scream was different. A child's..." A weight pressed me to the floor. "That's why he didn't hear me running to hide. Their screams covered up my sounds."

God.

My chest was going to collapse.

"I'm alive because they're dead."

Brett's hand found my shoulder. "They're dead because a sick fuck killed them. *Do not* take that shit on. Do not. That's his and *only* his. You got me?"

I couldn't look up at him. I couldn't move, but some of the pressure eased. Just a little. That's what I needed to hear and perhaps exactly the way I needed to hear it. He was pissed off and annoyed *for* me.

"What else do you need to do while you're here, Detective Dic—Dove?" Brett asked.

I looked up. Travis' gaze was burning above and behind me. His jaw clenched. "I need to question Billie about the last time she saw Ms. Walkins and Mr. Hibbley. Because of the nature of the crime and because of Billie's connection, we needed to come here."

"Have you questioned next of kin?"

"Yes, Mr. Jackass. Thank you for asking me how I do my job."

Brett grunted. "Just saying it might look a certain way if you came here first."

Travis didn't respond, but regret and anger swam over his face before he realized I was looking at him. He blanked it all in the next second. "We didn't come here first, but I wanted to get here before the news broke."

I hadn't considered the news. I was slow in remembering the *after* of everything.

They were going to blast it all over again. The Midwest Butcher was back, or a copycat was active, and what then? My name. My pictures. Everything dragged back up. All of it.

A sad laugh escaped me. "I thought I'd have to worry about someone starting with me first, and then branching off into his own thing."

Travis leaned forward. "Say that again."

I opened my mouth, but Brett squeezed my shoulder. "Don't make her say it again. You heard her."

Travis' eyes flashed in anger. He shoved up from his seat. "Stop bringing personal shit into this, Broudou."

"It's all personal, and you know it. It's going to be personal. And this ain't about you, Detective Dickhead. You delivered the second-worst nightmare to her doorstep right on the heels of finding out his lawyers are going to try to say Fowler's innocent. The timing's suspect, or at the very least, it's a karmic joke on

Billie and this family. You know what's going to happen. The press will eat this up. They will love saying the Midwest Butcher could still be at large and the man Billie put away as a twelve-year-old was innocent. Fuck. You know he's not." Brett's voice was low, and rage simmered just under the surface. Some started to leak out. "They're going to roast Billie alive."

"What do you want me to do about it?" Travis stiffened.

"Oh, I don't know." Sarcasm. "Maybe put a gag order on his lawyers? Saying they can't go to the press with their new idea because it could infringe on your investigation."

"How the fuck do you know I haven't already done that?"

"Have you?" Brett bit out.

Travis bit right back. "Yes. We delivered that order right before they were escorted off these premises. Any other bright fucking and unnecessary ideas, Mr. What The Fuck Do You Do Again? *Right.* You're an athlete. You run after a ball for millions."

"Wrong, asshole. I hit people for millions."

Travis' face twisted. He opened his mouth to speak, but Howard got in the middle.

"Okay, gentlemen..."

"Stuff it." Vicky was more direct. "What more do you need from us, Travis? It's already been a long day. I've no doubt that come morning, we'll be in a nightmare of a storm. Can you get to what you need and leave?"

He sighed. "We need to search your premises."

"No." That came from Howard.

"If there's someone—"

"I said no. Next?"

Travis paused before his next words. "I need to question you, Billie, about the last time you saw Ms. Walkins and Mr. Hibbley."

I nodded. I wouldn't have anything helpful to say, but... "There was a man," I suddenly remembered.

"What?" Travis said.

"What man?" Brett asked.

"Maybe a month ago, on Sunday. After..." I was about to say the same weekend we had our group date, but instead I went with, "The day of Brett's game against Minneapolis. It was thirty minutes to kickoff. Lo and I went on a walk down the driveway, and I saw a truck."

"What kind of truck?" Travis asked.

I needed to remember. These details used to be easier to pull up because I catalogued them. I focused a minute, and then I saw it again, almost clear as day. "A blue Chevy truck. White on the sides. Blue top. Open back."

"You didn't get the license plate, did you?"

I shook my head. "First three letters were GWB. Maybe a four after? An eight? But I'm not sure. I'm sorry."

"No. No." He wrote that down. "This is great, actually. Anything on the man himself?"

"I thought he was a hunter. Sometimes they..." I tried to remember what the driver looked like.

Howard finished for me. "Sometimes they come around, checking out the land. Ask if they can use it."

"Do you let them?"

"No. I'm saving it for myself and my son-in-law."

Travis barely hid a smile. "Howard." He inclined his head. "I know your son-in-law."

Howard grinned before it faded.

"He had a ballcap on." I could see him again. "Pulled low over his face. I was able to see his jawline, and it was clean. No beard. No mustache. White male. Trim body. Not skinny, just trim. Plaid shirt." No. I remembered this too. "Blue and white plaid shirt. Grey also. He matched his truck. I thought that was funny, but I didn't realize it until just now."

Travis wrote everything down. "Anything else?"

"Yeah." I squinted at the memory in my head. "He was

holding the steering wheel. No! He was tapping the steering wheel. I stared at him."

He stopped writing, his head rose.

"I stood on the hill and stared at him because I got a bad feeling. But I thought that was just because Brett had been concerned the night before, so that worry was in my head. Fresh. I shook it off, but yeah. I stared at him, and just before I turned around to go back to the house, he began to leave. I didn't see him go, but I heard him."

"You don't know the direction he went, do you?"

I shook my head. "No, but the girls were riding bikes in the yard that day. Luna was riding up and down the driveway. She might've seen..." I trailed off, seeing the fury that lit his face.

His hand tightened over his pad. "Lo's kids were outside?"

Oh no.

I swallowed over a knot. "Yeah."

Travis closed his eyes before breathing in through his nose. "Okay. Okay." He glanced to the living room. "Could we do the rest in there? Somewhere a bit more comfortable while Billie takes me through everything she knows about Ms. Wal—"

"Deandra and Martell." I stood and led the way to the living room. "Their names are Deandra and Martell. Dee was my friend."

31

BRETT

The detective sat down to finish questioning Billie, and once they got going, Howard cleared his throat and gave me a pointed look before disappearing into a back hallway.

Vicky sat down on the couch beside Billie.

"I'm good," Billie assured me.

Right. I went in search of Howard, finding him in a gun room. He had a rifle in one hand and searched for ammo with the other. "You know how to shoot?" he asked.

"I do."

"What type?"

I frowned.

He lifted his head. "Rifle, handgun? Something else?"

I felt a little foolish for taking so long to clue in. "We're going to clear the buildings."

He nodded. "We're going to clear the buildings." He sized me up. "Can you handle yourself in a fight?" He was all business and all soldier, nothing like the male fans I was used to.

"I can handle myself."

He continued to scrutinize me. "You ever been in a fight?"

"My pops was a drunk, and not a nice one. And my twin is

in prison for attempted rape." I didn't think I needed to say
more. "Yes. I've been in a fight."

His eyes sharpened. "Which do you feel more comfortable
with? Handgun or the rifle?"

"Handgun."

He passed me a 9mm, keeping the rifle for himself. Then
we headed out. I'd never had any official training so I listened
carefully as Howard clipped out commands, giving me a brisk
explanation of how we'd be moving through each building and
what our formation would be.

We did Billie's place first, then the coop and the rest after.

He turned to me as we moved along a walking path in their
woods, circling around the land and coming back toward the
house. "You know how to handle yourself."

I didn't ask how he knew that. When you're around
someone who knows violence, you recognize a certain quality. I
had that quality. "Didn't have a great first chapter in life," I told
him. "Football gave me a different path, you could say."

He grunted. "Billie said you were worried about her being
out here."

I considered my words, but I wasn't one to mince words
when shit needed to be said.

"You've got an open driveway," I pointed out. "No gates. No
sensors that I'm aware of. No security system. No dog. She's in a
separate building. Dead of night—"

"Dead of night, I'm going to hear if someone is walking up
on my home," Howard countered. "My family is here. No one's
getting past me."

I stopped, making him stop as well. We faced off, and I
didn't flinch. "With respect..."

His eyes went flat.

"You can't protect her when you're tucked up in bed, sleeping. You gotta wake if someone steps wrong on a blade of grass,
race down those narrow wooden stairs in an old house that

creaks, and beat him to her place in order to get between him and her. If that happens, you've left your wife in the open."

"I can protect my family."

"You're one man and again, *no* security system. I'm not trying to make you feel a certain way, but I'm going to do every goddamn thing possible to make sure Billie's safe. No bullshit, I won't sleep well knowing she's here alone."

His nostrils flared. He didn't like hearing that. "She ain't alone. We're here."

"Yes, in another building, on another floor. You move fast, and I can see your military training, but Billie's in the open, and you know it."

"I've protected her so far."

"You were protecting her against nosy and intrusive reporters, not a killer who won't be driving a vehicle or bringing a cameraman and a microphone with him. He'll come in on foot, and he'll be silent and fast, and if you're lucky, he'll try your house first. I've no doubt that you'll wake the second that screen door squeaks open, and you'll meet him with a rifle. It's not escaped my attention that you handle that rifle like it's an extension of your hand. But if he goes to her first? If he decides he doesn't think that shed is a shed? If he breaks down her door and grabs her in two seconds?"

His eyes glinted at me in the moonlight. "She's not as helpless as you're making her sound."

"I've no doubt, and it's reassuring to hear that, but there's a reason 'element of surprise' is a phrase. She could be dead before you hit the bottom step in your place."

"You got a better setup?"

"Maybe. Maybe not. I got a gate to get through, a second gate, and a third gate to my place. I got security patrols going through the neighborhoods. I got a security system that a buddy who was in Kandahar set up because that's what he does for a living, and he's the best in the nation. I know because I researched. And I can also tell you that I'll be getting a dog, one that's trained. I put in a call to a someone I know who trains K9 dogs. He's also trained them for the military. That dog is going to be her best friend."

"You know a lot of people."

"I know some, yes."

He didn't comment on that.

I relented. "I'm in the NFL Honors. Guys like to talk to me. Sometimes I talk back with them."

He gave a grudging dip of his head before indicating the house with his rifle. "I'm sure they're done chatting by now. Travis took off when we were done with the buildings."

We started for the house. "I'm going to do what she wants," I told him. "If she wants to stay here, I'll be here. If she wants to be at my place, I'll be there. I can't cover her Saturday nights."

"I got her." He glanced over at me. "When are you getting the dog?"

"It might be a bit, but my buddy said he's got one that might be perfect. Only reason he's not meeting the criteria for the K9 training is because he won't just sniff out what he's trained for. He keeps sniffing everything out. They can't use him for his specialty. He was going to ship him to a different department, but he said he'd look into it for me."

"And if that one doesn't work out?"

"I'll put in for another one. Might be a bit longer, but we'll get one."

We walked the rest of the way to the house in silence. When we got to the screen door, we could see the women in the dining room, hear the low murmur of their voices.

I waited for Howard to go in first, but he didn't. He stared at the door, looking like the world rested on his back. "She might want a rescue dog that can be trained how you'd like," he said. "She'll say those special dogs will find a home, but the rescues already need a home. Some rescues are damn smart. It's the people that are the problem. Expect that pitch from her."

"Then I'll make a few more calls."

He sighed. "She's going to love that dog."

"She will."

He held my gaze and gave me a nod.

I'd gotten his approval—and not just for the dog.

32

BILLIE

Deandra died because of me. Martell.

This was bad, so very, very bad. And it wasn't like the last time when it all happened at once.

God.

Pain seared me, and my knees almost buckled.

They were dead because of me. It wasn't supposed to be like this. I had never thought—I choked out a sob, covering my mouth with my hand to stifle it. No one was supposed to die because they knew me, because I cared about them.

No, no, no.

I wouldn't let it happen again. I *couldn't*, and that meant I had to go.

A copycat serial killer. He sent him. It's the only explanation. For this new killer to know how *he* killed, to have killed someone I knew, it was him. Cameron Fowler decided to come after me after all.

I wished so hard that it weren't true. It was all a very bitter and twisted coincidence, but I knew better. I had lived this before and survived. Everyone that I loved died around me.

My chest constricted.

I'd gone to the farm earlier to get what I would need. Vicky saw me, and I knew she was wondering what I was doing, but I lied saying that I was getting what I would need to stay at Brett's for the duration. For lies, it was plausible and she hadn't asked more questions after that, but when I drove away, she stood there, watching me the whole time.

I just hoped she hadn't made a call to Brett, though he was at work. He'd gone to the stadium. He wouldn't be able to leave any time soon. I should have another two hours before running into the risk of possibly our paths intersecting. That was just the possibility, if he left work early or something like that.

I needed to make plans.

I needed to send them down the wrong trail, and bought airline tickets to Jamaica. Then a one night stay at a resort, and another one night stay at a different resort. That should give me a few days to start.

Maybe I should've thought this far ahead before it got to this point, but I hadn't. Before, any attempt to hurt me had only hurt me, not people around me. The men who tried to kidnap me, they hadn't bothered with my loved ones. This was different. It was supposed to start and end with me, not Vicky or Howard or Lo or the girls. Not Roger.

I would not let this world touch them.

And Brett...

The cash I'd pulled out of my bank account was stuffed under my clothes, and I picked up my car keys. I'd have to ditch the vehicle at the airport, then try to see if I could pay someone to take me somewhere else. I'd need to pick up another car, but the more steps I could put between me and my next mode of transportation, the better.

This had always been in the back of my mind, the day when I might have to run because of the Midwest Butcher.

Bitter regret laced every step I took, and I flicked away the tears that were already spilling, but this needed to be done. If I left now, there was a chance everyone I loved would be left alone. And Brett, that was too new. He would be left alone.

God, please.

He'd been the universe's present to me. I got weeks with him. I got that window of time, and I would hold onto these memories. They would keep me company, but it was time to go.

I stuffed down the pain, the regret, and I let the numbness back in.

I wouldn't be able to do this if I wasn't numb. If everything wasn't blocked inside me.

I felt nothing. I couldn't. If I did...and I was already faltering in my step.

If I let myself feel, then someone I loved would die. That's what would happen.

The letter I left behind was a lie, telling him I was at the farm and would call when I was heading back. I hoped it'd give me another few hours before the questions started rolling in and the calls would start.

I picked up my bag and headed for the garage. Two steps away, and it was shoved open from the other side.

I braked, my heart leaping into my throat at the sight of a large and imposing body suddenly there. Then I heard Brett's savage growl.

"Did you leave me a note, at least?"

I relaxed, knowing it was him, but then tensed all over again for another reason.

His face had been in the shadows. He took a step toward me, stalking me.

"Brett." I began backing away, eyeing him. Wary.

His eyes flashed, taking in my movement. An ugly smirk came over his face. "Let me guess, it's a fucking 'Dear Brett' letter?"

I kept backing up. "It's for your safety. Vicky and Howard's safety. Lo's," I choked out her name, but stopped because he was moving with me. He stalked me.

"Bullshit." His head lowered as he drew closer until I came up against the kitchen counter. Deep anger rolled off him in waves, and it set me back. It was overwhelming. I was almost light-headed from the intensity of it, of him.

"You're going to fucking run? What lies are in here?" He crossed the room in two steps and snatched up the letter, reading it over. As he did, he grew still. More still. More locked-down. Angrier. By the time he was done, his cold eyes sliced to me, piercing me, before he took in my bag. "Vicky called me. She said she thought you might do something like this." He raised the letter back up, almost feral eyes glaring at me. "According to this, you're going to the farm. According to Vicky, you were already at the farm. She said you went in, acted off, and squirreled away a giant bag." His eyes fell to my bag. "Can't be that bag. That one's not big enough for all the shit she said you took from the farm. Where's that bag, Billie? Hmm?" He was taking in the car keys that I now clenched in my fist. "I'm betting that bag is already in your car, in the trunk. All fucking ready for you to *cut and run.*"

His last words were an accusation, and they landed. They were dipped in poison, and I felt it start to spread inside me, but I accepted that. It was fitting. Poison from him, but the poison was really me. It was inside me. It was joining the poison that I already had inside me.

Didn't he get that?

"Brett," I started, but stopped because he wouldn't want to hear any of that. He wouldn't say I was poison. Vicky wouldn't say that. Howard. Lo. None of them. But I was, and how did I get them to understand?

How did I get Brett to understand?

"You have nieces." I'd start there. My voice came out rasping. Weak.

His eyes snapped to slits. "What?"

My eyes closed. My head lowered. I had to try it this way. It was the only option. "You have two nieces and a nephew. You have a sister to fight. You have a brother whose relationship you need to build, and I know you want to build on it. I know it." This felt right because it was right. Knowing that, feeling that, I looked back up. Strength pooled in my stomach, helping me hold his gaze steady as he was still skewering me.

"What the fuck does that have to do with you *leaving me*?"

God. My heart squeezed. He sounded so hurt by that. I shook my head, whispering, "It's not like that."

He was in front of me again, almost in the blink of an eye. One moment reading the letter by the table and the next, in my space. Breathing me in. His eyes still drilling into me, burning from my supposed abandonment of him, and that made whatever hold was on my heart, that made it even tighter. My lungs were hurting.

I was failing.

"Brett," I choked out, reaching out to him. I was blind in that movement, just knowing I couldn't take the pain that was searing me. It was too much. His hatred. His anger. All of that was mixing in with the very real panic to flee. Somehow Cameron Fowler had sent a copycat killer after me, and he or she or they were going to come after those I loved. And even if I didn't know it, or fear it, it was too much of a risk for me to stay.

I *had* to go.

Why wasn't he seeing that? "I have to, Brett."

His eyes flashed, hotly. His mouth turned into a flat line. His face hardened. "Bullshit."

"No. It's not—"

Something in him snapped. I saw it, saw the flash in his eyes, before he leaned down to me, his mouth almost touching mine. His nose was centimeters from me, but he still had that letter in his hand, crumpling it in his fist. "You think anyone will be safe with you gone? That's bullshit. If Fowler is behind this, or if there's some other sick fuck behind this, they've been clocked in long before now. That means they already know us. They know Vicky. Howard. Lo. Roger. Your nieces." He paused, just a fraction. "Maybe me. Probably me. They *know*."

My heart was barely beating, it was being squeezed so hard. A death grip was on it.

His head stayed, but he moved his lower body against mine, and I felt him brushing against me. He wanted me, even during all this, he still wanted me. I leaned toward him without realizing it, my body needing the steadiness of his body against mine, his hands on me. His heat was driving me crazy, being so close, but not closing all the way.

Brett's hand cupped the back of my neck, holding it in an iron grip.

I blinked, staring up at him.

He was taking me in, his gaze scanning every single inch of my face before coming back to my eyes. His eyes, God. They were almost glittering from whatever emotion he was feeling right now. "You run, and this psycho will use anyone you love against you. He'll take one of your nieces. He'll let it become a big spectacle and then he'll use her as bait to draw you back into his trap. You run and you guarantee someone you love will die." His hand tightened on my neck. "*Don't* run, Billie."

There was a final click at his last words. Everything that I had let loose, ready to go, all of it was yanked back inside me, and hearing him, realizing he was right, the last seal was poured over my heart. He was right. I couldn't go. This killer had already been planning, long before me.

He already knew who I loved.

"Brett," I cried out, sheer terror starting to claw at me.

An icy hand was making its way up inside me, and I couldn't stop it. Every inch of me was freezing in place, the understanding that I might've insured the death of one of my nieces—Brett growled, his hand flexing before his mouth dropped to mine.

The fire from him surged in me, battling against that coldness, and I gasped under the onslaught of the battle happening inside me. Brett took advantage, his tongue slipping in, and he was taking over. He wasn't letting me feel what was happening in me. It was all him. Only him.

His hand grabbed my hair, twisting it, and he yanked my head back.

A cry came out from me, but he swallowed it whole, his mouth chasing me and not giving up control.

I was under his command. Whatever he wanted, I would give. I would want to give it. Needlessly. Seamlessly. Blindly. But then the fire from him won and desperate need reared out of me.

I needed him.

I needed him *now*.

Pushing at his shirt, I hungered to touch his skin.

Brett had paused at the connection, but when my hands fell to his pants, he came back alive.

He bent in one motion, picking me up with both of his hands cupping my ass. He didn't wait for my legs to wind around his waist, he just lifted me and deposited me on the kitchen counter.

"You were going to leave me?" His hands ran up the inside of my legs.

I looked up, seeing how angry he still was, and as our eyes met, he yanked my legs open as he moved between them, fitting right into place.

"Hmmm?" One of his hands lifted again, cupping the side of my face, his thumb running over my mouth. His other moved to my pants, undoing them, and as his thumb sank inside between my lips, his other hand shoved down, finding my entrance.

I moaned, pleasure taking me over. Lust. Desire. All of it was circling through me like a tsunami.

He looked down at his hand between us, but his other thumb kept hold of my mouth. "You were going to run. You were going to leave us all behind, and what good would that do?" He looked up once again, a haze over his eyes, as the need to submit his dominance was pounding through him. And I knew it was there because I was feeling it inside me, the same yearning was pressing out of my chest, wanting to connect to him, to cement his hold over me.

I began panting and ran my tongue over his thumb.

His eyes focused there, that haze widening, and as he sank a finger inside me, he switched out his thumb for two other fingers of his. I gasped from the sudden onslaught, but then I was swallowing on his fingers. I tasted them, desperate to taste whatever he was feeding me, but as I did, a second finger joined inside me, and he was thrusting them in slowly before drawing them back out. His other thumb pressed on my clit, rotating, as he kept moving inside me.

A different look came over him as he was watching me. I clenched around his fingers, not sure if I liked that look, but he flashed a wide and almost wicked grin as he pulled his fingers from my mouth, replacing them with his own mouth. He drank in my gasp as his fingers twitched on another thrust, and I yelled, my release coming fast and automatic and so strong that it shocked me.

Tremors rippled through my entire body.

Brett drank all of it up, his lips owning me, as his fingers pulled out of me. My pants were taken off. He lined up, pausing, his head lifting to look at me.

I nodded, licking my lips, wondering for a brief moment what his cock would feel like inside me, and then he shoved in, and I moaned all over again, because he felt so good.

He ate that moan up too, before pushing me against the

counter, his hand holding the back of my head so I didn't hit against the cupboard. As he did, he began moving hard and fast inside me. He was doing it with one purpose and one purpose only, to make me come all over again.

As I realized that, I began shaking my head. "I can't. Not so soon after—"

He caught my mouth, silencing my protests, his hips moving in and out of me in a beautiful but demanding rhythm.

I was almost dying inside. Brett felt so good inside me. I'd never experienced sex like this.

"Billie," he rasped out.

I opened my eyes, finding him watching me with a dark and intense look in his eyes. They narrowed, his hand flexing on my hip where he was holding me in place, anchoring me as he kept thrusting inside. "Are you going to run?"

My eyes widened. What was he doing? "What?"

He paused, as a delicious heat began building in my spine, swirling around me. "Are you going to run? Are you going to leave me behind?" His eyes glazed over and he lowered them, his mouth finding my shoulder as he yanked my shirt to the side, giving him more access to me. He tasted me, and I shivered from the sensations going through me. "Are you going to let the rest of us stay out in the open again?"

I couldn't answer. I didn't want to, but I also *couldn't*.

Carnal hunger and pleasure was wrapping itself around me and it was tightening on me, squeezing me for another release, and I fought against it, not wanting to come so soon again. Not when he hadn't come once.

"Billie," he snapped, his hand catching my jaw and pulling my mouth over to him, but I gasped as he did that and my lips brushed against his, distracting him.

He moaned, his mouth sinking over me again. "You're so tight. You feel so good."

I needed more skin. More of him against me, and I began

pawing desperately at his shirt. I wanted everything gone. My shirt. His. His pants. The rest of my clothes. I wanted nothing between us.

"Brett," I panted, blind again in this new frenzied need.

His mouth was gone, and I whimpered, but he was taking all our clothes away.

His shirt. Mine. They were tossed to the side.

His pants were shoved down and off, and he pulled out, just long enough to rip my thong off. Then his cock sank back in, right where it was supposed to be, but Brett lifted me up, carrying me from the room, still inside me.

I squawked but quickly wrapped my legs and arms around him, and as he went up the stairs, I began lifting myself up and moving over his cock, riding him.

He stopped in his bedroom's doorway, a hiss of air leaving him as his hands flexed into my ass, kneading me, I begun rolling over him, but a new primitive look flashed in his eyes, a stark and primal need hardened his face, but then I was on the bed and he was moving over me.

He didn't give me any more time to adjust to the new position before he pulled out, only to slam back inside, and then he kept going.

I didn't understand what was going on between us, but I wanted to battle him. I wanted to push back.

He felt what was going on inside me, and lifted his head, still moving inside me. He watched me, his eyes narrowing. "What are you needing, Little Billie?"

That name.

I came alive, hearing that name. One other person called me that and I hated when they did, but as Brett said it, he claimed it. He was taking it over, and I wanted that more than anything. I cried out, my voice sounding strangled, as I pushed up against him, my hands holding tight to his shoulders.

Brett frowned briefly before adjusting quickly.

He was sitting, and I straddled him, but he hugged me tight to him. We were both moving over the other, both riding our wave, our fronts brushing against each other.

A sheen of perspiration broke out over my skin, and soon the rubbing was smoother. Our bodies were sliding against each other.

I loved this. All of this. This was my man, and I was claiming him, but Brett was also claiming me right back. He held me over him, his arm clasped tightly around me. And then, I paused, my hand sinking in on his shoulder as I lifted myself up, then dropped back down.

He groaned, cursing, before he said, his voice sounding thick, "What are you doing, Bill—"

"No." My hand snaked up, grabbing the back of his hair and I pulled.

His eyes widened, surprised, but dark desire flooded them immediately.

"You use my name," I rasped out again.

He frowned before a smooth grin spread out. "Little Billie?"

I moaned, sinking down over his cock and holding there, grinding.

"You like that name?"

I couldn't respond. The ability to make words come out of me had left me, and it was only the feelings of him inside me, what he was doing to me.

He tipped me back.

I opened my eyes, about to protest, but he pushed me down and came with me, never stopping sliding inside me. "It's time you come, Little Billie."

That name.

I was writhing underneath him, the frenzy coming back over me.

"Are you going to run, Little Billie?" He was almost taunting me, but he wanted to come. I heard the need in his voice. He was barely holding onto his own restraint. "Billie," he snapped, "Are you going to run?"

I didn't answer. I didn't want to. I couldn't give in, for some reason.

Feeling that, he paused, in everything.

"No," left me in a succumbing sigh.

And also feeling *that*, he held himself above me. "Are you going to run, Billie?"

We held still, this question between us, this moment hanging there because it meant everything somehow.

We were both sweating. We were both breathing at once, together.

Fear slipped out, breaking through some wall inside me. He saw it, and his eyes grew tender. His touch softened. He said again, gently, "Are you going to leave me?"

He began moving again, slowly pushing in, going to the hilt and grinding against me, but he dropped his head down, his lips finding mine in the softest, the most loving kiss, as he breathed against them, "Little Billie."

That did it. I flooded over him, coming, and I cried out, "No."

"No what?"

My climax was exploding inside me, but I panted, "I won't leave you."

"Good," he growled, and his mouth dipped to my throat.

He began fucking me. He rode me through my tremors, and this time, it was for him. It wasn't long before his hand found my throat, resting there as his eyes found mine, and he grated out, "Because you're mine, Billie. Mine to protect. Mine to pleasure. *Mine.*" He pushed one last time inside me, before he groaned. "All mine."

I was his, but as I ran a hand down his back, I thought, *You're mine too.*

33

BILLIE

They were scared in the days that followed.
I didn't know if Brett said anything. I doubted he did,
but they were still scared. Brett too. After that night, the flood-
gates were opened. We had sex multiple times every night.
When we went to bed. In the middle of the night. Sometimes in
the morning before he left for the stadium. A few times, as soon
as he got home, he was reaching for me. There was something
insatiable in both of us, like we were both starving for the
other, needing to reassure the other that we were still there,
that we could still touch each other.

That the other wasn't gone, but I knew Vicky and the rest
were also scared.

Scared of how I'd react.

Scared that I'd shut down.

Scared I'd run away.

Scared I might collapse.

Vicky. Howard. Lo. Roger.

They all watched me.

I supposed I'd do the same in their shoes.

It was the worst during Dee and Martell's funeral. Martell's daughter and both of their extended families wanted to have their funerals together. Identical closed caskets were at the front of the church and Martell's daughter married them in death.

I lost it.

It was my fault—no. It was the killer's fault. It was the Midwest Butcher's fault. Martell's daughter didn't blame me. She made that clear to me, but it didn't matter because my mind knew where the blame should logically go, but my heart didn't.

They died because of me.

Brett slept at my place that night, and I just wanted all the emotions to go away. Every single one of them. I wanted no memories. I wanted no feelings. I wanted no thought. He helped erase them by fucking me until I was either burning from his touch or I was sleeping, passed out from sheer exhaustion.

Today was Sunday, and Vicky had decided to have a couple friends over—Travis and a few of his cop buddies. Roger was in heaven. Howard knew how to instantly man-speak to them, so there was a lot of that happening outside.

As I washed the dishes, I watched them from the kitchen window as they walked down the driveway, poking in the dirt.

"What are they doing?" I asked Lo, as she was helping dry the dishes.

"They're laying down wires for sensors."

"Sensors?"

"Yeah. You know, in case someone comes during the night. I think Howard's just trying to get better security."

"Mom!" a voice yelled from the other room.

"Hold on, baby. One second."

"MOM!"

"Agh. Okay. I'm coming." Lo gave me a look. "I love my children. I love my children. I love my children." She kept repeating this to herself as she went into the other room. That had to be the fortieth time either Charlotte, Cynthia, or Luna had called for her. They'd been fighting since they got here, and I was pretty sure I saw Luna put Cynthia in a takedown hold at one point.

Lo had called me yesterday after Travis had been over to question Luna and the others about whether they'd seen anything that day last month when they were riding bikes outside. According to Lo, Luna had seen the guy in the truck, but being questioned hadn't bothered her. She just thought it was a fun new game of testing what she'd noticed at random times, and she was convinced Travis was going to question her again about other things. So all day she'd been studying every person, dog, child, and vehicle they came across.

I still couldn't help but wonder if the girls subconsciously knew something was wrong. That would explain their behavior today.

Feeling a presence come to stand next to me, I assumed that Lo had come back. "Are we overreacting? Could it just be a coincidence?"

"Not one fucking bit," came a low voice in response.

It wasn't Lo.

Travis stood there, his back to the counter and a dishtowel in his hand. His eyes were hard, his jaw tight, and even if there hadn't been those tells, I would've felt the tension coming off him. He reached for a plate to dry.

He was here to check on me. I knew it was going to happen, and considering it was his job, I went back to washing. He continued drying until we heard the girls scream again from the other room. The screen door banged shut, and the girls spilled out into the backyard with Lo following. Vicky was out with the chickens, so for the moment, Travis and I were alone in the house. The television had been left on in the living room. The Kings were scheduled to play in the seven o'clock central time slot, but a different earlier game was currently playing.

"I'm not supposed to officially tell you this, but we found a trail," Travis said. "Similar families. An engaged couple with an adult child out of the house. All murdered in the same fashion, all with the telltale signs of the Midwest Butcher."

I went still. "Here?"

"The first was a small town outside of Kansas City, starting a path down here."

No...

"He's been doing a murder a day, but he took his time."

No.

Travis kept his voice low, and he turned toward me. "They're watching to see if he'll keep going. Maybe this was just a stop on the way."

"Was it?"

His chest deflated. "No. There's been no one since."

"Right," I said dully. "This was his destination. How many murders?"

"Does that matter?"

"How many?"

His lips thinned. "Seventeen."

Seventeen?

My blood ran cold.

"Families or people?" I whispered.

"People. Ten families. He's crossed state lines, so the Feds are coming in, but since you're here and there's no sign he's moved on, they're thinking he's staying put."

"Because of me?" I wanted it not to be true. I wanted it all to be a coincidence, even though I knew better. Even though I had already planned to run because I knew it wasn't a coincidence. "What if..."

"We're not overreacting," he said gently. "We're being cautious." He paused. "I gotta tell you some other stuff, and know that if this gets out, it could be my ass." A curse slipped from him. "A profiler did a workup. She met with Cameron Fowler on Saturday after all the murders came to light. We got her preliminary report today."

I'd stopped washing.

"Feds know it's bullshit what Fowler's lawyers are saying. He is the Midwest Butcher. His DNA was found at four other murder sites. He was smart, but messy in how he killed. He made a mistake. Your witness account was the one thing the Feds needed to catch up to him. I've looked at all the evidence. There were other things, too much to add up for a wrong-guy-in-the-wrong-place situation like they're saying. They also analyzed the new DNA his lawyers found, and it matches his, just not enough markers for an exact match."

"What does that mean?"

"That means the unidentified DNA belongs to someone related to him, which the state's attorney will annihilate by saying it was more than likely DNA he had on his person that transferred to the hatchet he used."

I ground my teeth. I liked when they were vague about what he used to kill people.

And about the other details.

"According to the profiler, she thinks he's a young male. White. Someone who was affected when the Midwest Butcher was captured. An event correlated in his life, bringing trauma as a result of the Midwest Butcher or because of an event that happened in his family, like a divorce around the same time. The profiler is leaning that way, thinking his mom was engaged, and there was another older child out of the house. Or that he was the older child out of the house when his parent and their significant other were murdered or died somehow, which left lasting effects on the boy."

I was still standing there, but my hands went to the counter. I held on.

Travis was gauging my reaction, but I wasn't giving him anything.

"She thinks he's alone, with few or no friends," he continued. "Probably attractive. People say he's a nice guy but not charming. They say he's nice as a courtesy, but if they think about it, they'll realize there's something awkward about him. She thinks he has a job that requires travel, like the Midwest Butcher did. Or maybe he lost a job and that spurred the beginning of these murders. They're looking for him to be originally from Kansas City or somewhere in Missouri. Considering the details he knows about the Midwest Butcher, what he did with the bodies, he's been in either direct or indirect communication with Fowler. Like maybe he was Fowler's apprentice."

"What did she say about me?" My nails scraped against the tile on the counter. There was a reason he was sharing.

"With the rate of his acceleration, she thinks he's working in a frenzy to an ultimate goal, one he needs to get off his chest before he can feel freedom. She thinks it's as if he's been tasked with a job, and he's not enjoying himself. These murders aren't for him, but for the Midwest Butcher, and the end goal is you." He hesitated. "She thinks he has his own method for killing, and you're not going to be killed the way the Midwest Butcher did his murders. She thinks he's going to take his time with you and use his own method, like you're a gift to Fowler, but also a fuck off too. Letting Fowler know that he's going to start doing things his own way."

My nails sank down, and one broke. I didn't feel it. "I'm a breakup gift?"

"In short, yes."

"And I *am* a target?"

"They asked ten profilers. Ten out of ten said you were a target."

"Why are you really telling me all this?"

He snorted a laugh, eyeing me. "You're taking this remarkably well."

He had no idea.

I slid my hands into the water so he didn't see any blood from my nail. "I've been under threat and a magnifying glass since I was twelve. Two men tried to kidnap me before I landed with Vicky and Howard."

"*What?*"

"Being threatened is nothing new to me. Hiding and living a very solitary life is not new. It's the other way that terrifies me." *Brett. His spotlight.*

"I'm not going to ask about Broudou." Travis' voice went flat. "He's protecting you?"

I thought of how he'd held me Saturday. How it was the first Saturday he got permission not to stay at the hotel with the team. How his cock sank into me that night, claiming me over and over again.

"*Mine.*"

How he'd continuously slid inside me through the rest of the week.

A tingle raced through me, up my arms.

"We're fine," I told him. "I don't need to be coddled. I may look tiny, and at times I get triggered, but I'm not going to fall apart." I stared at him, hard. "This is the warmup. The announcers are still talking about each team's chance at winning the game and giving their predictions. It's not even kickoff. I will fall apart when the last touchdown is made and that buzzer goes off, when I'm *still* standing and holding the fucking football. I need you to be my teammate, not my coach or my babysitter. And I need you to stop looking at me, wondering when I'm going to fall apart. I *can't*. You need to understand that."

I needed that from everyone because we had so much

farther to go. *No one* understood the full ramifications of everything happening. There were secrets.

More would come out.

"You're still on the investigation team?" My voice was hoarse.

Travis nodded. "Local asset. I know you and your family. I'm on the in-the-know team."

He'd not said anything to give this indication, but I had to ask. "Do you know who he is?" Shock showed before he masked it. "You do. They do."

"How the fuck—" He shook his head. "There's a person of interest, yes."

"Who?"

His jaw tightened. "I can't tell you that."

"Funny. That seems like the *only* information I should be told."

"Billie."

I changed tactics, hearing the resolve in his tone. He wasn't going to budge. "They can't find him?"

He didn't reply, but I got my answer.

They had a person in mind.

That was good. That was great.

A laugh bubbled out of me. I couldn't stop it.

"What?"

I shook my head, unable to hold back.

There was hope on the horizon. What if I was wrong? Maybe this was going to end soon. Maybe, just maybe, my heart would still be pumping when it did.

"What?" he pressed.

"It's just... If I'm his breakup gift to the Midwest Butcher, he's already lost. Fowler lasted so long because authorities had no idea who he was. He was only caught because I saw him. This guy is second best, and for a serial killer—that'll *piss him off* after he's caught. I almost can't wait to see his face when he learns he lost."

"He lost?"

I picked up the dishtowel again. "All serial killers are in competition with each other. You know that."

Maybe it didn't make sense to others. Maybe my words were insensitive, but they were true. This guy was already known, and he'd be caught.

He'd be beaten.

34

BRETT

One of the coordinators came over after the game. "They're asking for you in the press room. Coach said to go in and answer a few questions."

We'd lost against Chicago, and even worse, we'd lost because they got an extra field goal. We were lined up to either score or get our own field goal to tie, but our kicker missed. Still, the loss wasn't his fault, though he'd be blamed. It'd been a team effort that got us into that position.

But I was not the one to go in there, especially after a loss. What were they thinking, sending me in there?

Reeves saw me frowning in the direction the coordinator had gone. "You okay?"

"The fuck they want me in there?"

Stone Reeves and Colby Doubard were much better suited for this. It wasn't uncommon for me to still be on the field doing those interviews, while they'd shower and go to the press room. They were the better team spokespeople, though Reeves was hands-down better than Doubard. Colby typically gave shit answers and the sports channels spent half the next week deci-

phering whether he was being sarcastic or whether he truly felt
donkeys could play better than we had.

Colby burst out laughing. "Oh, damn. You piss Kim off
lately? She decides who does the press room."

Reeves glared at our quarterback before shaking it off and
lifting his chin toward me. "The kids are with my parents this
week, so Dusty is hoping to do a dinner Tuesday night. Want to
come?"

I shook my head.

Doubard groaned. "No, man. You gotta come. And we told
Dusty you're seeing someone. You gotta bring her too."

"I can't. Things are going on right now."

Reeves smirked at me. "Yeah. I'm going to tell my wife you're
coming, and when you don't show up, I'll play dumb. That's on
you, buddy."

I growled.

Colby laughed, patting me on the back. "Can't wait to meet
your woman."

Well, fuck.

No one wanted to go against Stone's wife. I was trapped and
everyone knew it.

I'd headed for my area of the locker room when I heard my
name shouted.

It was the same coordinator as before. He held up his arms,
a clipboard in one hand. "What are you doing?"

"I was going to shower, check my phone, and then go in."

"No. Go in now. You're up first."

"Why?" There had never been this urgency before. And
also, we lost. The winning team went first.

He turned, shrugging. "Just go. I don't know. I'm only told
what I'm told. Get it done, and then you can take off."

I still had my helmet in hand, but knowing Lawson, he'd
yell at me if I even tried to put it down, so I headed out with it
still with me.

Just as I left the locker room, Foreman, one of our running backs, was checking his phone. He looked up at me and froze. His eyes bulged out. "Shit!"

I gave him a look but kept moving. I'd decipher that later.

When I got to the press room, a spokesperson was at the microphone but waved me over when he spotted me. "Come in."

The room fell eerily quiet as I approached and took my seat. I was still in full uniform. Sweaty as fuck. As the spokesman stepped down, he gestured to my helmet. "Would you like me to hold that?"

"No." That was only for me or the people whose job it was to handle our equipment. I scowled at him, putting the helmet on the table.

A guy shouted from the back, "Brett, can you take that down? We can't see you."

Another reporter smirked. "Yeah, Brett. They want to see your pretty face."

I mean-eyed the second guy and glared at the first before I put the helmet at my feet.

Some laughter rippled through the crowd before a tiny beat of silence. I wasn't saying shit until an actual question was asked

"How'd you feel about the game, Brett?"

I leaned in and shrugged, then gave a polite response. "We obviously didn't do our best, but we put ourselves in that place as a team." Other players would go further and remark on how we'd learn from our mistakes and make the appropriate corrections for the next game. I stuck with the first reaction.

"Do you think your relationship with Willow Harm had anything to do with how you played today?"

I froze, my insides snapping to attention.

What the hell?

I searched for who'd asked the question, but the reporters

themselves were looking around. A bunch of phone alerts went off.

A buzz rose—shock, then hunger. I saw it on their faces, felt it in the air.

Anger rose in me, swift and fierce, but I was not going to lose my control.

I needed to repeat it three more times before I could focus on the next question.

A woman on the right side of the room asked, "Are you worried about Willow in light of the revelations that the Midwest Butcher is back?"

What. The. Fuck?

I sat back, scowling at the entire room.

The questions came in a flurry after that.

"Are you confirming you're in a relationship with Willow Harm, the Midwest Butcher's only survivor?"

"How long have you been seeing each other?"

"Did this start after the tripping incident?"

"Is Willow in danger?"

"Does this mean Willow helped put an innocent man in prison? Is the Midwest Butcher not Cameron Fowler? Has he actually been free?"

"Has he been murdering this whole time?"

"Why did he start up again?"

"Have you talked to law enforcement?"

"Are you worried for your safety?"

"How do you think this is going to affect the Kings?"

Kim shoved inside the door, her face pale. Her eyes were wide, panicked, but as she hurried to the platform, I shoved my chair back. We bypassed each other. Grabbing my helmet, I left and I could hear her speaking into the microphone before the door shut behind me, "No more questions will be answered. We'll have a statement within the hour—"

What the fuck?

What *the fuck?*

"Brett!" someone hollered after me.

I sent whoever that was a death look. A few others had started to follow me, but they took one look at me and scurried backwards.

I stormed farther down the hallway.

My blood was pumping and it was vicious.

It was out. Billie and I were out. That wasn't supposed to happen. We'd been discreet except for the first couple public outings, only once on purpose and the other two by accident.

Kim came running down the hall after me, the sides of her blazer flapping. "Brett! I didn't know."

I stormed past her, ignoring the looks from the team's staff, and went into the locker room. A lot of the guys were still there, glued to their phones, but at seeing me, they snapped to attention. Most took off.

"Brett, I swear I didn't know," Kim called from behind me. "I never would've sent you in there if I had."

I rounded on her. "You think I give a shit about you right now? This shit's out. That was just a taste of what Billie's gone through, and it's only going to get worse. I ain't giving you two fucking seconds of my attention right now, Kim."

She stopped in front of me, her chest heaving, her hair coming loose from her bun. "I—"

"Move," I snapped.

She jumped, darted backwards, and cursed before taking off. She went toward the elevator that went to administration.

Reeves, Bilson, Doubard, and Olvander were waiting for me near my locker. I skimmed the room. The guys who hadn't taken off were watching, silent, waiting.

Olvander was the biggest of the guys, his bald head still gleaming from the game. "Hey, man. This is the chick, huh?"

Bilson glanced his way.

"Yeah, man."

He held up his fist. "I'm real sorry about what she went through."

Dipping my chin up toward him, I met his fist with mine before I began changing. The shower would need to be bypassed until I got to Billie and got her home.

Reeves was waiting for me to finish. He tilted his chin up as I shoved down my shirt and reached for a ballcap, yanking it down over my head. "What do you need from us?"

"From us specifically or from the whole team," Bilson added. "Tell us, man. We'll do whatever you need."

Doubard ran a hand through his hair, flicking his eyes in the air. "Obviously we'll all shut the fuck up about this situation because none of it is our business."

"But ..."

My eyes shifted to the back, to whoever had said that. Foreman, the running back who'd probably just seen it on his phone when I was leaving the locker room, hesitated before rolling his shoulders back, thrusting his chest out. "There's a serial killer involved. This guy, whatever the fuck they're saying about him, is sick. He's connected to Broudou's woman, and she's connected to him. We're connected to him. Could we be targets? Let's be real here. We got families."

"You engaged?" Colby snapped.

"No." Foreman frowned.

"Anyone in your family engaged?"

"Not that I know of."

Doubard turned all the way around to face Foreman. "If you'd read the full article, you'd see engaged couples are being targeted. Now you just look stupid."

"Hey, man."

"That's uncalled for."

Reeves raised his voice over some of the other guys. "Right now, as a team, we gotta support Brett. The rest of your worries go to fucking PR. That's their job." He turned back to me.

"What do you need from us?" He raised his voice, purposively letting the team know he was also speaking for them.

While they'd been arguing, I'd grabbed my phone and checked the notifications. The world had gone mad. That's how it looked on my phone.

I ignored all of them, finding Billie's name and hitting call.

She answered after the first ring. "Hey."

Goddammit. Her voice said it all.

She wasn't sad. She wasn't falling apart. She was regretful. She was thinking of me.

"You okay?"

"Yeah." She sighed. There was noise on her end, but she moved somewhere. I heard a click, then the sound faded away. "One of his lawyers leaked everything. Feds are also here. They showed up an hour ago."

"What?"

"I'm sorry for what happened to you. We saw the interview. Roger got all pissed on your behalf, said it wasn't an interview, it was a press drive-by. He'd had two glasses of wine. To let you in on a family secret that's not a secret at all, Roger will use any excuse to have wine. You may now get to experience what we've lovingly nicknamed Wine Roger."

My lips twitched. *Jesus.* She was joking. She was thinking of me, feeling bad for me, and watching me on television. Her world was breaking wide open, and she was focused on me.

"I really want to say some things to you right now, but considering I got a decent portion of the team listening in, I better not. I wouldn't want to make their ears burn from embarrassment."

Doubard snorted before moving away. "The dude's joking. He's making a crack."

Olvander's big hand came down on my shoulder. "Tell your girl we're thinking of her. She's got our support." He left too after that.

Reeves stayed. He lingered until Billie and I ended our call. She was fine. She was going to be fine, but I needed to get to her because that was my job too.

No matter how she sounded, what she said, how she seemed, I needed to be at her side.

Reeves moved in as soon as I put my phone away and started filling my bag. "Bring her Tuesday."

I stopped. "Are you fucking serious? That is the last thing we're thinking about."

He held up a hand, a stubborn look on his face. "Bring her. She needs friends."

"She's got family. She's got a sister."

"She's going to need friends among the football wives and girlfriends. You know the deal. They have a group."

"*Not* the fucking time, Reeves. Christ." I shoved aside my impatience with extreme effort as I let go of my bag. "I'm not saying this to be a dick, but fuck off right now. The last shit she needs is dealing with what that group scoops out on a daily basis."

"Not that group. Dusty. Kayla. Emma." Emma and Kayla were Jake and Olvander's women. He held up his hands in surrender and took a step back. "I'm talking about them. They'll rally around her. She can bring her sister, and if she's got a husband, bring him too."

My chest burned. The need to get to Billie's side was the *only* thing I could feel in that moment. "I can't make any promises. This is a different scenario than anyone in here has dealt with."

"I get that. I do. We can be here for you and her, if you want us."

I stopped, studying him. I studied him hard, pushing aside getting to Billie, because this was important. Drinks with Olvander was the most I'd done with the team since joining. It'd been the same deal with my other team. I had acquaintances outside of the team too, but it was mostly buddies I could call on for a favor if I needed something. Vice versa as well. Getting friendly with the team just wasn't something I did, but Reeves had been trying and he'd been trying for a while. There was a different look in Stone's gaze today.

I slung my bag over my shoulder. "Maybe."

It was the best I could give him, and Reeves saw that. He jerked his chin before leaving.

My phone buzzed the whole time as I went to my truck. For the entire drive to Vicky and Howard's farm, my phone didn't stop making sounds. I was used to getting greetings, messages of support after a loss, and that kind of thing, but this was different.

This was insane.

This was just a *glimpse* of what Billie dealt with since she was twelve.

The thought of that almost brought me to my knees.

35

BILLIE

For all the chaos in the world, there was also magic. I didn't know how to explain it, to understand it, but as Brett drove up the driveway, it was there. Magic. A calm in the storm.

I'd felt it swirling around me with Vicky and Howard's concern, the way Roger took the kids to their house and Lo stayed behind because she didn't want to leave my side. When the news hit, the storm that was already brewing was just compounded.

Seeing the beams from Brett's headlights turning onto our driveway, a tranquil feeling settled in me. Over the week, I went through all the emotions. Numb. Being scared. Grief. Trying to run. Today, I was okay.

I was dealing. I was good.

It was Brett.

He wasn't the detective like Travis. He wasn't the one with military training like Howard. He was an athlete, but he'd grown up hard. He was like me.

I went out into the darkness with the house lit up behind

me. Everyone was up. Cops were still here, and a couple FBI people. They were all talking to each other, leaving me alone.

I knew they were watching me.

I wanted to get away from their eyes, but it was also Brett. He drew me to him like a magnet.

As he pulled up right in front of me, he held my gaze through the window. He'd not showered. He'd warned me about that, but he still looked delectable.

His lips curved up. His eyes warmed, and when he opened his door, I flew to him.

He caught me, and in the blink of an eye, he lifted me and his mouth fused to mine.

It was like this with us, every time. The same insatiable need for each other. We'd been starved of something that only the other could give.

He turned and sat me down in the passenger seat next to him.

His lips never left mine.

Moving his hand to the back of my neck, he anchored me as he took charge. Tendrils of lust pushed away any worry. Need pulsed through me, building with each throb. Growing. Rising. That hunger was almost its own entity, taking me over.

I surged up, wrapping my arms around his neck, pressing as close to him as I could get.

He groaned, resting his forehead to mine.

I panted a little, my heart racing. "Hi."

He flashed me a grin back. "Hi."

A light flashed behind him as the door to the house opened. Lo was coming our way, her head down, her hair tucked behind her ears. She glanced over her shoulder to the house, her bottom lip tucked between her teeth.

Brett rolled down his window.

"So they sent me out since you two were necking like

teenagers," she announced, rolling her eyes. "And also, ugh. Is that what I have to look forward to with my girls? I don't think I'll be able to handle it. Roger most certainly won't. He'll be pressed against the door every time the girls come back from the date, a fake rifle in hand. He's not a real gun guy at all. Though, that makes me love him even more. But anyway..." She stopped, probably trying to remember her original message. "Right. The two FBI agents are freaking out. They say they're stationed here to protect you. They want to know if you're going somewhere."

"I'm going to Brett's," I told her.

She looked over her shoulder. "I think they're going to argue with that."

No. "There's been no threat against me."

Lo shook her head. "There have been and you know it."

"The normal ones. Right?"

"There's one they're worried about. The Feds are still combing through the rest of Dad's computer. They wanted to take everything in with them, but he raised hell since he still needs that for work and stuff. So they're copying everything, but yeah, there's one standing out from the normal lunatics. I might've overheard all of that." She frowned. "Why are you fighting this? You know you're a target. All the profilers are saying you are. You, yourself, have said you are."

"Could they park outside your place?" I asked Brett.

His eyes narrowed, studying me.

Lo snorted. "They're going to have a conniption fit at that."

"Is that what you want?" he asked, but I knew that wasn't what he really wanted to ask.

I nodded, sighing. "Not in the house. Outside."

Brett turned to Lo. "They can walk through my place, see my system. I talked to Howard earlier. My place is safe."

She looked ready to argue but saw my face and swallowed

the protest. "Okay." She stepped back. "I'll tell them. Is it safe to send them out to talk to you, or are you two going to keep necking like you're teenagers?"

Brett chuckled.

I glared.

She noted my expression, the ends of her mouth turning up in a slight grin as she went back inside.

"I want to leave."

Brett's eyebrows rose. "Let's wait and talk to them. We can get a police escort to my place. Being safe isn't—"

No! I felt heat rush through me.

He paused, seeing my reaction. "What's going on?"

I shook my head, frustration settling in my chest. I knew what I should do. All the proper steps, knew what they'd say, knew their worries were valid. I'd lived this already. But there was a restlessness inside me now, and I was suddenly, so madly, so furiously sick of being this way.

Of being scared. Of hiding.

Of not living.

Of not being in the sunlight. Brett brought me the sunshine.

I just wanted to feel that warmth, his warmth.

What would that world feel like?

If I'd not gone to Jojo's?

If my mom hadn't—I couldn't go there.

"Just go," I whispered. "*Please.*"

The screen door opened again. The Feds were coming out.

Brett saw something on my face and clipped his head in a nod. He turned and yelled through his window, "I'll text you my address. We can talk there."

The first agent frowned. "Wha—"

Brett threw his truck in reverse, gunning the engine and swinging the front around like a drag racer, handling it as if he'd done this a million times before. He shifted gears, slammed down on the accelerator, and we were racing down the driveway.

A sense of freedom swept over me—the speed, his carefree handling of the truck, the wind from his window still open. It was irrational, but in that moment, it was a morsel of food after a lifetime of starvation.

A thrill sparked through me.

Brett was waking me up, in more ways than one.

We came to the road, and as if he was a pro, he braked and swung his end to the left. Almost without stopping, we zoomed straight ahead. We were out of sight before any headlights came following us on the driveway.

Brett watched in the rearview mirror, one corner of his mouth curved up.

He wasn't reckless. It might've looked that way, but his face was calm. His eyes were steady. He handled his truck with restraint, everything calculated for maximum control.

"We've got another three miles before cops will clock us for speeding," he warned me. "While I'm enjoying the random burst of teenaged rebellion, I'll need to slow down. Getting hauled in after a car chase would cause a certain publicist to have an aneurysm."

I grinned. "I know. Thank you for that, though."

"Not a problem. Care to share what bee got in your pants? Just so I'm on the same page."

I shared what I could, trying to explain it the best way possible.

After a little bit, he nodded. "I can get that."

"You've driven like that before."

He grunted. "It's called a controlled fishtail. Most have to rev their engine for maximum effect, but I figured a way to do it faster. I did a lot of crazy shit when I was a kid."

"Yeah?"

"Yeah. I'll tell you about it. Actually, I think there's a documentary that kinda covers where I grew up."

"Really?"

We were coming to the outskirts of the city, so Brett slowed to a normal speed. Once we hit the interstate, the phone started ringing through his dashboard.

Willy calling.

Brett cursed. "I gotta take this." He hit accept. "If this is about the news, I don't want to hear it."

The person on the other end was quiet a moment. "What are you talking about?"

"Nothing. What's up?"

"Uh... Okay. An update for you. The judge granted Shannon visitation."

Brett's mouth tightened. "Supervised?"

"Unsupervised."

"Shit! How?"

"Because we can only prove neglect. No abuse."

Brett's hands tightened around the steering wheel. "You told them about Sammy's protocol?"

"We did, and while the judge said he was also alarmed by that, there was no proof anything of that sort had happened."

"What the fuck does that mean?"

"They asked Sammy if a man had ever come into her room at night, and she said no. She said it was just a caution, course she pronounced it as a cahdish."

Brett shook his head, a slight grin showing before it was gone again. "When does that start?"

"Immediately. Judge said there's no reason to wait. Shannon's been acting like a good little parent. You know how she is."

"She's thinking of this as a long con."

"Yeah, but I'm also calling on behalf of Stevie. You guys play the Orcas in three weeks?"

"At San Diego, yeah."

"They want to come. Stevie, Georgie, Sammy. And they want my family to come with them."

"No Shannon."

"Of course not," the guy scoffed. "Georgie and Sammy might want their mom there, but Stevie has refused to have anything to do with her."

"Good girl."

The guy—who I was assuming was the half-brother—bit out an abrupt laugh. He wasn't sounding happy. "She's smart. I could see Stevie growing up with the mission of destroying her mother when she's older, and she's got the means to do so. And if Shannon does ever change and become a good person, Stevie may still move forward with her plan of destruction, just out of spite."

Brett shook his head. "She's got good reason. She's endured Shannon more than we ever had to."

"You going to tell me what you're talking about with the news? Is there something going on I should know about?"

"Nope." Brett raised his voice. "I'll have someone from the team reach out with tickets, and we'll figure out travel—"

"No. We'll cover travel expenses. We'll be bringing them. The tickets will help. It's almost impossible to get tickets to your games."

Brett's eyes narrowed. "You're going to stay and see me afterwards."

There was silence on the other end.

Brett let out a savage growl. "You're not fucking coming to my game, bringing my nieces and nephews, and not seeing me afterwards. You try that shit, Will, and I'll rip your head off."

"That went violent fast."

Brett growled again, his hands tightening over the wheel once more.

A sigh came over the line. "Yes," he agreed but sounding peeved. "We'll stay so you can see everyone."

"We're doing a meal."

Silence again.

"Goddammit, Will!"

"Fine. A meal. But we'll have to get a hotel room then."

"Even better. You can get a room at the same hotel the team uses. I'll have someone reach out to you with all the details."

"You don't need to do that."

"I don't care. It's done. Do not make other arrangements. We'll talk later in the week about the tickets and shit." Brett ended the call, rolling his eyes. "That was my half-brother. He's moving forward with trying to get custody of them so she doesn't keep fucking them up."

"She's out of prison, I take it?"

"She was in county, and yeah, she's out and raising holy hell. Will seems to be handling her."

We were almost to the exit for his neighborhood. The closer we got, the more relaxed I became. I rested my head against the headrest and turned his way. "You've not said much about this to me."

His eyebrows pinched down. "I haven't thought about it, to be honest. I'm just used to shouldering my shit and moving forward." He glanced my way. "You want me to share this stuff with you more?"

"I want to know everything about you."

His eyes were warm when he looked over at me again. I smiled back, feeling the sunshine again.

"I need to get some gas," he said, hitting the turn signal as we were nearing a gas station. "This place is lit up. There's usually cops hanging out there. Don't know why since I know they're usually busy. If they're not, would you feel okay stopping? Or I can take you to the house, come back myself. It's just easier for me to fill up at night than in the mornings."

I could see a squad car parked to the side. "We can stop now. We've deviated from our schedule, so I'm sure it's okay, even if he's watching us."

He. The killer.

At the reminder, Brett's face turned to stone. "Where I go, you go. You stick like glue."

I nodded. He made my heart flutter.

36

BILLIE

O ther vehicles were filling up when we pulled in.

As Brett got out, I went around to where he was and leaned against the side of his truck, watching as he fit the nozzle in the right place. He glanced over, the corner of his mouth lifting.

I mirrored his half-grin.

Would it always be like this? Where the world melted away? Where I felt lighter the second I saw him, like I could fly when he touched me, like I was off the planet when he kissed me?

My chest squeezed. God, I hoped so.

"What are you thinking?"

My cheeks warmed, and I bit down on my lip. "Nothing."

He grunted, his eyes darkening, falling to my lips. "You're lying."

My grin turned into a smirk, but a teasing one. "Maybe."

He laughed, reaching for the window washer and going over to do the windshield. I tracked his every move, hunger lighting inside me. His T-shirt was a little too small for him, and I was not complaining. No way. It showcased his stomach muscles, his bulging biceps, the thick, black band that went around his bicep. His beard was a little fuller. He'd told me once that he usually trimmed it before every game until play-offs. After that, he let it grow as long as they lasted, only shaving it after their last final game.

I liked the beard and loved how it felt, but a part of me wondered what he looked like with it gone. I kinda hoped he'd never fully shave it off.

The gas pump clicked off while Brett was still doing the other side of the window, so I returned the nozzle and closed the gas tank, following the directions and twisting so it clicked once. I was closing the outside shield when someone asked from my side, "Excuse me, ma'am. Do you have the time?"

The voice was polite but a little muffled.

I reached for my phone, pulling it out right before a dark shadow fell across me. A hand grasped my hand, and I froze, my eyes lifting.

He had a mask on. It was translucent, but it blurred what he looked like. Eerily.

His eyes were clear. They were so cold.

An emotion flashed there in that split second as we stared at each other. Then, we both burst into action. I opened my mouth to scream for Brett, and at the same time, he twisted my hand down and around, bringing my back against his chest.

He clamped a hand over my mouth, muffling my scream.

The smell was horrible, whatever was under his gloves.

I gasped, letting my phone go and grasping for his wrist, trying to get free.

But I couldn't. Black dots started to dance at the edges of my eyesight. I was going to fall unconscious. No. God, no.

Brett...

He had me against his chest, pulling me backwards. My body started to shut down. I couldn't hold onto him any longer and my hands fell. My feet stopped moving.

My body was going limp.

"HEY!"

He stopped, a curse came from him, and then I was free, but falling to the ground.

There was a thud.

Another.

They were fighting.

"Call 911!" Brett yelled, his voice savage. I'd never heard that tone from him. It was animalistic. I struggled to wake up, to see better, to help if I could. Brett needed me.

I tried sitting up, but everything swam around me.

My hand scraped against something and a dull pain pierced me. I fell all over again.

I tried calling for Brett, or for help...anything.

I needed to wake up!

You're safe, baby. I heard a soothing woman's voice inside my head.

"Mom?"

Someone came up to me, a dominant presence. Male. Definitely male. Strong arms swept me up, and I curled against a chest. *Brett.*

Something inside me uncoiled, and I gave in, surrendering.

You can sleep, baby. You're safe. You've always been safe.

That was my mom. I wanted to talk to her, to hear how she was, but also, why. After so many years, *why?*

Darkness took over.

A HAND SMOOTHED over my hair, a low voice crooning to me.

I knew that voice, knew that smell of lilac and lavender. It was the lotion she used.

Mom!

I opened my eyes. She was sitting beside me on the bed. So beautiful.

Smooth skin. Her eyes so clear and blue. A loving smile on her face. She looked healthy. Glowing. Her skin wasn't dry anymore—the reason she used that lotion so much. There were no stress lines under her eyes, around her mouth. No bags either.

She had laugh lines instead, like all she did was laugh, all she did was smile now. Even heaven couldn't keep the happy lines from forming.

"You're safe, Billie. He didn't get you."

I reached for her hand, but I couldn't touch her. She could only touch me.

I closed my eyes as she ran her fingers through my hair again before drawing away.

"Mom."

Her eyes were filled to the brim with love. "I'm so proud of you. You've endured so much, but you don't have to keep it to yourself anymore."

I frowned, not wanting to go there, not wanting to have this emotion with her. Not now. She'd been gone for so long. "Mom—"

"You need to wake up," she told me.

Muffled conversation rumbled from somewhere. Dark, angry, worried. Not angry—furious. That was Brett.

"I like him, but he's worried about you so you need to wake up. You can tell him, honey."

Mom started to leave.

I reached for her hand, my fingers sliding through hers. "Mom!"

"Billie, wake up."

"You need to tell me why, Mom. I have to know why."

She was fading.

She couldn't go. "Mom! Why did you leave me?"

She just shook her head, love shining from her face. "Wake up, Billie."

She said it again and again, her voice growing more firm. Insistent. "Wake up, Billie."

"Wake up, Billie." The voice changed, shifting so it was deeper, more masculine, and I jerked upright, trying one last time to reach for her. I crashed against a hard chest. A rough hand cupped the back of my hand, holding me close. "God, Billie. You're awake."

Brett.

Brett was holding me. Talking to me.

I clung to him, a deep sob working its way out of my core, up my throat. I let it out as I tipped my head into his chest.

She'd been right there. The answers were so close.

"Billie, you're okay. You're safe. You're safe."

It was Brett's voice, but they were my mom's words. I could hear her speaking through him, and I shuddered against him. Blinking, I pulled back, seeing more clearly. Feeling more clearly too. "What happened?"

It flooded back.

The gas station.

"Do you have the time?"

I repressed another shudder. The stench of death had clung to his hands.

"He used chloroform on you. I was almost too late."

"Did you get him?" I grasped both of his arms.

The regret appeared even before he shook his head. "I didn't hear a thing. I'm so sorry, Billie. The music from the gas station was so loud. He'd parked just behind us, to the side so we couldn't see his vehicle behind the post. He was starting to pick you up when I slammed him."

"You slammed him?"

His face was grave, his eyes haunted. He reached up, framing my face with his hands. His thumbs rubbed over my cheek, so softly, as if he thought I'd disappear. "I got him, but he dropped you, and I was worried you hit your head."

"There was a squad car there—"

He shook his head. "Empty. It all happened so fast. By the time I'd checked to make sure you were okay, he'd peeled out. Another guy came running over, so I yelled for him to call 911. I didn't know the cop was just inside."

"Did they do a search?"

"Yeah. He was gone by the time anything was organized. Shit, Billie. I'm so fucking sorry."

There was a knock on the door.

Brett turned to stone, his face hardened.

"Wha..." I looked at the door as it opened. We were in a hospital room. I could hear beeping in the background. A stale stench of disinfectant in the air.

Travis came inside, along with a woman I didn't know. Dressed in dark slacks, a blue coat, her eyes were bland. She held up her badge. FBI.

"Willow," Travis began, giving me a long and detached perusal.

He was here to ask me questions. I understood that, but I spoke before he could start the interrogation. To her. "Why weren't you at the house with the others?"

Travis stopped midstride.

The woman's eyebrows jumped up, and the two of them shared a look before she cleared her throat. She had dark hair pulled back in a wicked-tight hold. Dark brown skin, maybe five feet, eight inches tall. Slender build. Her blazer was tight against her body, showing the definition of her arms. She either lifted on a regular basis or did enough cardio to define her muscles. When Travis didn't say anything, she pressed her lips together. "I'm Agent Cardiman. Or Nikki."

"This is the profiler, Billie," Travis added. "The one I told you about."

She threw him a look before masking it. She wasn't pleased with him. As she stepped closer to the bed, her head tilted to the side. "I'm here to try to get as much information as possible about your experience." Her eyes turned inspecting, trained on me.

I shifted on the bed, drawing my legs up so I could turn and lean back against Brett's chest. She noted the sequence of movements, her eyes narrowing and her lips softening. They didn't smile or frown, they just weren't in a hard line anymore. Her eyes dropped to Brett's hand on my thigh, a strong and possessive hold.

Her gaze lifted back to my face, seeing that I was also watching her. A brief smile flashed over her face before it was gone just as quick. "You're comfortable around law enforcement." It was an observation.

I considered not correcting her, letting her have the wrong assumption, but instead I said, "I'm comfortable with Brett." That was all I'd give her, though the truth was that yes, I was familiar with law enforcement. That was it. That was *only* it.

She shared another look with Travis before her shoulders rolled up, back, and down. "With your permission, I'd like to take you through an exercise. You were so close to..." She hesitated. "...to our suspect, and while we've watched the security—"

My heart lurched against my chest. "There was a camera? There's footage?"

Travis nodded. "It's not super clear, but we got details."

"His license plate?"

"Out of range. He knew the camera was there. He waited until he was in the blind spot of Brett's truck."

"He knew Brett was doing the windows?"

Brett's body tightened. My hand dropped to his, turning it and lacing our fingers.

Travis watched that happen before he answered. "Yes."

"He didn't think I'd gone in to pay?" That question rumbled from behind me.

"No." Travis' eyes narrowed, the corners of his mouth turning down. "He watched you pay at the pump. He had a narrow window of a few seconds, and when Willow went to remove the nozzle, he moved in. It was his only opening, and he knew it."

"What does that mean?" Brett asked.

"That means..." Agent Nikki answered, moving so her feet were planted and slightly ahead of Travis. "He's smart. He probably figured he wouldn't be able to get to you again. That also tells us he was watching, most likely waiting for an opening. When he saw it, he took it. And he was willing to risk going against a professional defensive end."

"The slam was—" Travis started with a grin. But Nikki skewered him. He coughed. "I mean, he was willing to go against Brett."

"That means he wasn't worried," she continued. "He was willing to risk trying for you, that tells us he's confident in his abilities and that he could get away, which he did. He more than likely had an escape route planned ahead of time."

"Planned for the gas station? How would he know we'd stop there?"

Travis stepped up beside her, answering me. "Because we think he's been watching Brett as much as he's been watching you."

"And," Nikki said, "we think he either knew it was Brett's pattern to get gas in the evening or he has the ability to plan ahead. Serial killers usually only strike if it's within their script of planning. They control everything. The fact he couldn't have controlled what Brett would do means he's not a normal serial killer. He's either desperate or he's adaptable. A serial killer who's adaptable is even more dangerous."

"What were you saying about earlier, about taking her through an exercise?" Brett asked.

"Yes. We have the footage, and we'll get your statement, but there are more details we think you might remember if I take you through this exercise. It's to help open your other senses. An undertone of a smell you might not remember initially, or the fabric of his shirt. Stuff like that."

My mind was going back there at just her mention of it. "He's white."

Nikki nodded. "We assumed, but that's good to have confirmed."

All sorts of details flooded me now, things I'd picked up, but didn't want to remember. I didn't want to go back because somehow, I had a feeling that while she meant to take me back to that gas station, she'd end up taking me back to a bedroom, where I'd crawled under a bed.

I really didn't want to go back *there*, but I sighed. "When do you want to do it?"

37

BRETT

"You're going to need police escort when you go to practice tomorrow."

"Fuck that," I growled at Travis.

Detective Dickhead and I were now at my place, out at the guest house Callie usually used to study. We'd left the hospital once Billie was released. They'd checked her over, and because Billie wanted to do this while everything was still fresh—or most likely to get it over with—she'd insisted the two law-enforcement stiffs come to my place with us. Billie was now lying down inside, working with Nikki, while Travis and I were on the porch. There were a couple other officers waiting in the entryway so I could walk them through my place and show them the security system and upgrades I'd had done since meeting Billie.

Travis tried a different tactic. "Howard said you're getting a dog?"

"I'm still waiting on the dog. What the fuck does that have to do with a police escort?"

Dickhead bit back something before rolling his eyes. "You're in this now. He knows you're with her. He could try for you to get to her. You know she'd give herself up in a heartbeat if it meant keeping you safe."

"Again. How does that translate to me getting a police escort?" *Fuck.* I could hear my old high school buddies cracking up over this—me being followed by police for my safety. I'd been on the other side of something like this back then, the one doing my brother's dirty work—until he took it too far one time.

"You want to go to your job tomorrow, you'll be doing it with a police escort," Travis confirmed. "Otherwise you won't be going."

I was almost ready to throw down on this, but Billie made a sound from inside, something between a cry and a whimper. It was loud enough to penetrate the glass, and my attitude died instantly.

Travis turned to watch her too. "Do it for her."

I growled. "Goddammit. What if I got my own security?"

"That would work, but I got a call on the way over here. We've already reached out to the Kings, and they agreed to let police shadow you if that means you can make all your practices. They also approved having extra police around the stadium through the week."

My growl just got louder and deeper. Frustration pulsed through me. "Should've slammed the fucker better. Knocked him unconscious."

Travis bit out a laugh. "For what it's worth, the slam was impressive. You were worried about Billie. That's the only reason you didn't get a better hold of him. Also, don't be surprised if that gets leaked. It was epic."

I tossed him a dark look. He needed to shut up.

Sobering, his eyes cooled. "I'm just saying, if you want to be there for her and also there for your team, you need to expect some extra police around, at least until we catch him."

"Or until he fucks up."

"That too."

Billie made another sound, and every inch of me wanted to burst through the door and go to her, either stop the exercise or just hold her.

I wanted her to feel safe and only safe, nothing else—no fear, no worry, no more ghosts, because whether she knew it or not, I could see them. She was one of the most haunted people I knew.

"She's safe in there, and Nikki knows what she's doing," Travis said. "If there's something Billie can remember that will help us find him faster, she'll get it."

"She's a profiler. This is what they do?"

"This is what she did before specializing as a profiler. And because at her core, she's FBI. She'll do what she needs to find this guy. And a heads-up, we got your statement, but you were fighting him. She's going to press you again for anything you might've left out."

"I didn't leave shit out. He knows how to take a hit."

"You didn't mention that earlier."

"Just thought of it."

"See? That's why she's going to press you again. Tell me what you mean when you say he knows how to take a hit."

"I came at him hard, trapping his arms so he couldn't hit me with anything. After the initial contact, he loosened his body. He averted his head so I couldn't see his eyes, but it was more. He didn't want me reading him while we were fighting."

Dickhead nodded. "For a guy to do that, that kind of thinking—"

"He's a fighter or a quarterback."

He grunted. "Doubt he's a quarterback."

"Me too. So he has fighting experience, real fighting."

"A guy learns how to maneuver like that if he's gotten hit a hundred or more times. Mind and body are both conditioned by then."

"Shit." I scrubbed my hand over my face.

"Yeah." He sighed and turned away.

After a moment, he indicated that I should follow him. "Come on. Show us this fancy security system you got. Wow us so we don't need to be inside the house."

He'd thrown that my way as a challenge, but impressed or not, there was no way they'd be inside the house.

My system was flawless.

38

BILLIE

After Travis and Agent Cardiman left, Brett and I made a round of calls. The news would break in the morning, and we didn't want everyone to hear about it that way.

It was decided that I'd stay at Brett's while he went to work. His place was almost a fortress. Vicky, Howard, and Lo would take turns coming to me, and Roger and the girls would stay away until everything was sorted.

Lo had the first shift, bringing me everything I'd left at my place. My laptop. My printer. She also packed a large bag of my clothes in case this lasted a long while.

The next morning our phones started buzzing at four AM, and they never stopped. Brett got a call from the Kings, so he went in early, but only after making sure there were two squad cars outside.

Lo returned, and we sat in Brett's giant living room, watching TV. I'd propped myself in the corner of his couch with pillows, my laptop, and a blanket over my legs. Every channel was covering the attempted kidnapping. Lo was riveted, not by the terror of me almost getting taken, but like most everyone else in the world, she was riveted by the slam

Brett Broudou had given the guy to thwart the attack. I had to admit, I was too. Though I winced every time I saw my body lose consciousness.

The stalker had been about to lift me up, the back door of his truck open. It was idling there, ready for him. Then, mid-bend, Brett tore in from his side of the truck, a blur because he was moving so fast, and *wham!* The news slowed the video down, focused on how Brett was coming in, his head low, his eyes right on my attacker. His arms opened, and *slam!* He hit the guy square in the side, trapping his arms like he'd explained last night. My attacker was forced to let me go. Brett's eyes followed me as I slumped to the ground, but he somehow managed to get enough traction to lift my attacker in the air before slamming him down.

That slam was *everything.* It was violent. It was savage.

It took my breath away, and something deep in me, dark in me, stirred because that'd been by my man.

Mine.

I wanted to watch it on repeat.

Brett had almost broken the guy's head open on the asphalt. I wished he had, but the attacker tucked his head down so his shoulder took most of the brunt.

In the video, Brett wavered, seeming torn between going after the guy and checking on me. When I tried to sit up, he went to me, and in that opening, my attacker got away, though he was clearly hurting. He was gone in a second.

"God, I wish Brett had broken him in two." Lo shook her head.

I shivered, but it had nothing to do with temperature.

She glanced over and then did a double take. "You okay? You want me to turn this off?" She raised the remote. "I'll change the channel."

She clicked, but the next one was another news segment, and they were discussing the same incident. She muttered a curse, skimming through more channels, stopping on the sports network, which was also analyzing Brett's hit at the gas station.

Lo cringed. "Uh... Well, at least they're not showing your tripping clip. That seems to have finally gone away."

"Until *Dateline* does a show on me."

"Right." Lo cringed again. "I should try to make friends with hackers."

She was serious, and I started laughing. After a second, she started in with me, and then we couldn't stop. There was just so much tension to release. Finally, wiping our eyes, we were able to breathe again.

"I'm sorry about that," she said.

I swatted at her, chuckling. "Stop. I won't be able to do any work today."

She made a face, glancing at my laptop. "How are you working today? I mean..." She thrust a hand toward the television.

"Because I'm not Willow Harm on here. I'm Melanie Morning, and my clients think I have a normal life, which means no kidnapping attempts, no serial-killer fa—shit. I was going to say serial-killer fate, which doesn't make sense."

"Fate? You think you coming across the Midwest Butcher was fate?"

My throat burned. I refocused on my screen. "I need to work before something new happens and I really do fall apart."

Lo jumped to her feet. "This isn't your fate. This isn't some destiny shit. You lived. You survived—"

God. I stared at the screen, my throat scalding now.

Lo quieted. "Billie?"

I shook my head, my fingers shaking as I tried to type my password in.

I was denied.

I typed again.

Denied.

The burning sensation was spreading, moving down my chest, my stomach, my legs. I shoved my computer to the side and jumped up, starting to pace.

"Billie." Lo stood too.

I never fell apart. There were tears some nights, but when I was alone, when no one could hear. That was it. That was all I gave him. This new guy, he would get less than that. I couldn't control whether my arm would shake, or my fingers, but if I fell apart? I could control that.

"I'm fine," I said through gritted teeth.

"You can take a day, you know."

"No, I can't!" I yelled. "I can't, and you know it. If I take a day, then he got that day. And he might get another day and another. If he's watching, he's never seen me cry because of him. He's never seen me scared. I won't let him get off on seeing that power over me. I *won't* give it to him."

Lo's eyes were focused on my hand, and I looked down to find it completely shaking. Cursing, I tucked it under my arm. "I can't control that. I—"

"Maybe if you gave yourself a day, your body wouldn't react like that."

I stopped, but a surge of dark and nasty anger rose in me. "Fuck you, Lo."

"Excuse me?"

"You heard me. There's a hole inside my chest." I wanted to tear it out as I started toward her. "It's in there, and it's as big as an ocean. I can't take a day. I take a day, and I'll feel everything. I'll fall into that ocean, and I'll never come back out. I'm at the top, still hanging on. I am refusing to fall because there's no lifeboat for me there. There's no ladder to climb back out. I fall and I'm there alone, and I'm never coming back." I stared at her a moment, feeling my emotions rage. "He took my friend," I continued, "the only friend I was able to have. He took her dad. Her mom. Her siblings. And two days later—*two days*—my mom and brother were gone too. She—" I had to stop and catch my breath, my lungs were spasming so tight. "I don't know why it happened. If she was so shocked that she couldn't control the car?" My voice broke, but I forced it steady. I forced everything in me steady. "That week was the worst in my life, taking me into this new nightmare world, and in some ways, I've never left. This is just the latest shitty thing to happen to me, except this thing is shitty enough that the entire world once again knows how shitty my life is."

Lo stood silently, listening with tears falling down her face.

I made myself breathe in some calm. "I'm sorry. I didn't mean to unleash all of that on you."

Lo opened her mouth, but no sound came out. Her head dropped. She walked straight over and wrapped her arms around me.

Oh.

She held on tight as she whispered, "I'm so fucking terrified."

I reached up, putting my arms around her as best I could.

"I'm scared someone will kill Mom and Dad," she continued.

My hands flexed, holding her to me.

"I have nightmares that someone will find our house, and Roger will try to defend us because you know he will. But he's not a fighter and he'll get killed instead. And my baby girls..." Her voice broke.

I squeezed her as tightly as I could.

This was why I should've planned for this.

Why I should've run, no matter what Brett said.

That was all too late now. The only thing I had was regrets, and the only thing that could've stopped any of this terror from touching them was if I had left as soon as I legally could, if I

had lived with no family, no friends, and no loved ones that he
could take away from me.

I ached at just imagining that life.

"I'm so terrified of what could happen to them. If I'm taken.
If I'm killed. If they're..." She hiccupped through her tears. "I
can't go there. If I do, I will lose my shit in a way that I'll never
be able to unlose it. But Billie..." She pulled back, still holding
onto me. "I am absolutely terrified of losing my sister."

My hands trembled against her back. Her sister. Brett called
Charlotte, Cynthia, and Luna my nieces.

My family.

I'd fought so hard from letting them in that last wall, but it
was all for nothing now.

I loved them. They _were_ my family.

Lo kept going, not knowing my train of thought, "I don't
want to imagine what your life has been like, and I'm saying
that because I've done it. All of us have. Mom. Dad. Roger. You
have to do what you have to do to get through this shit. I understand that, but don't push to the point where something in you
completely breaks and I lose my sister a whole different way.
I'm not worried about some sick psycho trying to hurt you.
You're a survivor. You're going to survive whatever comes at you,
but you need to survive yourself too."

I sucked in a rattling breath and whispered, "I just told you,
I can't fall into that dark ocean world. I won't climb back out."

She shook her head. "That's bullshit. I'm obsessed with you.
If you go, I go. And if I go, Roger comes. Then the girls. Howard.
But Vicky will be the last, and she'll hold out. She won't go with
us."

A slight laugh escaped me. "You're right. She'd find a boat."

"Totally. She'd bring the Coast Guard to save all our asses."

"She would."

"See? If you go into that dark ocean, we'll make sure you'd
come back. And we didn't even consider what Brett Broudou

would do. Knowing him, he'd dive in under you to quickly make a raft so you never even touch the water."

I barked out a laugh. "I don't know about that."

"Or he'd try to punch into a different dimension. Maybe a different ocean. A pink ocean."

I shook my head. "You still call him Brett Broudou."

She blinked at me. "I do?"

I nodded.

"Oh." She finally let go of my arms, stepped away, and shrugged. "Well, I mean, a guy who slams your sister's would-be kidnapper to the ground is kinda legend in my mind. He was kinda legend already." Her eyes sharpened. "Don't let him know I said that."

She turned toward the hallway.

"Where are you going?"

"I need to do my sisterly duties and, you know, check out the place. I didn't get the chance after the hospital."

"You're going to snoop."

She raised her chin in the air. "Checking the place out. Snooping. It's all the same. Now, you going to be okay while I'm gone or do I need to stay and make sure I'm a lifejacket for you?"

I grinned, some of the tension easing, but that ocean was still in me. I didn't think it'd ever seep out. "No. I'm good. I need to work."

"Okay. Have fun working!"

I'd just settled in when my phone buzzed next to me.

Brett: How's the day?

Me: Good actually. Lo is snooping around your place.

Brett: Ask her to keep an eye out for a Mustangs jersey. I got that signed by Cutler Ryder, and after the move, I can't find it.

I smiled. It was easier and easier for me to do that. Smiling. Grinning. I hadn't done a ton of it before Brett.

Me: Will do. Is everything okay with the team? Why were you called in so early today?

Brett: They're worried. PR is having a meltdown, but the coaches and players are rallying around me. Reeves invited us over to his place for dinner tomorrow, if you want to go. I'm assuming no after what happened last night.

I gasped, almost dropping the phone.

Me: Stone Reeves?!

His text came in a few seconds later.

Brett: So you do want to go?

Me: Yes! Omg yes!

Brett: Now I'm wondering whether I should mention that Bilson and Ole will also be there with their wives. And Doubard might be too.

I was almost choking by now, but in a good way, the ocean long forgotten.

Me: OMG!

Brett: I should just always know this is how you're going to react. When push comes to shove, you're always going to be a football fangeek, aren't you?

Me: Yeah. Duh.

We texted a little more, and I was smiling almost stupidly wide when we said our goodbyes, but I needed to be Melanie Morning for a while still. After refilling my cup of coffee, I checked my emails.

That's when I saw it.

Everything went cold again.

The most recent one's subject line read: *You got away last night. You won't next time.*

I clicked on it, and there was only one more line in the email body.

I know who you really are.

39

BILLIE

I was sitting at the kitchen table, the email pulled back up on my laptop, when I heard the garage door lifting. It was a little after seven PM.

The door to the house opened a second later, and Brett called to me before he'd even entered the kitchen. "Babe!" He stepped in, saw me, and swallowed whatever he'd been about to add. He flashed me a grin, carrying a bag. "It smells delicious. What'd you cook?" He went to peer into the pot on the stove.

"Lo made chicken and vegetables."

He inhaled a whiff. "God, that smells good. Where is Lo?"

"I asked her to leave since you were on the way back." I watched him, waited until it clicked that something was wrong.

He turned to me. An alertness clicked into place. "What's wrong?"

My tongue suddenly swelled, but I shoved the computer back so he could see it as he came over.

As he did, his body tensed. "What the fuck does that mean?"

God.

My stomach was doing somersaults. "I don't use my real name for my work as a graphic designer," I told him. "I'm Melanie Morning to my clients."

"Okay." His eyes cut to me. "How does that work?"

"Most of my clients have found me through word of mouth, but he found me. He knows who I am." Frustration was building, threatening to seep out of me. "Work was the one area he'd never touched, that *they* never touched. I could be a normal person this way, but that's gone. He knows."

"Babe." Brett's hand came to my shoulder.

I shook my head. "I don't want to tell Travis. The more people who know—I'd have to give up being Melanie Morning to my clients. I just know it. Somehow they'd ruin that for me. Travis told me they think they know who he is. It wouldn't even matter." His eyes were fast darkening, filling with rage, but I was only half paying attention. My own panic blinded me. "They just have to find him—Brett?"

He was gone. There'd been a swift curse, and then he was gone. It happened so fast.

"Brett!" Panic replaced everything else as I shoved out of the bench, running after him.

By the time I got to the door, he was already through his main gate.

I ran across the courtyard to see him being held back by one cop while he shouted in the face of another. Two more cops came sprinting from another car—one was on the radio, the other had a gun pulled.

God.

No.

I ran to get between Brett and the cop. "Don't shoot him! Don't."

Brett bit back a curse, but swept an arm around my waist to lift me up and around him. "They're not going to shoot me. I don't have a weapon." He raised his voice so the cops could hear, would get the message.

One snorted. "You're a weapon by yourself, Broudou. Get in my face again, and we'll put you down."

Brett snarled, his face filling with rage, and he started for the guy again.

Now the other cops had their weapons out and pointed.

My heart threatened to stop any second. If even one of them pulled their trigger. "Don't! No," I pleaded on a scream.

I got between them again, my back to Brett's front. He bit out another curse, but again swept an arm out in front of me. He didn't move me out of the way this time. He held me in front of him.

"You shoot him, you shoot me," I said.

Brett started to try to lift me clear once more, but I held firm, staying between him and them.

A female cop made a frustrated snarl before yelling, "Holster your guns. Jesus. Put 'em away. Or switch to stun." She took charge, her voice rising. "What is this about, Broudou? You came tearing out of the house looking to attack us. We're trained—"

"I want to talk to Detective Dickhead." Brett had stopped trying to lift me away, but he was barely contained. His arm was like cement in front of me, and I held onto it, my fingers tightening around him.

"You mean Officer Dove? You have his number—"

"No. You call him. You can get his ass here quicker."

"And if he's in the middle of something?"

"Then I'm taking Billie, and I'm making some phone calls to old friends." His tone was ominous. "I'm not fucking around. Get him here, or I'm returning to my roots."

She frowned, not understanding that last statement, but Brett didn't care. He twisted, lifting me in a surprisingly gentle hold as he carried me back through the gate, hitting the button so it'd lock. When we got back into the house, he put me down, but only to bend in front of me so he could throw me over his shoulder.

"Brett!"

"Just easier this way." He took the stairs three at a time, going into his bedroom, where he set me on his bed. He disappeared into his closet, bringing out a bag.

"What are you doing?"

He put the bag on the bed, unzipped it, and went to his dresser. "I meant what I said. These fucks know who this guy is and they haven't told you?" He waited one second for me to affirm.

I nodded warily. "He wouldn't."

He pulled open the top drawer, taking out my clothes. He tossed them onto the bag, opening the second drawer. "That's what I figured."

"Brett." I reached for the bag, holding it to me. "What are you doing?"

He stopped, his gaze wild, his jaw clenched in a way I'd never seen before. He was *livid*. "We don't need their protection. I know people. You can disappear, and if this fucker wants to get to you, the only way is through me. If they don't share—"

"Which one are you going to call? Channing Monroe or Mattis Naveah?" a voice asked from the doorway, a strange voice that I'd never heard from Travis.

His gaze was hooded, his jaw clenched.

Brett's eyes narrowed. "Maybe one, maybe both. I know others too."

"That's right. You know all sorts of people. What'd you say to me again? 'I'm in the NFL Honors. Guys like to talk to me.' Or something like that? Am I getting that wrong?"

Brett grew still.

The tension in the room thickened.

"Who's the guy trying to kill Billie?" Brett asked.

Travis' jaw could cut glass. "That is information I cannot share, nor should I have said in the first place."

"Bullshit. You wanted her to know. You told her all about the profile. You wanted to share the details about the theory on who this guy is—"

"Profiles work. That's why we use them."

"So Billie gets to know all about this guy's fucked-up head, but not who he is? She's not given a picture in case something happens and she sees him before he sees her? Does he have computer skills? Is that in the profile?"

Travis' eyebrows dipped. His head tilted to the side. "Why would you ask that?"

"Is that in the profile?" Brett ground out.

He didn't answer at first. "Yes. We believe he has or used to have a high-level computer job."

"I thought you knew who he was?"

Travis' face was like stone again, giving nothing away. His eyes flicked to me as he answered me, "We have a name. We don't have anything else. It's not enough, even to you."

Brett seemed to know what that meant, but I didn't.

His eyes closed, and his hands balled into fists, one of them still holding a pair of my leggings.

"What?" I looked between the two of them. Neither would look my way. "What does that mean?"

Travis grimaced, raking a hand through his hair before he turned toward the hallway.

"Brett." I waited.

He wouldn't look at me.

"Brett!"

His eyes lifted, and a tsunami of anger, regret, and fear mixed in there together.

My voice quieted. "Tell me what that means."

"Don't," Travis warned, still not looking at me.

"Means he's government or he was government."

My heart lurched. "What *specifically* does that mean?"

"That means," Travis rejoined the conversation, his head turning to lock eyes with me. "He has skills that we're probably not accounting for."

"Thought you said he was a fighter," Brett remarked.

"It fits," he shot back. "He knows how to fight. He didn't engage with you because he didn't have time. Also accounts for why he was comfortable enough to even try at the gas station with such a short window."

Brett wanted to hurt Travis. I could see it in the way he watched him. That darkness was there, needing violence. I knew it now, seeing it on his face when he slammed my attacker to the ground. It was there on his face again, but lurking. Hidden.

I saw it because there was a part of me that could feel him inside me. My own darkness stirred, rising up, matching what was already in Brett. It was more than knowing how to handle himself or how to shove against a guy on the football line. This was deep. Did it come from his childhood? Or his own brother? He'd not gone into great detail, and I wanted to know. I wanted to know so badly that I could taste it, but yeah, whatever had created the darkness in him, I knew it was there because I had it too.

"Who is this guy?"

"Broudou," Travis clipped out. "I can't. It could be my job."

Brett went to a whole new level of scary. He didn't move a muscle, but somehow everyone in the room knew it. The hairs on the back of my neck stood up.

"A reminder here," he said quietly. "You guys want to find him. That's your job. Her job isn't being kept in the dark. She does not need to adhere to any of your rules. She has done nothing wrong—"

"He wants to kill her!"

"No shit. So give her a fucking fighting chance. Give us a name. Give us a *picture* of this guy."

"And if we're wrong? We could be destroying some guy's life if we're wrong."

"We won't say shit."

"I can't—"

"A picture."

"I can't! I don't even know his name. I just know we have a name. That's it."

I could barely breathe from the pressure in the room.

It was almost crippling, but I was with Brett.

We needed a name. We needed a picture.

I started talking, "I used to help out around the neighborhood when I was younger. Before I came to the Mitchells, but after that too. I wanted to make money, knew I needed to make money. Wherever I stayed, whichever foster home I was at, I'd go to the neighbors. Offer to mow the yard. Do dishes. Walk the dog. This one lady paid me to play cards with her granddaughter. Mostly it was that they took pity on me, I think. But I helped. Odd jobs. They paid me in cash. And no matter how nice they were, there was still a look in their eyes. Maybe at first they didn't know who I was, but it always got around. Foster kids whispered. That got to the parents, to the neighborhood, and then they were either scared of me—like what happened to me could happen to them—or they pitied me. They never took me seriously. Because of the way I grew up, I never really got treated like a normal person or a normal kid. Before Jojo's, people looked down on me and my brother. We were poor. Mom didn't want us to make friends. She said the less people who knew us, the better. I never understood it back then, but now, thinking back, I know some of that was because we were poor. She worried that because sometimes our meals were a little thin, someone would decide to take us away from her. She never gave herself credit for the love she had for us or how she made sure we had food in our bellies at the end of the night. She'd always sing to us. She had a real good voice. The way we grew up wasn't normal. I didn't know normal until I worked with Deandra. She didn't care about my past. Martell did, and he was cautious. Deandra always took up for me." My voice shook, just a little.

I took a deep breath before I continued. "She got me thinking I could do more than working in the grocery store. She noticed that I liked doodling on paper towels for my breaks. That was before we had all the technology available that we have now. And when we did, Deandra bought me an art tablet. It was over for me after that. Central Grocery were my first clients. It helped their business, so other businesses asked for my information. I chose at that moment not to be Willow Harm. I wanted a simple name, so I picked Melanie Morning." I paused. Both guys watched me with such intensity. "I've enjoyed being treated like a normal person."

Travis' eyes sharpened. "What are you saying?"

"He took that away this morning."

40

BRETT

She wouldn't sit still.

I wanted to stay home from the Reeves' dinner, but Billie wasn't having it. Once she found out about it, it's all she thought about. The FBI had taken her computer, so she'd spent the rest of yesterday and today using my computer to email all her clients, informing them she'd be changing all her contact information. She even took her website down, just to be safe.

"I'm nervous," Billie exclaimed now when I looked her way after the third time she'd shifted in her seat in the car.

"Nervous bad or nervous good?"

"We should've brought chili."

"Babe." We'd had this conversation three times today. "I asked Stone and he said no on the chili. He's just happy we're coming."

"Okay. That's good." She expelled a sudden and dramatic breath, pressing her hands to her stomach. "What if they're scared to be around me? That's a thing, especially now."

"They won't be scared."

"But what if they are?"

"Billie," I said softly.

She studied her hands at her stomach. "What?"

"They're just happy I'm coming. If there's any weirdness, it'll probably be about me."

"Wait. What?"

"I told you, didn't I? I don't have a lot of friends."

"And?"

I inclined my head, not really wanting to go there, but she was nearing the edge of inducing her own panic attack on something that didn't warrant any of that kind of stress. "So Reeves has been asking me over a few times. I went a couple times, but that ended this summer."

"Why?"

The reluctance was still there. Unmoving. I tightened my hold on the steering wheel for a beat. "How about we can get into my shit at some other point?" I slid a sideways glance her way.

It worked. She was fully invested in me, her cute little face puckered in concern. Her own worries were cast aside. She was fucking adorable.

She said, her eyebrows pinched together, her nose wrinkling up, "How about we get into your shit now. Why don't you have friends?"

"I thought I told you this before."

"Not having friends doesn't mean actually having no friends. There's always one or two. Right?" She was watching me, waiting.

I sighed, my hand relaxing on the wheel. "I got a few buddies, but I wouldn't call them friends. They're guys I know. We call each other if we need a favor."

"What about your half-brother? Or that guy who called you? I thought I heard you laughing."

I frowned, "Monroe?"

"Whoever he is. What about him? And your brother?"

The mention of my brother wiped everything out of me. I

was void inside. "My brother was a monster. He wasn't a friend to anyone."

Billie's head moved back, hearing my flat tone. She said, hesitantly, "No. I meant—"

"We're here."

We were pulling up to the Reeves' gate. Before I could roll my window to press their buzzer, the gate was already opening for us.

Well, there you go. Perfect fucking timing.

41

BILLIE

Olvander was the first to approach us in the Reeves' backyard, and normally I would already be in full geek moment. I wasn't. I felt off. I couldn't get Brett's words out of my head. That he didn't have friends.

He had buddies who he called for favors and vice versa.

That was... I didn't like that. I didn't like that at all, and he didn't want to talk about it. After he said it, I knew why he said it. He wanted to distract me, and he had, but he hadn't meant to say what he said. It slipped out.

But Olvander had an arm around a *very* beautiful woman. Dark brown skin and an angular face with high cheekbones. Kind eyes. Her braided hair was up in a bun set high on her head.

"Kayla, this is Billie," he said. "She let me cry on her shoulder one night about how I thought I'd messed up with you. Billie, this is my wife."

Sigh. This was totally a woman that I would have a girl crush on. Not in a sexual way, but in a friendship way. I'd crush on becoming a friend with her. I beamed at her, holding out my hand. "Hi. It's so nice to meet you."

A wide smile stretched over her face as she shook my hand. "If I'm to believe what Ole said, he received sound advice from Broudou's soon-to-be woman. That'd be you then."

Brett moved more firmly into my side, his hand on the small of my back, and I felt how the last of his tension melted. He was okay for now. I glanced up, sharing a look with him. We'd continue our conversation, but later. Not now. Now, as I caught the amusement in his gaze, he was letting me know that I could fully go into my geek-out moment. I plunged into that and my stomach acted like a rooster let loose for the first time in the hen house. I didn't know where to go, what to say, how to act, but I was giddy happy.

I also had a slight urge to hump Brett.

Kayla frowned at my silence, glancing to Olvander.

"Is she okay, Broudou?" he asked.

Brett let loose a hearty laugh, his hand pressing more firmly against my back. "She's a football geek at heart, so she's the opposite of okay. This is her adorable quiet because she's bouncing around inside of herself like a kid eating ice cream in a bouncy house. Give her twenty minutes before she remembers how to act normal again."

Kayla's smile was blinding. She linked her elbow with mine. "Then on that note, I'm taking over with Billie. You guys go and discuss how the grill works."

Brett and Ole shared a look.

Brett commented, "Beer?"

Ole grinned. "I'll show you."

I WAS SITTING at a table with Jake Bilson's wife, Dusty Reeves, and Kayla.

I was dying.

Not only was Kayla nice beyond nice, she was funny. She

was smart. And she wasn't fake. Neither was Emma, Jake's wife or Dusty. I knew about Dusty, since I'd followed her on social media, knew the effect she was having for ocean conservatorship and rescuing marine mammals.

Dying. I was so *dying*, in a good way. A great way.

I was still geeking out twenty minutes later too. Full-on. I couldn't stop smiling and saying, 'uh huh' to every question they asked me. At first, they were confused and then they found it endearing. Now they thought it was funny.

But because I had a lack of social skills while I was in my geeking out phase, the three women had been talking amongst themselves. Dusty finished telling a story where her little boy bulldozed into a neighboring football game, somehow got their football, scored on their endzone, and how both teams went with it. The one team tried defending against him while the other team, the one whose endzone he was running for, began helping to block him. His own team stood stupefied on their field, but the kids began cheering him on.

It'd been a whole thing, according to Dusty.

Kayla's eyes began shining with extra wetness, so Emma changed the subject, the first one cluing in on her reaction. She looked Dusty's way. "Is Colby coming tonight?"

Dusty reached over after noticing their friend's reaction and patted Kayla's hand. "You know, I don't know. He mentioned he might, but I'm not sure."

"Is he bringing—"

"Shhh..." Kayla nudged Emma, glancing at me under her eyelashes.

"Oh. Right." Kayla nodded.

Me. They were not saying something because of me. Oh no. I had to leave my geek-out phase. I'd been mute for too long. Taking a sip of wine, I stuffed all my ridiculousness down inside of me and coughed. I could be normal. I could. "Don't worry about me. I didn't want to interrupt the conversation, but I'm good now. What were you saying about Colby Doubard?"

All three stared at me. They didn't respond for a moment.

I looked around. "What?" Oh no. I'd let my geeking out go too long. It was weird now. Weird in a way where I couldn't come back from that. I'd messed up.

But Kayla flashed me a smile, the wetness in her eyes gone. She teased, "She says '*what?*' after sitting here for over twenty minutes when we've been forced to converse with each other."

"I—uh—what?" My neck got hot, and I knew my cheeks were probably flooded with color. "I just had a bit of fangirling to manage, over all of you. And your husbands, but not in the way you're thinking. I know all their football stats since they were in college."

They shared shocked looks.

"Yeah," I sighed, looking down at my lap where I curled my hands together. That was too much.

"Their football stats?"

I looked back up. "Yes." God. I hoped they didn't think I was geeking out over their husbands for other reasons? That was my worst nightmare. Or, well, maybe not my worst nightmare. "Stone had six hundred thirteen yards after catch. He was targeted one hundred eighty-four times last year with a hundred twenty-eight receptions. That was last year." I bit down on my lip because I could say more. I could talk all night long.

The women shared a look before Kayla leaned forward. "Billie."

I was still mortified. "What?" This was embarrassing.

Dusty cracked a grin. "*You're* the one *we're* intrigued about."

I frowned at her. Blinking. "What?"

Kayla was trying not to laugh and failing. "We've been trying to bring Brett into the group for so long, but you're the one who got him here."

I gave each a long look. "What?"

All three dissolved in laughter once again.

Kayla was shaking her head and trying to smother her mouth in her hand.

Emma, who'd I'd not spoken directly to yet, leaned forward across the table. "Brett wasn't going to come to dinner. Stone asked him more than a couple times, and all the guys have tried befriending him. Olvander's the only one who had success, but that's because they played together in Kansas City. Brett's a good guy and the rest of the guys want to keep him here. They don't want him leaving, but it's not just about the game. They want to get to know him too, and he has a wall up. Even now, he's got it up." Her eyes flicked behind me.

I twisted around. Brett was standing next to Ole, both holding a beer, and both talking. Stone Reeves and Jake Bilson were also there, but they were talking to each other. They weren't talking with Brett. I kept watching, seeing how Jake and Stone both would talk with Olvander. Their eyes touched on Brett, but he had shifted backwards. He wasn't totally in the group. He was putting himself in that position.

A pang went through my chest, and I reached up, touching the back of my chair. My fingers curled around it. No one should not have friends, even if it's by their own design. I'd know. That was a kind of loneliness that no one should know.

Feeling my gaze, Brett looked over. Our eyes caught and held, and I saw the unspoken question from him. He was asking if I was okay. My cheeks pinked again, and I gave him a little smile before nodding. He gave me the slightest bit of a nod back and lifted his beer for a sip. Olvander said something to him and Brett's attention returned to his teammate.

I turned back around, lost in thought.

Dusty cleared her throat. "We just want him to know we care. That's all." There was another note in her eyes.

"What?" I asked.

She blinked, frowning slightly before saying, "We—" She glanced to the other women as if drawing strength from them. "We know, obviously, about your situation." She rushed ahead, seeing me sitting straighter in my chair. "We don't want you to feel uncomfortable, but..." Her eyes closed, and she lowered her head.

She lost her nerve to say whatever she was going to say.

Emma said it, "Are you okay?"

Dusty and Kayla shot her grateful looks.

Emma added, "I can't imagine how people react when they recognize you, but we're not like that. As a human being, we want to make sure you're okay. Are you?"

The other two quieted, all waiting for my response.

An old conversation came back to me, one I had with Brett.

"People can get weird when they find out about me. You know about some of the more unhinged reactions, but there's other reactions too."

"Like what?"

"I once had a psychic who could feel him, and she ran away from me. Literally. She yelled over her shoulder that she couldn't handle the feel of death that hung over me so prominently. Imagine hearing someone say that in the mall, the looks I got. I didn't even know a psychic was there. That was the last time I went to a mall, no matter how much Howard likes their food court."

Of all people that could understand the price of fame, and in some circles, I was famous, it was these people. I could tell them stories. They'd understand. They'd probably nod in understanding or sympathy, but I didn't want to do that. I didn't want to talk about myself. Tonight was meant as a reprieve from my normal life, where the roles were switched and I could be a nobody around these new and very cool and very beautiful people because their fame wasn't like my fame. They'd earned theirs. They had adoring fans, people like me. They hadn't gotten notoriety because a serial killer didn't kill them when everyone else died around them.

It wasn't fun.

Dusty leaned over, her hand touching my arm softly. "You don't have to say anything, because in a weird way, we get it."

I didn't know what she saw to prompt her to say that, but a knot swelled up in my throat and I jerked my head in a nod. She gave me another smile before her hand dropped away. I caught it with mine, not thinking about what I was doing until her eyes lit up with surprise. I only squeezed her hand, the same softness that'd come from her before I let her hand drop.

I liked these women. A lot.

I wanted to be friends with them.

My voice cracked, but I still said, "I'm okay. Also, I don't just know football stats. I know chicken stats too. You know, if you ever want to learn about chickens." I pointed both of my thumbs toward my chest. "Consider me your hen lady."

There was a brief moment of confusion.

I asked, "Do you know who Sylvia Rivera is?"

That's when someone yelled out behind us, "We're here."

At the same time, all three around me stiffened with varied expressions of tension.

I took in their reactions.

Then I heard, "Oh. My. Gawd. Say that's not who I think it is?"

My heart dropped.

I turned around and two things happened at the same time.

One, I was rocked. Colby Doubard had arrived. A part of my inner geek wanted to start buzzing because he was the Kings' first string quarterback. He threw the football four thousand eight hundred thirty-eight yards last year, with thirty-seven touchdowns.

Oh yes. I was buzzing again, or starting to, but he wasn't alone.

The second thing that happened was that after the woman who accompanied Colby Doubard said what she said, she followed that up with, "Holy shit! It *is* Butcher Girl! I thought no way, but it is way. It's a sign from the universe."

Kayla had begun to stand up from the chair beside me, and this new arrival rushed forward, dropping into it, even before Kayla fully vacated it, and she gawked at me. Live and in person and three feet from me. Her hand went to her chest, to her heavily tanned skin that was showing because she was in a strapless dress, and she dramatically hunched forward. "You have no idea, but you and I were sisters from a past life. I swear to Mother Gaia."

42

BILLIE

The night had only started.

Dusty tried to intervene, but Doubard's date ignored her, shooting her hand instead toward me. "Goodness me. Where are my manners? I'm Brandi. How are you? Well, maybe don't answer that one. We all know how you're doing. Not good, right? I wouldn't be good if I were you."

She was beautiful. All the women here were gorgeous, each in their own way, but Brandi's beauty was forced. It felt brittle. She didn't have the natural glow like Kayla or Dusty. With long legs and slender arms, she was thin, but it wasn't healthy. Not like with Emma, who was also slender, but whose skin was a lovely cream. Both women were similar weight, but one glowed from the inside out and the other's glow was forced. Brandi's voice was husky, a sexy deep-throated sound that teased a slight Southern accent. Curly brown hair, green eyes. She had a little bit of a round face, and her makeup was done flawlessly.

At first glance, there was nothing that made her stand out from the other women.

At a second look, she was nothing like the other women.

Scanning around the backyard, it seemed everyone was

aware except Colby Doubard. He was holding tightly to a beer and scowling in the distance.

I shook Brandi's hand. "Yes. Hi. I'm Billie."

"Billie." Her lips drew into a wide smile. "God. I love it. Not Willow? Billie is such a heartwarming but hick-sounding nickname, isn't it?" She looked to Kayla and Emma for confirmation but didn't wait for it. "Tell me everything. You were, like, extremely poor, right? That's what the last documentary on the Midwest Butcher was saying. Did you interview with them? Do you get paid for that? How much do you get paid for each interview? Though, I suppose it's different with each one. I really liked the last documentary done on your life. They went more in depth about you and about, God forbid, what happened with your mom and brother. And no father? They never mentioned a father. Didn't your mom drive into a river? Were you in the foster system ever since then? Do you think your mom went into the river on purpose?"

"Brandi!" Dusty shoved to her feet, glaring.

I stilled.

She didn't notice. "The documentaries always say it was an accident, but they imply there was more to it. Was there? She was probably in such shock from what her daughter went through and wasn't paying attention. And your brother too."

"Oh my God." Kayla got to her feet. "Stop talking."

So still now. I was almost a statue.

She wouldn't stop. "I grew up with my grandmama. My mom, bless her heart, she gave me up to meth when I was twelve. The same age when you went through all your stuff."

My stuff.

My *stuff*?

Dusty yelled, "Shut the fuck up!"

Brandi wasn't reacting, like this sort of reaction happened all too often. "I've always felt that we were connected. You and me. We both went through similar things at the same age—losing our moms."

This was another reaction that I got in foster homes, at school, from neighbors.

I felt Kayla and Emma's horror. When I looked up, they were shell-shocked, and the old Billie—the person I'd been able to be when I got here, the fangirl, the awkwardly shy one, and the one starting to feel like maybe she'd met some new friends—that Billie shifted to the back.

I became Willow Harm.

I hadn't wanted to be Willow Harm tonight.

Then Brett was moving my way, and my body warmed, needing him, knowing he was coming to help in some way.

His eyes were stormy, his jaw tight, but Brandi preened as he stopped behind me. His hand went to my back.

I leaned into him. I couldn't have even stopped myself. My body jerked toward him, and he shifted, moving so his side was against me and I rested all my weight into him.

Brandi paid no attention to any of this, but she should've because Brett spoke, his tone flat, "Doubard."

Their quarterback's head snapped in our direction. He'd been in the back with the others, and they were all now taking in that something had happened. A dark look flickered in his gaze, but he stomped it down as he made his way to the table. "What's up?" He was eyeing the other women.

Brett's hand was solid on my back.

A little trickle of awareness spread down my back from his touch. It was pooling at my spine. It was waiting.

Stone moved closer. "Babe?"

Dusty seethed, "We're okay." He still went to her, and after a second, she leaned against him. He smoothed some of her hair back and pressed a kiss to her forehead.

"I'm aware this is more your friend group, but if you don't get your woman to stop talking to mine, I'm going to fix this situation my way. I don't think anyone wants me to do it my way." Brett's voice was low, but the warning in it got everyone's attention. His gaze went to Brandi and his voice matched his eyes as he said, "When I shut women up, I don't tend to be nice."

Doubard stood taller, his eyes filling with anger, but that glare was for Brandi. "What did you say?"

"Nothing," she clipped out, giving Brett a chilling look.

"No," Doubard barked.

I jumped, but Brett held me still.

Jake went to Emma's side, and Olvander stood next to Kayla, his hand on her hip.

Brandi gasped, then shrank back in her seat.

He rounded the table, coming to her seat. "I told you to leave her alone. I told you tonight was important." He took her purse, her phone, and he stepped back. "We're leaving."

"But—" she gaped, the blood draining from her face, before she looked around the group.

Everyone was watching.

"Colby, come on—"

"No." He held his beer out to Jake Bilson, who took it without a word, and Colby raked a hand through his hair. "I'm so sorry, everyone."

"You don't apologize—"

He ignored Brandi as she shoved to her feet. He finished, speaking over her, "—we will be leaving." He fixed her with a glare. "Let's go."

She didn't move. The two were in a heated stand-off.

Colby only raised one eyebrow, another kind of warning flashing in his gaze, before she broke. Muttering curses, she reached for her things, but he held them out of her reach, looking over her head again. "I'm so sorry again." His gaze fell to me for a moment, and he winced, before giving Brett a stiff nod.

Brett returned the motion.

The tension in the room lifted, almost dramatically, but Brandi was still trying to grab for her purse and phone. "Give me my things, Colby. Or I swear—"

His gaze fell to her, and that same warning flared again. "Finish that statement and we're over."

She pressed her lips together, a frustrated snarl slipping out.

His eyes held firm and narrowed, that threat not lessening, until she gave in.

The fight left her, and she warmed, pressing up against him. "Honey, what was it I said? I just wanted to get to know her. That's all."

He barely controlled his eyes from flicking up, but his hand lowered. He shared a last look with Stone before striding out of the backyard. Brandi was right on his heels.

Brett's hand stroked over my back.

That trickle of awareness that had been waiting spread to my front, and it turned into an excited flutter. And that began to warm me all over, including moving between my legs, where I began to ache.

A brief moment of silence followed in their wake, one that I paid no attention to, until Dusty cleared her throat. "Well, then. I now need a drink, and since I'm not pregnant, I intend to get drunk. Husband?"

Stone tilted his head towards her. "Wife?"

"You got baby duty tonight."

He chuckled, a promise of something else there that rang between the two, something loving, but also something exciting. "Sure, Dust. No problem."

She tipped her head back, a deep laugh coming from her. "I know what that means, but you're not deterring me. I'm drinking." Her eyes found me, sobering. "I'm so sorry for everything Brandi said. She," she winced. "It's her way with people. She thinks she's charming when she takes some of the darkest moments in your life and chucks them back at you as if they don't matter. I know I shouldn't say this, but I cannot wait until Colby moves on to the next girl."

"Dusty." Emma also stood. "I've decided that I'm also drinking." She said to Jake, "You also have dad duty tonight."

He grinned at her as she passed by him, her hand touching his chest as she followed Dusty to the bar. "I'll take dad duty any day if it means you're letting loose."

She tipped her head back, a very sensual and confident chuckle trailed out.

Brett slipped into the seat Brandi vacated, his arm resting over the back of my chair. He turned into me, blocking everyone else out. His eyes were heavy on me, making that ache start its own drumbeat. "You okay?"

Silent, I nodded.

His eyes darkened. "You need to go?"

Silent, I nodded again. That ache was growing.

His hand moved to my leg, sliding to the inside of my thigh, and held there.

We were both transfixed by the other.

My chest started rising and lowering, the need for him rising up, overwhelming me. I didn't understand it. I couldn't explain it. But it was there and I was feeling it, and Brett had picked that up.

His eyes fell to my mouth. I licked my lips. Slowly.

A deep guttural groan escaped him.

I was really hoping no one was paying attention to us. I had that fleeting thought before my leg twitched, closing Brett's hand between my legs, and that was enough.

Brett shoved back his chair, grabbing my hand. "We gotta go."

"But—what?"

I had no idea who said that.

We were fast heading out. I was trailing behind Brett just as Dusty and Emma were coming back with their drinks. I noted the margaritas and gave them both a thumbs-up. "Those look delicious."

"Where are you going?"

Brett looked over his shoulder, squeezing my hand. "We gotta go. We have a thing."

"A thing?" she repeated, confused.

"Yes." We were at the door in their fence and he reached for the knob. Turning so his back pushed open the door, he pulled me against him and spoke over my head as I was trying to still wave goodbye. "We got a text and we have to go. Thank you for the invitation. It was fun."

Her eyebrows shot up. "Fun?"

Emma started laughing, understanding. She elbowed Dusty, giving her a meaningful look.

We were stepping through the fence, just as I heard Dusty exclaim, "Oooooh! OH!"

Then Brett slammed the door shut.

I was pushed back against it.

And his mouth was on mine.

Explosions.

Those explosions were happening inside me, at the same time a barrage of fireworks were let loose, and there was the whistle of another bomb falling because I knew in that moment, as Brett was trying to devour me, as he lifted me in the air, his hands under my legs, and as I was molding every part of my body against him, that the bomb was me.

I'd been launched in the air.

So totally and so completely because I was in love with Brett Broudou.

43

BILLIE

A s soon as we were home and in the garage, Brett hauled me out of the truck. I was *drenched*, needing his mouth, his touch. I wanted his cock inside me, and he pressed me against his truck, my front against it. I gasped, my pulse pounding as he shoved his body against me. His mouth was on my throat, sucking me in deep, a desperate hunger coming from him, as his hands ran down my body, sliding to my front. My dress was shoved up to my waist as his hand dipped down, moving to my clit.

I moaned.

God, that felt so good.

A deep breath left him as he bit down on my neck. "You like my touch?"

His beard scraped over my skin, a torturous caress.

I pressed back against him, which made him moan. His other hand caught my hip, slamming us both back against the truck, and at the same time, his other finger slid up inside me. My thong was just moved aside.

He worked me over, his finger thrusting up. He kept going, a slow but steady rhythm, and he continued teasing me, his mouth making little nips at my throat.

An inferno rose inside me, taking me over. A hot, passionate twister made of fire that was *hungry*. I wanted all of it. Everything. I wanted every inch of Brett deep inside me, moving, claiming. A second finger slid inside, and my legs clamped tight. My hand moved down, wrapped around Brett's wrist, but I merely held onto him, needing a hold on the havoc he was creating in my body. But he only chuckled against my neck, his tongue continuing tasting me, until his fingers were moving so fast, digging in so deep, that my entire body seized in spasms.

Desire. Pleasure. Lust. All of it was mixing together in my body, creating the perfect sensual frenzy that took over my body. My mind was gone. It was only able to concentrate on the sensations Brett was giving me.

I broke, my entire body lifting up as my back arched. A guttural groan left my throat, hoarse and raspy.

God.

I panted, shivers wrecking me, but then Brett's body was gone.

He dropped to his knees.

His hands clamped on my hips.

"Wha—" I gasped, lifting up all over again as his mouth found my pussy.

His tongue slipped inside, and the first climax hadn't even dissipated before he was building another all over again.

"Brett!" I cried out, my legs unsteady. My whole body was shaking.

His tongue slid out, only to trace around my other hole.

I froze, but he just lightly licked around it before he moved back to my cunt. He thrust in.

One of his hands held my hip firm, keeping me in place as I was beginning to lose control of myself. "Brett, God." I cursed and moaned at the same time.

He pulled out of me, long enough to say in a deep command, "Hold, baby."

Baby.

Another shiver went through me, so delicious and addicting.

His tongue was back, and his other hand slid to my front, his thumb rubbing over my clit.

Another storm was building, rising, surging up, and I yelled out as my body exploded.

My release tore through me, and I was a mess, unable to do anything except pant as the waves pounded over me.

Brett was moving in the background, but I wasn't paying him much attention. I couldn't. I was still recovering from two mind-blowing orgasms. He picked me up, and we moved fast into the house, through and to his bedroom. My dress was whisked off. My thong was long gone, I had no idea when that happened. Brett was undressing, and then he gripped my ankle. I was tugged to the edge of the bed.

"Wha—" I lifted my head.

The lights remained off so it was dark, but I could see Brett wrapping something around my ankle. There was a crackling sound as my leg was suddenly yanked toward the bedpost and held tight.

"What are you doing?"

He moved to put a binding around my other ankle, the same thing. Both of my legs were now spread wide for him. I tested it out, but there was no give. I was laid out for him, and I sat up, my chest heaving and my heart still racing from the garage. I eyed him, as he stood in front of me, his own hunger coming out as he was breathing me in. All of me. All of my nudity.

He reached for his cock, fisting it, and he stroked it. A low groan leaving him.

His eyes met mine, and his flashed with intent. Dark

promises. "You were turned on at the dinner. What did it exactly?"

Surprise leapt in my throat, keeping me silent. I'd never seen this side of Brett.

His eyes were so dark, so alpha.

He climbed onto the bed, still stroking himself, and he knelt over me, rising so he was arched over me. "Hmmm, Billie? Little Billie."

A tingle raced through me.

I gasped lightly, not understanding my reaction at that name.

He noticed it, his eyes dipping down, trailing over my body. They darkened even more, sinful desire emanating from every pore in his body. His one hand reached out, cupping my breast, his thumb rubbing my nipple as his other hand continued to work himself. He bent down, his mouth falling on mine. I expected a hot, demanding kiss.

He was gentle instead.

My body began to tremble once more, but from the promise of what he was going to do to me.

A part of me was suddenly awake, suddenly alive. I was feeling in a way that I'd never experienced before, as if every part of my soul was spread out, wide open, claiming any and every bit of pleasure there was to experience. I wanted it all. Whatever Brett did to me, I would thirst for it and more.

I would yearn for this touch from him.

His tongue slid inside, rubbing slowly, purposely. He was taking everything from me, making it his own, branding me. He grazed against my lips, his beard brushing against my skin, before he lifted up so he could see me better. "Was it when I stood over you and threatened that woman for you?"

My body started to vibrate, low but steady.

He saw it, his eyes lighting up. "Was it that I moved in to protect you? Help you?" Bending back down to me, he moved to my neck, tasting me, slow and agonizing. I couldn't contain myself, my body was continuously quivering. Shaking. His words, how he was drawing everything out, how he had tied my legs apart, all of it was too much for me. I was close again, so close, just from all of this.

Brett lifted his head again, sweeping over my body. "I think I need to tie you up a lot more, Billie." His eyes flashed back to mine, and a slow grin spread. "Little Billie."

The tremors went up another level.

God. I was going to come again.

I'd never felt this before, not to this extent.

"Brett," I groaned.

"What, Billie?" He stopped stroking himself and moved between my body. One of his hands ran up the inside of my leg, ending between them and he dipped a finger inside me. He was watching what he did to me, how my body was responding to him, and he cursed. "I wanted to feel your lips wrapped around my cock, but I don't think I can hold out anymore." A second finger thrust inside, and he ground them as deep as he could go, his palm also pressing against my clit.

"Please." I panted, writhing on the bed, my legs unable to move anywhere. That was tipping me over, knowing I was powerless to him. I was here for his enjoyment, his viewing pleasure, whatever he wanted to do to me, but knowing he'd only make me explode, knowing we were doing this together, that I could trust him explicitly.

"Please what, baby?" But he pulled his fingers out of me and took his cock. He shifted up, closer to me, and ran the length of him between my folds. Up and down. Slowly.

I moaned again, falling back to the bed. My back arched.

"What do you want, Billie? Tell me. I want to hear the words from you."

I opened my eyes, and it took effort. This was sweet torture, and it was pure agony. "I want you to fuck me," I snapped, sitting up—and he slid inside.

I held still, holding my breath, because that felt so good.

He hissed. "Jesus. You feel good."

We both held still for a moment, adjusting to the feel of him finally inside me, before he fell back down to me, catching himself so his body didn't crush mine. He pushed me down to the bed from the motion, and his head turned, his mouth nipped my ear before he said into it, "I'm going to do delicious things to you. I'm going to tie you up. I'm going to bend you over. I'm going to make you scream until you beg for my cock inside you, and then we're going to do it all over again." He began moving inside me, and I bit down on my lip, trying to control myself, but my body was trembling from another climax coming so soon, too soon. He kept moving, a smooth glide of his body and dick, and he continued speaking into my ear, "That woman tonight was no one. No one, Little Billie. She was a gnat to you, to us. If she wasn't getting fucked by my teammate, I would've cut her down the second she dared approach you. You are mine. There is no limit to what I will do to protect you. No boundary that I'll adhere to. No law or territory or action that will keep me from violating, breaking, shattering, or destroying if it means that you are safe and you are at my side."

All his words, the intensity as he spoke, he was making promises that I was feeling in my soul. How all of that, with what he was saying, mixed with how he was thrusting inside me, branding the feel of him deep inside in my body, it was all too much and I screamed, my entire body jackknifing against him as my third climax tore through me.

"Baby, you are mine." Brett kept fucking me through my release. "There is nothing I won't do if it means taking care of you."

I couldn't speak. The ability left me from the ferocity of my last explosion.

Brett didn't seem to mind as his lips dropped to mine, and his tongue took control of my mouth at the same time, his cock began moving faster, deeper, rougher. All of a sudden, with a savage growl erupting from him, he rose, slid his hands under me, and he propped me up so he could hit at an even deeper angle.

Holy fuck.

He was going to the end.

"Brett," I gasped. "God. Baby."

His eyes snapped to mine at my last word, and he unloaded, coming inside me.

44

BILLIE

A phone was ringing, and I didn't want to hear it. That intrusion was not welcomed.

The cold blasted me as Brett rolled away, checking his phone, then cursed at whoever was on the other end. He was up and heading out of the room as he answered. "What is it?"

I sat up, reaching for my own phone.

Christ. An onslaught of memories came all at once. The dinner. Brandi. Then Brett, the extreme need I felt for him, and the rest of the night. I looked at the bedposts, feeling those restraints all over again. I had loved it. Loved the feeling that he could dominate me, that I would be in complete submission to him. He'd tied my arms down for the second round.

A delicious shiver went through me.

I was addicted to him.

My body already longed for the next time he'd tie me up, and how he would do it, but it was more. My heart was bursting. He'd stamped himself on every part of me, mind, body, and soul. I was his, whether he realized it or not. I was his, whether he wanted me or not.

I lay back down, letting myself remember the rest of the

night. We hadn't stopped. Brett kept taking from my body, and I gave it. Gladly. Completely. I stifled another groan, because my God, he could come back in here, and he'd be able to just slide right inside because I was wet. Then again, this was probably from the last two rounds, as I lay on my stomach and he took me from behind. I'd tried reaching for him, tried bending down so I could suck him, but he wouldn't let me. He said last night was his feast. I'd get to eat another night, and I was looking forward to that. Images of our very last round flashed in my head as I rode him, rising up over him, and as we watched the other the entire time, neither of us spoke the whole time, and I cursed, knowing, feeling it in my chest—back to my regular programming schedule of terror and murder.

I focused on my phone, seeing there were no new texts or calls. My family was still sleeping, no doubt, like normal people. Whatever had happened, though, I couldn't wait. There was an itch inside me, and it was growing, becoming more demanding.

Something had happened, something bad.

I slipped out of bed, grabbing the sheet to wrap around me.

Brett's voice was coming from his office, where he was sitting on his couch, one elbow resting on his knee and his head hanging down.

"What's he 'allegedly' saying then?" His gravelly voice ground out. He waited for their answer before biting out a curse. "Just fucking tell me. Should I listen to it and summarize for her or let her hear it?"

His head lifted, his eyes already guarded.

His mouth turned down. "I'll call you back."

Whoever was on the other end protested as he ended the call.

He didn't tell me anything, just held my gaze, and after a moment, I could see his suffering. He was hurting for me.

I crawled into his lap and took the phone from his hand. He

leaned back on the couch, cradling me, as I went through his call history. KIM KINGS PR was at the top.

"Kim is public relations?"

Brett nodded. His neck was stiff. His whole body was rigid under me, but I hit call.

"Billie—"

She answered immediately, her voice filling the room as I hit speaker. "Jesus Christ, Broudou. I'm not calling to ruin your day or Billie's, but what affects her now affects you, and that affects the team. We've taken a stance to support you. I need to know how to proceed. I'm getting calls from the press about this leaked call."

My heart had sank inside me, but now it swung like a pendulum. "What leaked call?"

There was a beat of silence before she sighed. "Thanks for the heads-up, Broudou."

Brett pressed his forehead to the back of my shoulder, his hand folding over my stomach. "Just tell her what you told me."

She hesitated.

"What leaked call?" I asked again.

"There's a report hitting the news today that the Midwest Butcher took a reporter's call, and it's going to be leaked."

My insides felt wooden. "Leaked?"

"It's leaked. It hasn't hit the news yet, but it's out there."

"Where?" I grated out.

"Brett?" she asked, a pinch of impatience edging in.

Brett reached around me to take the phone. He brought it closer. "Just tell her, Kim. She's been dealing with this shit all her life. You're not going to be the one to break her."

She was quiet again, and I didn't know this Kim person, but I wondered how often people talked to her like that.

"It's on social media," she said. "Take your pick. You'll be able to search for it and find it, and it's going to spread fast. Do you want me to tell you what he said or do you want me to wait for you to listen to it?"

Brett growled behind me. "Just find it and press play. You can listen to it with us."

I closed my eyes, shutting down in preparation. I was going to hear his voice again. I'd see his face in my mind.

But I wasn't going to let myself go back to that day, under the bed, seeing his bloodied boot stepping toward me.

I shuddered.

Brett's arms tightened around me. He placed the phone next to us and lifted me as he got more comfortable in the corner of the couch.

Cameron Fowler's voice came over the phone. There was some static, but his voice was clear enough. I knew it was him. "...I mean, this guy out there that's doing these new killings, he's not the real Midwest Butcher. I can say that because I know the real Midwest Butcher. He ain't me either. I've been talking to him since he reached out since I'm in here for his crimes."

A male voice asked, "You're saying you're in communication with the real Midwest Butcher?"

"Yeah. Sure am." He coughed, but I could hear his grin. He was enjoying this. "And yeah, he's got something to say to this new guy copying him."

"He does? What does he think of this new killer out there? Is he the guy you're talking about? Is he the real Midwest Butcher?"

Fowler started laughing, the sound high-pitched and grating. He was more than enjoying this call. "Oh no, no, no. That is definitely not the real Midwest Butcher. This new guy, he knows some of the Butcher's secrets, that's for sure, but it's because he *told* the new guy."

"So the Midwest Butcher knows who this new guy is? He's been in contact with him?"

"He knows exactly who he is, and why he's doing this. He's angry at the real Midwest Butcher. Angry and hurt. He feels rejected, but he's going about it all wrong. You see, there's something everyone's got wrong. He thinks it's time to clear it up."

"And what is that?"

"Butcher had been in that house just before me. There's new evidence that backs it up. But—"

"Mr. Fowler, what are you saying here?"

I started hyperventilating.

Brett held me tighter, a hand rubbing over my back in long, slow, soothing swipes.

I focused on that, timing my breathing with his motions, and then I was able to hear again.

"—real message from the real Midwest Butcher is that everyone got it wrong."

"What did they get wrong?"

Fowler didn't answer at first. "That the girl got it wrong. She saw me because I'd gone in there to check on the family. I was going to help them, but Butcher had already left. She must not have seen him. That's why she testified seeing me. She got the wrong guy. He's still out there and free. I'm an innocent man inside here. And since he's out there, if anyone were to do something on his behalf, he'd be real mad. It'd be his place to do something. Not anyone else's. No one else's."

The reporter was quiet. "Are you—are you talking about if something were to happen to Willow Harm?"

"No! No," he said sharply, before lowering his voice. "Just that if someone thought they'd be doing something for him, they wouldn't be. That's for him to do. He'd have to do something about *them*, and he said everyone could read between the lines with that one. He got a good laugh out of that."

I shoved out of Brett's arms and ran to the nearest bathroom, emptying my stomach in the toilet.

Brett said something on the phone before he came in, adding, "I have to go."

I was still bent over the rim.

"Do you want some water?"

I nodded, holding on as another round came up my throat.

He returned, setting the glass on the counter. He smoothed back my hair and sat behind me, his body blanketing mine. His head rested beside mine, a hand running over my hair and back before sweeping up for another circle. I lost count of how many times he repeated this motion until my stomach stopped seizing.

He reached for my water, handing it to me.

I sank backwards against him, taking the glass and my first sip. Then I waited. It felt good going down my throat, refreshing. When my stomach didn't clench up, I took another sip, and another.

But mostly I just sat there in his arms until I lost track of time.

His phone rang in the other room.

Neither of us mentioned it until he cursed and hit the door, shutting it, muting the sound a little.

"I can take a day off—"

I shook my head. "No. You'll get fined."

"Then I'll get fined."

"You're not taking a day off."

"Billie..." His arms flexed. He was about to launch into an argument.

"No." I was so tired, so weak. "No. I'm going to the farm. I want to be with Vicky and Howard. I want to hold Miss Sylvia Rivera."

There was exhaustion in my voice but also resolve.

Brett heard it and didn't fight. His chest seemed to deflate behind me. "Are you sure?"

"Yes. That call was leaked on purpose. He's trying to tell the copier not to move on me, but it won't work. He'll be even more determined now. I'm going to spend time with the people who love me. I'll be there when you're done." I turned to look at him but quickly moved away, conscious of what my breath must smell like. I leaned forward, hanging my head between my knees.

Brett continued rubbing my back.

"We'll sleep there tonight."

I didn't argue because as the nausea shifted aside, a new burn took its place. A scalding burn. Anger.

The Midwest Butcher. This new guy. Everyone else.

They wanted to break me? Well, fuck them.

No one was going to break me.

45

BRETT

I was leaving the stadium when I saw the detective in the lobby area.

"This is where they put the 'unwanted' visitors. You're not wanted. How's that feel, Detective Dickhead?"

He tensed, catching the extra meaning behind my words, before rolling his eyes. "Such a class act, Broudou. Like always."

"That's me. So classy and sophisticated, I've been to the White House three times."

He shook his head, some of his real anger flaring for a moment before he concealed it. "Does she know your past? Your real past? Does she know about your brother?"

This went serious real quick. I took one step toward him, knowing he'd feel the implied threat from it. "It was one of the first things she found out about me." I waited, seeing some of his anger slip out again. "Let's be clear here, Billie may not know every single bad thing I've done in my past, but she knows I have a past. She knows that if football hadn't come into my life, I might've ended up in a cell next to my brother. And guess what?" I flashed him a hard smile, a cruel one. "I still get to make her scream on my dick, every fucking night."

All the pretense vanished between us. He might've been here for his job, or some other reason, but he still wanted what was mine and he couldn't have her.

Because she was mine.

I raised an eyebrow. "I got the girl, Dickhead. When are you going to accept that?"

He scowled. I could see all the loathing, the disdain. It didn't matter what I did for a living, how much money I had, I was beneath him.

I almost laughed. "You just see me one way, don't you?"

"Yes," he lashed out. His nostrils flared. "I don't give two fucks what you've done with your life. You were a criminal growing up. It was in how you were raised. You were born to be a criminal and that part of you is so far deep in you, that'll never come out. You might be legal now, but you are still and will always be a criminal. She deserves better than you."

I stepped back, finally getting him to show his cards. He didn't say anything that wasn't true and in a way, I respected that. It was honest.

"We can agree on that, but she's better than both of us."

Surprise leapt in his eyes at my words, but they went flat again because I smirked, knowing it looked cruel, wanting it to look as cruel as possible. My tone taunted because by now, it was a conditioned response to this asshole. "Still doesn't change a goddamn thing because *again*, I got the girl."

He bit back whatever he wanted to say, and it took considerable effort. He grated out, "I didn't come here for this pissing match. I came to find out how she's doing. How is she?"

I narrowed my eyes, studying him. I wanted to see a crack, maybe a hint that he actually didn't care, but fuck this guy. He did. I wasn't sure when he'd finally detach from Billie.

"How do you think?" It pissed me off that he was coming to me, but it also would've pissed me off if he hadn't. Before he could retort, I said briskly, "Let's walk."

As soon as we got outside, I said, "She's at the farm today."

"I know. I called Lo."

So he'd checked up on her. "Why are you here then?"

"I need to run something by her and Lo said you'd be the one to ask for the most accurate barometer check on Billie."

I stopped abruptly, everything else instantly dropped. "You found something."

"I—" He gave in. "Yeah. We found something, but it's not much. It's not *enough*."

"What is it?"

"The name we had is a fake."

I waited.

He didn't say any more.

I raised an eyebrow. "That's it? Save your gas next time." I started walking.

He let go, staying behind. I got four paces before he said to my back, "We got a picture."

I braked. "You should've fucking led with that."

He shrugged, unperturbed, coming to pass me. "I'm leading with it now." Before I could ask, he held a palm up. "We don't have the picture yet, but it's coming."

"What the fuck does that mean?"

"Traffic cameras at four of the murder sites, and one near your gas station, all picked up the same truck—different plates, but the same guy. His face is covered in all the images except one. We're waiting for the last one to come through. It's got good quality, we've been told. I'm here to ask how to proceed with Billie. She made it clear she wanted to be in the know. Nikki approved that, so I'm asking your opinion. Do I tell her we have a picture coming or wait and see if it pans out into anything?" He hesitated. "I wasn't sure her mindset, considering the recent phone call leak."

That's why he was here. That was maybe the real reason he sought me out. "The call rattled her, but she's okay."

Some relief hit him and his shoulders lowered a little. "And the other thing?"

I chewed on it, but after seeing her reaction this morning to the call, I nodded. "Send the picture when you get it."

"Even if we can't get identification from it?"

I wanted to tell him no. I wanted to shield her from all of this, pretend none of it was happening. I wanted to pick her up, take her to bed, and not let her leave again until she was smiling and glowing and had that little giggle I loved.

But I knew my woman by now and knew what she'd want.

"Even if you can't see shit, you send her the picture." My phone buzzed, and it was actually a name I wanted to hear from. "Anything else? Any other realizations you've had over the last forty-eight hours that you need to get off your chest?"

He rolled his eyes. "Why are you such a pain in the ass?"

I smirked and began walking backwards, hitting accept on my phone. "We already went over this. Catch up. Because you're a cop, and I come from criminals. And also, because you have a boner for my woman, which *really* pisses me off." Then I pivoted, the detective forgotten and I raised the phone to my ear. "What's up?"

"Who was that?" my brother asked, sounding amused.

"Nice to know you'll always be a dick," Travis called from behind me. "At least you're consistent. Wait for your police escort too." He motioned toward the squad car parked in the lot.

I gave him the middle finger before unlocking my truck and getting in. As soon as I turned on the engine, I put my phone aside and waited for the escort Dickhead mentioned. They pulled into position and I eased ahead of them as the call switched so it was coming from my dashboard.

I replied to my brother, "Just some local pests. What's going on?"

Will was quiet. We'd had enough conversations over the last

month for me to know he was going to bring up something I wouldn't want to discuss. "Listen, you've not said shit about what's going on with your woman, but brother, we get the news too. You've been great about helping with this fight against Shannon, but if you need something from us—"

"I'm good."

"I know Budd's dead to you, and believe me, I'm learning how Shannon is the fucking reaper. You kill her and she keeps coming back to wreak vengeance. But you're not all alone. You and me, we aren't close, but I'm still family. Say the word and I'm there."

"You're helping Stevie, Georgie, and Sammy. You're already helping," I told him. "Can you imagine the alternative? Me having them here in all this?"

He sighed. "Yeah. I get it."

"What's the real reason you called?"

He bit out a harsh laugh. "There was something, but we can talk after your game."

"You sure?"

"Yeah. Stay safe out there."

I grew grim but bit out, "That's the plan."

46

BILLIE

The knocking started at four the next morning. Brett and I were in my bed at the farm. It was warm, cozy, and small. I didn't want to move, but Brett was the one who got up and went to the door. There was muffled conversation, and I snuggled into his pillow, breathing the smell of him in deep. It was almost ridiculous how much just the smell eased any little anxiety twisters inside of me.

His voice rose, saying, "Are you kidding?"

Annnnnd there went my momentary peace. It was time to get up.

My hair was a mess, and I was yawning as I made my way to the front area. Brett and whoever was at the door were outside, so I took a second to find my sandals. I'd pulled on one of Brett's Kings T-shirts and went back to trade my sleeping shorts for his giant Kings sweats. They barely stayed up, but I loved them. The waistband rolled over a few times, hitching them at just the right place before I slipped out the door.

Travis and Brett were on the patio of the guesthouse.

Brett looked over at me, a slight grin tugging at his lips, his eyes trailing over my outfit. He liked when I wore his clothes, and he really liked when I wore them to bed. There was an extra thrill in his eyes every time he stripped them off me.

This morning, right now, I focused on Travis.

He looked as if he hadn't gone to bed the night before. He wore a police-issued jacket with a bulletproof vest underneath. Wrinkled jeans. His hair stuck up in all directions, but his eyes sparkled with bags under them.

He was holding back a smile.

I stopped in my tracks. "What?"

"We got him."

My heart jumped up, but no... "What?"

He cleared his throat, his head dipping down. "We got photo identification, then we got his real name and location. We moved fast—had to because he was on the move again. But we got him. I was dispatched to tell you."

The door of the main house opened. Vicky and Howard came out, both in their robes. Since Howard didn't have a shotgun in hand and because Vicky approached us first, he must've checked to see what was happening before leaving the house.

"Travis? What's going on?"

He turned to tell them, and they both blinked in shock.

Brett moved to stand behind me, wrapping his arms around my front. I leaned back against him, my hands sinking into his arms as my knees threatened to buckle.

It couldn't be over.

There was no way.

That was too fast. Too easy.

"Who?" I croaked.

No way could this be done.

Travis tilted his head to the side. "It's true, Billie. We got him. We can place him in five of the murder sites, and I've no doubt that if we keep looking, we can put him at the others. His cell phone has pinged out here twenty-seven times over the last two weeks. And before that. We took apart his house. He had pictures of you plastered all over his walls, along with items taken from the other victims. There was a hair clip taken from Deandra and another item from Martell Hibbley. There's more that I can't disclose, but it's him."

Deandra. Tears burned my eyes. *Martell.*

"Did he have contact with—"

He nodded. "We've found letters. He'd been corresponding with the Midwest Butcher for the last seven years. There were details in those letters no one else could've known. In the last three letters to Fowler, this individual was becoming angrier and angrier. He wasn't receiving a certain approval that he thought Fowler owed him. That's how Agent Cardiman explained it to me. I can't disclose anymore." His eyes were intense before he blinked and they softened. "You're safe. That's the important thing here."

Safe. My hands tightened around Brett's arm and he held me closer, kissing my forehead, brushing a hand over me.

Travis faltered, seeing that. His face went blank.

"Who was he?" Howard asked.

Travis turned their way. "I'm unable to tell you his name, but it'll be announced later. The press finally named him. They're calling him the Copier Killer. We'll make an announcement this morning, saying we believe that we've caught the Copier Killer."

The Copier. It was an insult to any serial killer.

It got my approval.

"Do you guys have any other questions?"

Vicky let out an abrupt laugh. "My apologies, Travis. We're all just so surprised, and relieved. I'm sure as we process this more, we'll reach out."

He nodded. "You know my number."

I could feel their eyes on me, but I didn't say anything. There was nothing more to say at this point, not until we could get more answers. But I did wonder, was this how it had happened for others? They were waiting, half-living their lives, always waiting, and them *bam*, one day there was a knock at the door?

Did it happen like that?

"You're uncharacteristically quiet, Broudou." Travis frowned his way.

A short bark of laughter came from the chest behind me, his voice rumbling deep there. His hand smoothed down my side as I was still tucked back against him. "It's an abrupt change. Like Mrs. Mitchell said. Still processing."

"Okay." Travis skirted between all of us. "Let me know if you have more questions. Otherwise, I'll get going."

His foot scraped over the gravel as he started back to his vehicle.

A thought came to me, and I tore out of Brett's arm. "Wait. Can I see the picture?"

Travis nodded, his gaze locking on mine. "I can bring it out later, but I'm sure it'll be released at the press announcement. Feds like their presentations. They'll do a whole show to assure the public that we caught the guy and they're safe. The families of the victims are all being notified right now as well."

"But you'll bring it?" I pressed.

"I'll bring a copy."

"Thank you, Travis." Vicky reached out, touching his arm. "We'll let Lo and Roger know. The girls have been worried."

"Maybe we'll do a Sunday dinner again, after Brett's game so he can join?" Howard nodded in our direction. "You're invited, Travis. And Agent Cardiman. She told me at great length how much she liked Vicky's pecan pie."

"I'll let her know."

He didn't linger after that, but there was a moment of silence once he was gone.

I didn't know what to say.

I almost felt bereft. Like I'd been shorted from something.

Brett reached for me, pulling me back into his arms, and at the touch, at his smell and his heat, some of that empty feeling soothed away.

Howard spoke first, a slight laugh hitching out. "Well, damn." He scratched the back of his head as his robe started to loosen. "That's—that's—something, ain't it? It sure is something, alrighty."

Vicky snorted, tying it back up and patting his tummy. "I think you could've said that better, but I know there's no going back to sleep after that announcement. Coffee? Brett? An early breakfast before you need to leave for the stadium?"

47

BILLIE

They announced the arrest. Billy Haskell.

That was the name of the Copier Killer, and I noted the irony. His life was quickly uprooted. They found his social media, and suddenly people from his real life were doing interviews left and right. He fit Agent Cardiman's profile almost perfectly. A computer coder. Time spent in the military. Good looking, but also odd, according to what people were posting on his social media accounts. Caucasian. His father had killed his mother in front of him, and the timing happened when the Midwest Butcher was caught. Three towns away. It'd been a domestic abuse situation, but it didn't matter. A tragedy occurred in his real life at the same time.

There were too many similarities.

It was him, and I was still in disbelief.

More accounts were found from him that were dedicated to me. I'd only been able to stomach a momentary glimpse of them. There were pictures of me plastered all over those other accounts.

Things didn't happen like this, where it was wrapped up

with a neat little bow. Then again, because they knew me, I'd sentenced two people to death so maybe this one wasn't actually wrapped up with a pretty bow.

More would come out. It always did.

There was a brief knock on my door at the farm, and I called, "Come in!"

Vicky appeared, carrying a mug in her hand. "Hey-o. How's it going?"

She was being chipper, had been chipper all week, but she was also cautious. They all had been watching me, waiting for my freakout, but it wasn't coming. Or it was and I was in denial. I wasn't sure anymore myself.

I was desensitized to all of it by now.

I'd gotten a new computer with new accounts. My clients transitioned smoothly to the new ways to contact me, easily accepting when I relayed that there'd been a problem with my previous email.

Vicky took in my laptop, sliding into a chair across from me. "Did Travis get back to you about how he found you as Melanie Morning?"

I growled shortly. "No. He never brought over the picture I asked to see either."

"Oh." She sat down across from me, sliding my mug over. "I made you a cappuccino. Got that new machine yesterday, and it's a delight to make these."

"Thank you."

Her eyebrows furrowed. "That's odd, right? Or maybe he wasn't cleared to show you a copy?"

I shrugged. "I don't know, but he said I wouldn't get my old computer back. They're keeping it for the trial, just in case."

"That's frustrating."

"Yeah, but this time, I'm not that involved with the trial. Travis thinks I'll only need to testify about the attempted abduction, and I could do that on video."

"Well, that's something."

"It is."

I was aware of Vicky's scrutiny and knew she'd come over for a reason. Since the Copier had been caught, we'd gotten back to a routine, and that included coffee in the mornings if Brett and I slept here.

It was almost four on Friday, so this was something else.

"What's up, Vicky?"

She snickered, shaking her head. "You know me so well."

I gave her a slight smile back, just waiting.

"How's Brett with all of this?"

My stomach tightened, but I shut that down and shrugged. "He's okay." My tone was light, but I was lying. Vicky would know I was lying, but I was still lying. The truth was that I didn't know. After Travis' early morning visit, Brett turned quiet. I hadn't noticed, not then. Too caught up in my own turmoil, it wasn't until a few days later that I realized his silence.

"How's he really doing?"

I sighed, sitting back. "He's there. You know. In the background. He's being there for me." Which was the truth, but I didn't tell her how he held me in his arms every night with an extra tightness, or how there was a new edge when we had sex. Sometimes it was intense. Sometimes rough, which I liked, which I needed too, but as he was fucking me, there was a wildness in his eyes that hadn't quite been there before.

I flashed back to yesterday, how he'd taken me against the back of his kitchen door. My front was pushed against it, and he peeled down my sweats, his sweats, before he thrust up into me. Or how his hands braced against the door beside my head, pinning both of my hands underneath his as he pistoned into me.

Or how he reached for me at three this morning, pulling me to sit on his dick.

How he lay back, our eyes never breaking contact as he gripped my hips, watched as I rode him. How I felt he wasn't just looking at me, but he was seeing into me, seeing my soul. There was an extra frenzied emotion in every single one of those times, and a surge of adrenaline pierced me, just as I was remembering.

It was a two-way street. He was addicted to me, the same as I was to him.

My mouth started watering, and I needed to change the topic. "I'm sure he's processing, like me. Are you thinking about still going to the local VFW for Monday's game?"

Her eyes were sharp. I had no doubt she was aware of what I was doing, but she went with it. "I think so. Howard is excited to see his buddies. He wants to tell them about the Feds that were here. You're still planning on going to the game?"

The Texas Kings were playing the San Diego Orcas for Monday Night Football, and the game was in California. Vicky and Howard were concerned, though Vicky had been more vocal about it. This wasn't our first talk on the subject.

"Yeah," I confirmed. "Brett's got family coming. He's taking time to spend time with them afterwards. It's a big deal for him. I want to be there."

"But it's so soon after..." She looked down at her lap, where I could see her hands wringing together. "What if it wasn't the right guy? What if—what if he was framed?" She held up a hand before I could say anything. "I know. I know. That'd be a lot of details to frame because too many coincidences, but Billie, what if? Just, what if?"

I moved my cappuccino aside and reached over, taking her hands in mine. "Lo and Roger are coming with me."

"But—" Her chest rose. Her shoulders too. Fear flitted across her face. "I know. I know they're flying with you and sitting with you, and you'll be fine. And Brett's been so amazing, and you're going to be there for him. I get that too, but I just feel, right here." She pulled one of her hands away, forming a fist and pressing it to her sternum. Her hand was shaking. "I just feel something's still off."

It was too soon. I felt the same.

But the facts were starting to outweigh my fears. There was a very good chance that they actually had gotten the right guy, and with all the evidence... I needed to be there for Brett.

"We'll be smart," I promised her. "Travis is coming too."

Her chest rose again and held. Her eyes flicked up. She made the sign of the cross, which wasn't a motion Vicky made. I'd seen it happen three times since coming to them. She believed. She went to church, but she and Howard weren't ones to be vocal about their beliefs. They lived their values and preferred to lead by example.

They weren't showy or pushy.

"We're flying there on Sunday," I told her. "We're all staying in a shared suite. I'll take the farthest bedroom. Travis will be in a connecting room. I know Lo won't let me out of her sight. She'll even go to the bathroom with me. We'll be lowkey, only venturing out to go to the game, and right after, I'll be with Brett. I'm flying back with him the next day. I'll never be alone."

"I know, and you have your training, but we almost lost you. He almost got you. If Brett hadn't been there..." Her breath shuddered.

"We weren't expecting it," I countered. "We're on guard now. And again, it looks like they did get the guy."

Her hand lifted to her mouth, her fingers trembling. "I still just have this fear. Both my babies are going."

Both of her babies.

She'd said it before.

But there was a new shift inside me, and my heart started picking up speed.

Should I—but Vicky was saying, "No. You're right. Lo and

Roger will be watching you like a hawk. Travis too. And no one would mess with Brett." She laughed at herself before fixing a piercing gaze on me. "You stay safe and come back. Do you hear me?"

I heard her.

48

BILLIE

Lo and I wore matching airport outfits. That's what we called them. We were both in leggings, sneakers, and tank tops. I broke the mold with wearing a flannel overtop. If I got hot, I could wrap it around my waist. I also kept a ballcap on, pulled low over my forehead, and sunglasses. No one seemed to recognize me, even though I counted thirty television screens covering the Midwest Butcher and the Copier cases. My old picture flashed every now and then, the one they always used when I was twelve. There were two basic images that were used on a rotation. My school picture or the one where I was carried outside by a police officer, covered from head to toe in blood. My stomach churned every time I saw that one. I didn't understand why they used it—wait. No. I did. Shock value. The press had no regard for sensitivity levels among other people who might get triggered by that image.

The clip when Brett and I first met also had a surge in popularity. Me tripping. Him catching me. Me looking at him all starstruck and awkward. I still grimaced every time I saw it, but I was handling it better.

Lo commented on that as we settled into our seats on the airplane.

I shrugged. "I kinda have to, you know. Considering Brett..."

Understanding dawned. She nodded before flicking her gaze to where the two guys were sitting, the row in front of us. "That's part of the reason I was more pro-Travis."

"*Part* of the reason?" I teased.

"It never mattered, which I knew. One glimpse of how he looked at you and you looked at him, and I knew nothing I said was going to make a difference. You two are supposed to be. Anyone with eyes can see that."

I noticed Travis shifting around in his seat.

I was going to ask if he was okay, but the flight attendant came over to see if we wanted anything to drink before taking off.

Lo shot up her hand. "Don't mind if I do! And also, thanks to the B-man for giving us first class seats. I'm not usually one where money makes a difference, but free booze? That's a whole different level."

The people across from us snickered, but if I'd been worried about Lo bringing attention to us, it was baseless. By the time we were in the air and landing in San Diego, Lo got the entire story from the elderly couple across from us. They were going to cheer on their two granddaughters in a gymnastics competition. Lo lit up, sharing about Charlotte and Cynthia's gymnastics, and phone numbers were soon exchanged.

When we got off the plane, hugs were exchanged. Roger got involved, hugging them.

As soon as they separated from us, he asked, "Who were those people?"

Lo filled him in, and I pulled out my phone to text Brett.

Me: We arrived. How are you doing?

Brett: Good. You feel okay still?

Me: Yeah. No one could recognize me. I don't think, anyway.

I snapped a picture of myself, sending it to him.

Brett: You look good. *Fuck.* Those leggings. The first chance I could get, I'd be rolling them down your legs, pushing you against the nearest counter, ripping your panties off, and sinking deep inside you. I'm fucking hard for you right now.

My cheeks got a little warm. Lust fluttered in me.

Me: Brett...

Brett: What, Little Billie? Fucking what? Tell me.

My mouth watered, and I shifted as we were standing, waiting for Travis to grab his checked bag. Seriously. My cunt started to throb for Brett.

Me: Where are you?

Brett: I'm in a meeting with the team. If I wasn't, I'd be stroking myself and pretending it was your hand. Or better yet, your mouth. I want to feel your lips wrapped around my cock. I want to feel you taking me all the way, and as I sink down inside, as you'd lean down, relax your throat and I could go even farther. I want to violate you in thirty different filthy ways, all dirty and all delicious.

I shifted again, the throb growing. The back of my neck was heating up.

Me: I'd like that. All of it. I'd sink down to my knees for you, and I'd suck you inside my mouth. I want your taste, right now.

Brett: Christ. I want you right now.

Me: Me too.

"What are you doing?" Lo's voice came out of nowhere.

"Agh!" I screamed, my hands and phone flying in the air. Then I screamed for a whole other reason, because my phone! It was in the air, and I was watching it go down, where it was going to fall to the floor and it was going to break apart, and yes, I was watching it in slow motion, until a hand appeared and plucked it out of the air.

"This yours?" Travis arrived, his checked bag in hand.

I gaped, my lungs concaving.

He frowned at me, his eyes glancing to my phone's screen.

"NO!" I rushed over to him, grabbing it away. God. Had he seen anything?

I quickly looked. Something happened and the texts were gone. All my apps were pulled up, but my shoulders relaxed. Thank goodness. I quickly pulled up my texts.

Me: I almost dropped my phone. We're in the airport, about to head to the hotel. Pause this for now?

Brett: I was wondering if something happened. And yes. Me and my dick miss you.

Me: I miss you too. How are you feeling about the game tomorrow?

Brett: Guys are hyped. Everyone is saying Orcas will win —it's their revenge game from last year's Super Bowl, but that shit's not going to happen. We're heading in for meetings, then are doing dinner tonight and going to bed. I'll call you when I get to my room. Pick up where we left off? My dick's already excited.

Me: Okay...

Brett: ....? What's the ...? Don't leave me and my dick hanging. Him, not so much. He's at a full salute.

Me: Nothing. It's nothing. I was just wondering if I could sneak into your room tonight or you into mine, but we shouldn't. You could get fined.

Brett: Don't think that I haven't thought of that, but they gave me a roommate tonight. I'm going to kick him out while we finish our sexting from earlier so don't worry. We'll both end the night satisfied.

I chuckled, feeling a little better. He'd been quiet all week, but this Brett seemed like normal Brett. Some piece inside me clicked back into place, the one that had been worried about him.

"Stop sexting your man," Lo hollered, waiting for me beside our Uber. "Let's go, woman. We got a hotel to explore and a bar to hit. This mama and her man are on holiday, and we're going to introduce San Diego to Wine Roger. They'll never know what hit 'em."

Me: I gotta go. Lo is on the fun bus and I cannot miss this. I love when she and Roger both get on the fun bus at the same time. Love you. Kick ass.

I thumbed it off, not thinking.

It wasn't until later, much later, when I realized what I'd sent.

He never responded.

49

BILLIE

W e were in the stands the next day, slightly buzzed, and I was fully stressed from this game.

Or, we were very buzzed.

Okay. Extremely buzzed.

Drunk. I was drunk.

So were Lo and Roger.

They got drunk first.

Brett and I weren't able to finish our sexting conversation last night. He did reply later, but he didn't comment on the 'l' message I'd accidentally and completely hadn't meant to send, saying his roommate refused to leave. The timing wasn't ideal, but Brett wasn't a liar so I believed him, and some of the nerves there smoothed away.

Some of them. Not all.

I'd told him the 'l' word and his response was no response. No matter how I sliced that, it wasn't good.

But we were here and the game was tied, and I was back to stressing. I couldn't handle this. The back and forth. They were up. We were. They kicked a field goal. We did too. Hence, I was drinking. Travis was our sober bodyguard. Lo deemed him that title since the rest of us were already six beers in, and these beers were *big*. Roger went off on a whole tangent relating the depth and girth of the Orcas' beers to certain body parts. Lo couldn't stand, she was laughing so hard. The people in front of us heard Roger's tangent, which turned into a lecture (somehow), and that transitioned into a pep-talk, and by the end, it was a motivational speech. Almost every person around us listened to him, and as he stood up on his seat, his beer raised, twenty-three other people joined him in a salute to the mighty Super Bowl defenders.

We were Kings.

As the group chanted together, I got goosebumps.

Wine Roger was now Beer Roger. I forgot how beer affected him.

Someone from the Orcas administration found out I was here and offered a private box. I didn't think this was normal for the opposing team's fans, but then again, I didn't know. It was my first NFL game, much less the first one where I personally knew one of the players.

Brett hadn't mentioned the use of a private box.

I turned it down, to Lo's chagrin. It was for the best. Being in a box would've put more of a spotlight on me. Camera lenses would and did go there. I'd asked if Brett's family could use it instead of us, which quieted some of Lo's drunken whines.

Pun intended, which cracked Lo up so all was good.

Besides Roger's motivational speech, I wasn't concerned about being recognized in the stands. My outfit was excellent camouflage. Leggings. Ballcap pulled low over my forehead. Sunglasses. My hair was in a braid. Kings jersey. I'd wanted to wear Brett's jersey, but wondered if that was pushing my luck. But man, oh man, I was excited for when I could wear his jersey. As a football geek, I was salivating over the chance. Until then, I'd make do with sleeping in it, which I had last night.

Roger was the one wearing Brett's jersey. (His own. Not the one I slept in. I'd *never* surrender that to Beer Roger.)

"Let's go!" Lo surged to her feet, her new beer in hand, and her Kings foam finger in the air. "Come on, Doubard. Make some magic happen."

We were in the third quarter. Orcas now led seventeen to fourteen. Our offense was having a hard time getting yardage. The Orcas' defense was one of the best, which showed that their shocking rookie franchise trip to the Super Bowl was not a fluke.

The Kings were mostly running the ball. Their running backs were getting pounded, but they were inching the ball forward. We'd just gotten another first down.

"Doubard hasn't been able to connect to Reeves all night." Travis groaned.

"I know." I shook my head.

They snapped the ball. Lo started laughing as Doubard tried throwing again, but no one was open.

He went out of the pocket, and I shot to my feet, holding my breath because he was scrambling.

Combs, the Orcas' defensive end who was a nightmare, Brett's counterpart, went right at him. No one blocked him.

I was screaming, my beer long forgotten.

Doubard kept running, twisting, and—

"He's going for it!" Travis was up, yelling next to me.

I could breathe again.

The ball was passed to Foreman, and he got three yards.

These plays gave me heart palpitations. All the crushing and roughness until a play worked and then a magical opening appeared, and *boom*. The running back broke free and ran for it. I loved those plays.

We were on our third down and only gained two more yards. If they didn't make something happen with the next play...

Doubard got the snap, fell back, and launched it.

I was yelling. Travis was yelling.

It was gorgeous to watch, a perfect throw dropping to his chest like a baby to cradle. The defensive back assigned to him was behind by three yards. Stone had him. The guy wouldn't be able to catch him.

Thirty.

Twenty-five.

Twenty.

Fifteen.

Ten.

Five.

Touchdown!

The Kings fans in the stadium erupted.

Roger cried out, "Oh hell yeah!" and launched himself at us.

"Dude." Travis moved in, grabbing Roger and hauling him off us.

Lo was laughing, tears in her eyes, and she had to hold on to me. "I'm so sorry about my husband."

Travis was irritated, but catching our reactions, he shook off the anger.

It was almost mesmerizing to see how he could discard one façade and pull on a new one. Like discarding a shirt and pulling on a new one. So easy. He puffed out his chest, shaking his head, and took hold of Roger's shoulder. "Let's not cause any injuries here. Maybe stop fucking your wife's foam finger with your foam finger. We're trying not to attract attention, remember."

Roger laughed it off.

I glanced in Travis' direction, still grinning, but spying his face, that faded.

He was pissed.

A darkness flashed briefly as he shook it off, a grin flashing to me. I was startled. It hadn't been the first time I witnessed that from him. There was something underneath his cop exterior, and my gut twisted together.

I frowned, seeing him through a new lens.

I rewound through my interactions with him.

He was fine. Protective. Pissed when Brett had crashed our two dates, but the second one... I hadn't looked closely enough. Thinking back, remembering how he'd looked when he came outside and saw us, I now could remember darkness there too.

I'd been too caught up in Brett.

A bad feeling took root in my core. I wasn't able to shake it.

I wanted to, as Travis now turned back to the game, cheering as we got the extra point. Then we sat down while the teams switched.

This was my favorite part now, not my favorite part before I started boinking Brett. Before boinkage happened, that'd been when our offense was on the field.

Post boinkage, it was now.

Brett was coming out.

Travis checked his phone, reading a text, then leaned my way. "A buddy said the announcers keep talking about Broudou, how he's dominating the game."

They were right. Brett had sacked the quarterback three times.

The Orcas' QB was frazzled.

I wasn't surprised they were talking about Brett. *Good.*

"That's lit," I quoted Luna.

Roger overheard and cracked up.

Travis gave me a tight grin before focusing back on the game.

A little voice began nagging me, sticking to the back of my mind.

Neither team put any more points on the board.

Brett had effectively shut down the Orcas' offense, which

wasn't an exaggeration this game. He got to their quarterback three more times. Only one was a sack, but the other two forced the quarterback to throw the ball away. (Which wasn't allowed, but it happened.)

We were moving with the crowd when a security guard and an Orca staff person appeared through the crowd.

"Are you guests of Brett Broudou?" one of them asked.

Travis stepped forward. "Yes, we are."

Both the security guard and staffer turned our way, noticing me. Recognition flared in the girl's eyes. "We were asked to extend an invitation to come to the family section," she said. "The visitors have their own area."

Travis' hand came to the small of my back as he started to answer for us.

I stepped to the side, raising my voice. "That'd be great. You'll show us?"

She was eyeing Roger and Lo, who were...I wasn't sure what they were doing. They were giggling uncontrollably together, obviously intoxicated, but they'd stopped finger foam fucking each other.

I'd stopped drinking after that last touchdown so I was better.

But the security guard edged toward them.

I moved forward, taking both Roger and Lo's hands in mine. "They'll be fine. I promise. They don't get out much. They're parents."

Lo whispered behind me to Roger, "Quick. Do your donkey laugh."

Oh, God. I closed my eyes, preparing.

A second later, "HEE-HAW. HEE-HAW, HAW, HAW."

Lo and Roger dissolved in laughter.

"HEE-HAW. HA. HA. HAAAAAW-HEEEEE."

Ignoring them, I smiled at the security guard and staffer. "Let's go. Please."

50

BRETT

"Brett." Callie found me after the game, after the interviews.

"Hey." I just finished dressing after a shower. Putting my things in my bag, I pulled out my phone. "What's up?"

She looked around, biting her lip, hugging herself.

I'd told Callie a while back to steer clear of the house with Billie's stuff going on. It was for her safety, which she understood, but since then, we'd not seen much of each other outside of the usual physical therapy conditioning.

I straightened, giving her my full focus. "What's going on?"

"Can I..." She raked a hand through her hair, whipping it around. "Can I stay at your place for a bit?"

My eyebrows went up.

She cursed, dropping her eyes. "It's... I got kicked out of my place. I've been staying with my friend. You know, the one from Jack's, and well, that's not going so well."

"You what? You were kicked out?"

"I know. I know." She held her hands up. "I feel like such a loser asking, but would that be okay? I don't know what you've told Willow about me, but I can stay in just the one part so I wouldn't bug her. There's a small kitchen in there. I can totally make do. I just... I need some time before I figure out my next steps."

Callie made decent money. I knew she did, and she wasn't a big spender. She studied for school or she was working. That was her life, and I doubted she'd suddenly developed a gambling problem in the last month. This didn't make sense, none of this, but Callie was as much of a closed book as I was.

Maybe more.

Probably more.

"Are you okay?"

Her eyes jerked to mine, widening. "Yes! Yes. It's nothing like this. I'm still trying to save up money. If it's a problem, I don't have to—"

"Callie." She started to walk away, but I caught her arm. "Of course you can stay, but I have to ask. If something's going on, if you're in some kind of trouble, you can tell me. I might be able to help."

Her eyes fell to my chest, and she gulped before gently pulling her arm away. "I'm okay. Really."

She wasn't. She was as far from fine as we were from Texas right now. "You can stay, but you need to tell me what's really going on. You don't have to today. Tomorrow. Or even next week, but eventually. Just loop me in. You're in my house. You can trust me."

She gave in, her eyes swimming in tears as she nodded. "Yeah," she croaked out, tucking some hair behind her ear. "Yes. Okay, I will. Later."

"Okay."

My phone buzzed.

Callie edged back, gesturing to it. "I know you have people waiting for you, so I'll leave you to it. Thanks, Brett. I mean it. You're a lifesaver."

I threw her a look. I'd never go that far.

Willy: Where are you? Awesome game, by the way. We went back to the hotel.

Brett: It'll be a while. You're at the Rothchelton, right?

Willy: Yes. Kim from your team helped set up the family suite. She was very kind.

Kim was kind? *Kim?*

Brett: Why don't you guys do dinner and plan to meet up after that? I'll come to you guys.

Willy: Okay. They don't know you're coming. We didn't want them to get crushed if something came up and you weren't allowed to stay after. Your team travels together usually?

Brett: Yes, but I explained the situation to Coach. He okayed it. Give me your room number and I'll text when I'm getting ready to head your way.

Willy: *thumbs-up emoji*

I wasn't far from the family visiting area and could hear the buzz when someone yelled out my name. Glancing back, I came to a stop. "Mason Kade."

Still tall, but slimmer than when he'd played in high school, Mason Kade was one of the best wide receivers in the league—him and Reeves. He still was, even though we were both nearing the age where retirement was getting thrown around more and more. Most players at our positions retired long ago. As he got closer, I saw the exhaustion in his eyes.

It was a look. I had it too.

That's where our similarities stopped.

Mason always played football. He's always been known in football, and he went to one of the top teams right off the bat. But he went free agent and decided to move closer to where we both grew up. He was Fallen Crest. I was Rousseau. The neighboring towns had been rivals, and it was the same with Mason and his brother with my brother and myself. Enemies. That changed after high school. Things had never been copacetic between Kade and me, but I didn't particularly hold anything against him either. He and I had just been on opposite sides all our lives. Except after the Super Bowl last year, we went to dinner. It'd been a turning point, and since then we'd occasionally been in touch. I'd gotten a text from him a week ago letting me know they were thinking of Billie and me.

"Hey, man. How are you doing?" he asked, holding his hand out. "That's twice you guys got us."

I shook it, a nice sturdy handshake. "Good, good. And you know, it was a team effort." I smirked, which he saw and rolled his eyes while biting back a grin.

"Do you have people here? Sam came. She's hoping to see you."

"That's be nice to see her. My half-brother came today too."

He nodded. "Will, right? He went to Fallen Crest, didn't he? He wasn't in Roussou with the rest of your family."

"No. Different mom. He's still in Fallen Crest, actually."

"He is?"

I nodded. "Your wife's here?"

He shot me a look. "You're playing. What do you think?"

I grinned. If his wife had gone to my school, and if she'd never met Kade, there could've been a scenario where she and I might've had a situation. Beyond that, I couldn't say. She and Kade were meant to be, and that's how it was always supposed to end up.

We began walking together. "Billie's up there."

Mason ground to a halt.

For the first time, maybe ever, I saw Kade at a loss for words. "She's...here?"

I inclined my head. "They caught the guy."

"Shit, Brett. I—we, fuck. Sam's been—you don't know. You helped her once, and she's never forgotten that. I've never forgotten that. Now your woman..." Emotion I never knew Mason Kade was capable of washed over his face before he blinked a few times and swept it away. He cleared his throat. "We're here for you. Anything. You name it, it's done. I mean it."

I nodded. "I appreciate that."

"I mean it."

Now I started to feel things I never would've acquainted with Mason Kade.

"Tell the truth." I eyed him, half-smirking. "This emotion is more because we spanked your asses for the second time, right?"

He shot me a look, but the emotion was gone. His lip twitched. "Pretty sure I could still kick your ass."

"Pretty sure you never could. I'm twice your size, Kade."

"You're not that big, Broody."

"Speak for yourself," I countered, ignoring how conversations quieted when we walked into the family area. "I'm *always* that big."

Kade snorted, but I ignored him.

Billie was in the corner, and I only had eyes for her. I went right to her.

No one else mattered in that moment.

51

BILLIE

I thought Brett was a little nuts when he offered to pay for our rooms. The Rothchelton wasn't just any hotel. It was the definition of luxury for all hotels, what those hotels looked up to. This place catered to celebrities and the uber rich.

So, yeah. Brett was nuts.

We were waiting for the elevator as two other guests joined. Both men were in business suits, and considering the clientele for the Rothchelton, I'm sure these two weren't normal businessmen, but it took two seconds for their football fanboys to come out.

They asked for selfies.

Then autographs.

When the elevator arrived, they rode with us and wanted to talk football with Brett.

I tuned out, remembering the look on Brett's face when he came into the family section. Everyone had stopped talking because the image of Brett Broudou walking beside Mason Kade stunned people, but in the midst of all that, Brett couldn't give two fucks because he only had eyes for me.

He went right to me and hauled me in for the tightest hug, lifting me off my feet.

It took me a second to react and then I had my arms wrapped around him. He soothed something in me that I'd been ignoring, or trying to ignore. The booze helped today, it helped a lot, but there were still some nerves.

I loved him.

I told him.

It was in a text, and it was said without thinking about it, but it was still there. He gave me no response so was this my response?

I tilted my head back, trying to see him better, and when his eyes met mine, my whole body came awake. His eyes were dark, stormy, and *heated*. A shiver went down my spine, knowing what he wanted to be doing at that moment. Feeling it, his eyes flashed. His hand moved to my spine, as if he could soothe that shiver away, but it was one of those delicious ones.

Things happened after he set me back down on my feet, but it was all a blur. I was in a Brett daze. It was so strong that Lo and Roger were shooting me looks because I wasn't geeking out when Brett introduced me to Mason Kade, and then to his wife. Normal Billie wouldn't be able to talk. I'd be staring, geeking out inside myself, with the whole fangirl look on my face. Instead, I was cool, calm, and collected.

I was normal by most people's standards. Totally not Normal Billie.

Which Lo and Roger picked up on, but comprehension clicked when Brett and I couldn't move a foot without touching each other.

He kept an arm around my waist, or a hand looped in the back of my pants, or slid his hand down my arm to take my hand in his. If he wasn't touching me, then I was reaching for him. Always in contact.

At the end, my back was plastered to his front, and his arms were in front of me. One of my hands hung onto his arm with our other hands playing with each other.

Cue another one of *those* shivers.

I'd been having them the whole time we were in that family section. It was almost all I could concentrate on, barely hearing Lo and Roger excusing themselves when we got to the hotel lobby. They were heading for the bar.

Travis said his goodbyes even before we got to the family room, saying he needed to get to the airport. He was needed back in Texas so as Brett and I moved to the elevator, it'd been him and me.

We were alone, until those two guests joined.

The doors opened now on their floor, and when Brett didn't move, neither did they. He hit the hold button on the door and stood in front of me. I reached forward, my fingers slipping underneath his shirt, feeling his skin. His heat.

His voice dipped low, the beginning of a warning from him, "Gentlemen, I believe this is your floor, not mine."

They would've ridden all the way to our floor and accompanied us to our room, but Brett wasn't going to let that happen. The words were fine, but the tone was an assertive command. *Get off on your floor.*

Both snapped to attention, reacting to him instinctively before they could catch themselves. They hurried off the elevator, but as the door was sliding shut, one yelled, "Do us a favor? Switch to the Orcas when you're out of contract."

The other guy thought that was hilarious.

But then the doors were shut, and Brett slowly turned to me.

Oh, boy.

He dropped all pretenses of normalcy, and he was letting everything out now.

If there was a beast in him, it was out. It wanted to play. It wanted to do dark, dark things to me.

Big, burning, intense eyes. Ones that were back to smoldering and making my body feel all the sinful promises he had
for me.

"Brett," I squeaked, my body already vibrating with
excitement.

I took a step back as the elevator began moving again.

He moved in, looming over me. His heat enveloped me.

His presence filled up the entire elevator. The tension from
him kept rippling out, multiplying, building on top of itself
until I could see translucent tendrils curling in the air, making
the tension spike. The feel of that elevator shrank until I was
almost gasping, desperate for air.

He moved close, a hand to my stomach, and backed me
against the wall.

Pine drifted over me, surrounding me, and my nostrils
flared as I wanted more of that smell, more of him.

"Are you okay?" the words came out soft from me.

My entire body was writhing on the inside because I knew
what he was going to do to me, and a part of me wanted that,
but a part of me was scared at the same time. Brett was so
much. So powerful. He filled the room as soon as he entered it,
even if he didn't say anything. Everyone knew on a primal layer
inside themselves that he was dangerous. That he could and
would do whatever he wanted to. I'd gotten used to that pull
from him in a way, but this was on a whole other level. There
was an edge to him, a restlessness that he'd kept trapped inside
himself, that beast, and he was letting that wild part of himself
out. It was the first day that side of him was tasting freedom,
and all that intensity was focused fully and solely on me.

His eyes slanted, glittering with intent. "Okay? You want to
know if I'm okay?"

A new awareness trickled in, sliding down to pool at my
feet.

Something was wrong.

"What's wrong?" I tried to shove aside the nerves, the flutters, the lust that was swirling in me.

"Wrong?" His own nostrils flared and he took a deep breath just as the elevator stopped. "I'm going to show you what's wrong."

The doors slid open, and Brett bent down in front of me.

In the next instant, I was over his shoulder.

Then the world turned upside down, and I gasped. "Brett!"

He ignored me, stalking down the hall to our room.

He used the key, and we were inside.

The door slammed shut behind us as he didn't stop. He stalked inside the suite, to the bedroom, and ducked, throwing me on the bed

"Brett!" I sailed in the air before landing, then bouncing on the bed.

What was going on?

I needed to catch my bearings for a moment, but in that slight pause, his hand wrapped around my ankle.

I held still. What was he going to do?

I met his gaze as he was half arched over me, his beast trying to control himself.

I went still, a part of me knowing that in that moment, he was a predator. I wasn't scared in the way where I worried he would hurt me, but I *was* his prey. I knew it. He knew it. I was his to do with, to play with, to command, to give pleasure to, to become *drenched* with need, to fill with his release.

I was his.

But he was also mine.

I was breathing so hard, my chest rising and lowering at a fast rate. And because of that, I rasped out, in a clipped tone, "What is this?"

His eyes snapped.

That'd been the wrong thing to say.

52

BILLIE

"What is this?"

He repeated my question, almost hissing. Then suddenly, he pulled on my foot, dragging me to the edge of the bed. His gaze bore into mine as his hand slid up the inside of my leg, all the way to the top of my leggings. He slipped underneath my jersey, and his gaze flickered down there for a second.

He drifted closer to me, pulling me closer to him at the same time where I was only a few inches from the end. My leg was still propped up on the end of the bed, he leaned down, draping his arm around my knee, holding me anchored there for him.

His eyes went back to mine, and I was pierced all over again. The storm in his gaze was moving around, twisting. He was not happy, but as if following my train of thought, he ground against me. He would've been in me if our clothes were gone.

I bit down on my lip, holding back a moan.

"You feel that?" He'd started rolling my leggings down at the top, but he paused, his one hand sliding down my leg, wrapping it around his waist, plastering my cunt against his dick, and he rocked into me.

I sucked in some air. That felt *so good.*

"I've been hard for you ever since you sent me that little text yesterday."

He kept rolling his hips so a whole new cloud of pleasure was taking me over, so it took a little bit before his words penetrated.

Wait.

My text?

I opened my eyes—when had I closed them?—he was glaring back down at me, his face right over mine.

My text...

Oh, dear God.

My text.

I gulped. "Brett—" I tried to sit up, but he took my hands, both of them, and pinned me in place, lying down on me. My hands were pinned beside me, and he began grinding into me, going slow, going purposeful, going at a rate that was tortuous.

I was burning up. Wanting. He wasn't giving me what I wanted, but I still swallowed, waiting for him.

"Love you. Kick ass," he clipped out. "That's what you sent me. At the end of a text. When I was already rock hard and trying to keep from losing my shit and storming out of there, hunting you down, and bending you over the nearest counter so I could sink in, knowing your pussy was built only for me. And you send those words to me? 'Love you. Kick ass.'"

He was angry.

My chest deflated.

I started to try to pull my hands out from his, but I couldn't move. At all.

He drew back, then thrust back against me, his eyes glazing over for a second before they grew alert once again. His fury crystal fucking clear. "You love me?"

He was still grinding into me, and I forgot all about needing to get away.

Back to panting.

Back to only feeling those sensations he was building in my body.

"Brett, please," I whimpered, moving back against him and moving with a rush. Yearning for more.

"I asked you a question." He stopped, breathing harshly over me. "Do you love me?"

My eyes snapped back to his.

He was serious. He was asking me.

At seeing something in me, his whole demeanor softened. He let go of one of my hands, his thumb pressing gently against my bottom lip, rubbing it before falling away. He also softened his tone, asking again, "Do you love me, Billie?"

Fear filled up my chest, and it filled and filled and it kept filling. The pressure there building until I knew it was only a matter of time before I'd break open.

"Yes," I whispered, the word detonating a dam inside me. All the emotions that'd been rising burst free, and I was saying it, saying it in a rush as if to save my soul, "Yes. I don't know when it happened. I don't. Maybe when you caught me from falling, let me ramble about Miss Sylvia Rivera, took me to goat yoga, or when you held me in your arms surrounded by bikers protecting us, or you started following Nellie Bly around and she didn't know what to do. Or Jesus, maybe it was all the fucking orgasms you gave me and we had to stop one time because I was losing my voice from all the screaming. Or I don't know, maybe because you brought the sunshine back. And I know that as long as you're standing next to me, I'll only feel the sunshine. No matter how dark it might get. I don't care if you don't want to hear it." Tears were sliding down my cheek by now, and I was *not* meeting his gaze. I couldn't. I'd shatter when he'd pull away from me.

Why I thought he'd do that, I wasn't sure.

But he would. I was so very sure of that.

He couldn't love me. He was angry I'd told him. I had changed everything when I sent that text.

"I'm sorry. I'm so sorry." More tears slid down. I needed to get away. Both of my hands were caught in one of his, and when I tried sitting up, he lay back down over me, holding me in place. "God, no. Please, Brett. Let me go."

"No," he roared, deep and primal and low, coming straight from his chest. "I will not let you go."

I went still again, looking at him.

He relaxed, visibly, when my eyes met his. As he let go of my hands, both of his went to where he had stopped pulling free my leggings. He continued rolling them down my body. His hands worked between our bodies because he wasn't letting me up as he began, his voice so tender, "You tell me that you love me as an afterthought. Like you'd been feeling that for a long time and kept it to yourself. Kept it to yourself for so long that when it slipped out, it was normal. Comfortable. As if we'd been saying it to each other at the end of our phone calls for months, years even."

He paused, my leggings down to my knees, and his one thumb began rubbing over my exposed knee. A tingle trailed over my skin from his caress. He readjusted and whisked them off the rest of the way and leaned back into me, rubbing his dick against me, the ache was unbearable.

I wanted him inside me so bad.

But he wasn't done talking, and he tore his gaze from mine, his head folding as he looked between where he was grinding up and into me, against me. He kept moving, rotating his hips around before pushing, and holding as if he really was inside me to the hilt.

"You think I don't know what those words cost you?" He caught my gaze again. "You have an entire family who loves you, but you won't let them have that last bit of ownership over you. That you're someone's daughter. That you're someone's sister. You're someone's aunt. They've claimed you. They love you the same, it makes no difference to them. It's you. You won't let them all the way in, but you love them. I know you do. You can't let them in, and it bothered me. I couldn't figure it out. Why wouldn't you? It wouldn't make a difference. They wouldn't change." He stopped pushing into me and held still, rising up so his hands rested on my hips.

There was so much distance between us now.

I ached from the separation.

His thumbs began moving in circles, rubbing over my skin. "It hit me one day. You loved your mom. She died. You loved your brother. Died. Your friend, dead. Was it just them, baby? Were they the only ones you loved and lost? Were there more?"

No... I needed out.

I needed to be away.

I began to twist, but Brett caught my hands and pulled on them. "Hey."

My eyes went back to him. And at the mere look, he had captured me. I couldn't pull away anymore. That wish was leaving me as quick as it came.

He drew one of my fingers into his mouth, sucking it deep before pulling it back out of him. He watched me all the while, that darkness flaring bright to me. "I'm not angry you told me, Billie. I'm angry you said it as an afterthought. I'm angry you said it in a text. I'm angry you sent me that text when I was in a room with fifteen other football players and I couldn't leave to strip you of your clothing and show you how I feel."

Had I—had I heard that right?

My heart was pumping so loud, so fast.

Had he just said... "Wait." I tried to sit up but couldn't because of how he was holding my legs in place. I collapsed down again on my back. "What are you saying?"

His hands went to my panties, and he simply tore them off. His hand moved to my pussy and he dipped in a finger.

Oh, God. I couldn't think when he was doing that to me.

He dipped a second one in, both sliding as deep as he could go, and he pressed down on my clit at the same time.

Or when he was doing that.

"Brett," I said.

He continued as if I hadn't said a word, both his fingers starting a smooth rhythm in and out of me, "I had already prepared myself. You don't know that, but I thought that since you weren't letting your family past those last walls, that you couldn't. You wouldn't let yourself love. Maybe that's why you love those chickens so much."

Oh. Miss Sylvia Rivera. My heart clenched.

He kept on, his fingers too, "So you see, Little Billie." He pulled his fingers out, ignoring my pained protest, and he began undressing himself. His shirt. His pants. Everything else. And he bent over me, unsnapping my bra and moving back in place between my legs. One of his hands went to the inside of my thigh, pushing it wider, giving him better access.

I was soaking the bed. My need was dripping out of me.

His other hand went to his cock. He gave it a couple short strokes and then lined it up at my pussy.

He held my gaze. "I had prepared myself to go through life being okay that you wouldn't love me. But then you told me in a text, and you can't take that away. Even if you want to. Even if you regret saying it. I won't let you. You love me. I'm taking it. It's mine, just like you're mine, because I love you too."

He shoved inside, and I cried out, my body instantly arching from the sensation of him finally being inside me, but it was him. His words. The frenzy he had created, stoking it, poking it, turning it over, adding the right caress, the right gaze, the right word until I was absolutely fucking dripping for him and he was inside me, and he'd told me he loved me, and I loved him, and it was too much for me.

"Brett!" I screamed, ripping myself out of his hands and jerking up to wrap my legs and arms around him, and he groaned, his hands picking me up from under my ass. He moved me farther up the bed, laying me down, coming down with me since I was in a ball, twisted around him, and he began shoving inside me.

Fucking me.

"God, baby. I love you," he whispered, peppering me with feathered kisses to my forehead. My face. His lips falling to my mouth and opening over me, his tongue taking over the whole of me, sliding inside there as well.

We moved together.

He loved me.

I was riding the wave of that.

I couldn't believe he loved me.

"I do. Believe it." He pressed hot kisses to my throat. Gripping me harder as he sank back into me. He never stopped. "I fell the second your face lit up talking about that damn chicken. A hen. I wanted you the second I saw you. Wanted to fuck you, was making plans to make that happen even before you tripped in front of that camera. Then I touched you, and I sizzled, baby. Fucking burned from just that one connection. By the time your interview was done, I was almost obsessed. Then you started talking about chickens in that elevator and whatever that's inside you, that falls when you fall in love, that happened. A piece of me broke off and fell at my feet, a goddamn chunk. That was you. That part of me had your name on it.

"That's why I wanted to rip the heads off of those guys on the street. They were interrupting me. I only had a window of time because you were going to run away. I felt it. Knew if I didn't claim you and made it where you felt me in your soul, that you would leave me in the dust. I could feel how scared you were, even then. And I needed to know you. I needed to have you because I was already in love with you."

"Brett," I could only gasp, tears coming back to my eyes because it was all too beautiful. What he was saying. What he was doing to my body.

"I got scared in that vehicle afterwards. Convinced myself you were too good to be true, but not because I was in love with you. A part of me was still in denial, though I know that's what I was feeling. I convinced myself you were too good to be true because you were perfect for me." His head tucked down into my neck, and he kissed me there before holding me tight and moving faster. His voice was hoarse, the effort to keep talking was choking him, but he kept talking and he kept fucking. "I ain't the guy who gets anything perfect for him. You need to know that moving forward. I got a break with football, and I took it, even knowing I shouldn't, but I did. I was too greedy, needing another lifeline to pull myself out of that hell I'd been living in all my life. Hell that was me too. But I never got anything else. Just the football. I knew that too, and I was okay with it. If I just had football, I'd be okay. Then in you came, strolling into my life like a fucking demolition team, tearing everything down inside me. I knew nothing would be the same, and I got scared. If I hadn't gotten the chance to get you again, I would've deserved all the bad shit the universe would send my way as a punishment. You brought more good to me, and I'll never know what I must've done in a past life to get the shot at you."

He was saying all of it. All the words. Beautiful words. Heavy words. Words that were making me soar, but he kept thrusting in, and I was going to break. I couldn't speak.

"Brett!" I broke, my release flooding my sensations. My body snapped back from the ferocity of my climax.

When my body calmed, the waves still crashing over me,

Brett continued thrusting inside me. I reached for him, needing to tell him all the words back because everything he said, I felt too. All of it. Every single word.

We were made for each other.

Then his dick surged inside me, unloading, and he let out a deep groan and lay on me.

I welcomed his weight. All his smells that were just him.

They wrapped around me too, and the next thing I knew...

53

BRETT

B illie fell asleep and I didn't have the heart to wake her
up.

I lifted her up, putting her under the covers with a bottle of
water on the nightstand. She'd been clear that she wanted to go
with me to see my brother, a visit that I'd almost forgotten
about until I caught the time and my phone's alert light was
flashing from where it'd fallen in the rush to get Billie naked as
soon as possible.

Shit.

To go from this, from pouring out my heart, and laying
claim to every single inch of Billie that I could—I wanted her to
feel me in her toes—and then go to a meeting with my nieces
and nephews? Plus Will. Two completely different envi-
ronments.

I was raw. Truth be told.

Getting Billie's text yesterday ripped my heart out and
slammed it back inside with renewed vigor. It wasn't anything
I'd realized until I saw those words from her. I loved her. I was
obsessed with her. I knew all of that, but I hadn't known the
extent until those two words appeared on my phone.

Love you.

My phone buzzed. I took it, grabbed my bag and stepped into the bathroom.

Willy: WTF? Dinner's been eaten. Where are you?

Me: Leaving my room in three. Keep your panties on.

Willy: Dick.

Me: Yes, I have one. Thank you.

It buzzed again, but I ignored the rest, jumping in the shower and quickly washing up. It was a little longer than three minutes, but not much when I was dressed and leaving the room with a note behind in case Billie woke up. I didn't think she would. She'd been *out* out when I moved her under the covers, but if she did and if she wanted to join us, she was supposed to text me. I'd come down to get her.

54

BILLIE

I woke with a jerk and knew something was wrong.

Not bad wrong, or really wrong, but just wrong. Something that should've been there wasn't, and rolling over, reaching, it was Brett. He was gone.

The day came back to me, followed by the event of Brett and me. The whole 'love you' event because that's what it'd been. I loved him. He loved me. Holy Christ. I still felt Brett inside me. I felt him in every inch of my body and I groaned, wanting him by my side *now*.

I spotted a note on the nightstand as I rushed for the bathroom, realizing that I must've fallen asleep almost immediately after the Love You Event because I was naked. Buck naked. And pretty sure Brett's cum had dried, sliding down my legs.

I kinda loved that, knowing I still had him on me.

After washing my hands, I read the note.

I went to see my brother and fam. If you wake up and want to join, text me. I'll come and get you. Do not come up alone. I'll worry. I don't care if they caught the guy.

-Brett

There was no room number so I was sure he did that on purpose, forcing me to text him to find out where they were.

I could've texted him. I should've. An easy text and Brett would come get me, but after the onslaught of pleasure and all the emotions from the Love You Event, and waking up without him here, I didn't text him.

I texted his PR person instead.

Me: This is Billie. What's the room number for Brett's brother?

I assumed I might need to wait for her response, but it came almost right away.

Kim, Kings Public Relations: I'll give it to you, but you did not get it from me. I am fully aware that if Brett wanted you to have it, he'd give the number to you himself and since you're asking me, that means he didn't.

Her next text gave me the number.

Kim, Kings Public Relations: Delete these texts in your history.

I dressed, using a washcloth to clean up a little, but there was one area I left alone. When I headed out for their room, Brett's cum was still on me.

———————

SINCE I WAS GOING up a few floors, I didn't run into anyone else, but I still pulled the hood of Brett's Kings' hoodie up when I knocked on their door. I could hear sounds of kids inside. Running around. A few shouts.

Footsteps came over, pausing on the other side of the door, and a muffled curse was said as the door was opened. "Brett, found something of yours." The guy barely skimmed me with a look, shutting the door behind me and walking back around as Brett came over.

A thunderous expression was on his face, but as he drew closer, I held up a finger and tipped my head back.

He stopped just inches from me, waiting. His eyes firmly latched onto mine.

We were in a doorway. Brett was blocking the view of us from everyone else, no one could see around his back so I closed the distance and lifted up on my tiptoes. I held my finger still in place until I could curve it around his neck as Brett moved with me, fitting his body to mold around mine, and as our lips touched, we both exhaled a deep breath.

It'd been wrong to wake up without him.

It was right to be back in his arms.

His arm tightened around mine, and a low growl ripped from him before he deepened the kiss.

"Keep it PG," came a flat female voice, younger.

Brett froze for a second, then lifted his head and held my gaze for a moment longer. His arm moved so both of his hands held onto my hips and his fingers flexed, keeping me against him. "You smell like me still."

I grinned, slowly. "It is your sweatshirt."

His eyes darkened, as his fingers flexed again. "Something tells me it's not just the sweatshirt."

"Okay, okay. My wife is threatening bodily injury if you don't step aside and let the rest of us meet your woman."

Brett held firm for a second before stepping back.

I'd not taken the time to really take in his brother when he opened the door. It happened so quick, and I'd only seen Brett after, but now, studying him, it was a little surreal seeing parts of Brett in him.

But not.

Will looked younger, and on the outside, he had dark blond hair that was tussled, and with a white hooded sweatshirt and faded jeans, he looked almost the exact opposite of his brother.

Brett was rough. He had his beard and some tattoos, but it was more. It was the air around him. At first glance, Brett could've been cast as a villain, or at the very least, an anti-hero. At first glance, anyone who met Brett knew that about him. They sensed it.

His brother looked the opposite, like he was the hero.

Smooth skin. Clear eyes. He was classically handsome except for a nose that was crooked, just a little like it'd been broken a few too many times. Will was the guy who went to church on Sundays. Brett was the guy who threw on a worn leather jacket and hit the road on the back of a Harley Davidson. The two were so opposite, but on a second glance, a second feel for them both, and that's where the similarities lay.

Underneath his almost preppy exterior, the same edge of restlessness clung to his brother, and then there were the eyes. Will's were sky blue, but it wasn't the color. It was the look in them, that he'd seen too much in life. As I pulled my gaze away and took in his wife, then their kids, I knew instantly whose were his and who were from their sister.

His wife and his children were untouched. There was an innocence to them, and as Will moved back around to stand beside his wife, the rest of what I'd felt from him clicked into place. That was the edgy restlessness.

He saw things he did not want to see again, and he would do anything to keep his family from viewing that side of life as well. *That* was where I knew he was Brett's brother.

It was the promise that if someone hurt their family, they would kill that person. They would *relish* killing that person.

Brett stepped close to me again, his hand resting on the small of my back. "Billie, this is my family."

HIS NIECES WERE ADORABLE, the fourteen-year-old and the eight-year-old.

Stevie was almost Goth with dark lipstick and dark eyeshadow. Pale skin. Dark hair, but it was dyed blonde with the roots showing. She had a lip ring and a pierced nose, and she stood at the back of the room in an oversized dark plaid shirt and black leggings.

She was Shannon's.

She was also beautiful, though she was trying to cover it up.

If I made eye contact, she'd avert her gaze every time. Her eyes tracked Will's wife, Harmony, constantly.

The irony of that name was not lost on me.

The eight-year-old, Sammy, was the opposite. She was the definition of sunshine. Bright blonde hair. Bouncy curls. Smooth brown skin. Dark eyes, and she was all smiles. She even wore a yellow top with a white lace overlay over leggings, also yellow. She couldn't stop throwing herself at Uncle Bread, which was a hysterical nickname. Brett caught her every time and swung her in the air, her delighted shrieks convulsed into giggles and once he set her back on her feet, she'd back up, run, and throw herself at him all over again.

Georgie was shyer, though I got a glimpse of him. The little boy. Deep dark eyes, wavy black hair, and his skin was also light brown. He stayed in the bedroom, playing video games with his two cousins, Brett's other nephews. All of them came out to see who arrived when I arrived, but quickly returned. None of them had come back out to our room.

The three of them—Stevie, Georgie, and Sammy—were very much a unit. I noticed it when it came time for everyone to go to bed. Harmony was the first to mention bedtime, but everyone ignored her until Stevie stood up. Georgie was the first of the boys to stand from the floor, putting away his game player. Sammy extricated herself from Brett right after, skipping over to Stevie and taking her hand. They went into the back bedroom.

Harmony moved between the rooms, but it was obvious
that Stevie was handling everything with her siblings. When
they were ready, she lingered in the doorway as Sammy first
came to hug Uncle Bread goodnight. Georgie was next, holding
his uncle long and tight. After they disappeared into their
bedrooms Stevie came over to give Brett a hug. She was fighting
tears as she pulled back.

"Hey." Brett stopped her, his hand on her arm. "I'd like to
talk to you."

She looked at it, and he dropped it away. She took a shuddering breath, her head down. "Thank you for everything,
Uncle Brett." She raised her head, squared back her shoulders.
"But no—" Brett opened his mouth so she spoke over him. "I
know what's going on with Mom. I know that she's trying to get
me back." She looked at Will and Harmony, who came out of
their boys' room, shutting the door gently. "You're not going to
take me away from them. I don't care that I'm almost an adult. I
ain't going back to her, and if you try to make me, I'll run." Her
gaze skimmed over me, and she shuddered. "I'll run and I'll
take them with me."

"Stevie," Will said.

She backed away from him, toward me, toward the door.

Her whole body was trembling. "I'm not going back to her.
You can't make me."

"Stevie, honey." Harmony started for her, holding a hand
out.

Stevie jumped and jerked around.

I was between her and the door, and she paused for one
second.

I saw it all. Everything.

She was terrified, panicking, and determined.

She would've bulldozed over me if it meant not going back
to her mother. That truth ached inside me, because no matter

who my father was, I was lucky enough to get two good moms in my life.

"Do you know me?" I asked.

I'd been quiet for most of the visit, making pleasant small talk with Harmony as the two brothers conversed together in the main sitting area, looking a little awkward. I'd been introduced to everyone, but I'd only nodded and smiled. Stevie hadn't said a word, but she'd watched me from time to time. Then again, she watched everyone.

It'd been fine talking with Harmony, but it was obvious she was nervous about meeting Brett. And she was overwhelmed with everything. I caught that a few times when she slipped, saying how tired she was. It wasn't just the words, it was in the way she said it and the worried looks she sent to Stevie and Sammy.

Harmony had grown up with money. It was in the clothes she wore, and I didn't think she realized that had an impact on others who didn't have the money to wear name brands, like Stevie. She had the newest phone model, rings on her fingers, and perfectly styled hair with the right products and sun-kissed highlights. But I also caught the other looks Stevie had cast in Harmony's way.

Stevie was aware of how different she was from Will's wife.

There was a disconnect between them. Harmony was yearning to be Stevie's new mother and Stevie was throwing everything up between them to keep her away.

She held my gaze for a beat before moving her head up and down in a brisk nod with a coolness in her eyes. She didn't care who I was.

That was fair. I forged ahead. "I lost my mom and brother the same week I lost my friend. The rest maybe you know. It's better if you don't, but I've been through things. I don't know you, and I don't know what you've been through, and I have no idea why you got it so wrong, thinking they want to send you back to your mother." Her eyes flared at that last statement, but I continued, "But being as someone who just met you all, I can tell every adult in this room is crazy about you. Whatever you're thinking, you got something twisted wrong. Are you not seeing how crazy they are about you? I mean, look." I nodded to them. Will and Harmony stood together. Brett was slightly ahead, coming closer to me. All paused as Stevie turned, a slight frown on her face.

This was so totally not my place, but I guess I was going there anyway.

I stepped beside her, saying, "I'm fairly certain each one of them will shit themselves at the thought of you going back to wherever you say you won't go." Hearing Stevie giggle, just a little one, and she gasped almost right after, every cell in me relaxed.

Catching Harmony's gaze, seeing the love literally swimming there, I moved close to Stevie and lowered my voice, "I had a great mom, and I lost her. Then I hit the mom lottery when I got a second chance at another great mom. She's been my mom ever since, and that woman behind you? I am pretty sure she is bursting at the seams to try to be a great mom to you as well." Stevie tensed, but I quickly added, "You do what you need, but I'm telling you. Every girl should get a chance at having a good mother. Or a woman who will love you like a mother. Those are just as great too."

I stepped back, but I'd scored.

I could see it.

I got in there and I got Brett's niece to start thinking, and when she looked Harmony's way, I swear there was a shift. "Uncle." She gave in with that one word, everyone heard it.

Brett caught her up in a hug first.

Will soon followed.

Harmony was last.

By that time, Brett joined me, tugging me so I stood in front of him and he looped an arm across my chest. I leaned back against him, and held onto his arm with my hands, half-tempted to prop my chin there to watch this moment.

Brett tugged me backwards, holding his hand up in a silent goodbye. Will tipped his chin up, his eyes finding mine and holding, a silent thank you to me. Reading it, I gave him a little nod, and he turned back to his wife and niece. No one else existed for them.

As soon as we were in the hallway, Brett swooped down, picking me up and carrying me to our room. "Goddamn." He buried his head in my neck, nuzzling once we were through the door. His beard tickled me. "You helped in there. You have no idea. Thank you, Billie." His voice broke off, and he wound his arms tighter around me.

He was in his feels.

So was I.

I gauged his mood. "Brett."

"Hmmm?" He looked down, his eyes smiling. His hands flattened on my back, shoving up under my shirt.

That was a good enough sign for me.

I reached for his pants

"Wha—" His hands covered mine.

"Oh, no. This time, I'm the one getting you worked up. Let's see how you like it. Now." I stepped back. "Strip and get on the bed."

55

BILLIE

Brett's phone buzzed at some point during the night. He answered, rolling out of bed, but when I stirred, he touched my arm. "Go back to sleep."

Since it was three in the morning and we'd been busy until two hours ago, I was happy to incline. As he was moving to the bathroom, I faded back out.

The next time I woke, Brett was slipping into bed behind me. The covers came back down, and his arm pulled me to his chest.

Oh yes. So happy.

An abrupt knocking woke us up again. I was on my third time, this was Brett's second. The knocking wouldn't stop. Hard. Insistent. Brett cursed, stalking over. He opened the door, barking, "Fucking what?"

A muffled conversation happened after that.

I was awake. Barely. But I was up, and squinting at the clock, saw it was after five in the morning. The other call had been two hours ago. What was going on?

Brett was still in the hallway with the door slightly closed, so I grabbed my bag and slipped into the bathroom. I took a quick shower. The door was closed when I came back out and Brett was dressed, rifling through his bag.

I stopped in my tracks. "What are you doing?"

He threw a distracted look my way, his eyes skimming over me before returning to his bag. "I have to go."

A knot rooted deep in my sternum. "What?" I stepped toward him.

"I have to go." He zipped up his bag.

His wallet and phone were next to his bag on the bed.

"Where are you going?"

"I have to go—"

Something in me snapped. I rushed over and just as he was about to pick up his bag, I snagged it, walking to the other side of the bed. Holding it on the other side of me, as if he would lunge across the bed for it, I leveled him with a look. "Okay. We're going to start over because it's obvious you're forgetting a very important key phrase we both said to the other not long ago."

He scowled, but it was me so he was trying to hold most of it back. "I don't have time for this—"

"I'm aware. So stop wasting both of our time. You and me? We're together. You said it yourself unless you were lying when you informed me how much you loved me as you slowly inched that giant dick inside me?"

His eyes heated, but his mouth went into a flatline. "You can't come with me."

"Well, that's bullshit and we both know it."

"Billie," he sighed, running an impatient hand through his beard.

"Where I go, you go. You stick like glue," I quoted him. "Remember those words? How does that not apply here?"

His hands were in fists. He growled, "Because that guy is caught—"

"So all the other people out there, who are highly

disturbed, and unhealthily fixated on the Midwest Butcher, and who knows how many others are now obsessed with the Copier Killer? All those people don't matter? Now, what? You're off to do whatever the fuck you're off to do and I get to go my merry way back to Texas? Lo and Roger are right now on their way to the airport. Travis left yesterday. I was supposed to go back with you."

Some of his glowering dissipated. "I made arrangements for your own private plane—"

Oh my God. I wanted to scream and throw things at him for two reasons. One, a private plane? I've never traveled on a private plane. And the other, he did it now? When it was so apparent I wasn't going to leave without him. I met his level of growling with my own, and it quieted him.

"You have anything breakable in here?" I held up his bag.

His head raised, wary. "No. Why?"

I let loose with the most aggravated grunt I could muster as I slammed his bag down on the bed. "You got me a private plane now? Now? I'm not going. Where you go, I go. Where you move, I move, and now I'm going to have that song in my head all day, but if you try to take one step out of this hotel room without me going with you, I will—"

Brett's gaze flared, darkening. "You'll what?"

I swallowed my threat, not totally sure myself what I was willing to say, but this would affect me. He had to know that. "If you leave me in the dust here, there will be consequences."

"You can't say that shit without backing it up. Put it out there. I need to know what kind of woman you are when you don't get your way?" he tossed back, so icily.

I was stung by those words, but swallowing past the pain, I just shook my head. "Nice to know that's the kind of guy you are when your woman's not doing what you want. You throw out stereotypes. Like it when I do it back? Trust me, I've met my fair share of creeps. I could do this game all day long."

Anger flared over his face. His jaw could cut glass, he was clenching it so tight. "You're saying I'm like those—"

"No!" I exploded, my hands went in the air, and he moved at that small opening.

He was so fast. He was across the room and he got his bag back, grabbing his phone and wallet as well. He started for the door.

"Brett, if you go out that door—" I cut myself off because what?

What was I willing to say because I needed to mean it. I couldn't threaten something and not follow through. But it would affect me and he wasn't hearing that part. He needed to hear that and understand it. This wasn't the Brett I knew, the one who said he'd do anything for me.

Where was he going? It must be that bad for him to go against what he vowed to me not long ago.

He stopped, his hand on the door, his back turned to me. He was waiting for me to finish what I started.

Anger surged through me, heating me up. "This is going to affect me, if you leave me here. Are you understanding that?"

He turned back to me, slowly, but locked down. A wall had come over him. "Why are you not getting this isn't normal? That where I'm going, you can't—" His voice broke. The wall came down, but I only saw how hardened he'd become. This was almost a stranger.

"You can't go there. Ever. I vowed to myself that I'd never let you see—"

Some of my hurt was starting to shift aside. There was an opening, though it was small. I came around the bed. "See what? See where?"

Haunted pain that I'd never seen in Brett showed suddenly. He didn't shove it back. He let me see it. "I have to go home."

"Home?"

"To Roussou. After we left last night, something happened

and Stevie had a breakdown. Will texted me at three putting me on guard in case they might need me to go to their room. Ten minutes later, he said everything was fine. Then he showed up down here because it's not. Whatever Stevie initially said to them, she must've changed her mind because he came to let me know they're leaving. I'm going too."

There was a pit in my stomach. "Why you?"

He opened his mouth, but I could see he wasn't going to be honest.

This was Roussou Brett.

I didn't know this Brett, and he didn't want me to know him. That was blaringly obvious. Let me in, say all the pretty words, when he's fine. When his shit is good and he doesn't need to be the vulnerable one, but the minute the shoe shifts to the other foot, it's a whole different story. Suddenly I'm supposed to be jetted away where I'm sure he has people to escort me to his place, where I could go back into hiding, while he was going home to bleed.

No fucking thank you. I was so mad that it was burning me up.

"Someone needs to deal with my sister, and there's no way in hell I'm putting Will or Harmony through that. So far she's stayed away, but this is different. My sister is toxic. Will's stayed away. He hasn't needed to handle her, and I know my sister the best. I—"

My head was whirling, but I nodded. "You have to be there. I'm hearing you." I'd already washed and dressed. Reaching for my sandals, I pulled them on and started putting together my own bag.

"What are you doing?"

"I'm going with you."

His eyes flashed again. "Billi—"

"Don't," I clipped out, continuing to gather my things. My

heart was pounding, and I raced as if I didn't get everything ready in time, he would literally leave.

"Don't do this. Go back to bed. I know some people. They're going to take you to the airport and go with you until you get on the plane, and I have other people who'll pick you up when you arrive. They'll escort you to my home. You'll be safe until I get back."

He was still in the room, that meant he wasn't ready to cut and run. Not yet.

I moved faster, grabbing my Kings sweatshirt at the last minute. This one was my favorite. It was Brett's with his last name, and for a moment, I hesitated before picking it up. A heavy silence came over the room as Brett watched me, and then I grabbed it. No matter what happened next, it'd always be my favorite.

I'd always want to keep it close.

I pulled it on and it fell just past my thighs, over my pants. Reaching for a Kings ballcap, I pulled my hair through it, letting it fall down my back as I pulled the cap low on my forehead. It was too early for sunglasses, but I still kept them in my hand. If needed, I could slip them on. With my bag on my back, my purse inside, and my phone in my hand, I lifted up my chin and gazed coolly at him.

"I don't care what you say, I'm coming with you." I motioned for him, for the door. "Let's go. I'm right behind you."

His jaw was still so clenched. He went back to glaring at me.

I met his gaze head-on. "I don't care how much you're pissed at me. I'm coming with you, so let's fucking go."

He pivoted sharply, going first through the door, but once out in the hallway, he fell back to walk next to me, his hand going to the small of my back. I was tempted somewhat to shrug him off, but who was I kidding? It hurt that he tried to ice me out and if he kept up this way, it'd erode what groundwork he'd already laid with me.

I wouldn't be kept contained. That wasn't going to work with me.

He either trusted me enough, let me all the way in, or this wasn't going to work in the long run. And because of that, as a dull ache took root in me, I knew this touch from him might be the beginning of the *last* touches from him.

I'd take all the touches from him I could get.

56

BILLIE

It was early in the morning, but there were still a few other guests leaving for the airport, their suitcases in hand. A couple of the guys did a double take when they spotted Brett. One looked ready to come over and talk, but Brett flashed him a death look and the guy rethought his idea. Smart guy.

"Good morning, Mr. Broudou." The woman behind the front desk lit up as we approached. Her demeanor froze over when she saw me, but her smile warmed back up as she only focused on Brett. "Your rental vehicle is outside and ready for you, sir. Was there anything else I could do for you?"

Emphasis on the *anything*.

I fixed her with a glare.

She ignored me, only focused on Brett.

"No. This is all, thank you. I won't be needing that other service either." His eyes flicked my way.

Two guesses what he was referring to.

Her smile faded a little. "Oh. Oh, yes. Of course." She studied the screen, seeing what that other service was and as soon as she did, her eyes widened, flashing to me. "Miss Harm, I hope you enjoyed your stay here as well."

I struggled from rolling my eyes. "I'm good. Thank you."

I didn't answer her question, and I didn't care. How fast her attitude changed.

Brett picked up the fob she set on the desk between us, signing a piece of paper next to it.

She said, "Raul is bringing your vehicle around as we speak, and he'll have another fob set in there for you. Congratulations on your win yesterday. Miss Harm, have a good rest of the day."

Brett was all business, stepping back, his hand going to the small of my back, and he herded me out the door. The same businessmen were outside, waiting for their rides, and the same one who'd considered approaching Brett was eyeing us all over again. Another guy was eyeing me until Brett pressed closer to me, moving with me almost so his front was molded to my back.

A younger man, dressed in a Rothchelton uniform, got out of an SUV and came around with a professional smile as the back was lifting open. "Mr. Broudou. His guest. Let me help with your bags, please." He took Brett's, putting it in the back.

I eased away. "I want mine with me."

He dipped his head down. "Of course." He said to Brett, "The other fob key is in the vehicle already. All the necessary paperwork is in the front. Will you be needing anything else?"

"No. Thank you." Brett handed over some cash.

The man took it, giving another nod before going toward one of the other business men.

Brett went to the driver's side. I got in the front passenger seat, and we were off after that.

"Do you want to stop to get anything before we leave the city?" Brett's tone was still cold to me, but he glanced sideways to me. "Coffee or food for breakfast?"

I could've gone for coffee and I knew Brett needed food, but gah, he was so distant. It stung. "No," I said stiffly. "If you want something, you can stop."

I knew people did that, said no to things that they'd normally want when they were in an argument. I never understood it, but I did it just now. It felt good, seeing the flare of irritation as his jaw hardened again. "You're saying you're good to ride six hours in the vehicle with me without water or coffee? Be reasonable, Billie."

That had my back sitting up straight. "I am being reasonable. If you want something, you can stop and get it." But also, six hours? I needed to search where Roussou, California was on Google maps.

He bit out a curse, and that knot twisted up inside me all over again. I knew that was me, irritating him, but dammit. I wanted him just to open up, tell me what was going on with him. Not with the situation at hand, but inside him. Where were all these thoughts in his head? What was he scared of?

How could he not see that he couldn't be so open, making me fall in love with him, with how protective, how caring, how loving, how fierce, how giving he'd been to me and turn around and let a cement wall slam in place between us.

That was not love.

If it happened now, if I let it happen now, it would happen again, and again, and it would keep happening until that wall was so thick between us that I wouldn't see the Brett I loved anymore.

A shudder went through me.

I couldn't let that happen.

But we were just starting on this trip, and he was letting me come with him, so there was hope. I'd wait to start chipping away at that wall. Six hours in the car was a long time to remain stubborn.

When he'd stop to get food, because I knew he would, I'd get coffee *then*.

57

BRETT

The drive was brutal. Six hours of almost total silence from Billie. I almost broke a few times, but it was there. An impasse. We were both at it, but the thought of taking her to Roussou sickened me.

She couldn't see that side of me.

She couldn't meet Shannon. My sister couldn't ever see Billie. Once that happened, Shannon would go in for the kill. And it'd be so easy. I gave her enough ammunition from all the bad shit I did when we were kids. Most of it was done for Budd, but it didn't matter at the end of the day.

I did it.

When Billie found out, it'd be over for us. She'd never look at me the same, but leaving her at the hotel and forcing her to return home without me, I saw that it was going to rip us apart. My conscience was yelling at me to do just that. If this was what would make me lose her, then it was going to happen eventually. Especially when I knew what was going to happen to Shannon. She would be out for blood, and I was the one standing between her and her kids. It wasn't really Will and Harmony. If Shannon got through me, the next line of defense was Channing Monroe. After him, it'd be his wife, Heather. The last line was Will and Harmony and neither would stand a chance against Shannon. She was that vindictive and poisonous.

"I thought you lived in Roussou?" Billie spoke for the first time since we stopped for gas a little after leaving San Diego. Even that, she'd only said that she was going inside to grab coffee and snacks.

I parked outside the hotel that was set up next to the Fallen Crest Country Club. It was relatively new and they also offered a lot of anonymity here. I didn't think Shannon would dare come here when and if she found out that Billie was with me on this trip. "It is, but we're staying the night here. Roussou's just next door to Fallen Crest, and of the two towns, Fallen Crest is the better one to visit."

I was going through my phone, making sure all my bases were covered before I reached for my wallet and anything else I'd need. I hadn't noticed that Billie went still until I glanced toward her, reaching for the door. "Ready?" My voice trailed off.

A look of pure hurt, pure longing, pure agony all were mixed together and in her eyes.

Oh, shit.

She swallowed before her voice came out, raspy, "I wanted to see your hometown."

The hurt won out, and I could feel how dejected I was making her feel. Anger flared through me, right after knowing that I was continuously disappointing her today.

I made myself look at her, long and hard, because this was what I might eventually only see on her face. It could take months, or years, or decades, but eventually, I'd stop playing football. Would I return to my roots then? Would I become the Brett that I used to be, and even though I would fight it, it might happen when I wouldn't even realize it.

I'd just one day be me again.

I should end it now with her, give her a chance to find someone else. Someone who would always be good, who'd never make her feel disappointed.

No. I couldn't. I just couldn't. She was mine. I couldn't let her go. She made me hope for good things. She made me start believing that I deserved something good in my life, because I got her and that said something.

"Let's go." I shoved open my door, climbing out.

Billie was slow to get out, but I waited by her door until she did. Taking her bag from her, the trek inside was slow as well, her head was folded down, her hands stuffed into the front of her Kings sweatshirt. The sight of her would be burned permanently in my mind because I did that to her, I made her feel like that. I just kept doing it, over and over again, and I didn't know how to come out of this hole I'd dug.

She was falling into it with me.

I hated that.

I said once we were in the room, "I'm going to get my bag and food. Did you want anything specifically?"

She'd started to open the patio door. "You're leaving?"

"Just to get food. Fill up with gas again. Anything you want? They have everything around here. You could look up Manny's. It's a favorite local spot. I could pick up food and bring it back."

Her lips parted, the ends curving down. "You don't want to go there tonight? We have time."

"How about you order some lunch in? We're still in the late lunch hour. I'll be back by then, unless I run into someone I know."

Her eyes narrowed. "Are you going to see your sister now and you're lying to me?"

A frustrated sound ripped from my throat. "Why are you pushing this so much? It's my family. It should be my decision when you meet them."

Surprise lit up over her face before she closed it all down, and she raised her chin up, though her bottom lip was trembling. She didn't know that happened when she was particularly distressed, or when she was particularly aroused. Both emotions made her bottom lip shake. "You're keeping me out. It's not about meeting your family. It's about whatever that's going to happen to you when you see them, that's why I'm here. It's my *job*, to be at your side so I can help you get through this. And don't lie to me again. I know coming here is a big deal to you. I know there's things or people or memories that haunt you. And I know that's what you're trying to keep me away from, but Brett, you're stopping me from doing my job."

"That's not your job, to handle that stuff."

"It is too!" she cried out. Her hands went into her hair, balling it in fists, before she forced her hands to let go. "You can't do this. You can't be all up in my business, knowing the worst that's happened to me, and shut me out when it comes to showing your skeletons. That's not fair to me or you. You want this relationship to work? You're either all in or you're all out." She delivered that as a silent bomb, letting it drop between us. "You had six hours to think about it. It's your decision. Let me in or I'm out."

58

BILLIE

I regretted my words as soon as the door closed behind Brett. What was I doing, issuing ultimatums? I was wrong. So wrong. He could let me in at his pace. I shouldn't be kicking down doors and throwing threats around. It was wrong of me.

I was an ass.

Though, I was thankful that I forced him to bring me along. No matter what, I would've felt hurt if he'd sent me home and kept this whole trip away from me. There were things, people, memories that haunted him. Those wounds were still there and deep and still fresh or he would've shared about them. It would've been easier for him.

I threw myself back on the bed. What had I done?

My phone beeped.

I lunged for it, hoping it was Brett, hoping we could fix this thing that I'd created.

Lo: Are you guys back?

Me: No. We're still in California.

Lo: What? I thought you'd be back by now. I went by Brett's house.

Lo had been put on the guest list at both of the gates. She

also knew the code to get past his own gate, and I'd given her one of Brett's extra garage remotes so she could get into the house if she needed. With everything happening before the Copier Killer was caught, it seemed prudent that one or two members of my family could access Brett's home, just in case of anything. We'd planned for worst case scenario.

Me: Was the house okay? Why didn't you just call first?

Lo: House was fine except there was a girl there.

Me: A girl? What girl?

Lo: Or a woman. I couldn't get a good look at her, but neither of your vehicles was in the garage so I reversed out of there. I wasn't sure what to think or do.

Me: Brett's with me. That's Callie. She sometimes spends time at his house.

Lo: That's a relief, but also that's weird. She's gorgeous. And what are you still doing in California?

I groaned, eyeing the mini-fridge. It was stocked full of alcohol, and well...if there was any time that called for booze? It was now. Brett wouldn't mind the extra charges and if he did, I'd cover them.

Grabbing a full bottle of wine, I searched for the opener and poured a healthy glass before I curled my feet underneath me. Then I hit call.

Lo answered a second later, "If you're calling me, this isn't good. What is going on?"

I settled in. "I fucked up."

59

BRETT

The vehicle was gassed up, and I was walking out of a grocery store. Besides water, I grabbed a few other items, but also a couple deli sandwiches. Billie liked to take apart her sandwich. She'd lay the turkey to one side, remove the lettuce, the tomato. Then she'd apply a generous amount of mustard before relining everything exactly how she liked it to be, and the top of the sandwich was left off. It was too much bread, but then she'd also cut off half of the bottom and lay that on top. After that, she'd cut the sandwich in half before taking one of those halves to start eating.

It was a whole show and the first time I saw it, I was amused but also amazed. Now I couldn't wait to watch her do it all over again. There were a few packets of mustard in the bag as well.

Right when I got to the rental, my phone started ringing.

Getting in, putting everything to the side, I shut the door and took the call. "What's going on?"

My brother's voice came over the phone, sounding stressed. "Are you here yet?"

My alarm bells went off. "What happened?"

"Stevie divulged more. This shit, Brett—this shit doesn't

stop. She sent some texts to Shannon and now Shannon is calling us, threatening us. She's threatening Stevie. This is a mess, but Brett," his voice dropped off, strangled at the end. "This shit, what Stevie is telling us? It's all so fucked."

I grew cold because there was only one place my mind went, and it couldn't be. Not my *goddaughter*. "What's she saying," my voice was just as rough as Will's.

His tone went so low. "You don't want to kno—"

"Will, tell me."

He was quiet for a long time, a real long time. "Will," I said again, clearer. "I have to know."

He sighed before cursing. "Fine. Yeah. I—there was an incident with Shannon's boyfriend."

"What incident? Did he touch he—"

"No! God, no. I should've said that right away."

"What happened then?"

He still hesitated.

"If you don't fucking tell me—"

"He's a drug dealer."

I got quiet.

"He'd been forcing Stevie to sell drugs for him at her school. She just told us and she's terrified she's going to get arrested."

I closed my eyes. Will had said Stevie was starting to talk about what living with Shannon was like. I never thought *this*.

"How long had it been going on for?"

"She said two years."

Jesus.

"Did anything happen with Shannon's other boyfriends?" I didn't recognize my own voice. "How many other boyfriends did she have?"

Goddammit. I wanted to kill this guy.

"We don't know, but we're now worried about what else might've happened. Shannon dates real losers. We're preparing for the worst. We called in a counselor. Someone we know from school. She's good, and she's coming over to help us through all this."

"I'm coming over."

"I—" he hesitated. "I don't think that's a good idea."

"Will," I warned. "Don't even think about keeping me away from my niece."

"It's not that. It's that this is a really pivotal moment right now. If you come in or if you bring Billie, I'm worried too many people will be here. Stevie might close up again."

I understood what he was saying, but I was railing inside. I wanted to hurt someone. I needed to hurt someone, preferably whoever hurt Stevie. God help that guy because I was going to find him, and then God help me because I'd need His help to stay out of prison.

"Listen, I wanted to let you know what's going on. We filed for a temporary order of protection against Shannon on behalf of Stevie. With Shannon's recent threats against her, we had enough that we felt we needed to do the restraining order. Harmony was on the phone with the lawyer as he submitted it, and the police should be delivering it today. I know you're here and you came to handle Shannon, but our lawyer and the police are saying we should steer clear. We need to let the courts handle everything. I think that's the right course of action."

Right.

He was right.

Of course he was right.

Whatever was best for Stevie.

But Shannon's boyfriend was going to die.

"Brett?"

"Yeah," I barked into the phone. "Yeah. I'll steer clear. Just, give me a call if you need anything."

"If you're staying the night, maybe come over in the morning. I think Stevie would appreciate it."

"Of course. Anything, Will." My voice broke again. "Anything."

"Yeah," his was strained again. "I'll keep in touch, update you."

We ended the call after that, but I didn't see anything in front of me. Not for a long time. My phone was ringing once more, and I looked at the screen. It was Monroe.

I declined that call.

Then I drove, leaving town. My phone lit up again when I was entering Roussou.

It was Billie this time.

I was wrong in getting involved with her, not with what I was about to do. Her boyfriend made her sell drugs.

I knew all the bad shit that came along with selling drugs. I knew it because Budd forced me to be a part of that world too. History was repeating itself and I'd be damned before I let anything else happen to my niece.

I'd need to stay away from Billie after this.

A drug dealer had a boss, and they had a boss, and they had a boss so once I found Shannon's boyfriend, I knew what it would take to get all the information out of him. Knew how long it would take. The blood that'd be shed. The screams I'd ring out of him, and only when I was satisfied with all the names he could give me, and after I'd make him plead for his death, then I'd end him.

I was like my sister. I was like my brother. There was more bad in me than good, and that bad just surged over the line, overtaking me.

I'd had a good run, but it was time to return to my old roots.

I should've stayed away from Billie from the beginning.

60

BILLIE

K*nock, knock!*
I gasped, jerking upright from the couch, my phone still in my hand.

Lo gasped too, from the other end of the call, "Who is that?"

Knock, knock!

But it sounded more like, *bang, bang!* It was that hard and that quick.

"Someone's at the door, Lo."

"No shit, Billie. Who is it?"

It sounded again.

"Oh my God, what are you going to do?"

I stood, my knees were shaking. I clutched the phone tighter. "I don't know. What should I do?"

"You could call the police."

"I could." I frowned, looking at the emptied wine bottle on the table. "I think I'm drunk."

"I am too. Brett never got back to your room, did he?"

"Come on!" a male voice yelled from the other side.

"It's a guy," I raised the phone, speaking into it in a hushed voice, my head folding down. My shoulders hunched too.

"Again, no shit. I'm on speaker, Billie. Are you going to call the police?"

"I can't."

"Why not?"

"I'm on the phone with you."

"Oh, yeah. Do you want me to call the police for you? Where are you again?"

"How are you going to call? You're on the phone too. With me." She'd been drinking with me. We'd been commiserating together, but after Lo reassured me that I hadn't been totally wrong because Brett was all up in my business, and not returning the favor, so a part of me had been right. The ultimatum part, which I never meant as an ultimatum, was a bit harsh. We came up with a plan on what to say to help ease the sting of that threat away because I loved Brett. I had no intention of leaving his side anytime soon, except now in the very literal sense.

"I can have Roger call. Where are you?"

I migrated closer to the door, whispering into the phone, "Fallen Crest."

"Where?"

"Fallen Crest." Only a little louder this time.

"Where?"

"Fallen Crest!" I shouted this time.

"Hey!" came from the other side of the door.

"Shhhh. He heard me."

"I didn't say anything." Then, on her end, "Roger! Roger!" Lo cursed into the phone. "I swear, if I'm not talking about sports, alcohol, or golf, the entire house could fall down around him and he wouldn't hear."

Knock! Knock! "Seriously, woman. This isn't a joke."

I whispered into the phone, "He's getting impatient. We've talked too much. I need to do something."

"My God, I can hear that too. You're not being quiet." That was the guy again.

"Did you hear that?" another hiss into my phone.

"ROGER!" She muttered another curse before, "Billie's on the phone. She wants to know what kind of wine you want her and Brett to pick up on the way?"

A squeak sounded, and then, "What?" Roger's voice came over the phone next. "What'd you say? Billie's coming over with wine?"

"No! You need to call 911 for her instead."

"No!" I shouted into the phone.

"911? Is she okay?"

I was fully yelling now, "If he calls 911 where you live, that'll go to your local dispatch. I'm not in Texas. I'm in California."

"Oh, shit. WAIT! YOU NEED TO CALL 911 IN CALIFORNIA WHERE BILLIE IS. SHE HAS SOME GUY TRYING TO BREAK INTO HER HOTEL ROOM!"

WHAT?" Roger yelled right back.

"For fuck's sake." The guy on the other side pounded against the door once more, but he was losing momentum. "I'm a friend of Brett's. I'm coming for *you*. You're Willow Harm, right?"

"He knows who I am."

Lo added right after, also horrified, "He knows who you are." She must've turned her head away, "HE KNOWS WHO BILLIE IS!"

"WHO BILLIE IS? WHAT? I don't understand what's going on. Where am I calling 911 for? How do I do that? I've never had to do that before."

"I don't know."

And from the other side of the door, the guy said, frustrated but resigned, "He'll need to look up the phone number for the

Fallen Crest Police Department, but honestly, woman, you're killing me. I'm here for you because I got a call from Will, Brett's brother. He thinks your man is going to do something stupid, and if I'm remembering Broudou correctly, only a couple people will be able to get through his head if he's in his old head-busting mindset."

"Wait," I said into the phone.

"What?" Lo squawked. Then yelled, "SHE SAID TO WAIT, although still get the number for Fallen Crest Police Department, just in case."

I inched closer to the door and yelled through it, "What's your name?"

"Channing Monroe. I have no idea if Brett's mentioned me or not. We're not super friendly."

I was racking my brain, trying to remember. It was all foggy up there. "I had a bottle of wine. I don't know if I would remember even if I hadn't."

I could hear his sigh, then he was muttering under his breath.

"What's going on?" Lo's voice cut in.

Roger could be heard in the background, "I found a Fallen Crest Lane in Arlington, Texas. Is that where she is? Should I call the Arlington Police Department?"

"What?"

I tuned Lo out as she could be heard talking to her husband, took a deep breath because to me, this stuff was scary, opening a door to a stranger, and I peeked through the opening. "What happened to Brett?"

The guy shifted so he could see me better, but he was inspecting the opening between us, and seeing something or not seeing something, he suddenly kicked open the door.

I yelled, scrambling back.

He smirked at me, motioning to the door. "Never open a fucking door without the chain attached."

Right. That's what he'd been looking for. Apparently I got stupid when I had wine.

"Did you open the door?" Lo yelled. "Who's there? Are you okay? Are you still alive? I'm shitting my pants."

"What's going on?" Roger's voice came closer.

I was eyeing the guy now, who had remained standing in the hallway, an eyebrow raised up, waiting for me to do something.

"Billie just opened the door for the guy." She told me, "We gave up on the number. Please tell me you're still alive. Who is it? What's the guy look like?"

He was... I considered the best phrase to describe him. The dirty blond hair. The ripped and lean body. The gun holstered on his hip, which was making my stomach feel a certain way because nothing was between us. The taser gun and handcuffs hanging on his other hip. The loads and loads of tattoos all over him. And then there's his face, which didn't seem right that he'd be that pretty with all that weaponry on him. I didn't know why that made sense to me, but it did. "He's a dirty golden tattooed warrior god." He crossed his arms over his chest and I saw a badge hanging there on a chain from around his neck. "He's a cop."

"He's what?" Lo barked.

"I'm not a cop."

"He's not a cop," I repeated.

"I'm a bounty hunter." He glanced away, muttered, "Fuck's sakes."

Roger must've grabbed the phone, his voice came out so much louder, "A dirty golden tattooed warrior god? Take a picture of him, just so we have it on hand."

I did, also saying, "He's *not* a cop. I don't know if you heard that. He's a bounty hunter."

"A bounty hunter?" Roger was impressed.

The guy, who could hear everything, had tipped his head

backwards. His hands were braced at his sides. I sent it to them.

Roger saw it first, "*Oh*. He's good looking."

Lo sucked in some air, like I had earlier. "Good looking? That guy is *hot*. And he's a bounty hunter? If he says he's there for Brett, I say go with him. And normally I wouldn't ever say that, but if he'd been there to abduct you, he already would've. Plus, if it's true and Brett's in trouble, you need to go to him. What's he doing now?"

"He's still standing there."

He rolled his eyes, his hands lifting up in frustration. "Your man is probably already doing something seriously fucking stupid and you're *still* discussing this? My woman would've been out the door carrying a baseball bat and grabbing a bulletproof vest on the way the first second I mentioned anything."

I lowered the phone and scowled. "Okay. One, I don't know you. I don't remember Brett mentioning a Chandler Montag—"

"My name is Channing Monroe."

"—and Brett told me to stay put unless he himself came for me. Don't know if you're aware, but I had a couple run-ins with serial killers. That makes me cautious." I caught sight of the door, that'd been kicked open. "Normally makes me cautious. Plus, I've already maybe pissed Brett off beyond repair which was why I was drinking that—" I swung around to point at the wine bottle, and I forgot that I'd opened a second one too. "—because I needed to calm my nerves. Not the best idea, but I felt really bad. And I was talking to my sister on the phone and she was making me feel a little better about it all."

Lo gasped again through the phone.

"What?" Roger was now squawking. "What? WHAT? Why are you gasping?"

I could hear her tears. "She called me her sister. Roger, she called me her sister."

I looked down at the phone. I was going to be a blubbering mess in two seconds. "I did. I—" I yelped as the guy crossed the threshold, grabbing my wrist, and he pulled me after him. "Ow! Ouch. I can walk, you know."

"What's going on?"

The guy plucked the phone from my hand, shutting the door behind us and tugging me after him. "My name is Chandler—" He cursed. "My name is Channing Monroe." He rattled off a bunch of information. The phone number for the police department, then the phone number for the Roussou police department. He also gave his own personal phone number, followed with instructions to call his wife with her name and her phone number. For some reason, he gave the number of a restaurant called Manny's, which I perked up about because Brett mentioned that place too, but for the love of me, I couldn't understand why he was giving that information to Lo and Roger. Also, I doubted they were able to get everything down by the time he was done because he said it all so fast.

We got to a truck, and he finished the call with, "You can stay on speaker with your sister, but when we get to Roussou, you both need to shut the fuck up." He unlocked his truck, opened the door and didn't wait for me to climb in before he hurried to his side of the truck.

I climbed in, shutting the door as he was already starting the engine.

I asked into the phone, "Did you get all that?"

"Yes," Lo said in wonderment. "With bated breath too."

Roger added, "We got it because Luna ran in and hit record on my phone. I was still searching for it when he got to the second town's police department."

"Thanks, Luna."

"Oh, she's gone," Lo sniffed. "We need to get them to bed,

but I can't leave this room. I'm so wired. Also, I hope Brett's okay."

The guy cast an annoyed look at my phone, and his mouth flattened, but he didn't say anything.

I frowned. "We're not usually like this. It's just—the thought of Brett being in trouble isn't totally computing with us. It's Brett." That knot was back and sinking lower in me. "And also—"

The guy shook his head, holding up a hand. His voice came out softer, "I get it. The shit you've been through and a stranger's busting down your door? I get it."

I finished, "—the quickest way to draw me out of a hotel room is to tell me someone I love is in trouble. I needed to wait a little bit, think it through. The door part without the chain was a drunken mistake."

He cast me a sideways look, his hand resting on the steering wheel. "There's a case of coffee in a can at your feet. Drink as many as you need to sober up. Will briefed me a little on what's going on and he said that although Brett sounded okay when they got off the phone, he wouldn't put it past him to do something stupid. Hence his call to me. When I called Brett, he wouldn't pick up."

"Billie," Lo said, her voice now very somber. "Get off the phone with me and call your man." She ended the call from her side, and I had so much dread and fear and panic and all of it was now hitting me at once because I wasn't the one in trouble. Brett was, or might be, and I'd wasted time in getting to him.

I'd been so foolish.

I went to my call history, went down one name, and called my man.

Please, let us not be too late.

61

BRETT

I turned my phone off as I broke into Shannon's trailer. She wasn't there, and based on the looks of it, she hadn't been back in a long while.

I gave no fucks about breaking in.

Old cigarette stubs were in a can. The toilet hadn't been flushed and stank up the place. Old needles were discarded on the table. Empty beer cans littered the floor everywhere.

Jesus Christ. This was where my sister lived? The last time I'd been at her place, it wasn't like this.

I took pictures of everything, along with a video as I walked back through the place, before stepping out and relocking the place. Keeping the extra key, I walked back to my rental when a door opened behind me. "Little Monster? Is that you?"

Jesus. Little Monster. I'd not been called that since I was eleven, when I let the other kids call me that. That got changed to Monster in high school, and then all of it went away when Budd went away.

"Brett?" she asked again, trying to see me. An older lady's head poked outside her door, her head lowered as if that would help her see who I was in the shadows.

I moved her way. She heard the crunch of my feet over the gravel and sticks. Her thin shoulders tensed, but as soon as I stepped into her own trailer's light, she relaxed. She cast a hand over her graying hair, but it did little to tame the frizziness of the strands. It was still long, pulled back behind her. A smile spread over her face, moving her wrinkles aside. "It is you. How are you? You've gone and made us all so proud, you know. Our own boy, coming from this trailer park, going all the way to the big screen. The Super Bowl. Real proud."

"Hello, Mrs. Neverroo. I thought you would've pulled out and gone to Arizona to live with your kids? You got grandbabies down there, don't you?" Mabel Neverroo. She'd been one of the kind neighbors. She liked baking cookies, taking care of any kids in the park, in her own way. If we needed a place to crash after school, she'd let us watch her television as she put some popcorn in the microwave. She liked making lemonade too. It was one of her staples.

She laughed, her voice more gravelly than I remembered, and waved a hand toward me, still smiling. "Oh, you know me. I like my drink too much. I put up next to my kids, they're in my business, telling me what's healthy or not healthy for me. Love my grandbabies, but I like having my freedom at the same time."

"You're not tied down anymore? No more Wallace?"

A slight glimmer of pain showed in her gaze, and she let it shine. A sheen of tears appeared. She only blinked those away, moving so she was standing in the doorway, and hugged her jacket tighter around herself. She was pale. Her skin was usually kept tan from sitting outside in the sun so much, but it'd lost that color. "No. Wallace passed on a year ago. Cancer." She cursed, her hand flicking away one of her tears. "Damn things. I don't know why I'm crying. He was an abusive asshole most days. I spent most of my time keeping him out or keeping him away from here. Nothing good, was he." She drew in a deep breath, shaking her head slightly. "Guess you miss what you know, right? Enough about me." Her eyes flicked past me. "You won't find your sister there, if that's who you're looking for. Last I saw, she'd been holed up at her boyfriend's."

Yes, *that* guy. "What's his name?"

Her eyes narrowed a bit. "I was relieved when those kids were taken out of there. Considered reaching out, but you know the situation. Your sister's gotten worse since this last boyfriend. He ain't a good one. He was around a while back, then was gone. He's been back again. I tried convincing Stevie to live here, or sleep here, but she was too worried about the other ones. Then your sister stopped showing up, and around a week later, vehicles pulled up and those kids were taken out of there. I hope everything's being made correct regarding them."

"His name?" I repeated.

She was studying me, knowing the situation, which a new surge of fury lit through me. She knew and she hadn't said anything? Course she wouldn't reach out, that'd make her a narc.

"I've no doubt you'll find him." She raised her chin up. "You'll get his name then."

She fully knew what I was planning on doing.

God, this life. It had a way of always pulling you back unless you got out and stayed out, and look at where I was. Back here. "I need the boyfriend's name, Mabel."

Her gaze continued to hold mine for a good thirty seconds as she was weighing whatever she saw in me, what she heard from me, and maybe what she remembered of me as a kid. I'd been one of those sitting at her table, the sound of popcorn popping in the microwave.

The buttery and slightly burnt smell wafted over me.

I felt it all again.

The fear. The desperation. I didn't know what was right back then. I only knew how to survive.

She drew back inside her trailer. The door shut. A long minute later, she came back out and extended me a piece of paper. "Once you get there, you burn that."

I took it, seeing a street name. It was enough. I could find him from this.

"It's nice seeing you, Little Monster. I've no doubt you'll do what you need to do." She went back inside, shut the door, locked it.

The outside light turned off.

62

BILLIE

I still wasn't quite sure who the guy was driving me to Roussou. Chan...d—no. I was blaming the wine still. I couldn't ask his name again, but he told me he knew Brett from school. I'd asked if they were friends and he just laughed at me. He might've mentioned something about that, but he'd not elaborated on the laugh. I hadn't asked any more questions.

We drove the rest of the way in silence until, as we entered Roussou, which Brett was right, was so much smaller than Fallen Crest, when his phone rang.

He hit accept. "Did you find him?"

Another male voice said, "Got a couple calls from different sources. He was at his sister's trailer, but the last tip said he's parked out front of a house, down on Boll. Shannon's current boyfriend lives there. Cory Hughes. He's got a bad rap sheet. Domestic violence. Restraining orders." The guy got quiet before clipping out, "He's a drug dealer."

"Text me his house number."

"No problem. Texting now."

They ended the call, right as another beep came through his phone.

Since entering Roussou, he'd grown harder and harder. He'd been hard to begin with and I was surprised at how I could sense that considering I'd only gotten irritation from him, but this was different. The call helped, adding a cold feeling that would normally have my alarm-senses tingling, except they weren't. The only thing I was alarmed about was getting to Brett now.

I surveyed the street as we slowed and took another turn.

He was slowing down, looking from house to house.

I picked up his phone, swiping the screen to see the last text.

"Hey," he balked.

I let go of the phone, now searching with him, telling him the house number.

I saw Brett first, pointing at him without saying a word.

He pulled in, parking next to Brett's rental and as I rounded the truck, I heard Brett's tone. "Why the fuck did you bring my woman, Monroe?"

I faltered, not recognizing that voice from him. I'd heard Brett when he was angry, happy, about to release. I'd heard his growls. His savage curses. His fear and alarm when I'd almost been taken.

That was *not* this person. I didn't know this person.

He was so far from human that a part of me broke.

I paused, just slightly, before I surged ahead.

Monroe didn't respond. Smart of him.

Brett almost stopped me in my tracks, "I wouldn't, Little Billie."

My heart clenched. He had no idea why him saying that name, how it came from him, affected me so much. I would need to rectify that.

"What are you doing, Brett?" I kept going to him.

"No," a savage growl burst from him, and it stopped me in my tracks, but only for a second.

I leveled him with a look and surged forward. My hands went into my sweatshirt, pulling his hoodie tighter around my frame, but my eyes were on his. They weren't moving from him. I could feel the other guy lingering behind me.

"Stop." I closed the distance. If I swayed just a little toward him, we'd be touching. My front against his knees, since he was sitting on the top of a picnic table, his feet on the bench between us. A baseball bat was beside him. Seeing that, my heart sank. "What are you doing here?"

"Go away, Billie. I mean it. You gave me an ultimatum and I'm choosing." His eyes sliced through me. "I'm not choosing you."

My chest swelled, and I let myself sway the rest of the way. We both stilled at the contact. I savored it. He was here. He was solid. He hadn't gone anywhere. He hadn't done anything yet. I could take back my words. He couldn't take back his actions. "Don't do this." I moved in closer, pressing harder against him.

"You have no fucking idea who I am."

"You're Brett Broudou—"

"No fucking idea who I really am."

I leaned back, cocked my head to the side and repeated his own words. "Your twin's in prison for attempted rape. Your mom never left the trailer park. Your dad was a drunk all your life. Your sister—"

"My sister is going to prison for letting her daughter be around a drug dealer and whatever fucking else she failed to protect my niece from because I know this is just the beginning." His words were so ugly, filled with hate. "And, baby, it's about time you realize something because I'm just tuning in myself." He shoved in against me, ignoring my gasp as he quickly reversed our positions. He jumped down, caught me, and lifted me up so I was on the top of the picnic table, and Brett shoved my legs apart, moving in and leaning over me. His hands went down to the table on either side of me. He was pushed up so close to me, I could feel his dick, feel him hardening for me.

I closed my eyes at how good he felt as he slowly began rubbing against me.

I didn't think he was aware of moving. His eyes were so heated, the need to hurt was spitting back at me. "Stevie was selling drugs for her boyfriend. I know that world, know what else he might've been making her do for him." Torment wrung from him. He hissed, a low snarl coming next. "I had no clue. Not one damn clue, thought Shannon would never go back there because baby, that's the world I used to live in. Budd sold drugs and I enforced for him. A part of me *liked* it. I liked hurting people. It made sense to me. That world's not going to touch Stevie. I won't let her get pulled back in by him, by his boss, by his boss's boss, because that's how it works. Once you're in, they don't let you leave." His eyes burned at the same time they were dead. "I know what it takes to get out. I won't let that land on my niece."

Pain sliced through me.

"Not this time." He started to pull back, his words so icy. "It's time for you to leave. You don't want to be here for what's going to happen next."

My hands clamped down on his arms, holding him in place, although we both knew that was a lie. I wasn't strong enough to do that, but my touch on him had the same effect.

He froze, still wrapped around me.

"Billie," he sighed, tipping his head back.

"You think words like that are going to scare me?" I leaned in close and he looked back down to me. An inch separated us. "You forget who you're talking to."

His nostrils flared. We continued to battle each other, silently, until he clipped out, "I'm going to do what I was born to do and I'm going to protect Stevie as I do it. I know what'll happen to me after. Prison or death. That's where we end up in my family. It's my time, my turn. I'm okay with that. If I survive whoever this asshole's boss sends after me, then Budd's going to be fucking ecstatic when I show up in the cell next to him."

The guy jerked ahead, starting for us.

I stopped him with a look, mouthing 'no.'

He stopped, but his face twisted up. He really did not know Brett that well. That was now obvious, but I did and I ran a hand down the side of Brett's arm. He tensed, but he didn't move away. His head moved down, his mouth and beard nuzzling against my throat. I tilted my head to the side, giving him more access, and he pressed in harder to me, his dick nearly entering me through our clothing.

I felt him shuddering.

And I felt this different beast in him. This one was different from when he took control of me, giving me sinful pleasure, but he wasn't too far away. If they were a coin, this beast was on the other side, and whether he realized it or not, whether that guy who knew Brett realized it or not, my Brett was coming back.

I could feel him.

He was less animal, less stranger, and more mine.

"I'll tell you again because I don't think you're hearing me. I hurt people. If they looked at me wrong. If they didn't move out of the way fast enough. I'd deliver a beating, sometimes they'd go to the hospital. I *never cared.* Not one moment. I used to think my dad made me into that kind of person, but it wasn't just him. That's *who I am.* You can't be with me, Billie. I ain't any better than the killers obsessed with you." He suddenly tensed, his head raising, then he said, "One way or another, that piece of shit is going into the ground. I'm here to speed up the process."

The door opened behind us.

I stiffened. Brett had heard him coming somehow. The guy still waiting with us cursed under his breath, before he was moving, but he went back to his truck.

Light from the house shone over us, and we heard a female exclaim, "What the hell is going on here?"

"Babe?" another voice from behind her, a male this time.

A shiver went through me, a bad one, at just hearing his voice. She hadn't sounded good, but he made me feel that dirty inside. This was the boyfriend.

Brett was still arched over me, and as he began to move, I clamped my legs tight, trying to hold him in place. I reached around, my arms wrapping around his back too.

"You're going to leave me?" I breathed against him.

He stayed in place, just for the moment. My time was running out.

I lifted my chin up over Brett's shoulder so I could see better.

The woman was heavy-set, a tank-top stretched over her front and belly with scrub pants, the kind a nurse would wear to work. She wore no bra and her dirty blonde hair was long, but messy. A portion stuck up on the side of her head, as if she'd been sleeping on it. The rest was flattened in the back. Her makeup looked old, applied days ago and forgotten. She had a cigarette in her mouth, and she'd stepped outside to smoke it. Her hand was rising with the lighter, but she paused at seeing us.

That was Shannon.

There were slight similarities to Brett, but not much. They were big-boned. That ran in the family. The way their jaw and chin were structured were the same. There was a flattening from their eyes to their hairline that also looked the same.

Nothing else, though.

The guy, I didn't even want to look at him.

Tall. He lumbered over her, also big-boned, but not heavy-set. He was solid. Mostly muscle, but not ripped how Brett had worked his body into being. He had a white T-shirt, stained yellow in giant splotches. Baggy jeans hung off him. Dark greasy hair that stuck up all over as well. He'd not shaved in a day or two. His skin, a weird red and white pallor, was flushing red as he also stared at us. He flicked an impatient look over his face, rubbing at his eyes briefly before blinking multiple times, then leaning forward to squint at where we were.

"Who's there?" she barked, not sounding scared. She lit her cigarette now, taking a puff and holding it to the side before she exhaled.

I hated her. She was too smug. Too comfortable.

She was going to piss herself when she saw her brother, who had tensed all over again. He was getting ready to pull back, but I held him in place. He wasn't staying because I was forcibly making him. He was staying in place to indulge me, and I used this time for my advantage.

I began whispering into his ear, as I pulled one of my hands between us, running it over his chest. I was using any weapon in my arsenal to bring back the rest of my Brett because once he turned around, she couldn't see her old brother. She couldn't have him.

He was mine.

"I love you because you've only called me Willow one time."

I felt Brett go solid.

I wasn't letting him go. "I love that you didn't play with my mind when we first met. You asked me out. You told me you were interested in me. You laid it all out between us. I love you because you crashed two of my dates. I love you because you know how I love being pressed against things and being trapped, but how I *only* love it because it's you who's doing it. I love that you like sleeping under the stars, because it's one of my favorite things to do too. I love that you drove me around to see Halloween decorations. That you took me to goat yoga. That we slow danced in the middle of a group of bikers."

Some vehicles were approaching, then slowing down to park.

Doors opened and closed. Heavy footsteps thudded on the pavement.

I touched his cheek, pulling his head back so he could see me, only me. "I love how much you love your nieces and nephews, and now that you've met Will's children, you love them just as much. How you've kept tabs on your family members. How you continue to support them even though they have no idea about it."

There were voices talking.

I ignored them all because I hadn't gotten all of my Brett back. There was a feeling, a warmth that wasn't full blast yet. I didn't have my sunshine in my hand, not all of it.

He was close. So close.

He tensed, fighting against himself. His hands were rock hard. His stomach was a cement wall. He was breathing harshly. His hand moved to grab onto me, curling around my back, half splayed down over my ass.

"I overheard your phone call the other day. I know you're setting up a scholarship so Stevie can go to some rich private high school. I didn't mean to overhear, but I was walking past and your office door was open. And your voice carries." I readjusted my arms around him, moving higher around his neck, and I pressed my forehead to his chest, speaking, "I know that's not the first scholarship you've set up and it won't be the last. You seem to have *absolutely* no idea, but you *are* a good person. Present day. Now. Today. You are not who you were back then. You might've almost slipped tonight, but I'm here and I am not letting you go. You got that? I'm *not* letting you go. You had one job back then and it was to survive. Which you did. Congratulations, but you're not that person anymore. Your twin isn't here. You got out and Stevie will too, but *not* at the expense of me losing you. Are you getting what I'm saying? You do something stupid and I'm doing it with you. I'm right there with you. Where you go, I go."

"Billie," he murmured.

That was my Brett. He was back.

Relief started to trickle in.

My hands remained on his arms. His slid to my hips, as he straightened.

"You want the ugly truth?" I asked, studying him. At his brief nod, I said it, "I don't give *one fuck* what you've done in the past. I. Don't. Care. The only thing I care about is what you're planning on doing or not doing right now because you're mine. You're my future. Nothing and no one is going to take that away, including you. So get that shit out of your head because I need you."

He flinched, and he started to step all the way back.

I held onto him. "No one in your family could scare me." One day I'd have to tell him why that was the case. Today wasn't that day.

He stared down at me, his eyes darkening and deep emotion showed as he cupped the side of my face, so gently. "Thank you."

I clasped his hand, one last time, before I let him go.

It was time to handle his sister.

63

BILLIE

We flew back to Texas two days later. Brett missed an extra day of practice and he'd be fined. He'd pay the fine. Nothing and no one would've and could've pulled him from California with his family. After Brett stepped back from me that night on the picnic table, the exchange had been heated between his sister and him.

The guy too.

But Brett hadn't used that baseball bat he brought with him. Whether that was because of what I said, because those extra vehicles that showed up had been other bounty hunters coming in as backup, or because two police squad cars showed up not long after, I didn't know.

He just hadn't picked up that baseball bat and that's what I cared about.

They parked in the middle of the street. We were on one side of the street and Shannon and her boyfriend were on the other. We found out later that not only Will and Harmony spent the entire day with a counselor, but she called in a detective she trusted. With Stevie's accounts, her own testimony, and with enough other evidence and testimony that came together fast, they were able to move fast in bringing charges against Shannon and against her boyfriend.

Shannon thought the cops were there to protect them, so when the cuffs were pulled out, I pulled my phone out to record it all. I never wanted to forget the look on her face when they started reciting their Miranda rights.

They were taken away, one in each squad car, but more cops showed up because when they went through their house, they found another kid inside. A little boy, the son of Shannon's boyfriend. Shannon was charged with being a part of the drug dealing business since it happened under her roof, but there were more charges.

A lot more.

I didn't even understand them all.

That night was brutal and heartbreaking all at once.

Neither of us was hungry so we went back to the hotel after Brett talked with Monroe for a bit. (Channing Monroe. I remembered his name after that night.) The next day, we went to Will and Harmony's, and that was one of the rawest days I'd ever experience.

I knew the look in Stevie's eyes when she saw everyone there for her.

I recognized it because I'd had that same look one day, long ago.

It was in the afternoon when we were on the couch, she and I. We were just sitting, not even talking. Stevie was talked out. The boys were on the floor, their legs folded in front of them as they played video games. Sammy was next to her brother, playing with two dolls.

Stevie kept watching the adults, who were talking in the kitchen. Her mouth tightened, and I saw the regret on her face.

I leaned over, and said, "They're not upset at you."

She went eerily still, before her eyes jerked to me.

"They're upset because what you were put through. You

were hurt and they hadn't stopped it. They're mad at who hurt you, at who should've stopped it, and also at themselves. Not at you. Not because of you. They're upset because they love you."

Her mouth started trembling. Tears shown from her eyes. She quickly looked away.

I pretended she hadn't, saying, "When that man killed my friend and Jojo's family, and when my mom and brother died, it took me a long time to figure out what that weird reaction was that people had around me. Course not all people had that reaction, but some did. The good ones. They'd get all tense and have this odd half-twisted expression on their face. Sometimes they just got real mad, their whole face getting tight and swollen. But it's because they were mad at what happened to me, not at me. Took me a long time to figure that out. Don't take that on. When people get like that, it's because they're just mad you got hurt. Shows they love you."

It was worth repeating.

She began picking at the pillow in her lap, and she mumbled, "But I did it, what he made me—"

"No." I made sure to look her straight in the eyes. "You think about what would've happened if you hadn't done what he wanted you to do? What might've happened to Georgie? To Sammy? Would he have hurt them in retaliation?"

Her eyes clouded over.

"You were twelve." Jesus Christ. The same age as when I'd—

"Don't put that on your shoulders. It doesn't deserve to be there."

She tore her eyes away and went back to picking at the pillow. "Still. Not their fault. Any of them."

I relaxed a little again. "Yeah, but they're adults. They all think they're superheroes and think every bad thing that happens is their fault. It's easier to blame someone than accept they were powerless, including blaming themselves."

She didn't react anymore or respond. I wasn't sure how she

took my words, but Brett and I left the next morning after breakfast, and she'd hugged me so long and so tight.

She'd heard me.

Now we were back in Texas and we were driving to the farm.

I wanted to grab some things and see Vicky and Howard for a little bit before going to Brett's for the rest of the night. We'd just turned onto the driveway when his phone lit up.

Callie calling.

He frowned, but took the call. "Calli—"

A blood curdling scream cut him off. "Brett! BRETT—"

"Callie?" He jerked forward, hitting the acceleration and closing the distance between us and the farm in record time. "Callie!"

"Brett," she was sobbing. "Help! I need help. He won't stop and—" she choked off as another scream came over the phone.

He cursed but braked at my place. He threw open the door, shouting at me, taking his phone with him and speaking into it as he yelled at me, "Grab your bag."

"My bag?"

He was at my place and through the door.

I'd gotten my bag and my phone in my hand when he came back out. "Your place is safe." He stepped to me, grabbing my shoulders, and pressed a firm kiss to my forehead. "I love you. I love you so much, and we've not talked about all the heavy shit that happened this weekend, but know that I love you with everything in me. I have to go." He began running back to his truck.

"Brett!"

He started to get inside but stopped in the door and pointed at me. "Get inside. Be safe. Call 911 for me. The cops will get there faster than me."

My heart was pumping, strongly and loudly, and my hands were sweating.

I was having a slightly delayed reaction.

It happened so fast. Callie's call. Her screams. And now Brett was going to rescue her. It took one minute for all of that to transpire.

And I needed to call 911.

Shit! I needed to call 911.

I sank down on the bed, and did that.

"911, what is your emergency?"

I told them everything, gave them the information they needed, and as I did, I held up my hand. It was shaking. Not a slight tremor or tremble. The entire hand and wrist were uncontrollable.

The screams.

It'd been Callie's screams.

It brought it all back.

Of course, it would've come back.

They hung up with me almost right away and were going to call Brett's landline. I didn't have Callie's cell number to give them. After that, I took a few deep breaths before I realized I could call someone else.

I called Travis.

64

BILLIE

I went out to see the ladies. Vicky's car was here, so was the truck that Howard used, but the house was locked and their phones weren't on. They only turned off their phones if they were in church or at some church-related event.

Brett would be okay. Travis reassured me, said the police probably got there before him. They'd secure the house. Brett would show up to be there if Callie needed anything, but Travis was also going to run over to double check as well.

I felt better hearing that, but I was hurting and my family wasn't here. Plus, I had missed the ladies so much. I needed to hold Miss Sylvia Rivera in my arms. I needed all the hens around me. There was a flurry of activity when I opened the door, but I made sure to shut it quickly. I fumbled to pull out the light I'd brought, a solar flashlight. Vicky and Howard had a bunch sitting outside in case we needed them. I shook it and it lit up, and right at my feet was Miss Sylvia Rivera.

The rest were on the roosts they used for sleeping.

I made sure to hunch down and not hit my head on the nesting boxes or roosting bar.

In the far corner was just enough space for me.

I grabbed a broom from outside and got to cleaning that area, and when that was done, I laid a blanket out.

As I sat there, I yawned. Miss Sylvia Rivera moved into my lap and settled in, making a low clucking sound. It was like her purring.

I leaned back against the wall for a bit.

With Miss Sylvia Rivera in my arms, I didn't think about Brett, or whether I'd been wrong about what happened.

I just held her.

After a bit, my eyelids got heavy. I curled into a ball on my side.

Miss Sylvia Rivera clucked and moved to sit next to me on the ground. That said so much. The hens slept in the air. It was their way of keeping safe from predators. So if she was beside me, that meant she was guarding me.

I started to feel bad. I didn't want her worried about me, and I told myself I'd get up.

I needed to check on Brett.

My phone was back in my place, charging.

Five more minutes, then I'd go.

The hens were clucking their alarmed sound.

I jerked upright, which sent Miss Sylvia Rivera jumping away from me, flapping her wings. But I settled, my pulse calming a little. The solar light had fallen over, and my blanket covered it up, so there was no light in the coop.

Instead, I could see headlights flashing outside through one of their netted windows.

It was Brett!

Or Vicky and Howard were getting a ride back wherever

they'd gone. I didn't know the time or how long I'd stayed in the coop. I hadn't brought my phone with me because I hadn't meant to stay long, just a little. Get some comfort. Spent some quality time. A part of me wanted to stay out here, or bring Miss Sylvia Rivera with me inside, but I couldn't.

Grabbing my blanket and the light, I headed for the door. Or I tried to.

Miss Sylvia Rivera stayed at my feet, slowing every step because I didn't want to step on her. When I got to the door, she clucked louder and louder. The others joined in, feeling whatever she was feeling.

She was alarmed or she wanted me to stay.

I appreciated her support, but I needed to deal with the real world. Brett was probably losing his mind. I needed to check on him, let him know I'd fallen asleep.

I reached for the door, but Marsha P. Johnson had moved to the roost right above my head, and she started flapping her wings.

What is going on?

I moved Miss Sylvia Rivera aside.

She ran right back, stopping me.

I did it again.

We repeated this cycle until I was sure Vicky and Howard wouldn't be able to fall asleep and Howard would be coming out to make sure the chickens were okay. *Were* they okay? Was there a predator outside? I bit back a slight laugh at myself because this was probably the issue. Why was that just now occurring to me? A coyote? Or a snake?

Either way, I needed to find it and take care of it.

I scooped up Miss Sylvia Rivera and put her on her rung of the sleeping roost. Marsha P. Johnson soon joined her, and then I dashed for the door, getting out before Miss Sylvia Rivera could come with me.

I heard her wings moving, but got the door closed in time. I made sure they were all inside, and grabbed for a flashlight, the one to shine around if we really needed to see what was going on. I swept it around the coop, expecting to see grass rustling as whatever had them alarmed scampered away.

Nothing moved. There were no threats from outside the coop.

The headlights...

I'd assumed those were Vicky and Howard, but maybe not.

Brett would've been yelling for me, and he would've come down here to find me. He knew me.

An alien feeling settled over me.

The hens were still in a tizzy.

I moved toward the house, turning my flashlight off.

What did I have on my body?

I'd only brought a blanket and the solar light, but that was too small, too flimsy.

The flashlight was all I had.

I kept it gripped in my hand, my arms loose at my sides so I wasn't locked up.

Step by step, my heart pounding louder and louder in my eardrums, I edged toward the house.

When I got past the shed, I stopped and exclaimed my relief. There was no new vehicle, but a light was on upstairs in the house. It *had* been Vicky and Howard getting a ride back. The car must've left when I was leaving the coop, but then why were the ladies going crazy?

Was there something inside the coop and I hadn't realized?

Oh, God. Miss Sylvia Rivera hadn't wanted me to leave. Maybe it'd been just outside, and I was the one who let it in?

Horror speared me. I turned to run back to the coop—but a hand wrapped around my arm and pulled me back.

I screamed, reacting on instinct. I twisted my arm down and out of their grasp and swung with the other one, the one holding my flashlight.

"Hey—whoa!" a male voice barked as he twisted to catch my other arm right before the flashlight would've hit his head. His face scrunched up in anger and he shoved me back, taking several steps away from me. He held both hands up in surrender. "Hold on. It's me, Travis. I'm not here to attack you."

Travis.

Not...whoever I thought it might be. I jerked backwards, bent over and sucked in some air before I was steady enough to speak. "Holy shit, Travis! Holy shit!" I shook my head and pretended to hit him with the flashlight. "Announce yourself. Jesus"

He laughed but kept an eye on the flashlight. "I thought you'd be in bed. I pulled in and shit went nuclear in the coop. I thought maybe a coyote was trying to get in or something."

"No. Or..." I looked back. They were still worked up. "I don't think so." I walked back that way and I went in through the cage first, so if the hens ran out, they still wouldn't be loose. Travis was right behind me.

I threw open the inside door, and the hens ran out. Every single one of them.

I wasn't able to count them, but I went inside, my heart in my throat about what I was going to find. But there was nothing. No predator inside at all.

"Are you here about Brett? I fell asleep in the coop. I haven't checked my phone. Is he okay?" I looked around. "Is he here with you? Wait..." Where was his truck?

Travis stood in the middle of the cage, the hens running around him, and he had the coldest look on his face.

A chill went down my spine. "Travis?"

He continued to stare at me, hard. He looked like a stranger.

I didn't know this Travis.

A chill sliced through my whole body, and pieces began connecting to one another.

"Travis? Is Brett okay?"

He'd been interested in me for a long time.

But no... The killings had started north in the Midwest, leaving a trail to here.

The truck on the road, the guy watching...

I would've recognized Travis. Wouldn't I?

"Little Billie, you need to know my secret." My mom's voice came to me, echoing through my mind. I frowned. Why was I remembering her at this moment?

"Travis? What are you doing here?" I asked again, a wholly different tone in my voice. I felt detached from everything, already knowing and feeling the cold that only death could bring.

"You know how we move from place to place all the time?" my *mom asked me.*

I shook my head, needing to clear that voice from my memory. It wasn't the time right now.

But I heard my own voice respond, like I was twelve. *"Yeah?"*

"Things are out of my control now, sweetie. I need to tell you the truth."

"Mom?" I started crying.

"Brett sent me." Travis' voice was off. His demeanor was off. "He couldn't get ahold of you and he needed to stay with that girl."

Right. That made sense. It was something Brett would do.

I couldn't focus. I was distracted by the flashback in my head.

My mom was crying too. "We didn't move around so much because I kept getting fired, sweetie. I didn't want you to get attached. I told you it was because I didn't want you to have friends. That wasn't the truth."

"It wasn't?"

"No, honey. I would've loved it if you could have friends. You and

your brother. You were both so full of goodness and love, and you both deserved to have that in your life. You know that, right?"

I'd been so young back then, and it was the day after I lost my friend.

"Billie, are you okay?" Travis asked.

"What?" I couldn't focus, yet every fiber of my being screamed that I could not be distracted in this moment.

Travis was talking. From a distance I heard him say, "Did something happen after the game? Broudou seemed off tonight..." He kept talking, but I couldn't hear him.

I could only hear my mom.

"It's your father, Billie."

"Dad?" I whispered aloud.

Travis stopped abruptly.

"He's not a good man. You know that," Mom continued. "He keeps finding us, and he's never done anything to you, but yesterday..." She trailed off, more tears cascading down her face. Her hands shook and she tried to draw in some oxygen. She tucked my hair back, smoothing it before she forced herself to move away. "He hurts me, sweetie. And he did something with your brother yesterday—"

"What'd he do?" my voice was so flat. The panic was locked up, real tight.

My emotions needed to be off.

It all came back to me. I used to do that. That's how I would get through those visits with him. I'd shut everything off and become a rock. I'd pull all the way inside myself, turning into a robot when he was around.

Travis came closer to me.

I needed to step back, but I couldn't make my feet move. This, whatever had been unleashed in my mind, I needed to remember it first.

I made a choice and went back to the memory.

"What'd he do with Ben?" I asked my mother.

"He took him somewhere, and I can't let it keep happening. I have to go somewhere, Billie."

"Where, Mom?"

She bundled me in her arms, hugging me so tightly before she set me down again. She rocked back on her heels. "I can't take you with us. I'm so sorry, Billie. You need to be here because of what you saw yesterday. You know what I'm talking about, right?"

Pain burned me, and it jolted me in the present again.

"Jojo," I managed to whisper.

"What?" Travis asked.

My mom nodded, her tears wouldn't stop. "I'm going to take your brother with me so he won't turn out to be like him. Okay? He's going to go with me, but you can stop that bad man."

"The bad man?"

Fear gripped me now—fear of the bad man, fear of whatever my father had done to my brother, fear of what my mom was saying. What was she talking about? I couldn't understand.

"Mom," I said aloud. "What are you going to do?"

"Billie!" That was Travis' voice. Sharp. Angry.

"You're not going to see me again, or your brother, but don't for a second think it's because we don't love you. We love you so much. I will always love you. And in his way, your father loves you too, but you need to stay away from him. Okay?"

She spoke more urgently, pressing my hand in hers. "You need to listen to me so that you're safe. You need to go to the police, and you need to tell them who you saw yesterday. I know you saw the bad man. You can describe him. It'll be enough. They'll catch him. I know you didn't tell the police you saw him, but you did and you need to be brave. You need to go to the police, tell them who you saw. And, Billie..."

She started choking, hiccupping on the words. "There will be a time when they ask you who your parents are because they won't be able to get in contact with me. Listen to me very carefully. You do not tell them your father's name. You need to forget who your father is.

They'll take you away, and they'll put you with other people, and I will do everything in my power to make sure you get a good family. He won't come for you. That's the only thing he's ever promised me. So you'll go with other people. Good people. People who will love you and protect you. I'll make sure of it, okay? But you can't tell them who your father is. That way you'll be safe. Okay? You can do it. I know you can do it. You're a very brave girl. You always have been."

She looked over her shoulder, as if someone was coming, then turned back to me. "I love you so much. Never forget that. Ever, Billie. Ever."

She tore herself away, and after a moment there was a cry in the distance.

"Mom!" I wanted to go after her, but she was already gone.

I opened my eyes and ached. It was happening all over again. I was back there, back outside the police station as she was leaving me behind.

I wanted to go after her.

But no, that was back then.

Ben had been in the car with her. She left me at the bench across the street, then ran to our car and took off. She and Ben.

That was the last time I saw them.

Time spun around, bringing me back to *now* with a sob in my throat. I folded over. It was like losing her all over again.

"You need to start talking, Billie," Travis demanded. "Or I swear to God, I'll—"

I lifted my head, and for a moment, I hated him. I hated where I was. I hated everything because I *just* had her back. I'd give anything to have her back in my life. One more hug from her.

Travis cursed, his face pale. "You scared the shit out of me."

I gulped, my fingers curling around my flashlight. "What are you doing here, Travis?"

I expected him to drop the wall, show me his true self.

But he only shook his head in confusion. "I told you.

Broudou sent me. That girl who was staying at his place, her friend and a guy showed up. He was threatening them. They're fine now. The officers took the guy in, but Broudou felt he needed to stay back. He couldn't get ahold of you. Neither could I. Plus, I was going to see if Vicky and Howard were here. I couldn't get ahold of them either."

Wait. I was confused now.

"Vicky and Howard just got back. I saw their light on. They're probably in bed by now." I stopped, looking him over. He seemed normal to me again. The same Travis as before. He wasn't...

I was losing my mind. I *must've* been losing my mind.

But the flashback from my mom—until now I'd forgotten that conversation.

My brother.

God.

Ben.

What she'd done after that...

Their car accident.

I couldn't concentrate on Travis anymore.

My mom and my brother. I'd lost them that day, and I'd been so wrong.

"I FEEL weird leaving you here tonight. I could sleep on the couch."

Travis was inside my place, glancing around. The place was small, really small, which I loved. It felt right and cozy when Brett was here, but with Travis, who was smaller in size and height, it felt suffocating.

"I'll be fine. I promise."

My phone was ringing. "I'm sure that's Brett anyway."

"Okay. Well...are you sure? I can stay. I'm getting a weird feeling here."

The phone stopped ringing. It was charging in the other room so I hadn't grabbed it yet, saw who was calling.

It started ringing again.

"Travis, I need to grab that. Go. I'll be fine."

I started for the phone and heard Travis saying behind me, "Well, okay. Oh! Hey."

I stopped, looked back.

"Brett mentioned you still wanted to see the picture of the guy. Right? Or was I wrong and you don't need to see the picture anymore?"

It took me a little bit to remember what he was talking about. "The picture?"

"From the traffic cams. We got Haskell, but I promised Broudou I'd show you. It took me this long to get it cleared for your eyes only. You still want to see it?"

"Yes. Right. Yes, I want to see it."

"Okay. I got it in my truck. I can send it through on your phone. Type in the last four digits of your birthday to open it. Helps with the clearance."

My phone stopped and started again.

I was distracted and said to Travis, "Uh huh. Sure." I got to the phone and snatched it up, not looking at the screen before I swiped it open. "Brett?"

There was silence on the other end.

I frowned, pulling it away to see who'd called. It was a blocked number.

Ice lined my insides, and I hung up.

What to do?

Travis.

But I heard his truck starting and ran to the door, throwing it open.

He had parked on the other side of the yard, closer to the

driveway. No wonder I hadn't noticed his truck. It blended in with the shadows. His red lights shone brightly, then switched to a lower setting as he pulled out, heading back to the road.

My phone beeped a second later.

I glanced down, still distracted, that uneasy feeling starting to eat more of my insides, but it was the image Travis promised to send.

I clicked on it, my hand starting to shake. I typed in the last four numbers of my birthdate, and the picture popped up on my phone.

My blood ran cold.

I almost dropped the phone.

No! No, no, no. It couldn't be.

I grabbed my key and tore out of my place, letting my door slam against the side as I sprinted for the main house. I already knew it'd be locked. They were in bed. Unlocking it, I threw it open and yelled out, "Vicky!"

I stepped inside, and just then the living room lights turned on.

I crossed to the doorway, still speaking, "Howa—"

They were there, and they were awake, but their mouths were taped shut. They were lying on the floor. Their hands and feet were bound. And standing by the light switch was the man I just saw in the image Travis sent me.

Everything went flat inside me, like I used to have to be when our father would show up.

He smiled, brandishing a butcher knife, as he motioned to me. "Come in, Billie. Join us."

I said, my voice dull, matching my insides, "Hello, Ben."

My brother was alive.

65

BILLIE

"How are you alive?" I asked.

He shook his head, tsking me. "No, sister dear. We don't skip over the meat before going to the dessert. Try again." He wagged his finger at me, then wagged his knife in the air at me.

I couldn't stop staring at him. A part of me had stepped out of my body, but that also, couldn't stop staring at him. There was nothing about him that stood out. He would've been described as a cute guy, but nothing more. Lean. His shoulders were slightly wider than his frame. Brown hair that was cut short where he could just comb it and leave it alone.

He wasn't ugly. He wasn't handsome. He wasn't quite plain either.

He was nondescript.

Blue flannel shirt. Jeans. Work boots. He had some gruff on his chin, having not shaved in a day or two, but I recognized that jawline.

"You're the one who tried to take me from the gas station," I said, dazed, because this couldn't be true. This couldn't be happening.

God. My brother.

He laughed.

He wasn't right. An unhinged look was in his eyes, but he smiled at me. "We've been waiting for you all day. I was about to come and get you, but now that the cop is gone, we can get started." He lowered his head, a mischief gleam coming from him. One side of his mouth twitched up. "Should we hug, Billie?"

"I'm going to take your brother with me so he won't turn out to be like him."

Mom!

If he was alive—hope lit up in me. "Is Mom alive too?"

A dark warning cast over his features. He grew still, an ominous grumble deep in his throat. "What did I tell you, Sister? All Mommy talk for the end. We eat the meal before we get the dessert."

There was nothing inside him. His corpse was here. He was here, but the Ben that I knew was gone.

There was no soul inside him.

He gave me my name. He couldn't pronounce Willow when he was little so he called me Billie. I became Billie to everyone I loved after that.

"It was you? This whole time?" I whispered, my voice raw.

"No, Big Sister." The playfulness was long gone. He grew grave. Mean. Cold. "It wasn't all me."

...young male. White. Someone who was affected when the Midwest Butcher was captured. An event correlated in his life, bringing trauma as a result of the Midwest Butcher or because of an event that happened in his family, like a divorce around the same time.

He fit the profile.

An event that correlated in his life was me, when Cameron Fowler could've killed me.

His eyes narrowed, his head turning almost sideways. He

began playing with his knife, swishing it through the air like it was a light saber. None of this touched him. He was used to murdering, bloodshed, evoking terror in other people.

The pieces began to fit together, horrifyingly easy.

"You were the one watching the farm. I saw you."

He went still, his eyes cutting back to mine. He lowered the knife, stopping his gameplay. "Yes."

Two men. It was the only thing that made sense. Two killers.

"Did you kill all those people?"

"No, but I had a hand in it. I molded him, you see. A Billy for a Billie. Appreciate the irony, Sister? Your name. My face. He looked like me. He was the perfect mix of us. He was already obsessed with the Midwest Butcher. That's how we met, in an online forum. It was easy after that. Easy to get him to write to Fowler. Easy to get him to step over the line. A first kill. He already knew he'd like it, but he needed to learn how to do it properly. Fowler primed him, got him ready for me. After that, it was about waiting for the perfect moment." His head lowered, his eyes remained on me, and it was as if he were bowing to me. "We waited for you, Sister."

The perfect time. "What are you talking about?"

"I watched you your whole life. You were hiding, like me. I waited for you, waited for you to step out of the shadows and you finally did when *he* came along."

Him? Who? "Brett?"

His eyebrows furrowed before smoothing back out. "Billie with the IE, not a Y. I couldn't have him completely have your name because there can only be one of you. There'll only ever be one of you. Only one Billie." He smiled, the image of a child demon playing in a man's body. "Better than Melanie Morning. Did you forget? That was a fake name our mom used to use. You preferred the name I gave you. I liked that." His smile vanished. "Most would've taken the name our father gave you."

I didn't want to talk about our father. He didn't matter.

I wanted to hear about mom.

Was she alive? That hope was there, battering against a cage in my chest.

"We were never allowed to say Dad's name."

"What?"

Ben's eyes flashed again, snarling. "You're not listening to me, Sister. Don't make me give you an incentive." He leapt to where Howard was laying and picked him up by his ear, dragging him over.

Howard started yelling, his voice muffled through the tape. His face was gauntly white.

Vicky was yelling too, her voice muffled as well. Fresh tears streamed down her face, laying over dried tears, dried blood.

Ben dropped him on the floor, in front of where he'd been standing. He was beside the stairway, the front door behind him. I was just in the doorway of the living room and kitchen. Nothing was between us, and Ben wanted it that way. No barriers.

Except now the man who'd become my father.

Ben bent down, and before I could act, he sliced his knife over Howard's head.

There was a pocket of air, of silence, before the ramifications of what he did was comprehended.

As he stood back up, he straightened with Howard's ear in his hand. Fresh blood poured over his knife, dripping down to Howard's face as more blood burst from the side of his head.

Vicky was screaming, still muffled.

I—a scream was caught in my throat. I couldn't scream. I didn't know why that was. I didn't know how I knew, but I just knew that I could not scream. Ben was watching, waiting. He was judging me, waiting for something.

I wasn't sure.

His eyes were latched on me, and he was eerily still, an evil smile starting to tug at the ends of his mouth.

I didn't scream, barely. Sweat formed on my forehead from the effort not to let out how I really felt. Howard was moaning at his feet, rolling over. The blood spewed as he did.

"I thought that would be an incentive, but you surprise me, Sister. I can do an eye next time? Or maybe below his knee?"

I shuddered. "What do you want, Ben?"

His face suddenly darkened, and he stepped over Howard, lunging two steps to me before stopping. Standing at his fullest height, he thundered, "You will not call me that name. Ben is dead. I'm your *brother*. I'll be referred to as your brother."

He was close enough I could reach out to him. I could grab him, fight him, and as if he read my mind, he retreated back on the other side of Howard, making himself so he was dramatically smaller. His head and shoulders both hunched down. "It's been so long, Sister. We have so much to catch up on."

I didn't know what questions to ask him, which ones would set him off.

"What happened to you, Be—Brother?"

His eyes jerked to mine, but he relaxed as I used the appropriate term. "You'll need to be more specific, Sister."

My mouth pressed tight. He was boxing me in. He didn't want to talk about Mom. "After...what happened with you and..."

Another warning lit from him.

"Where've you been this whole time?"

He shifted to the side, his mouth pursed before he rolled one shoulder back, tightly. "Some people raised me, the ones who found me. They kept me for themselves, said I'd grow to be a backwoodsie like them. They taught me to shoot. To kill. To hunt. They beat the shit out of me every Saturday night. It was their entertainment. They taught me other things too. How to live off the land. How to be a ghost. There were things they couldn't teach me, where I would need to leave to learn those skills. They didn't want that, but they didn't realize who I was. They thought they were turning a stray dog into a killing machine. They didn't know they took in a cub that would grow into a wolf. That was their mistake." He raked his gaze over my face. "I killed them. I did it the way he used to."

He. The Midwest Butcher.

We'd come full circle, back to the start.

I didn't care about Cameron Fowler. He'd already destroyed my life once.

I wanted to talk about Mom.

I wanted to ask, so badly.

Is she alive? Please, Ben.

Maybe it was time, or maybe he felt my silent pleading because Ben all the sudden dropped the murderous gusto. He wouldn't look at me. He was more than half turned away from me, turned away from the entire room. If he lifted his head, he would've been looking directly at the stairs.

Layers left him, lifting off him, and vanishing away until he was someone else.

My lips parted. A sense of longing filled me. Ben... Now I saw him.

There was my brother.

"She lied to me." He half turned back to me, before swinging away. His back was almost to the room. "She left you on that sidewalk and told me that we were going to get ice cream. But we kept driving, and driving, and driving. We drove for so long." His voice thinned, sounding like a little boy, one that was scared. Confused. "I don't remember when I realized she lied to me, but it hurt. I didn't understand what was going on. Then she told me to get excited." He paused again, frowning slightly. "She was crying, but she was smiling. She said we were going to see the Mississippi. She told me I'd never see a river so big, so grand. I was excited." The last was breathed out, as if he was reliving it. That he felt something wondrous was happening.

He stopped again. His shoulders slouched so far down.

"We just kept going. The car went off the road, and Mom, she—" His voice was thick, so sad. "—she turned around as we were going down and told me to 'close your eyes, little angel, because we're flying.'"

Close your eyes, little angel, so we can fly.

I heard her, clear as day.

A tear trickled down my face.

He still wasn't looking at me, and his voice grew harder, more bitter, "I missed you, but I was excited for ice cream. Then I was confused and I wanted you. I kept asking to go back to you. She told me we were letting you go. She said the time had come when we could all be free. She told me we were letting you go live with another family."

He turned my way, the soulless eyes had returned.

I shifted back, readying.

"I never agreed to that." His eyebrows furrowed together, and an ugly resentment gleaned from underneath them. Joining that cold mean glint that'd been there in the beginning. It was back. A belated thought skipped in the back of my mind, if this was the last thing his victims saw before he killed them?

"That was her gift. Not mine, Sister. I did nothing wrong. I was a victim, just like you." His lip lifted, showing his white teeth in a snarl. "Except *are* you? Actually a victim?"

I went cold again and took a step back.

He began to follow me. "She died on impact. Her neck snapped when we hit the water. It happened in front of me."

Mom knew what he was going to become. This was what she tried to stop. She knew before anyone else.

"What do you want, Brother?"

He ignored my question, a fleeting smile on his face, and held up that knife again. He turned it over to show me the jagged edge. "It's a hunting knife," Ben informed me. "I use it mostly for big game. Elk. Bear. Special occasions. I thought about using it on you. I learned how to use this from the people who raised me." Suddenly, he dropped his hand and he stared at me, hard. "I was going to kill you, Sister. I came here to do that, but I admit," his eyes skimmed over me, a softness appearing. "seeing you now, in front of me—I forgot what it was like."

"What was what like?"

He ignored that too.

Vicky was rolling around, trying to get my attention. He had moved forward enough, toward me as I had edged backwards so she did this behind his back. Her eyes went to the window, and back to me. To the window, back to me. Howard was doing the same until he couldn't keep looking. The movement was too much for him. He only stared out the window.

Their message was obvious, but if I ran, I needed a plan. I had no weapons on me. None close to me. I couldn't run from him. He'd come back to them.

That *would not* happen. If I ran, I'd stop him. That was the only option.

Ben was talking, and he got my attention again, "...saw you on the screen and you're a star. It's why mom chose you in the end, because she saw it too. You're a star. I thought so when we were little, but this was different. These people already love you." He motioned toward Vicky and Howard, starting to turn.

I opened my mouth, needing to say something, do something. I had to distract him.

He didn't turn all the way, his gaze quickly averting to me again. He sneered as he said, "Your *new* family. But you still went into the shadows with them. I watched you so I know what made everything change. *He* changed everything. When he came into the picture, you stopped hiding. You no longer went into the shadows. I couldn't have that. Too many would start loving you. I won't share anymore. You're my family. You're my sister." He leaned forward, his face eerily calm. Peaceful. An unnatural possessive look shone from him.

I edged back a step another step.

I never closed the door. I'd let it go in my haste to find Vicky and Howard.

I could make a run for it, draw him away from them.

I glanced down, saw both Vicky and Howard watching me. Pain-filled eyes wide, the terror so evident, but there was more. A plea.

Vicky gave me the slightest nod. She was telling me to go.

Travis said the killer had real fighting experience. Brett had added, "... *how to maneuver like that if he's gotten hit a hundred or more times.*"

I had skills, but they wouldn't have been on Ben's level. He got the shit beat out of him every Saturday night for entertainment. If he took the beatings, he learned how to give them.

Sweat trickled down my spine.

Whatever I was going to do, I needed to do it soon.

Ben was peering at me, solemnly. He wasn't blinking. "Do you know what I'm saying to you?"

I drew in a breath, but something switched in me. If he was going to kill me, I was going to take him with me. If he was going to try and kill Vicky and Howard, I'd fight like hell. He messed up.

His head twitched, seeing my change.

"I don't care what you're saying."

He snarled.

I took a big step backwards.

His eyes flicked to my feet.

"I told you my rules about that name. Ben died in that river, Billie. I'm only—"

"I don't care," I clipped out, again. Another step backwards. "You messed up, *Ben.*"

Another step. I was almost to the door.

His eyes bulged out.

I said, my voice rising, "You caught me off guard. I needed to process that you're alive. You gave that to me when you talked to me. You let me *hear* you. In doing so, I made a few decisions."

One last step, and I was outside. My pulse was in my eardrums.

Ben's eyes narrowed to slits. His entire face twisted from fury. "Stop moving, Billie. I mean it."

"Or what?" I lifted my chin. "You'll do what, Ben?"

A light turned on in his gaze, and I knew what he was going to do. I read his intent as he started to go back.

"If you harm one more hair on either my mother or my father, I will take that knife and I will gut you with it." I meant it, every fucking word. I let him see it too. I wasn't scared anymore. I wouldn't be intimated anymore. There would be no more threats either. I was done being anyone's target or obsession or pawn.

I was done with it all.

He froze at my words. "Your mother?"

That's what got him?

More sweat ran down my spine because this was it. I wouldn't let him hurt the people I loved and that was all he was here to do. No one else was coming to our rescue. It was just me, and I had no weapons. Howard's guns were locked away. Ben would be on me if I even took a step in their direction.

The only weapon I could see was that knife, though I'm sure he had more somewhere.

That meant it would be a fight to get the knife away from him, and remembering how he took that hit from Brett at the gas station, what Travis had said about him having real fighting experience, let alone what Ben himself said about how he grew up.

I could only focus on what I had: I had everything to lose. That's what I had.

I tipped my head back and drew in a breath, then I had to laugh a little.

"What?" Ben frowned.

"It's just a dichotomy. I've wished all my life that I still had my mom and my brother. And I also feared this very scenario, of a killer showing up and going after the people I love. The fact that my wish came true and delivered my worst fear is a real fuck you from the universe." I had nothing else in me, no more bullshit to summon.

He was either going to die or the rest of us were.

He lowered his knife, a startlingly real sadness coming over him. "I was going to take you with me. I wanted my sister at my side again." A new look showed, a new determination. His jaw clenched and he raised that knife back up. "That will happen, Billie. I know you're on a suicide mission, but I won't let that happen. I'll take you away from here. I'll try not to hurt yo—"

I ran at him. Enough talking.

He changed his stance, and once I got to him, he ducked my first punch, but I landed my second. As he fell back a step, I was on him again, yanking one of his feet out from him. He fell hard on the floor. I raised my foot up to stomp down on his balls, but he rolled to the side, sweeping my feet out from under me. As I fell, he was on me pinning me.

Oh, hell no.

I snarled, twisting out. Trying to.

He had my legs pinned and one of my arms, but he didn't have the other one down because he was still holding his knife.

"Stop, Billie. I don't want to have to hurt you."

He was ridiculously strong. Did all serial killers get an extra strong genome in their DNA? Was that why they were psychopaths?

I panted and raged, but I kept twisting.

He cursed, readjusting his hold, but in doing that, he gave me an opening. I rolled to my side, my feet free, and he cursed again, more savagely, as he rolled completely off me.

I jumped to my feet, ready to attack, but I braked.

My world flipped upside down.

He'd gone to his collateral, and he had Vicky up on her knees. He stood behind her, the knife at her throat. He was panting too, sweating too, but his eyes were a stone-cold killer's. "Do—don't, Billie! Don't. I will kill her. I'll do it now in front of you or I'll do it later. It's up to you, but if you go with me, peacefully, she'll have a chance then."

I scowled, but God—I couldn't beat him in hand-to-hand. I wasn't skilled enough.

I shot back, "Howard too."

He grinned, darkly approving. "You're a smart girl, aren't you? What did Dad like to call you? Litt—"

The sounds of clucking started, at first quiet, timid. Then louder. They grew, and I looked behind me, to the opened door. Miss Sylvia Rivera was leading the flock. I'd left the coop door and cage open when Travis had been here earlier.

That seemed so long ago.

The ladies came looking for me, and running right to me, Miss Sylvia Rivera sped up, her clucking getting louder and louder. The rest swarmed around me, going to Howard, and then bypassing to Vicky. She was their other mother. They knew her, and apparently they decided now was breakfast time, despite it was still at night.

Ben was distracted, and Vicky surged to her feet, throwing her head backwards.

Thunk!

Cluck, cluck, CLUCKCLUCKCLUCKUCKCUCK! All the hens were in an uproar. They didn't like bodies suddenly almost landing on them.

She got him, and both were dazed for a moment, but it was enough.

I lunged over the couch where they had landed, and grabbed Ben's wrist, yanking the knife away. He didn't have a strong enough grip and as it came free, he paled.

I twisted it in my hand, moved my body so I went away from him and as I did, I tucked the knife under my side and it sunk in. I threw my body to the side, still gripping that knife. It was all engineered into one motion where I'd use my body's momentum to drag the knife across his stomach.

He howled, jerking forward. He clutched his stomach.

As that happened, I grabbed Vicky and dragged her across the floor.

She was yelling through the tape but raised her wrist up. I used the knife to cut her free.

"No!" Ben started for us, but he was bleeding too much.

I quickly stood in front of her, and I held the knife up, testing it in my hand. "Ben, I've taken lessons on Arsin knife fighting. I'm not the best, but I know enough—"

He stood, his chest heaving, the blood quickly pooling around his feet, but he was still steady and he exhaled a deep breath. "You should know better considering our childhood." He bent down, and pulled out a gun that was in a hidden ankle holster.

I couldn't do anything.

If he'd been a lesser fighter, I could've thrown the knife at him. Maybe.

Ben was too good. I'd recognized it when I fought him, and he raised the gun toward me, a flicker in his eyes before he aimed it at Vicky. The safety was turned off, and his finger went to the trigger.

I couldn't—no. Not again. I lunged toward him, and at the same time—BANG!

I was in front of him.

Time slowed down, and I looked up, my eyes meeting his. His were alarmed, but mine—I didn't know what mine looked like, but I wasn't just seeing Ben anymore.

Images flashed in my mind, coming at breakneck speed.

Brett telling me he loved me.

Us kissing.

Me crying.

As we held onto each other on the picnic table in Roussou.

Talking to Stevie on the couch.

At the football game, laughing with Lo and Roger.

Travis grinning at us.

Brett sacking the Orcas' quarterback.

Then they sped up even more...

The first time I slept at Brett's.

The first time he slept at my place.

The day Lo and I walked and talked on the driveway.

Luna crashing her bike into the fence, on purpose.

Brett coming for Sunday night dinner.

Jack's BBQ with Brett.

The alley with Brett.

The street where Brett protected me from teenagers.

When I stumbled and Brett caught me on the show.

When I walked past and saw Brett for the first time.

Coffee with Vicky, with Miss Sylvia Rivera in my arms.

When I first met Miss Sylvia Rivera.

When I got my first graphic design client.

Moving into the guesthouse.

Meeting Deandra and Martell for the first time.

Getting my high school diploma with Vicky, Howard, and Lo there to celebrate.

Laughing with Lo in her car as she drove us to the movies.

The first time I met Vicky and Howard.

Sleeping over at Jojo's and sneaking out into a fort we'd made in the backyard.

Laughing with little Ben.

My mom kissing me.

My mom holding me.

Christmas with Ben and my mom.

Ice cream with my mom and Ben.

Holding baby Ben.

When Ben was born.

My mom tucking me into bed.

My mom kissing me on the forehead.

My mom telling me she loved me.

Then the last one, which should've been my first happy memory, but it wasn't.

I went back in time, to the one and only time my father showed that he loved me.

And I gasped, coming out on the other side, because movement shot past me and I watched as Brett ran past me, so fast. The bang had been him kicking open the front door behind me.

My brother couldn't react in time.

The gun was knocked away, and Brett grabbed my brother around his chest, taking him with him, his momentum sending both of them out of the house through the back door. Brett rolled once with him before he launched my brother clear from the house.

I gasped, shoving to my feet. At some point I had fallen. My arm gave out and I fell down again, so I rolled, needing to see what happened.

Brett stood, standing between my brother and us, and even though Brett filled the doorway, there was a small opening where I could see my brother getting back up.

He started for Brett, and then *bang! Bang! Bang! Bang!*

Bullet after bullet hit Ben's chest, his body jerking from the force. Whoever was shooting stopped, but Ben remained on his feet. His eyes were wild.

I already knew, having heard him, but there was no humanity left in him.

He took a step toward Brett, and the shooter unleashed more gunshots again.

Over and over again, Ben's body jerked from each bullet as he took one more step, before finally falling to his knees, then stopping. He held himself there, somehow, and those crazed eyes looked past Brett, to me.

He was dying.

A tear welled up and slipped free before I could stop it.

He'd been my brother.

I loved him.

I raised him.

He'd been mine just as much as he'd been our mother's.

Emotions welled up in my chest. Ben was so crystal clear in the moonlight and I whispered, "I love you."

Ben faltered, just for a fraction of a second, relief showing over his face.

Then he died.

It was over.

66

BILLIE

Police sirens lit up the air, coloring it red and blue almost as soon as Ben's body hit the floor.

Brett ran to me, dropping to his knees, a sob in his throat. "Jesus. Baby. Billie."

I was fine, but he looked scared to touch me. "Help Howard."

Vicky was just finishing untying Howard, pulling the tape off his mouth and holding one of their couch cushions against his head. "I'm fine. We're fine. Take care of Billie." But seeing a plea from Howard who was looking from him to Vicky, Brett ignored her, picked her up in his arms. She was protesting as he stood, saying to me, "Don't move. I called Travis and he called the rest of his people. We got twenty squad cars out there and five ambulances. They're all coming down the driveway so sit tight."

He took her outside, bypassing Travis who was kneeling beside Ben. As Brett disappeared from sight, Travis felt for Ben's pulse.

There'd be none. I saw my brother die, knew it the instant it happened. I felt it. A weight lifted off my chest and I swore I heard my mom's voice whisper, "It's done now." An odd sensation of peace and warmth wrapped around me before that also lifted away.

Travis came in, holstering his gun. His eyes were hooded, his face like granite. His gaze skimmed over me, a question in there. I shook my head, just slightly, and cut my eyes to the side toward Howard. Travis raked a hand over his face as he seemed to have aged five years in one night. Giving me a brief nod, he went to Howard's side. "I'll help you outside."

"No, you won't." Howard said it loudly and proudly. His Adam's apple was bobbing the whole time, and he was so pale. There was a slight yellowish tone just underneath, which was worrying. "I am just fine. You help my daughter, you hear m—"

Travis wavered, knowing I wanted him to help Howard first.

Brett came in, striding to Howard, and he didn't give him an option this time. He knelt and picked Howard right up in his arms. He paused once, gritted his teeth, but readjusted Howard in his arms, and looking like freaking Superman, he carried him back out the door.

Travis said under his breath, watching them disappear, "Jesus."

I pulled myself up, resting against the back of the couch. It was nearest to me.

I wasn't quite ready to go out there, whether I walked, Brett carried me, or if the paramedics transported me. It'd be a scene so similar to another that I couldn't stomach.

So, stalling.

I was doing that.

Plus, Brett would want to carry me out. He was doing his thing where he needed to help but in a way where he could deny it later.

Travis eyed me, but as if reading my mind, he didn't come over to help me. He leaned against the wall behind him, sliding down to the ground. "Brett called me. He couldn't reach you on the phone so he logged into Howard's security system. He wasn't human when he called me. I'd only ever heard another person talk how he did, and that guy was jacked up on drugs and it took thirty cops to stop him from going on a rampage. I don't know how your man reined himself in, but he did."

"You're the one who was shooting Ben?"

Guilt flared in his eyes. He looked down. "I killed your brother. I'm so—"

"Do not," I said it swiftly, so swiftly that his head jerked back up. I leaned forward, letting him see everything I was about to say, letting him see how much I meant it. "It is a fucking tragedy what happened to my brother, and I'm not talking about today. I'm talking about when my mom drove into the river, when she died and he didn't, when he was saved by the worst possible people who could've been there at that moment. I'm talking about how he was then raised by them. They helped create him into this, but..." I couldn't go there, what I now realized my mom had known and why she made the decision to drive into the river. It was ghastly and horrible and no mother should do what she did, but she did it for a reason. That wasn't for Travis to know, not yet anyway. "It morphed him into who he became, which was a killer. He told me Ben died in that river, and I believe him. That guy out there —" I gestured to him, not looking because a part of me was still aching at the loss of what could've been, "—he's not Ben. He had no soul, and putting him down was the most humane thing you could've done." A tear slid down my face, and dammit. I turned away, saying, my voice dipping, "The brother I loved would've been horrified at the man he became. You put him out of his misery, and you brought justice to all the people he's killed. Don't ever feel guilty about what you did."

Brett was coming back.

I felt him before I saw him.

He stood in the doorway, his eyes on me, so dark, and Travis was right. His beast was there, but Brett was doing what he needed to appease him. A nerve in his jaw twitched before he came to my side. As he bent down to me, we both heard Travis say, "I shot him in front of you. You shouldn't have to watch your brother die, no matter what kind of man he became in the end."

Both Brett and I looked his way, but he didn't notice. A distant expression was on his face.

"I would've had it no other way."

Travis' head snapped to me, surprised.

"I saw my brother at the end. I was with him. That's all that matters to me. I got my brother back, and it doesn't matter how short it was, I still got him back for a brief moment. I would've had it no other way."

Wetness pooled on the bottom of Travis' eyes, but he blinked rapidly, clearing that away. His jaw turned rigid and he looked away as it seemed our moment was done. Brett gently slid his arms under me, and just as gently stood with me cradled against his chest.

He took me outside, saying gruffly, "Look away."

He wouldn't know this until later, but I tucked my head into his chest because I didn't want to see the police. The ambulances. I didn't want to see the chaos that my brother created. That's what was making my heart so heavy. He thought he was saving me from looking down as we walked past Ben's body, but that didn't bother me.

I peeked.

Goodbye, Ben.

I ASKED BRETT LATER, "Is Callie okay? What happened at your house?"

He shifted closer to me, lying on the bed with me until that wasn't enough. He reached over and deposited me on top of him, his body relaxing almost dramatically. I'd been given the all clear from the hospital and Howard had been taken back for emergency surgery to see if they could reattach his ear. Vicky was being taken care of so Brett pulled me into an empty room and held me as his giant body slightly trembled against me.

I breathed him in, balling his shirt in my fists. His beard grazed against my neck as he answered me, "She's fine. Her friend got a ride to the house by her brother. Callie said she was only supposed to drop something off for her, but they talked for a little bit. And something must've sent her friend's brother off because he suddenly started making threats. He's got some deeper struggles going on. It got scary and that's when she called me. The cops arrested him, but I guess that family member was the reason Callie stopped staying at her friend's place. With him in jail, she went back there."

"Are they going to be okay?"

He began kneading at one of my hips. "I think so."

The door opened. A nurse stood there. "You can't be in her —" She stopped when Brett lifted his head, and her eyes got big. "Oh. *Oh.* Mr. Brett Broudou. I—hello." She blinked a few times, her face getting serious. "I'm guessing the plethora of men wearing badges and carrying guns are here for one of you?"

Brett bribed her with an autograph and a promised video message to her son if she'd hold them off for another hour.

She sighed, looking back out the hallway. "That's going to be a team effort sort of thing. Order some pizzas for the nurse's desk and we can probably get you two hours."

The two hours went too fast.

After that, the questions started.

So many detectives and FBI agents and other kinds of government people came to question me. Then the press.

There was so much press.

People became obsessed with how my brother who had been thought dead turned out to be the mastermind behind the Copier Killer. A floodgate of cold cases were reopened as police all over were now matching my brother's DNA to unidentified DNA found in their cases.

There was a count of how many victims my brother had killed, but I didn't want to know. I couldn't bear to know. I'd learn it one day, probably from walking past a room as a report would be discussing my brother on the news. I was resigned to it, having lived through this maelstrom of events once before.

———————

HOWARD HAD to stay in the hospital for a week because he was suffering from internal damage we hadn't known about, but he got his ear back. Vicky looked ready to either cry or beat someone up when she saw the scars Howard would have for the rest of his life.

Howard winked at me. The scar didn't bother him that much.

———————

IT TOOK MONTHS LATER, but we buried my brother in a grave next to my mom. His headstone was unmarked and the ceremony was private. I couldn't stomach thinking about asking Vicky and Howard, or Lo and Roger if they wanted to come for the ceremony. So with a local minister, just Brett and I were there.

Until Travis walked up behind us, admonishing me, "Are you serious? You think we wouldn't want to be here for you?"

I stiffened, then shock spread through me as I saw Vicky, Howard, Lo, Roger, and my eyes began watering because there were so many more behind them.

"Don't get mad at your man, but Broudou told me what was happening." Travis shrugged. "I made a few calls."

"Brett?"

I was already plastered against his side, but at his name, his hand slid around my waist and he pulled me to stand in front of him, his arms firmly holding me in place. His head dipped, and he said next to my ear, "He was your brother, Billie. They're here for you." He pressed a kiss to my forehead, brushing some of my hair back.

My family was here. They'd come for me.

Vicky and Lo gave me hugs, and right after, I returned to Brett's shelter, almost sagging back against him as I took in the entirety of people who now surrounded my mom and brother's graves.

Olvander and Kayla.

Dusty and Stone Reeves, some younger men that I hadn't met were also with them.

Jake and Emma Bilson.

Colby Doubard.

These people were here for Brett, which almost had me crying all over again because following the showdown Brett had with his sister, which was more of a showdown between who he is now versus who he was before, and what I had to say all about that, he started letting people in.

As this happened, the biggest surprise was that Colby and Brett were almost inseparable. Everyone had been surprised by that, but I wasn't. I knew Brett and I was starting to understand Colby behind the mask he showed to everyone else. The two were similar in so many ways.

More people were still joining, more of Brett's friends.

Channing Monroe and his wife. Mason Kade and his wife. Two other men were also with them, both giving Brett a nod in acknowledgement.

Will and Harmony were the last ones to join, filling in the

last spot in the circle everyone had created. I didn't think it was done on purpose, but as Will's brother closed it up, somehow, it was perfect.

My hand found Brett's and squeezed so hard. Grateful.

But a shudder went down my spine because there was one more thing I needed to tell Brett.

EPILOGUE 1: BRETT

THREE YEARS LATER.

"Hey, man." Channing slapped me on the back after Will and I brought in the last of our things. He held out a beer, holding his own up for a salute after I took it. He handed a non-alcoholic one to Will since we both knew my brother didn't drink. "Are you all done? How's it feel?"

I took the beer, and all of us touched our cans together, but I gave him a look before taking a drag. "How's what feel, Monroe? Me? I'm fucking tired, but I also know we got a lot more shit to do yet."

Channing hid a grin as I skimmed through the house.

It was ten-thirty at night and the house Billie and I were moving into was riddled with boxes, packing paper, bags, and the furniture was spread out in every room. For the most part, Billie had already walked through the house before our trip with an interior designer. They mapped where they wanted everything put. I wasn't sure how much Billie was leaning on the designer, but she liked having a partner to go over everything together.

Me? Tell me to put our bed in the living room, and I might've given her a funny look, but I would've done it. Whatever made Billie happy made me happy, an edict that we'd been living by for the last three years. We'd finished the trip today with Will flying down and doing the drive with us. I drove the bigger truck with the last of our items while either he or Billie drove the other vehicle. If Billie was tired, he switched with her and she rode with me.

We had movers take the bulk in an earlier trip, but this was the last of it.

Vicky and Howard were flying in tomorrow to help unpack everything, but in all honesty, Billie didn't need the extra hands. She had enough here with Harmony, Stevie, and there were others who were waiting to jump in and help. They were holding off, waiting for the go-ahead. That was Channing's woman and also Samantha Kade. There were others in their group, and Billie had met them all during a few of our trips here to visit my family. We'd come more during Shannon's trial, and my sister pleading not guilty was a given, something she'd do no matter the evidence that'd been built up against her. I'd not been shocked. She kept turning down any deals offered to her, and the whole trial had been a shit-show. The Shannon shit-show, though in the end she was found guilty of every charge they threw at her. There'd been things inside their house that the police found, dark things, dreadful things that ensured both Shannon and her boyfriend would be gone a long time.

Everyone felt better knowing she was there and she couldn't get out.

"I was referring more to your decision about football. You and Mason retired at the same time." His mouth turned up in a crooked grin. And because Monroe was Monroe, I knew he was baiting me. Seeing if he could get some form of reaction from me, just so he could get a feel on how I was really doing. He'd done it in high school when we were enemies and that habit never went away. Channing liked to rile people up in general.

Since Billie got in my face, literally, or technically as I got in her face when I'd almost done something stupid that might've put me in prison, I took her words to heart. She wanted me to let people in, so I did. Or I worked at it. It was still a struggle because that's how I had been all my life. But I trusted Billie and she said she wanted me to have friends, so I had friends. If she said it, I did it.

Channing laughed for five straight minutes the first time I called him and explained what Billie wanted, hooting how 'adorable' I was, doing what my woman wanted. I tossed shit right back at him because he was wrapped tight around his own woman's pinkie and he knew it. Since then there was a friendship between us, but we'd always been on the opposite side of things for most of our lives so that push and pull between us wasn't going to go away. It helped that I'd been paying him to give me updates on my family, which paved the beginning of our friendship long ago.

I grunted at his comment, though I'd been just as surprised as everyone else when Mason Kade's announcement to retire broke the day after mine.

And we both moved to Fallen Crest.

Will grew quiet, listening to our conversation.

Channing smirked. "It's kinda funny, though. You and Billie moving to Mason and Logan's old neighborhood. You're just down the block from Mama Melinda and Sam's dad."

I gave him a look. "Stop fucking needling me, Monroe."

He laughed, taking a drag from his beer. "Or what? You'll take back my friendship bracelet?"

"I'll break your wrist so it'll heal so you can never wear another friendship bracelet."

He and Will both started laughing.

I was joking.

Somewhat. Kinda.

I wasn't really joking, which both knew and that made them

laugh harder because in the end, it wouldn't matter. After the initial phone call when I told him Billie wanted me to have friends, something switched in Monroe. He would't have let me not be friends with him after that, and me breaking his wrist, he'd still show up the next day. He'd demand an apology as he'd also be unloading things to help me build a treehouse, which he would tell me that I needed to do for my nieces and nephews, because he'd done it for his own kids.

"Where did they end up moving to? Are they back in this neighborhood?"

Channing was loving this conversation. There was a look of amusement but also a twisted grin on his face. "They moved to a different neighborhood, but their dad's old house is in this neighborhood too. I can't get over how everything is just coming full circle."

He was referencing old shit from when we'd been in high school. It was in the past and had no bearing on the now. None of it mattered.

I was getting tired of the direction this conversation was going. Channing got a kick out of it all, but I didn't. We'd only be here half the year anyway. Six months here for my family, especially since Stevie had taken to Billie in such a strong way.

Stevie was almost obsessed with Billie.

It worried Harmony a little, who was more tentative in her own relationship with Billie, but that's because of Harmony's family. Her parents considered themselves in the 'old money' society of Fallen Crest. They adored their new grandchildren, but Billie's past with the Midwest Butcher and how it came out about her brother made them decide they were in some place where they could approve of Billie or not. A lot of people were hesitant to form friendships with Billie. The part where they decided they were in a place to *have* an opinion was something I'd be clearing up to them, and shortly. They were in no place to approve of Billie or disapprove, and I was looking forward to the day I made that abundantly clear to them. I'd already started making moves to help me when I'd solidify that fact to them. The sooner the better.

However, the funny part of all that was that Billie didn't care. She truly didn't, and said it took off the pressure of her having to be friendly with them. She was good with the circle she had, with me, Lo, and now Stevie.

I only cared where no one had any fucking right in deciding not to accept Billie, unless she decided she didn't want to be accepted by them. But Billie reassured me this wasn't a fight I could or should take on. It was useless because narrow-mindedness wasn't something I could break, like Monroe's wrist.

Still, it pissed me off, and the few times we'd come together for a holiday, Harmony's parents and the rest of her family knew exactly how much I didn't like them. Will wasn't a fan either, and it'd affected his own relationship with his in-laws.

That was family shit that would happen no matter where we lived, who we were, or how old we got. Family would be up and down, as far as I was concerned, but Will and I were good. Will and Billie were good. Billie and I were good with Stevie, Georgie, Sammy, and now Will's two boys, so in that regard, I was content as fuck.

"What's this I hear that Stevie decided to transfer to FCA?" Channing sensed I wasn't going to react to any of his questions, so he let it go, throwing his next question to my brother.

That got my attention.

Will faltered as he was in the middle of taking another drag from his na-beer. He glanced my way before coughing and nodding. "Yeah. Uh. She originally wanted to do public school here, thought Fallen Crest Academy would be too different from Roussou. That's what she was used to, but she made the decision a week ago."

"She's going to FCA now?" I asked him.

He frowned at me, watching me carefully.

I'd extended a scholarship to Stevie years ago. If she wanted to go to the private school in Fallen Crest, she could go. It was her decision. Will and Harmony were financially maxed out in a legal fight against Shannon for custody before she'd been sentenced to prison. I helped cover Stevie's therapy fees, but I found out later that they decided to have Georgie and Sammy both see a therapist, and they were also covering those fees themselves. They hadn't wanted to use their insurance, hence why I set up the scholarship. Though, I would've set it up regardless and already had started before they told me.

Stevie turned the scholarship down, though she didn't know I was the one behind it.

He nodded. "We checked. The scholarship she was originally offered said they'd cover her. They said it was set in stone for whenever she wanted to use it. Real generous of them."

Channing's head moved back an inch. "I'll say. I had no idea there were scholarships for kids to go to FCA, though it makes sense. That school is expensive."

Will and I both shared a look.

Channing was talking as if they weren't in the way where they could afford to send their kids to that school. They could. They could afford to send thirty kids through that school if they wanted. They'd franchised his wife's local bar in other locations and they were doing well. They were doing very well, but I shook my head slightly to Will. We didn't bring it up. I didn't care about it enough *to* bring it up.

Seeing Billie trying to hide a yawn as she was going through some boxes, I said briskly, "It's time for you to say goodnight, Monroe."

He paused, his eyes skirting my way and then toward Billie before he dipped his head down. "You're right. It's that time." The goodbyes happened quickly, no fuss about it because it's how we were. He finished his beer, then headed out, holding up a hand to Billie. "It was good seeing you again."

Billie looked up, swallowing a second yawn. "Hi! Yes. Thank you for your help, Chandler."

It was a joke now between them, and Channing flashed her a grin. "Heather will kick my ass if I don't remind you that she'd love to come and help you unpack."

Billie flushed before nodding. "I—yes—I'll give her a call in the week. Just need to get my bearings until then."

Channing held up his hand in another wave before he was gone.

I was watching Billie, but Will was watching me. I felt his attention and wasn't surprised when he noted quietly, "Something going on there? Between Monroe's wife and Billie?"

I shook my head. "No. Billie's just content with keeping a small circle. It's how she operated growing up. That's all." That was true, but Channing's wife made it known she'd love to befriend Billie and all that would come with that. She had a group of friends that came with her, but there'd also be a load of support that would also come with them. Billie wasn't used to it. Took half her life to finally accept Vicky and Howard as her parents and Lo as her sister. Small steps. That's how Billie was right now.

Whatever Billie wanted. Whatever made her happy.

"That's nice of them, though. To extend that friendship branch."

Will was watching Billie now. She was moving around in the kitchen by herself, but she was doing it happily. He spoke quietly even though Billie couldn't hear. The house was that big. "Stevie wanted to come over to help Billie so bad. We just felt with school starting tomorrow, and it'd be late when we got here, it was better for her to wait to come over later in the week."

"Solid thinking."

He flicked his eyes up. "Harmony's coming around—"

"Will."

He stopped at my sudden firm tone.

I said, "Don't do that. Don't start to say some shit that'll be some excuse why your wife isn't coming around when our niece would move in here if all of us allowed that. We both know what's going on, and while it doesn't make me really like your wife that much, I probably wouldn't have liked her anyway because she's got a personality where she cares what other people think about her. I'm not like that. Billie's not like that. She's not hurting because your wife is scared of befriending her. It is what it is. I know your wife is getting some asinine opinions put in her head and I know who's putting those asinine ideas in there. So let's just say that we'll make sure to come to family holidays when certain people make their leave. However, Harmony isn't a bad person either. You love her. She loves you. She also loves Stevie, Georgie, and Sammy, so there's no bad blood between us either."

Will picked up on who I wasn't including, and who else might've been at their family holidays.

He nodded, sighing. "It bothers me, though."

"But it doesn't bother Billie."

We were in agreement there, sharing another look.

He said, "We need to have a talk about how much we're going to let Stevie come over here. She'd come over tomorrow before school if we let her."

"Sure."

"Just talk it out with Billie about what you guys want, and I'll talk to Harmony too, see what she's okay with as well. We know Stevie will be here a lot, and I know it somewhat hurts Harmony's feelings, but we'll deal with it. We can all tell that it's good for Stevie to be around Billie."

I agreed.

He left after that, finishing his non-alcoholic beer before going over to hug Billie and say his own goodbyes to her, whispering something to her which got him another tighter hug and lots of smiles from Billie.

She swung her eyes my way, still smiling, but I also caught a shadow there. She didn't come over so whatever it was, she'd tell me later. If she didn't, I'd be bringing it up. I didn't like seeing that shadow over my woman.

She liked the sunshine, and I'd make sure to remind her of that tonight.

No more shadows.

Just sunshine.

EPILOGUE 2: BILLIE

I was happy and wired and so tired that I'd progressed to hyper level three thousand. I liked my little home at the farm, but I also got used to Brett's big house and now we were in Fallen Crest, and if I were going to have a dream big house, this was it.

It was past midnight.

We'd gone to bed shortly after Will left, but again, I. Was. Wired.

Brett tried holding off from falling asleep until I went first. He did that all the time, but this time, he finally faded a few minutes ago and I slipped from the bed.

God. I couldn't believe how far we'd come with everything.

There were shows about the Midwest Butcher, and now those shows were revamped to add the last section that involved my brother and me. It spurred a whole new frenzy of the obsession people had with serial killers, and there was even a show coming out on Netflix loosely based off my life, including my relationship with Brett. They approached me to do the show, but they could've done it anyway, so I signed off with it as long as my name was never included in any line of the show or in the credits and if I got financially compensated. Brett had lawyers look over the contract, so there was no loophole to screw us, which at first and second pass, there'd been some items that needed to be smoothed out. In the end, my secret hope was that the show would either crash and burn and no more shows would come out or the opposite, where it'd get so big that people would forget it was even inspired from my life.

Fingers crossed.

I'd made peace that the show was happening, and after Ben's death, I hadn't been hated along with him. That'd been my biggest fear. It hadn't happened, and I finally felt like I could breathe easier. The rest would be fine.

I was content with my world how it was. With Brett. With Keanu, the dog Brett gifted me two years ago, a rescue German Shepherd. He was named after Keanu Reeves, but Brett talked me into dropping the full name policy for our future pets. So Keanu, and he was gorgeous and lovey-dovey and the bestest of the bestest best friend a person could get.

I was currently on my knees getting all sorts of licks and kisses from him because when I slipped out of bed, he came with me, and we were on the first floor of the house. I was in giant sized wool socks and I snagged Brett's Kings shirt he'd thrown on the chair, and standing, I backed up, eyeing Keanu who was prancing on his front two paws next to me.

We backed up, and backed up, until we were at the end of the long hallway on the first floor and then—bam! We both took off. Or I took off, running as hard as I could in these socks. Keanu was bouncing along with me, his giant tongue hanging from the side of his mouth, until...*woosh.*

I turned and let the socks let me slide the rest of the length of the entire house.

This was awesome.

As soon I as stopped sliding, we went right back for another trip.

It'd be cool if I could find some sort of engine just to propel me around the house. The whole first floor was either hardwood or a fancy looking tile that looked like real rock. The kitchen had a giant square island in the middle. The cupboards were European style, which I didn't know what that meant, but I liked the look. They weren't typical cupboards and one of them even lifted up.

Plus, there was a hidden door.

Actually, there were two hidden doors and a safe room. Brett had the safe room installed especially for me, but I knew in my heartest of hearts that it would never be needed. All the bad stuff was done, or I hoped because the rest was all sunshine, smiles, and sex. Lots of sex, my favorite part.

Brett was so good at it too— "What are you doing?"

I'd been about to let loose for another slide but stopped.

Brett had come down the stairs and stood in the giant doorway leading to the kitchen, stroking his beard, which he trimmed after playoffs every year, but this was his first year in retirement so we'd have to discuss his new policy. It had grown out again after he trimmed it last year.

"Hi," I was breathless and panting a little bit. The whole running to slide part was some work.

"Hi." His hand dropped from his beard. He fixed me with a serious look, his hand automatically dropping to pet Keanu on the head because every time Keanu saw Brett, he went nuts and acted as if it'd been ten years since their last meeting. "What are you doing?"

I motioned to the hallway. "Sliding."

He looked where I gestured. "Sliding?"

"Yeah." I lifted up my feet. "See? These are perfect for sliding on this floor."

"You're having a Tom Cruise moment?"

"What? No." I was slightly aghast at that. "There's no moment I'm having. This is a Billie moment. A Happy Billie moment. I'm happy."

He was back to studying me. As he did, his shoulders lifted up and back down, and his eyes began darkening. A slight tingle was starting to warm me because I knew what that look meant.

The sex was going to happen.

"What'd Will say to you before he left?"

Oh. The tingle went flat. The sex wasn't going to happen. I misread that look.

I lost the tingle for another reason too, which I was nervous to bring up, but since Brett had asked... "He told me that Harmony is pregnant again."

His eyebrows shot up. He'd not been expecting that. "Really?"

I nodded, my throat swelling up because of the other part I wanted to bring up to him.

Seeing it, because he was Brett and I was Billie and we were each other's person, he asked, gently, "What is it?"

Okay.

My pulse skipped a few beats, but brave face. I could do this. I blurted out, "So, I know we're not married."

His eyebrows went flat.

"We've not talked about making anything official, I realize—"

His eyebrows started to fold down.

"—but we're living together and it's been three years and now we have Keanu together, and Nellie Bly is really more your chicken than she is mine or Vicky's, so we kinda have two pets together now. Which are like our children, so it's like we have children together and..." I was so nervous. My palms were slick with sweat. I began toying with the end of Brett's shirt, which

was super big on me, which made me love it even more. "And
—well—"

His eyebrows were pinched together and that wasn't a good
face.

I stopped talking. If just the mention of our pets as kids
were making him look like that, I couldn't go through with it.

"Billie," he rasped.

"What?"

"What were you going to say?"

"Nothing. It's nothing." I needed a moment to collect
myself. I'd been wanting to bring it up, but I couldn't. Not if it
meant there was a possibility Brett wouldn't be okay with it. I
couldn't lose him, ever. Hugging myself, I stopped keeping track
of Brett until he was right in front of me.

He bent, put his head against my side, and lifted me up as
he stood.

I grabbed onto him from instinct, though he'd done this so
many other times, I didn't squawk like I normally would. "What
are you doing?"

With me hanging over his shoulder, he turned the lights off in
each room as he went back upstairs, then into our room, and he
tossed me down on the bed, but he came with me. Which I always
loved, and we'd negotiated the throwing me over his shoulder
stuff. My policy was that I was okay with it, as long as he put me
down in this manner. Always on the bed and he always came with
me, and there were addendums added if sex followed right after.

I was hoping for that addendum to happen tonight.

It wasn't happening this time because Brett propped
himself on top of me and raised himself to look down at me.
"What were you going to say?"

I slid a hand around his neck and tried to pull him down to
me. "Nothing. Come here—"

He resisted. "Billie."

I sighed, my hand falling back to the bed and I let it thump with a bounce because I was trying to distract him here.

He ignored it, only raising an eyebrow at me.

The nerves came back to me, fluttering in a tizzy all around inside me. They were worked up. "I—" Tears formed at the corners of my eyes. Did I really want to say this? Once I said it, it would either happen or it would definitely not happen and I wasn't sure which would break my heart.

"Billie," he said again, softer. He moved my legs apart, settling between them, but he only held himself there. "We've been through literal hell and back. You can tell me. There's no secrets between us."

My eyes held onto his, almost clinging in a way.

He frowned slightly, brushing some of my hair back from my forehead. Still in that soft tone, he said, "We've not married because you wanted to wait. Remember?"

I bit down on my lip. He was right about that too. "When we talked about that, it was right after Ben." I looked away.

"Yeah, but I've just been waiting for you to bring it back up. I'll marry you tonight if you said the word."

I looked back. "You would?"

"Of course I would." A gentle smile tugged at the corner of his mouth. "You're my forever, Billie. You were my forever the second I saw you at the news show that morning. I just didn't catch up until you began talking about chickens. But you're it for me. There'll never be anyone else. It's always been you for me. You want to get married tonight?"

My heart was going to burst out of me. To go from being so nervous to this? The sunshine. He always made me feel it in these moments. "I don't want to get married tonight."

"Tomorrow?"

I smiled a little. "I don't want to get married tomorrow."

"The day after?"

I laughed, reaching for him again, both of my hands sliding

around his neck and lacing together. "Not the day after."

"Okay."

"Okay?"

He relaxed more on top of me, and he moved against me where I could feel his dick. He was hard, and the sunshine grew more inside me because I also *really* loved his dick. So much.

And I loved how he began moving it against me, rubbing and grinding.

I groaned, my eyes closing, beginning to move with him, loving how I'd learned that if I pushed my hips off the bed and began rubbing up and down over his dick, clothed or not, Brett went still because he *loved* that sensation too. I was about to do just that, but he stopped moving.

My eyes popped open. "What? Why'd you stop?"

His eyes were dark with lust but also narrowed on me. "You need to tell me what's going on with you." He pressed a hand to my chest, his palm flat, right over my heart. "Let me in, Billie."

I melted. Who wouldn't at that move?

"Not fair," I retorted, but he only chuckled and waited. Here we go. I blurted out, "I know you're old."

"What?"

"I don't mean like that, but I mean in child-rearing age. You're old, but I'm not. I'm younger than you, but I'll be too old soon and—"

He sat up, all business now. He knew where I was going with this. "You told me you didn't want kids."

I went back to chewing on my bottom lip. This was stressful. "Well, that was before you. And when we had that talk, Ben had just happened and I told you my secret. Having a kid would— well, you know the reasons I was nervous about having a kid."

He said it bluntly, "You were worried about your father's reaction, if he found out."

My throat was searing, especially when I heard him say my other fear back to me, putting it in words. It was different feeling it, thinking it, then hearing it spoken out loud. "Well, yeah. He's not a good person and there's a reason my mom did everything she did. But yeah, if he found out, how would he react and would he want to be in some part of our kid's life? I mean, there'd be no way. You and I would never let that happen, but he might try, and if he did..." I couldn't say it.

If he did, chaos would ensue, and it'd be really bad chaos.

We survived the chaos my brother put us through and my dad would be a different storm altogether.

Brett went back to studying me. He murmured, "It'd be okay." When he saw I couldn't say anything, he moved to the side of me and pulled me into his arms. He cradled me, relaxing down on the bed, and I was half lying on top of him. One of his hands rubbed down my back. The other began toying with my hair.

I let one of my legs slip between his, resting completely against him.

He spoke again, his voice vibrating through his chest underneath me, relaxing me even more, "No matter what your father did, I'd never let him hurt you. Vicky wouldn't. Howard wouldn't. We all know Lo would go insane on him. Roger. Their girls. My nieces and nephews. Will. Even Harmony wouldn't let him. You'd have a wall of people between you and him. We just got here today, but I know that once we get settled, Heather, Channing's wife, is going to adopt you and you'll have all their protection too. You've met that group, but I don't think you realize how protective they are of each other. You have almost an army of your own to rally around you, protect you, and that's in any facet needed. Either literally or through going to the press. I know you've been scared all your life, but you don't have to be anymore."

He was saying all the right words. How did he always know the right thing to say? It was like his superpower, besides the sex, and besides his usual athletic abilities, which the entire nation could attest to how great those skills were.

But his best superpower was in how he loved me.

"I know after Ben, you went back into hiding, but you don't have to. You really don't. You can say and do whatever you'd like. You want to go to Congress on how they should better protect chickens, I'm with you. Just like you're with me. You got me to pull my head out of my ass and here I am, not just letting Monroe come over to help carry our furniture inside, but I called and *asked* him to help. Monroe is not a buddy that'd do that as a favor, be okay with some small talk over a beer before he'd head out for his own place. Monroe's an all-in type of friend." I wasn't looking, but I could hear his glare. "Which is annoying, but knowing that, I'm still friends with him. That says everything about you. Whatever you want to do, you have your army behind you."

I lifted my head to look at him, and I whispered, "I want to have a baby."

He didn't blink. He didn't react. He held my gaze and his own warmed at the words. He smiled after, slowly, and I saw how genuine it was. He framed my face, both of his hands cupping the sides of me and he half lifted me as I raised myself, my mouth going to his, and just before they touched, he whispered, "Will you marry me, Billie Harm?"

I gasped, jerking out of his hands and sitting up.

My heart was in the middle of its own stampede. "Are you serious?" I frowned. "Or is this a joke? Are you teasing me?"

He held my gaze, long and serious and drawn out. That tenderness never went away. It only increased, and he sat up too. Reaching into the nightstand beside our bed, the nightstand that was just put there today, he pulled out a little box.

I started crying. The tears I'd been trying to keep from shedding, even though I knew I was going to shed them, they were free-flowing now. I was smiling so hard, so wide, that it

was actually hurting. I cupped both of my hands over my face
as he got off the bed, kneeling down and he held the box up to
me, opening it.

I had no idea what the ring looked like.

My tears were blinding me.

It was there and it was sparkling and it was so pretty.

He asked again, "Will you marry me, Billie?"

I nodded, everything in me was overflowing, and as he
lifted the ring and slid it onto my finger, he paused once again
as he said throatily, "I would love to have a baby with you, and I
don't care what comes first. The marriage or the baby. Just as
long as you're included."

I laughed, still sputtering out my tears of happiness, but
Brett stood and picked me up, then he laid me down and
crawled on top of me.

We didn't do the sex that night.

We did the lovemaking, which was also known as the slow
sex, which was so good too.

ONE MORE EPILOGUE: BILLIE
THREE MONTHS LATER

I was nervous. Really nervous.

If I'd been nervous thinking about telling Brett that I wanted to have a baby, then that'd been a—no. They were different situations and different reasons for being nervous.

This one was about telling a secret I'd had all my life and waiting for them to hate me, condemn me, or get mad that I'd lied to them as long as they knew me.

Brett and I were in Texas and we'd just parked at the farm where everyone had gathered. Or the adults. I'd asked everyone to be here, even Travis, but had asked for a babysitter to take care of the kids. It wasn't appropriate to have them here, not for today.

And thinking all those thoughts, as Brett turned the engine off and started to get out of the vehicle, I didn't move. I couldn't.

I couldn't tell them.

I'd lose them.

I'd lose everyone.

Everyone who supported and rallied around me when it came out who Ben was, what Ben was.

I'd been lying to them too.

I told Brett right after because he needed to know every-thing. I knew there were new DNA testing measures, and they would've taken Ben's DNA, but I hadn't known what would happen after that.

But when I told Brett, I also explained to him why I loved when he called me Little Billie.

"Our father was abusive. He hurt our mom. He's the reason she didn't want us to have friends. She didn't want us to get attached because we kept moving to get away from him. He'd find us and then when he'd leave, we'd run again. It happened over and over until, well, until Jojo died. That was the end of it. My mom saw a way where I could be safe from him." I hated talking about my father. It was easier to talk about him as another person, as someone I didn't know. When I referred to him as someone related to me, it twisted up all my insides. It sickened me. He sickened me. Which was why I said, "He used to call me Little Billie."

Brett had tensed, looking distraught for a brief moment.

I shook my head, needing him to understand. "You took that name from him. It's yours. That's why I loved when you said it the first time, because it was like another part of me was stripped away from him. You claimed that piece of me for you. He couldn't have that anymore." My voice shook. "When you live in fear for so long, you don't realize all the pieces that get taken from you. That was a piece I didn't know I'd lost to him, until I got it back. Thank you."

He was still frowning. "I call you that during sex. That's—"

I laid a hand to his arm, hoping, praying, he'd understand. Really understand. "I know and because you did, it's in no way connected to him anymore. It's not his at all."

"But—"

"My dad wasn't abusive *to* me. He hurt my mom, but I didn't know that. And my mom said he took Ben with him somewhere. I didn't know that either, not until the last day I saw her. But he never did anything to me or with me. He was just cold. That's what I remember feeling around him. Cold and distant, but I could always feel his anger. It scared me. *He* scared me. I grew up associating fear with him, so when he called me Little Billie, there was no bad association with it. It was his nickname for me. My mom slipped one day and called me that same nickname and he got angry." I stuffed down a shudder. "Really angry. I think he hurt her that day because she sent Ben and me to the park. She said we could stay there all day and get ice cream on the way back." Regret sat on my shoulders. "I wish I'd known what was really going on."

"Your mom protected you from that for a reason. Don't take that away from her."

He was right. I nodded, drawing in some air. "Do you understand about the name? It's not his anymore, and because you use it mostly during sex, there's absolutely no association with him. You burned it all up and now I love when you call me that. I love hearing it from you. It's *only* your name for me. No one else's. Just you and just me and it makes me want you every time I hear it now. You did that. Do you understand?"

He had, but like everything and anything that was connected to my past or my brother or now my father, there was a time period afterwards where I couldn't quite breathe freely, wondering how much could Brett take, how many more truths before he decided he didn't want me anymore?

It hadn't happened.

Today, I needed to tell the rest.

The back door opened and Lo ran out first, going right to my door.

She hauled me out, hugging me tight and declaring, "I decided. You're never going to California. Never again. Brett can go and you guys can have a Zoom relationship. Zexting. You can make it a thing. I'm not letting you go. Also, Roger really wants to go to that place you and Brett go to all the time now. What's it called?"

"Rinascita." I hugged her back.

I hope you feel the same in an hour.

I HAD two things to tell them.

I started with the bad one first.

Everyone was sitting down in the living room. We'd gotten through the hugs, and all the beverages and snacks had been passed around. Everyone was comfortable. They were ready.

I sat in a chair in the corner. Brett was behind me, half sitting on the chair so I felt more than just his hand. I needed as much of him as possible, but I started.

"I—uh—I always thought my mom gave me up back then."

Someone gasped. I was guessing Lo because Vicky wasn't a gasper.

I hoped it was Lo and not Vicky. I didn't want to start this out with her already feeling betrayed by me.

I was looking down. I could do that, for this first part, but when I needed to tell them the end, I'd look. I'd look them all in the eyes. I was strong enough to do that.

"I just never knew because she left me at the police station and then she died. I didn't know if it was an accident where she was trying to run away, her and Ben going on the road when she knew I'd be safe from my dad."

A second gasp.

My heart hurt because that was Vicky. The first gasp had been her too.

I kept going. "I never told you guys about him, and I know you only know what was in my file, which was that I told the police I didn't know who he was. That was a lie. I've known who my father is all my life. I've known him until I turned twelve. That was one of the last times I saw him in person."

"What?" Lo asked. "You saw him another time? When?"

I glanced up, fleeting, before I looked back down and continued. I told them a brief summary of what I'd said to Brett three years ago. That he hurt my mom. That he took my brother away with him one time. That my mom was doing the best she could.

This next part hurt to say because why had it been me? "I do think he loved me, loves me still. He could've come forward, said he was my father. My name's been in the press so much, but he never has. My mom told me one time that he promised to stay away from me. She said it was the one thing he promised her. So far that's been true."

"Maybe he's not alive?" Roger said.

I didn't reply because I knew that wasn't true.

Here was the hard part. I closed my eyes and took a moment.

Brett's hand curled over my shoulder, giving me a squeeze before he reached down and took my hand in his. When he felt me trembling, he cursed under his breath and stood abruptly, but only to grab me, lift me, and he sat down underneath me, then pulled me onto his lap. His arms circled me, that hand finding mine again and lacing our fingers.

I settled back against him, a little of my tension easing. Just a little.

"Billie." Vicky's voice was so hoarse.

I looked up, seeing her leaning forward, her gaze shining with such strong emotion. "Whatever you have to tell us, we aren't going anywhere. I mean it. Anything. You are my daughter. I don't care that you don't have my blood. I love you and nothing would tear you away from me. You got me?" Her eyes flashed with intensity. "Now you say what you need to say because I need my second daughter to be able to breathe without it hurting. When you told your brother that I was your mother and Howard was your father, that was one of the best days of my life."

Two tears streaked down Howard's face as he blinked, nodding vigorously. His hand was clasped in Vicky's and I could see how tightly they were holding onto each other.

Maybe they already figured it out, or maybe they were preparing for the worst, but it helped me tell them the rest.

I didn't think about the movement. I'd think about it later because Vicky and Lo's eyes both got so big when I moved my hand and Brett's to my stomach, both of our hands opening to spread over my for-now flat tummy.

"After I found out what happened to Ben, who he'd turned into, I realized what my mom meant by needing to take him with her. And now I really understand. She couldn't choose between one child and the other. She didn't want Ben to become who our father was, so she decided to go with him. She chose to set me free. Ben told me the night he was here that Mom chose me because I was a star. That wasn't the truth. She let me go and she chose him. It just didn't turn out how she intended and we both lost her in the end, but she tried to go with him."

It hurt to keep going, to say the rest, and somehow I flashed back to that day.

I was hiding under Jojo's bed. The screams cut off, and there was a pained moment of silence.

I was so scared, every part of me was shaking. Even my teeth were rattling against each other, and I bit down on my arm to keep quiet as much as possible.

A floorboard creaked.

Another.

His pants swished.

He was drawing near.

The door opened, and he stepped inside.

He opened the closet.

Then to the bed.

His boots stopped right in front of me, shifting as he kneeled down.

He lifted the bedspread, and a face came down to look at me.

A face that I knew.

"I never understood why she did what she did, or why my father did what he did, but I do now. Ben and I were both loved. I know that now. My mom loved Ben. That's why she chose to die with him. And my dad loves me."

A deep breath.

My last secret.

"That's why my dad chose to let me live that day. After he had killed everyone in the house."

If you've enjoyed My Anti-Hero, please leave a review! They *truly* help so much.

If you'd like to read mores stories or some deleted scenes from My Anti-Hero, go to my website.

www.tijansbooks.com

If you'd like to read Stone and Dusty's story, check out Enemies.

If you'd like to read Mason and Samantha's story, check out Fallen Crest High.

(The ebook is free.)

If you'd like to read Channing and Heather's story, check out The Boy I Grew Up With.

RESOURCES

If you'd like to learn more about Sylvia Rivera, Marsha P. Johnson, or Nellie Bly, you can click on their names or check the sites below to learn why Billie loves them so much.

https://www.womenshistory.org/

https://www.glsen.org/

Other links:

National Domestic Violence Hotline
1.800.799.7233

Love Is Respect
1.866.331.9474

ACKNOWLEDGMENTS

I have had this book in my head for five years. Five years! Billie came to me first, and then Brett popped in when I was showering. No joke. I'm not an author who gets ideas in the shower. Other authors do this, but not me. So yep, Brett decided to join me and I still remember the moment.

But, I knew it would take a while before I could write their book.

A year later, the title for their book came to me and this was before I became aware of the entire anti-hero trope. I went back and forth if I should still use it, but I decided to go with the title that has been in my mind for so long.

And then when I finally started writing their story, the chickens! The chickens. (Side-note here: I am firmly an author who lets the characters speak in my mind and I am the tool to share their stories.) Because of the side-note, I was concerned about Billie's love, respect, obsession with naming her hens. I wanted to make it very clear that this was meant with the upmost respect and Billie genuinely holds these women and so many more so dear to her heart. I considered going with more typical names, but this wasn't being true to Billie so I chose to remain true to the character.

I truly hope that how genuine Billie was with her hens, that this was received with love by the readers.

I'd like to thank my editor, all my proofreaders, and my beta readers. Your feedback was so appreciated. Thank you to Mavis for letting me interview you about your hens. It's still been my favorite interview that I conducted for one of my books.

Thank you to all the goats I knew growing up. (This was a lot.) They are mischievous, but also very patient, serene, and loving. Though, stay away from most adult male goats for safety reasons.

Crystal, Tami, and Amy, thank you ladies so much for all the help you give me behind the scenes. Thank you to Becca for your input and also putting up with me.

Thank you to all the Fallen Crest readers! Thank you to the ladies in my reader group, Tijan's Crew.

And like always, thank you to my pup, Bailey, for hanging out with me while I'm reading and greeting me with a smile every time I move, or look his way, or stop typing for a second, or glance out the window—thank you for smiling and being happy. Always.

I hope you guys have enjoyed Brett and Billie's story.

ALSO BY TIJAN

Latest books:

My Anti-Hero

Pine River

Hockey With Benefits

A Dirty Business (Mafia, Kings of New York Series)

A Cruel Arrangement (Mafia, Kings of New York Series)

Aveke (Fallen Crest novella, standalone)

Sports Romance Standalones:

Pine River

Hockey With Benefits

Enemies

Teardrop Shot

Hate To Love You

The Not-Outcast

Rich Prick

Fallen Crest and Crew Universe

Fallen Crest/Roussou Universe

Fallen Crest Series

Crew Series

The Boy I Grew Up With (standalone)

Rich Prick (standalone)

Hockey With Benefits (standalone)

Nate (standalone)

Aveke (standalone)

A Kade Christmas

My Anti-Hero (standalone)

Motorcycle club romance:

Frisco

Series:

Broken and Screwed Series (YA/NA)

Jaded Series (YA/NA suspense)

Davy Harwood Series (paranormal)

Carter Reed Series (mafia)

The Insiders

Mafia Standalones:

Cole

Bennett Mafia

Jonah Bennett

Canary

Paranormal Standalones and Series:

Evil

Micaela's Big Bad

The Tracker

Davy Harwood Series (paranormal)

Young Adult Standalones:

Ryan's Bed

A Whole New Crowd

Brady Remington Landed Me in Jail

College Standalones:

Antistepbrother

Kian

Enemies

Contemporary Romances:

Bad Boy Brody

Home Tears

Fighter

Rockstar Romance Standalone:

Sustain

Christmas novellas:

A Kade Christmas

A Christmas Song (Ryan's Bed holiday novella)

More books to come!

THE NOT-OUTCAST

CHAPTER 1

I was lit, weak, and horny.

That was not a good combination for me. Usually my willpower was strong, like industrial-strength super-latexed condom strong, but not tonight. Tonight, the combination of the booze and cocktails had melded together and taken down my last holdouts of willpower. I was gonzo and then I got this text.

Dean: Mustang party! Now! Where r u???

Dean was my colleague, but let's forget about why he would be texting me because we are not 'texting' colleagues. Kansas City Mustangs. That was the important part of that text, and it was getting all of my attention.

Dear God. I could hear the whistle of the impending bomb right before it hit.

That was the professional hockey team that *he* played on.

Party.

Did I mention the *he* that was him? He, as in the only rookie drafted for Kansas City's newer team? He signed his contract after he had one year at Silvard.

The *he* that the team's owners were hoping could be grown into one of the NHL's newest stars, but that'd been a three-year plan. Nope. *He* had different ideas because once he hit the ice in their first debut game, he scored a hat trick in the first period. First. Period. Playing against five to ten-year veterans, and that had not gone unnoticed. By everyone. After that *he* exploded into the NHL scene and in a big fucking way.

They started calling him Reaper Ryder after that.

It was the same *he* that I perved on during a brief stint in high school, and then again during that one year in college before he got whisked away to superstardom. Though, he didn't know any of that 411 about my perving habits.

The second text from Dean gave us the address where to go, and the whistle got louder, target hit...direct implosion.

It was two blocks away.

He was two blocks away, and there went my restraint because I'd kept away from him for the last four years when I moved to the same city he was living in—of course he didn't know that—but this city was totally amazeballs by the way.

I was doomed. I might as well start digging my own bunker at this rate because I was already downtown partaking in some celebratory boozetails, so here we were. Here I was, well *we* because I wasn't alone. My main girl since Silvard days, Sasha, was on my right, and Melanie on my left. Melanie came after Silvard, but that didn't matter. She was one of my girls. The three of us. We were awesomesauce, and we were walking into this building that looked like a downtown loft, one that was probably the humble abode to someone not so humble, but someone with old-money wealth who enjoyed partaking in their own boozetails as well.

I already felt a whole kemosabe camaraderie with whoever owned this joint.

"This place is *fucking* awesome."

That was Melanie. She enjoyed coffee, girls, and she was an

amazing barista at Dino's Beans.

"Girl."

That was Sasha. She owned a strip club, told everyone she was an angry Russian, even though there wasn't one Russian strand of DNA in her body, and she enjoyed using one word for everything. That's not to say she didn't speak more than one-word answers, but those were her go-to for speaking.

"Whoa." That was me.

Melanie had jet-black hair. Sasha had ice-queen white hair, and me—I was the in between. My hair was usually a dusty blonde color, but today it looked a bit more lighter than dusty blonde. I still enjoyed it, and I also had super chill electric-blue eyes. The other two both had dark eyes so I figured I was still the 'in between' for the eyes, too.

When we entered that party, all eyes turned to us, and not one of us was fazed. We were used to it. Where we went, we got attention. Guys loved us (sometimes), girls hated us (usually), and we didn't care (ever). We weren't going to tone down our awesomeness because of their insecurities.

But we were all works in progress, or at least I was.

I was known to have entire conversations and whole other worlds and every version of apocalypses in my head. That was just me. You'll understand the more you get to know me, but trust me when I say that I'm a lot better than I used to be. Meds, therapy, and a dead junkie mother will do that to you.

But enough about me.

Melanie was the shit, and she really loved the word 'fuck.' A-*fucking*-lot.

Then there was Sasha, she'd been my roommate from college, and here we were, three years out of graduation (well, four for me since I graduated early, and don't ask me how that happened because it still shocked the hell out of me) and going strong. But we were on a mission.

That mission was more boozetails.

There were people everywhere. Stuffy people. One woman who had a tiara on her head. There were guys in suits, some in hella expensive suits, and tuxedos, too.

Whoa.

This wasn't just a party party. This was like a whole shindig party.

Fake Stanley Cups were placed all around with mucho dinero inside.

Crap.

I started to mentally shift through the emails—easier said than done when one was halfway to boozeopolis—that I liked to avoid and I was remembering some of the subject lines of those that I had skipped. There'd been a bunch from Dean lately, though, and one was about some 'Celebrity PR for Come Our Way' and I needed to double down on the crapattitude because I had a feeling we just waltzed into a fundraiser.

"Cheyenne!"

Dean rushed over to us, holding a boozetail in one hand, and his eyes glazed over. He was medium height with a more squat build that he easily could buff up more, but I didn't think Dean went to the gym. He was always at work and because of that, I usually saw him with his hair all messed up. That's how it was now, and his eyes glazed over.

My dude coworker was lit.

I started smiling, but then no. Not good. What corporate espionage was he up to by telling me to come here?

"Where's the bar, Deano?" Melanie.

I was impressed she hadn't used her favorite word.

"There." Directions from Sasha and like that, both my buds moved away.

I settled back, knowing they'd have my back. They'd be bringing the boozetails to me—even better—so I had the time to grin at Dean. "What's happening, hot stuff?"

He never got my quotes. Or jokes.

He didn't react and he grabbed my arm. "Have you read my emails?" Then he looked at me, his head moving back an inch. "What are you wearing?"

Nothing appropriate for a work event, that's for sure.

But I only upped my grin wattage. "I was going for a Daenerys theme. Felt like wanting to tame some dragons tonight." Except I took my own liberty with the outfit. Instead of her flowing robes and dresses, I was wearing a leather, almost corset-like top, one that wrapped around my neck and hung off one of my shoulders. The bottom was more Daenerys theme, a chiffon skirt with a slit up one thigh. And high heels strapped to my feet.

It shouldn't work, but it did. It so totally did, and I had woven colored threads in my hair so they were swinging free, free and lit.

He took another step back, looking me up and down again.

"You are," a pause, "something."

I scowled. "Dude. Insulting."

He had to blink a few times because he hadn't realized I spoke again, then he refocused. "Wait. You're downtown. There's no way you could've gotten here this fast, even if you were at the shelter, but I know you weren't at the shelter. And your place is an hour out."

Case in point, my outfit.

He was right.

Come Our Way. The name of our kitchen had been a marketing and genius ploy, one put in place by Deano himself, because while I wrote the grant that got us five million (not a common thing to happen for a start-up) and got us going, his job was actually to work on marketing and promotions to keep the money, spotlight, and volunteers streaming to our little kitchen. I maintained our grant, and I helped with literally everything else. I was the final say-so on all executive decisions, except for matters that we needed the board to oversee. We had another full-time staff member, but she liked to Netflix and chill (and really Netflix and chill with wine, not the other Netflix and chill) on her evenings. But all three of us manned our little kitchen that fed a lot of the downtown homeless in our corner in Kansas City.

And Dean knew I wasn't known for one to partake in alcoholic libations, but we were here, and I was thirsty.

It was my last day on my medication vacation. I was taking advantage of it.

It was a thing that happened to help cut down on build-up immunity. Sometimes I enjoyed it, but it was usually a whole struggle to get back on and make sure everything was smooth running.

But that wasn't something I was going to think about tonight, though my brain was already starting to go there. Tomorrow I'd go back to living almost like a saint.

Where were my girls with my drinkaloo?

Also, I was firmly not letting myself think of the *he* and that took mundo restraint because he had been a big major part of my daydreams since my junior year in high school through now—especially now since I've been living in the city where he was hockey royalty.

I didn't answer Dean, but spying another Stanley Cup filled with cash, I asked instead, "What's the funding for?"

"Oh!" He perked up, throwing his head back and finishing his drink. A waitress walked by with a tray loaded with fully filled champagne flutes. He snagged two, for himself. "That's why I'm here. I got the final acceptance that the Mustangs are going to dedicate an entire two days to Come Our Way. Two days, Cheyenne. Two days? Can you believe that?" He leaned in, excited, and I could smell how excited he was.

Booze breath. It's a thing.

I edged back a step. "Totally."

So not totally.

"That's awesome."

Really so not awesome.

It was a great PR day for the kitchen and for the team, I was sure that's why they agreed to do it. It wasn't uncommon for Come Our Way to have local celebrities pop in for a day or an hour to volunteer, but the media that followed them was always too much for me. I either stayed in the back kitchen, or I took a personal day. Media days were something *extra* extra. Flashing cameras. Razor-sharp reporters. Sometimes you got a good one who just wanted to spread good news about our mission, but sometimes you got the reporters who wanted to swing things to a more controversial article for the click-baits.

I wasn't down for that poundage.

Plus, the extra buzz in the entire building was like hay fever for my meds. I couldn't handle it, and therapy had taught me to avoid those types of situations, so hence why I usually disappeared—and if the entire team was coming for two days, it'd be insane. I was already not looking forward to it, and yes, I wasn't letting myself think of *him* being in my place of business. At all.

I thought he'd known me in high school, but that turned out to be a result of some slight delusions from my undiagnosed hyper disorder, so that was embarrassing, and then when college rolled around, I intentionally stayed in the background. But if he was going to be at my place for two days—forty-eight hours—there's no way he wouldn't see me, and that information was already bumbling through my head like an intoxicated bee hooked on coke and champagne. It just didn't know what to do or where to sting. Super painful.

Dean was still talking. "...and that's why I'm here. They reciprocated with an invite here, and by the way, it's so on-the-down-low that there's no security outside. Did you see that? To even get in here, you had to know about it."

That made no sense.

Dean didn't care. "And I've already met half the team. Oh!"

His eyes were bouncing around just like my intoxicated inner bee. "I got tickets to their game on Sunday. They rocked preseason, did you see?" He kept edging closer and closer to me the more he talked, something that was so un-Dean-like that I was having a hard time processing all this newness of what was happening around me.

Dean was around the same age as me, a few years older. Coming straight from grad school with a masters in reinvigorating the world to give a fuck about homeless and runaways, he had an axe to grind and an agenda to save the world. He liked to cut loose. You had to in our profession because burnout had the highest success rate, but seeing him this tricked out had that bee flying sideways. He didn't know if he was in my bonnet or my hair braids.

Then I remembered; Dean was a hockey fan.

I was, too, but I kept my undying adoration on the downlow like a lot of things.

Not Dean. He was out of the closet and loud and proud about his love for the Kansas City Mustangs. He also turned traitor and was a Cans fan, as well as the Polars (boo, hiss), but both those teams weren't in this current building or city. So yeah, it made sense now. He was geeking out on the full freakout reader.

That, and I was wondering how much champagne he had already consumed because he just downed both those two flutes in front of me. He was so drunk that my own lit meter was heading down into the empty zone. Not cool. Not cool, indeed, and where were my girls?

Just then, I saw one of them.

And my lit meter skyrocketed right into the red zone.

The crowd parted. I had a clear view right smack to the bar, and there she was. And she wasn't alone.

Sasha had her sultry and seductive pose out, clearly liking what she saw, gazing up at *him*.

Keep reading the rest of The Not-Outcast here or
go to www.tijansbooks.com